After Hours: Royal Duty

KATE HEWITT

MAYA BLAKE

CHRISTINE RIMMER

MILLS & BOON

First Published in Great Britain 2021
By Mills & Boon, an imprint of HarperCollins*Publishers* Ltd
1 London Bridge Street, London, SE1 9GF

www.harpercollins.co.uk

HarperCollins*Publishers*
1st Floor, Watermarque Building,
Ringsend Road, Dublin 4, Ireland

AFTER HOURS: ROYAL DUTY © 2021 Harlequin Books S.A.

Desert Prince's Stolen Bride © 2018 Kate Hewitt
Married for the Prince's Convenience © 2015 Maya Blake
Her Highness and the Bodyguard © 2013 Christine Rimmer

ISBN: 978-0-263-30055-0

MIX
Paper from
responsible sources
FSC™ C007454

About the Authors

Kate Hewitt has worked a variety of different jobs, from drama teacher to editorial assistant to youth worker, but writing romance is the best one yet. She also writes women's fiction and all her stories celebrate the healing and redemptive power of love. Kate lives in a tiny village in the English Cotswolds with her husband, five children, and an overly affectionate Golden Retriever.

Maya Blake's writing dream started at thirteen. She eventually realised her dream when she received 'The Call' in 2012. Maya lives in England with her husband, kids and an endless supply of books. Contact Maya: www.mayabauthor.blogspot.com www.twitter.com/mayablake www.facebook.com/maya.blake.94

A *New York Times* bestselling author, **Christine Rimmer** has written over ninety contemporary romances for Mills & Boon. Christine has won the *Romantic Times Book Reviews* Reviewers Choice Award and has been nominated six times for the *RITA®* Award. She lives in Oregon with her family. Visit Christine at http://www.christinerimmer.com

After Hours

DESERT PRINCE'S STOLEN BRIDE

KATE HEWITT

CHAPTER ONE

HE CAME IN through the window.

Olivia Taylor looked up from the blanket she'd been folding, her mouth dropping open in wordless shock. She was too surprised to be scared. Yet. He was dressed all in black, his body underneath the loose garments tall, lithe and powerful. A turban covered his hair but beneath it Olivia saw his face and the determination blazing in his steel-coloured eyes.

She drew a breath to scream when he moved swiftly towards her and slipped a hand over her mouth. 'I won't hurt you,' he said in Arabic, his tone brusque and yet also strangely gentle. It took her a moment to make out the words; she'd learned some Arabic living in the Amari household, but it was still of the schoolgirl variety. She'd been hired to speak only English to the three youngest Princesses.

He continued speaking and her shocked mind struggled to understand. 'That is my solemn vow, and I will never break it. Just do what I say and no harm shall ever come to you. I swear it on my life.'

Olivia stood there rigidly, his hand on her mouth, the scent of his skin in her nostrils. He smelled of horse and sand and sweat and musk…and, strangely, it was not unpleasing. Her mind was spinning with terrifying numbness, around and around, unable to latch onto any coherent thought. She couldn't think. She could barely breathe. Shock gave way to fear, making her dizzy. It was as if everything were happening underwater or in slow motion, yet far too fast, because already the man was propelling her to the window, and somehow she was going, going, her legs weak as water, her insides sliding around like jelly, her mind a blank canvas of fear and shock.

Halina was in the next room. The door wasn't even closed, not properly. She could hear her friend humming under her breath. How could this be happening? She'd only come in here, to Halina's bedroom, to put away her evening gown and tidy up a bit. Halina had just returned from what she'd claimed was an interminable dinner with her parents to discuss her future. Her fiancé. Olivia knew Halina didn't want to get married, and certainly not to a rebel prince she'd never met.

'He's practically an outlaw,' she'd said as she'd thrown herself on the sofa in her sitting room with a gusty sigh. 'A *criminal*.'

'I heard he went to Cambridge,' Olivia had countered mildly, used to her friend's theatrics, and Halina had rolled her eyes, determined to play up to whatever audience she had.

'He's been living in the desert for ten *years*. He's probably gone completely savage. I don't even know if he speaks English.'

'If he went to Cambridge, I'm sure he speaks English. And in any case your parents don't want you to marry him until his title is fully restored and he's back in the capital, in his palace,' Olivia had reminded her. She'd been governess to Halina's three younger sisters for four years, and she was well versed in all the family's hopes and plans.

Halina had been engaged to Prince Zayed al bin Nur

since she was ten years old, but a decade ago his family's rule had been overthrown by a government minister—Fakhir Malouf—and Prince Zayed, only just returned from university, had been forced into exile in the desert to fight for his throne.

Civil war had happened in spurts and bursts over the years, Zayed's band of rebels to Malouf's crack troops. Halina's father had insisted on honouring the betrothal, but only when Zayed's power was fully restored...and who knew when that would be?

But surely this man had nothing to do with that. Why did he want her? Why was he here?

Already he was at the window, one hip braced against the ledge, one hand gripping her upper arm, the other still over her mouth. She could taste the salt on his skin. His breath fanned her ear as he spoke, making her shiver.

'Please, do not be afraid.'

Strangely, she believed him. He didn't want her to be scared—and yet he was *abducting* her. Her frozen brain finally thawing into gear, Olivia started to struggle, her body arching against the man's as she attempted, uselessly, to free herself from his hold.

'Don't do that.' The words were quiet and lethal as his grip tightened on her, his hands like iron bands on her body. Inflexible and impossible to break, yet still strangely gentle. Olivia stilled, her heart thudding, knowing instinctively if she didn't escape now there would not be another good opportunity. And if she didn't escape...

Her mind blurred and blanked. She could not imagine what this man wanted with her, what he intended.

'I said I wouldn't hurt you.' The faintest edge of impatience had entered the man's low, steady voice. 'This is for the best, for both of us.' Which made no sense at all. There was no best for her in being kidnapped. *How* had this man been able to climb in through the window of Halina's bedroom?

The royal palace in the desert kingdom of Abkar was several miles from the capital city, remote and guarded by a high stone wall, patrolled by dogs and soldiers. Hassan Amari took no chances with his precious, beloved family. And yet here was this man, dark, strong, utterly in control. Something had gone very wrong at some point and Olivia couldn't imagine why or how.

The man turned her towards him. His face was very close, his lashes surprisingly long and lush, his eyes not merely grey, as she'd first thought, but a startling, mossy grey-green. His cheeks, nose and mouth were all hewn of harsh lines, giving Olivia an even stronger sense of the grim determination and inflexibility she'd seen in him from the moment he'd come through the window.

'I will keep you safe.' Looping a rope around her waist, he heaved her over the window to plummet down into the desert darkness.

The breath whooshed from Olivia's lungs and she was too startled to scream as the air streamed past, her heart suspended in her chest. Then the rope jerked taut and she landed with a heavy thud in another man's arms. He righted her quickly, her feet on the ground, but before she could scream he had covered her mouth with a scarf and tied it.

The man who had come in Halina's bedroom was scaling down the side of the palace wall, as stealthy and graceful as a panther. He landed lightly on his feet, his grey-green eyes narrowing at the sight of the gag on Olivia's mouth.

'I'm sorry,' the other man said in a low voice. 'I did not want her to scream.'

The man nodded shortly as Olivia's mind whirled.

What was going on? Why had they taken her?

The man looked back at her, a faint smile curving that rugged mouth. 'Come,' he said and, taking her by the elbow, he drew her towards several horses that were tethered by the palace wall.

Horses? How on earth were they going to get out of the palace on horses? The only way was through the front gates, tall and towering, topped with iron spikes and guarded by Sultan Hassan's private soldiers.

The man heaved her up on a horse and Olivia sprawled inelegantly across its back. She'd never ridden, unlike Halina and her sisters, who had been practically raised on horseback. The man quirked an eyebrow, seeming almost amused by her ineptitude, and then righted her, swinging up to straddle the horse behind her so she was nestled closely between his hard-packed thighs.

He snaked one arm around her waist to draw her even more tightly against him; Olivia could feel his heart thudding against her back, the heat of his body warming her right through. His scent invaded her senses. She'd never been so close to a man before.

'Let's ride,' the man said in a voice that managed to be both soft and commanding, and they headed off, Olivia watching in disbelief as they rode right through the palace gates, not a soldier in sight. Had these men taken over the palace? Had there been some kind of attack and no one had even realised?

As soon as they were clear, the man took off her gag.

'I am sorry for that. I did not want you to be treated so roughly.'

Which made no sense. He was her *kidnapper*. But Olivia couldn't ask any questions now, not with the wind streaming past and the sand flying into her eyes. The man slowed the horse down to tie the scarf around her hair and cover her mouth. 'There. That is better,' he murmured into her ear, sending shivers racing across her skin.

Olivia was conscious of the hard wall of the man's chest she was leaning against, his arm wrapped so snugly around her she almost felt safe. He kicked his heels into the horse's flanks and they were off again, flying across the sand.

The hours blurred into one another as they kept riding, the man holding her all the while, her body starting to ache from the constant jostling.

The moon was a silver crescent high above them, the sky a garden of stars sending silvery shadows across the desert sand, the only sound the steady thud of the horses' hooves.

At some point Olivia fell into an uneasy doze, her head resting against his chest, which seemed impossible, considering her precarious situation, but the constant, teeth-jarring movement had exhausted her.

She woke with a jolt when their gallop slowed, the man's arm relaxing on her only slightly. Olivia blinked warily; a few flickering lights emerged like pinpricks in the darkness. She heard low, murmuring voices but couldn't make out the words. It had taken concentration to understand everything the man had said to her in Arabic, and Olivia thought she must have missed or misunderstood some words.

The man slowed the horse to a stop and slid off it in one easy movement before turning to her.

Olivia gazed down at him, uncertain and suddenly desperately afraid. They had arrived at some kind of destination, and she had no idea what was going to happen now. What this man was going to do with her. He'd said he wouldn't hurt her, that he would keep her safe, but why on earth should she believe him?

'Come down,' he said quietly, and his tone reminded Olivia of the way Sultan Hassan talked to a frightened mare. 'No one will hurt you. I gave you my vow.'

'Why...?' Her voice came out in a croak; her throat was as dry as dust, sand speckling her lips and skin. 'Why have you taken me?'

'For justice,' the man replied. He reached for her, his hands gripping her arms with that gentle strength she'd felt before. 'Now, come down. Eat, drink, refresh yourself. And then we'll talk.'

Olivia's feet hit the ground and her legs nearly gave way. She hated being so feeble, but she'd never ridden a horse before and they'd been galloping for several hours. Her thighs chafed and her muscles ached. She felt as if she could collapse right where she stood. The man caught her, swearing under his breath.

'I thought you knew how to ride.'

'What?' Olivia blinked at him in surprised confusion. *Why would he think that?* 'No, I don't know how. I never learned.'

'It seems my intelligence was wrong on one point, at least.' He turned away before she could reply. 'Suma will see to you.'

Zayed al bin Nur strode towards his tent, his body aching from the hard ride and his heart thudding with the heady pulse of triumph. He'd done it. He'd actually done it. He'd successfully kidnapped Princess Halina Amari from behind the seemingly impenetrable walls of the royal palace. All that remained now was to seal the deal and make her his bride.

His mouth curved grimly as he thought of his future father-in-law's fury. Abducting Princess Halina had been a massive risk, but a calculated one. Hassan Amari knew Zayed's cause was just. And Zayed knew he needed the full support of the neighbouring kingdom of Abkar to wage war against Fakhir Malouf, the man who had taken his throne…and murdered his family.

The old rage settled in Zayed's gut, ice-cold and iron-hard with the passage of time, a familiar and almost comforting weight as he ducked under the flap and went into his tent. His advisor and friend, Jahmal, scrambled to attention.

'My Prince.'

'Have the preparations been made?'

'Yes, My Prince.'

Zayed shrugged off his travel-stained cloak and tore the turban from his hair, running his hand through the spiky mass to dislodge the grains of sand. 'Thank you. I am giving my bride half an hour to rest and refresh herself, and then we will go ahead with the ceremony.'

Unease flickered across Jahmal's face but he nodded. 'Yes, My Prince.'

Zayed knew his closest advisors had been deeply unsure about the risk he was taking. They were afraid of invoking Hassan Amari's wrath, even of starting another and far more damaging war with a neighbouring country they counted as their ally. But they didn't have the same fury and fear driving them as he did. They didn't remember the tortured screams of his brother and father as they'd burned to death in a helicopter that had pirouetted to the ground in flames. They didn't see his mother's shocked face when they closed their eyes, feel her unending grief, the memory of her dying in his arms a burden they would carry to his last breath. They didn't wake in the darkness, a silent scream of terror and rage bottled in their throats as the vestiges of a nightmare clung to their shattered minds and they were forced to face another bleak dawn, an unending day of fighting for what always should have been theirs.

No, they didn't understand. And no one ever would. This civil war would go on and on with no end in sight unless Zayed did something drastic and definitive. Fakhir Malouf would continue to set his country back decades, oppressing his people with his hopelessly backward schemes. Zayed *had* to act. And this had been the only option open to him.

There were worse things than a rushed wedding. He was honouring his betrothal vow, that was all. Halina would learn to accept it. Shrugging out of his dusty garments, Zayed prepared to meet his bride.

Half an hour later, freshly bathed and shaven, he ducked into the tent where he had ordered Suma to bring Halina to wait. His eyes adjusting to the flickering candlelight, he saw that she sat on a silken pillow with her back to him, narrow and slender, her hair streaming down it in a dark, damp river. She wore a loose robe of deep blue embroidered with silver thread that engulfed her slender figure but still reminded him of how she'd felt in his arms, slender and light. A surprising surge of desire arrowed through him. This marriage was about politics, nothing more, but it had been a long time since he'd lain with a woman.

Zayed let the tent flap fall closed behind him with a rustle and she turned, scrambling to a standing position, her eyes wide. She had incredible eyes, a deep, stormy blue, fringed extravagantly with sooty lashes. He hadn't expected those eyes, somehow.

Of course, he'd never seen a proper photograph of his bride, merely a few blurry images taken from a distance, since she'd been raised in virtual seclusion. They'd been betrothed when he was twenty and she ten, although it had been done formally, with a proxy, so they'd never met. Now did not seem like the most auspicious of introductions, but there was nothing to be done for it. Zayed squared his shoulders.

'You have been made comfortable, I trust?'

She hesitated, her gaze searching his face, looking for answers. After a pause, she finally answered. 'Yes…' Her voice was both soft and husky, pleasant. That was good. So far he liked her eyes and her hair, and he knew her body was both slender and curvaceous from being nestled against it on horseback for several uncomfortable hours. Three things that he could be thankful for. He had not expected so much. Rumours had painted Halina as a melodramatic and slightly spoiled princess. The woman in front of him did not seem so.

'But…' Her throat worked convulsively, the words coming in stumbling snatches. 'I don't… I don't…understand why you've…'

From behind them the tent flap rustled again and Zayed met the subtly questioning gaze of the imam he'd chosen to perform the ceremony. He would have preferred a civil service, but Malouf would dismiss a marriage that was conducted by a notary, and the last thing he could do was have Malouf dismiss this, the most important diplomatic manoeuvre he'd ever make.

'We're ready,' he said to the imam, who gave a brief nod. Halina's confused gaze moved from him to the man who would marry them.

'What…what are you…?'

'All you need to say is yes,' Zayed informed her shortly. He did not have time for her questions, her concerns, and certainly not her protestations. They could talk after the vows were performed, the marriage finalised. Not before. He would allow nothing to dissuade him. Halina's eyes had widened and darkened to the colour of a storm-tossed sea, her lips, rosy-pink and plump, parting soundlessly.

'Yes,' she repeated, searching his face, looking for answers. Did she not understand what she was doing here? It seemed obvious to Zayed, and it would soon be so to Halina when she made her vows. He could not afford to explain why he'd taken her, why they had to marry with such haste. Although his desert camp was well hidden, already Sultan Hassan could be sending his troops to take back his daughter. Zayed intended to have the marriage performed well before then.

Sensing his urgency, the imam moved forward and began the ceremony, speaking with quick fluidity. Zayed took Halina by her arm, firmly but with gentleness. She looked dazed, but Zayed hoped she'd adjust quickly. She knew they were engaged, after all. His methods might be unorthodox, but the end result would be the same as if they'd been surrounded by pomp and circumstance.

A silence descended in the tent and Zayed realised it was Halina's turn to speak. 'Say yes,' he hissed and she blinked at him, still seeming confused.

'Yes,' she said after a second's pause.

The imam continued twice more, and twice more Zayed had to instruct Halina to speak. *'Say yes.'*

Each time she murmured yes—*naaam*—her lips forming the word hesitantly.

The imam turned to him and Zayed bit out his three replies. Yes, yes, yes.

Then, with a little bow, the imam stepped back. Zayed's breath rushed out in a sigh of satisfaction and relief. It was done. They were wed.

'I'll leave you alone now,' he told Halina, who blinked at him.

'Alone?'

'For a few moments, to ready yourself.' Zayed hesitated, and then decided he would not explain things further.

Not now, with the imam listening and Halina seeming so dazed. Later, when they could talk, relax even, he would explain more. There would be food and wine and conversation—a little, at least. Then he would tell her. Tonight was not merely the marriage ceremony but its consummation.

CHAPTER TWO

OLIVIA FELT AS if she'd fallen down a rabbit hole into some awful, alternative reality. She had no idea what was going on; in the tent she'd only understood one word of Arabic out of three, if that. It had seemed as if some official kind of ceremony had been performed, but Olivia had no idea what it could be. And the man had insisted she keep saying yes—but to what? Perhaps he was preparing a ransom demand to the royal family, and wanted her to proclaim she was unharmed.

And she *was* unharmed, but she was also confused and more than a little scared. Who was the man with the terse manner and the gentle eyes? What did he want from her? And what was going to happen next?

The woman who had helped her to bathe and dress earlier, Suma, fetched her from the tent and led her to another, this one luxurious in every detail. Suma handed her some gauzy fabric and Olivia took it uncomprehendingly. Judging by the way Suma mimed her actions, she was meant to change once again. Olivia glanced down at the garment she held, a nightgown of near-diaphanous silk embroidered with gold thread. She had no idea why she had been given such a revealing and exquisite garment but she was afraid to think too much about it.

She couldn't ask Suma; the older woman spoke a dialect

of Arabic that was virtually incomprehensible to Olivia. They'd communicated by hand gestures, clumsy miming and the occasional understood word; there was no way she could ask the smiling, round-faced woman what was going on, or why she'd been given this nightgown. Not that Suma would tell her, anyway.

The tent she'd been led to was both sumptuous and spacious, with a mattress on a dais that was spread with hand-woven quilts of silk and satin and scattered with pillows. Candles flickered in torches and the desert wind made the tent rustle quietly. In the distance Olivia could hear the nickering of horses, the occasional low voice.

Suma left her alone to change and Olivia stood there, clutching the nightgown to her, wondering what on earth she was supposed to do now. Escape seemed unwise in the dark; she couldn't ride and they were hours from anywhere. Putting on a slinky, near-transparent nightgown also seemed unwise; the last thing she wanted was to be less dressed.

She put the nightgown on the bed, running her damp palms down the side of the blue robe she'd changed into earlier as she tried to think of a way out of this. Would the man come back? Did he speak English? If he did, perhaps she could demand some answers. Not that he seemed a man to acquiesce to anyone's demands, and Olivia doubted she'd be brave enough to give them.

Suma returned with a platter of fruit and cheese, as well as a jug of something, a carafe of water and two golden goblets. It was all very civilised, Olivia acknowledged with wry incredulity. She was being treated as an honoured guest rather than the prisoner she was...but she still had no idea what her abductor intended to do with her, and thinking too much about it made her stomach churn and bile rise to the back of her throat.

The older woman caught sight of the nightgown Olivia had left on the bed and frowned. She gestured to Olivia to change, and Olivia shook her head.

'No...*la*,' she said, speaking as firmly as she could. Her Arabic was clumsy but insistent. 'I do not want to wear that.'

Suma's frown deepened and she made wild gestures with her hands as she let forth a stream of incomprehensible dictates. Clearly Suma wanted her to wear the gown very much.

'Yes,' Olivia cut across her, having understood at least one word she'd spoken: *jamila*. 'It is very beautiful. But I do not want to wear it.'

Suma scowled. Olivia almost felt apologetic for disappointing her. Was she being reckless, by refusing the nightgown? What if it made the man angry? But why on earth would he want her in it in the first place? A question she could barely bear to ask, much less answer.

With a huff, Suma shook her head and then disappeared. Olivia let out a gusty sigh of relief. She really did not want to parade around a desert camp of strange men in a diaphanous nightgown that looked like something a bride would wear on her wedding night.

She paced the luxurious confines of the tent, wondering if anyone was going to come in to see her and explain what on earth was going on. What did they want from her? If they thought Sultan Hassan would pay a hefty ransom for her return, she suspected they would be disappointed. Hassan was fond enough of her, but she was just an employee.

And if they wanted her for something else...

Swallowing convulsively, she tried not to give in to panic. She wanted to see the man with the gentle eyes again, although something about his fiercely determined manner made her half hope he wouldn't come in. When he was near her it felt as if he were taking all the air, making it hard to breathe. Hard to think. And Olivia knew she needed all her wits about her now. Somehow she had to figure out why she was here…and then she had to figure out how to escape. Both felt impossible.

Then the tent flap opened and there he was, those grey-green eyes glinting in the candlelight. He was dressed as he had been before, in loose trousers and a long shirt of bleached linen that emphasised the powerful, rippling muscles of his chest and thighs.

Olivia tried not to gulp. She folded her arms and lifted her chin, which was just about all the defiance she had in her. Gazing into that penetrating stare felt like looking at the sun. 'I wish to know why you have taken me here,' she said in English. Surprise flared across the man's face like a ripple in water and then was gone.

'Your English is very good.'

That was because she was half-English. Although as the daughter of a diplomat she'd been raised around the world, her father had been English and that was the language she'd always spoken. 'I prefer English to Arabic.'

'Do you?' His own English was flawless, his tone impossible to decipher. A frown marred his brow for a moment and then smoothed out. 'Why have you not changed?' he asked, with a nod at the nightgown discarded on the bed.

'Why would I want to wear that?' she flung at him. His mouth quirked, impossibly, into a smile. He was actually amused.

'Because it is comfortable? And beautiful. You are, as a point of fact, very beautiful.' He moved past her to a low table flanked by two chairs and the tray with the platter of food on top of it. 'Come, have something to eat and drink.' He gestured to the low folding chair across from him. 'Sit down, be comfortable.'

Olivia could only gape. She was beautiful? No one had ever said that to her before. No one had ever even noticed her before. Why him? Why now? *What did he want?*

He sat down himself, seeming utterly relaxed…and utterly appealing. A tingle went through Olivia just from looking at him. Dark, close-cropped hair, those beautiful eyes the colour of peat, a straight nose and a mobile mouth, the lines and angles of his face both harsh and arresting. As for his body…it was lean and long, every inch of it pure, powerful muscle. Even sprawled in a chair he radiated strength and energy, power and grace. He was like a jungle cat, ready to spring, eyeing her with a sleepy, knowing, hooded gaze. He could devour her if he wanted. The knowledge flashed through her, certain and strangely thrilling.

She felt a tremor of fear, but with it a pulse of something else. Something almost like desire. He had such a *languid* look in his eyes. No one had ever looked at her like that. She'd spent her life in the shadows, half pretending to be invisible, ignored by her busy, widowed father, and then keeping to the sidelines of school life.

Since becoming the governess to the Amari Princesses four years ago, she'd been even more in the background, which she hadn't minded. That was where she was used to being, making sure she was quietly useful, keeping out of the way of people who were busier or more important than she was. Blending into the background felt both safe and comfortable, and it was only in this heightened, surreal moment she realised how dull it had always been. How dull her whole life had been, as if she had been waiting all along for something to happen. And now it had.

You've been kidnapped, she reminded herself with both fierceness and panic. *This is not some romantic adventure. This man has abducted you. You need to escape.*

'I want you to release me.'

The man arched an eyebrow. 'Where? Into the desert?'

'Back to the palace.'

His expression shuttered although he remained relaxed. 'You know that is impossible.'

'How would I know that?'

He made a gesture towards the entrance of the tent, one Olivia couldn't decipher. What, exactly, was he referring to? 'Too much has happened. Now, come.' He reached for the jug and poured them both goblets of what looked like water, but when he added something from another jug the liquid turned milky-white. Olivia eyed it askance.

'What is that?'

'Arak, mixed with water. It changes colour when diluted. Surely you have had it before?'

'No.' The only alcohol she had had was the occasional sip of champagne at Christmas or New Year when she was a teenager.

'Come, taste it. It is quite refreshing.' He smiled at her, flashing very white, very straight teeth. Olivia stayed where she stood. She could not sit down and have a drink with this man. He'd *kidnapped* her. 'Well?' He held the glass out for her, waiting.

'For understandable reasons I am reluctant to take any food or drink from you.'

'Is that so?' Irritation flashed across his face. 'I think the time for such petulant gestures has surely passed?'

Petulant gestures? Olivia bristled even as she recognised a grain of truth in the words. She was hungry and thirsty, and she didn't really think he'd drugged the food. There was no point spiting herself as well as him.

Her chin tilted at a haughty angle that belied the trepidation she felt, she walked over and sat down opposite him. She took the glass he held out, her fingers brushing his and sending another tingle like lightning through her. Her arm jerked in response, everything in her flaring white-hot. The man noticed; Olivia saw it in the brief gleam in his eyes and she felt a rush of embarrassment. She was so innocent, so *gauche*. She could not even hide it. And the fact that she should be attracted to him, her *captor*...

It was both weak and wrong.

'Taste.' His voice was a low, lazy drawl.

Olivia raised the glass to her lips, conscious of the man's gaze resting on her, so languorous and speculative, and she took a cautious sip. 'It tastes like liquorice.'

'It is the anise. Do you like it?'

She took another sip, feeling the fire blaze down her throat and into her belly, warming her right through. 'I... I don't know.'

He laughed softly, the sound winding seductive tendrils around her. She took another sip, craving the courage it provided even as the practical part of her told her drinking more was most unwise. The last thing she wanted to do was let her defences down in front of this stranger, magnetically appealing as he was. He was also dangerous—that Olivia knew for certain, felt all the way to her bones—and getting drunk was definitely not a good idea right now.

'So you have never had arak,' he mused. 'I am pleased to introduce you to a new experience.'

'Are you?' With a slightly unsteady hand Olivia returned the half-drunk glass to the table. She'd only had a few sips and yet already she was feeling the effects of the alcohol, her mind pleasantly blurring at the edges, her body relaxing. That was undoubtedly a bad thing, especially with the way the man was looking at her, with a mix of speculation and, yes, desire. Just as she, impossibly, unwisely, desired him.

A thrill ran through her like an electric shock at the

realisation. She was naïve, yes, and completely innocent, but even she could see the heat in his eyes, although she could hardly credit it. That such a man, a powerful, sensual, attractive man, would want *her*...

But she shouldn't want to be wanted, not by a stranger who was most certainly a threat. Confusion chased desire, leaving her emotions in a ferment. 'Where are we?' she asked, looking away from that heat-filled gaze.

'In the desert.'

'I know that, but where? Are we still in Abkar?'

There was a pause while he cocked his head, his gaze sweeping over her thoroughly, leaving heat and awareness in its wake. He wasn't touching her and yet everything prickled; it was as if parts of her body were stirring to life for the first time. Her breasts, her thighs, her lips. She felt weirdly, achingly conscious of them all, that persistent tingle going right through her, impossible to stop or ignore, obliterating common sense, rational thought.

Disconcerted, Olivia reached for her glass. She'd have just one more sip of the anise-flavoured arak, that was all. She needed a distraction from this unwelcome and overwhelming reaction.

'No, we are not in Abkar,' he said, his gaze still resting on her, considering, assessing. 'We are in Kalidar.'

The country of Halina's fiancé, Prince Zayed al bin Nur. Was her abduction related to Halina's impending marriage? Was the minister in power, Fakhir Malouf, behind it? Fear trembled in her breast at the prospect and her fingers clenched on the goblet. She had heard terrible things of Malouf, a man who seemed to possess neither mercy nor kindness. This man hardly seemed like a minion of Malouf...but who was he?

The man must have noticed the fear tensing her fingers and flashing in her eyes, for he leaned forward, his gaze blazing silver for one heart-stopping second. 'I have told you, you need never be afraid of me. I know we have had an inauspicious beginning, but you can trust me on that.'

'You kidnapped me from the palace,' Olivia pointed out, glad her voice didn't tremble as her insides did. 'Why shouldn't I be afraid of you? And why on earth should I trust you?'

'Such means were necessary. Unwelcome, I grant you, but very much necessary.'

'Why?'

'Because I had waited long enough and I could wait no longer. But we need not concern ourselves with politics tonight, *hayete*.'

My life. The endearment caught her by surprise, made her feel weirdly exposed, as if the careless words had revealed a need in her she'd been trying to hide. Olivia blinked at him, wishing she hadn't drunk so much of the arak. Her whole body was buzzing, but not just from the alcohol. The effect this man had on her was far more intoxicating than the arak. It hardly seemed possible that she could react so instantly and overwhelmingly to a stranger, and a dangerous one at that, yet...

She could not deny it. He affected her, and he knew it.

With a small smile flirting with his lips, he leaned forward and cut off a wedge of cheese from the platter with a small, wicked-looking knife. He handed the wedge to her, his lids half-lowered, his smile glinting, making Olivia feel another insistent throb of desire, a pulse going through her whole body. 'You should eat something. You have drunk much of the arak, considering you have never tasted it before.'

'I—oh.' Fumbling a bit, Olivia replaced the glass on the table. She would drink no more. After a second's hesitation she took the slice of cheese from him, her fingers brushing his once again, and nibbled it. It was delicious, fresh and tangy, and made her realise how hungry she was. The hours of riding had sapped her strength and given her an appetite.

'Good, yes?'

'Yes, it is very good.'

He cut a wedge for himself and popped it in his mouth. 'Have some grapes,' he said after he had swallowed, and he took a bunch from the table.

Olivia finished her cheese, mesmerised by the sight of his long, lean fingers tearing off a bunch of the grapes. Everything about the man was sensual, *sexual*. She couldn't escape it, couldn't ignore the heat snaking through her, pooling low in her belly, the tension and expectancy shimmering in the air. It was all so unfamiliar yet felt so... wonderful.

There was no other word for it, strange as it seemed. She felt as if she'd imbibed some secret elixir and it now flowed through her veins. She craved even more of it, the fizzing fireworks, the slow, molten uncurling inside her, even as a part of her insisted she stop, she back away, she stay safe.

She reached for the grapes but with a smile the man gave a little shake of his head and plucked one from the bunch, holding it out between his fingers, a sleepy challenge now in that heavy-lidded gaze. Olivia stared at him uncertainly.

'Open your mouth,' he said softly, and her eyes widened with shock. The invitation was so blatant, except it wasn't an invitation at all. It was a command, and one she should most certainly refuse. She should demand he release her; she should be acting outraged and angry, or even just afraid. Anything but this meek and wilful obedience, already enslaved to her own desire, and yearning for his.

She was complicit in whatever was happening here, unspooling between them in a golden thread of sensation. Wordlessly, her gaze fixed on his, she opened her mouth.

Triumph and desire flared white-hot through Zayed as Halina parted her lips. She really was the most beguiling creature, seemingly without artifice…and perhaps she truly was. Perhaps he should take her at face value, although heaven knew that was not something he did, ever. He trusted no one, not even those closest to him. He could not afford to. But his bride's innocence seemed total, her wide blue eyes utterly without guile, every reaction refreshingly honest, even a little gauche. She hid nothing. Perhaps he could at least trust that.

Letting his gaze linger on hers, letting her see the heat and need in it, he slid the grape into her mouth, brushing her full lower lip with his thumb. Halina gave a soft little gasp as she jerked back, her lips closing over the grape, her eyes heartbreakingly wide, reflecting every emotion as sensations chased through her—the taste of the grape, the touch of his fingers.

'Delicious,' Zayed said, his voice caressing the syllables, his gaze still on her. Her dark hair tumbled in silken waves about her shoulders, sooty lashes sweeping down to hide those stormy eyes. Where her tunic top gaped he could see the shadowy curves of her breasts and hips and it made him ache. She was utterly delectable, and he found he couldn't wait to taste her.

And wait he would not… With every minute that passed, Zayed knew Sultan Hassan could be coming closer, sending out soldiers to rescue his daughter. Zayed needed their marriage to be unimpeachable by then. He needed it to be consummated. And, judging from Halina's trembling reactions, she was not averse. Shy, perhaps, and undoubtedly innocent, but most certainly not averse.

She swallowed the grape with a gulp, lashes lifting as she gazed at him in obvious confusion. 'Why are you doing this?'

Zayed leaned forward again. 'Because I find you so very desirable, *hayete*.' The endearment came naturally— she was his life, the key to all his ambitions, all his desires. And, while his body stirred and strained with sexual need, that was what he had to remember. This marriage was essential to retrieving his throne. His inheritance. His life.

'But…' Her tongue darted out to moisten those full, lush lips. Zayed nearly groaned at the artless gesture that had lust arrowing through him. 'But you don't even know me.'

'I know enough. And this was always going to happen, *hayete*, was it not? It was decreed long before now. It was written in the stars.' Flowery language for what had been a businesslike betrothal when they had been both so young, but it was a means to an end. His bride's eyes widened and she seemed startled, and then shyly pleased. The words worked.

'Was it?' She shook her head to clear it. 'Was that why you kidnapped me?'

'But of course.' He had taken her out of desire, but of a different kind. 'Come,' Zayed said and, standing, he reached for her hand and drew her towards him, letting his fingers slide along and then twine with hers.

Her whole body trembled as she stood before him, her head lowered, her lashes fanning her cheeks. 'What…?' Her voice was no more than a thread of sound. 'What do you want with me?'

'I want to make love to you.' Zayed rested his hands on her shoulders, felt how impossibly slender she was, how fragile. 'Slowly and sweetly.' He bent his head to brush a kiss against her temple; her skin was soft and cool. 'Is that what you want?' His lips moved lower to press a kiss to the side of her neck. A shudder went through her body.

'I… I don't… I haven't…' In her nervousness she stuttered, and Zayed laughed softly, kissing the nape of her neck, letting his mouth linger. She smelled of lemons.

'*Hayete*, I know.'

'But…but…surely you didn't bring me here for this?' A soft moan escaped her as he placed one hand on her waist, fingers splaying to brush her hip and the underside of her breast. Her reaction to him was so complete and overwhelming it made the need arrow even more strongly inside him.

'What if I did?' he murmured, stroking the side of her breast with knowing fingers. He needed to go slowly, of course, but it was hard. Harder than he'd expected. His body was demanding to be sated, his thirst slaked. And his bride was so very willing in his arms, trembling as she was, her gaze wide and wondering as she tilted her head to gaze up at him.

'You *did*…'

Was she painting some romantic picture of him as a white knight coming to steal her away because he couldn't resist her? The prospect was laughable, yet so what if she believed it? If it helped in the moment, then so be it. He did desire her. Immensely. And that was enough.

'I did,' he assured her, and then he captured her mouth in a kiss.

CHAPTER THREE

IT WAS A kiss that stole her breath as well as a little bit of her soul. It was the first kiss Olivia had ever had, and she swayed beneath it as the man's mouth moved persuasively over hers.

Her body was awash with sensation, her mind dazed and reeling. She'd never expected this to happen. She'd never expected to feel this way. She was being seduced, ruthlessly and thoroughly, and she couldn't even resist. She didn't want to. The pleasure coursing through her in a hot, honeyed river was too strong for that.

The inner protestations that this man was a danger, her enemy, her abductor, fell utterly silent. She no longer cared. Even if this was merely a night and the man, stranger that he was, used her and then tossed her aside afterwards, Olivia knew she could not turn away from this. Not when she'd finally woken up, after a lifetime of sleeping. Not when every sense and nerve was tuned exquisitely, acutely. She *felt*. She felt so many wonderful things.

Tentatively, learning the steps of this new and intricate dance, she reached up to grip his shoulders, her fingertips grazing his skull. She pressed her body against his, thrilling to the feel of his hard, muscled chest and powerful thighs. And more than that…even in her innocence she recognised the insistent throb of his arousal against her stomach. She'd seen enough films, read enough romance novels, to recognise it and she thrilled to it, to him, all the more.

A groan escaped him as he tore his mouth from hers and took a step back from her. His expression was nearly as befuddled as her own, Olivia thought. They were both breathing heavily, staring at each other in dazed desire, the very air between them seeming to shimmer.

'Come to bed,' he said, and reached for her hand.

For a second Olivia hesitated. Here was the moment of clarity, of choice. Was she really willing to give up her virginity to a stranger? Would she do this, the most intimate and sacred of acts, with a man whose name she did not even know, who had kidnapped her, who had to be merely using her, no matter what flowery language he used? And yet he wanted her. That was no lie, no trick. He wanted her…and she loved the feeling of being wanted.

His fingers found hers and he tugged gently, a smile curving that mobile mouth. 'Do not be afraid, *hayete*. Remember when I said I would never hurt you. That is, and always will be, my solemn vow.'

He spoke as if he knew her, as if he had been waiting for this moment. Waiting for her. Olivia knew he couldn't have been. It was just words, sentiment, yet she believed him in this at least: he wouldn't hurt her. She wouldn't let herself get hurt. A night and no more. How many women had made the same bargain, the same promise? There need be no regrets. She didn't care who he was. All that mattered was what he made her feel right now.

He must have sensed her acquiescence for his mouth curved in a deeper smile, and Olivia saw the triumph flare in his eyes along with the desire. He pulled her gently towards him and she came, hips swaying, heart beating. Their bodies nudged and bumped and he gazed down at her, standing so close she could feel the beat of his heart against her own.

'You are very beautiful. Very desirable.'

No one had ever said such things to her before. She was too skinny, too quiet, all hair and eyes. She didn't have Halina's generous curves and lush mouth, her engaging smile and contagious laughter. She always stayed in the background and no one ever noticed her at all. Until now.

Shyly she laid her hand on his chest, felt the steady thud of his heart underneath the press of her palm. 'As are you.'

He laughed softly at that, and then he took her hand and raised it to his mouth, kissing her palm, his gaze never leaving hers. 'Then we are well matched,' he murmured, and his mouth moved from her palm to her fingertips, kissing and nibbling each one in turn until Olivia's knees went weak.

The man drew her to the mattress, bringing her down to its feathery softness, the silken covers slippery beneath her. He stretched out alongside her, his body relaxed but his gaze so intent.

'So very beautiful,' he murmured. 'But I want to see all of you. May I?'

Everything in Olivia trembled. 'Yes,' she whispered, unable to say anything more. He tugged at the ties of her robe so it fell open, revealing the simple chemise she wore underneath. Keeping his gaze on her, he reached out and cupped her breast, his thumb sliding over the peak, making her shudder. She'd never been touched so intimately, so knowingly.

'You like that?' he murmured, and she nodded jerkily. 'Yes.'

He lowered his mouth to where his hand had just touched, and Olivia jerked again, arching off the mattress as his mouth closed over her breast, damp and hot, sending darts of intense sensation through her. She gripped his head, unsure if she wanted to anchor him to her or push him away, because it was so much. All her nerve endings felt flayed, yet she wanted more of him.

He moved his mouth to her other breast and she gasped out loud. The novels and films had never described it like this. And then he was moving lower, placing lazy kisses along her abdomen, her navel, and then lower still.

Olivia tensed as he nudged her thighs apart. Surely not…? But he was, his warm breath fanning her very centre, and she let out a long, shuddering sigh as he kissed her in the most intimate way possible. Pleasure licked through her veins and her hips arched helplessly, her fingers threaded through his hair, her body on fire. She'd never, ever felt anything like it; it *consumed* her. He did.

And then she felt as if she were burning right up; she cried out loud, a jagged sound, as pleasure exploded inside her, took her over, blazing through her. When she came to, everything hazy around her, he'd come up to rest on his forearms and was smiling down at her.

'And that's just the beginning.'

The *beginning*? He'd kill her, at this rate. Kill her with pleasure. He laughed softly. 'Don't look so disbelieving, *hayete*. I intend to make this a night you shall never forget.'

He already had. Still smiling, he shrugged out of his own clothes and then rid her of the rest of her own. Their bodies came together, naked, skin on skin, limbs twining and tangling. It felt so intensely intimate, to be pressed against someone like that, every part of herself on display, on offer for him. And he took it, his gaze roving over her, his mouth curved, his eyes gleaming with pleasure. He liked what he saw, and that thrilled her.

'Touch me,' he commanded, his voice a throb, and she gazed at him in surprise. Then, hesitantly, she let her hands drift from his powerful shoulders to the satiny skin of his back, and then down to his hips. His arousal pulsed against her, exciting and terrifying her all at once. But he'd told her not to be afraid, and somehow she wasn't.

'Touch me,' he said again, his voice ragged, and Olivia knew what he meant. Feeling shy and bold at the same time, she moved her hand from his hip to curl around the pulsing length of his arousal. His breath hissed between his teeth as she stroked him, hardly able to believe that she could create this response in a man so fierce and beautiful.

He kissed her again, hard, the lazy sensuality he'd shown earlier now becoming something far more raw and primal that Olivia matched, the heat and need an insistent pulse inside her, an ache that demanded satiation—again.

He slid his fingers to her core, moving against her slick heat, making her moan. 'You're ready,' he said and Olivia tensed, knowing she was, of course she was, and yet…

Slowly, surely, he slid inside her, an invasion that felt both shocking and overwhelming, the smooth slide of him filling her right up. She gasped out loud, her hips twitching in instinctive discomfort as she struggled to accommodate the sheer size of him.

Sweat sheened on his brow as he braced himself on his forearms and held himself still inside her, waiting for her to adjust to the entirely unfamiliar sensation. 'You are not hurt?' he asked through gritted teeth. Holding back was clearly a huge effort.

Wordlessly Olivia shook her head. She felt too overwhelmed to speak, too emotional. The dazed pleasure that had drugged her senses was trickling away, replaced by a tidal wave of realisation at the enormity of what she'd done. What could not be undone.

As if sensing her thoughts, he brushed a tendril of hair from her forehead and then pressed a kiss against her temple, the gesture almost as intimate as the pulse of his body inside hers. 'It is all right, *hayete*. This is right, what is between us. There is no shame in it. None at all.'

Her body was relaxing into him, instinctively learning his shape, accepting it, and his words were the balm she so desperately needed. She put her arms around his taut shoulders, drawing him closer, bringing him even more fully into herself, gasping at the feel of it. It was as if he'd gone right into her centre, invaded her soul.

'Please,' she whispered, needing something more from him, craving it. *'Please.'* And then he began to move, each slow thrust creating a delicious friction that had the pleasure rushing back, lapping at her senses in wave after wave of sensation and then engulfing her entirely.

Her cry shattered the still air as he pulsed inside her and her body felt as if it were dissolving into sated fragments. She cried again, a sob of joy and wonder, as she pressed her face against his damp shoulder, her body shuddering underneath his as the waves subsided but the wonder remained.

Zayed held his bride in his arms as she shuddered and wept, clearly overwhelmed by what they had experienced. Hell, but he was overwhelmed too. It had been a long time since he'd lain with a woman, a very long time. Yet he didn't think it had ever felt like this.

Was it different, perhaps, knowing his life was linked with this woman for ever? She would bear his children; she would stand by his side. She was his bride, his wife, his Queen. Yet none of that had been in his mind when he'd held her, when he'd been inside her. The need to consume her had been too overpowering—and that was a dangerous thing.

He didn't need people, just as he didn't trust them. Betrayal had taught him the latter; grief had taught him the first. Zayed rolled onto his back and stared up at the roof of the tent as Halina lay quietly beside him, faint tremors still going through her body.

'You are not in any discomfort?' he asked eventually and she pushed her hair away from her flushed face.

'No...no.' She looked rosy and satisfied and a little bit uncertain. He wanted her all over again, so he rolled away from her, into a sitting position.

'Good.' It was done. Nothing could break the bond they'd created; she was his wife both in name and physical fact. Zayed rose from the mattress in one fluid movement and shrugged on his clothes.

'Where are you going?' Halina asked. She suddenly sounded very young, and Zayed was reminded that she was only twenty-two—ten years younger than him.

'I have things to do.' His voice came out brusque so he tried to moderate it. 'I will see you later.'

'You will?'

'Of course.' He suppressed a flash of annoyance. Already she sounded needy, clinging, and that was the last thing he wanted. 'If you need anything, you can ask Suma.'

'Suma? But I can't understand her.'

The flash of annoyance came again, and with it an odd sense of unease. 'What do you mean?'

'She speaks a dialect I can't understand.' She was clutching a sheet to her breasts, her hair tumbled around her face. Zayed fought the urge to climb back into the bed and take her in his arms all over again.

'I did not realise she was so difficult to understand,' he said stiffly. 'You will have to get used to it. She is the only woman here to serve your needs.'

'But...what...what are you going to do with me?' Her voice was both tremulous and brave.

Zayed's gaze narrowed. 'What am I going to do with you? I have already done it, *hayete*. It is finished.'

She bit her lip. 'I know that. I mean, I wasn't expecting more than...than this. But now what are you going to...? Why did you kidnap me?' She lifted her chin, holding her gaze steady as if steeling herself for a blow.

Zayed stared at her, completely nonplussed. '*Why* did I kidnap you?' he repeated. 'Surely that is obvious? I told you I could not wait any longer.' He blew out a breath. 'Your father will not be pleased, I grant you, but he will not be able to affect the outcome. Of that I am certain.'

Now she looked genuinely confused, her brow creased, her lips parting. 'My father...' She shook her head slowly. 'But my father is dead.'

'*What?*' Zayed stared at her in complete shock. Sultan Hassan *dead*? When? How? But no; surely he would have heard of it? He would have known. His informants in the palace would have said something. Still, a cold fist clutched his heart. If Sultan Hassan was dead, all his plans fell apart, crumbled to dust. To nothing. The man had no sons, and his heir was a distant cousin, someone Zayed could not rely on to help him. 'When did this happen?' he bit out.

His bride stared at him in wary confusion. 'Years ago. Five years now.' She frowned. 'I don't understand. What could my father possibly have to do with any of this?'

'Wait.' Zayed felt as if he'd entered some weird, alternative reality. How could Halina be saying this? Sultan Hassan had most certainly not died five years ago. What the hell was going on?

'Why do you care about my father?' she asked, her voice trembling. 'Who *are* you?'

For a moment he could only stare. She knew who he was. She *had* to know. 'I am Prince Zayed al bin Nur,' he said, biting off each word. She'd wed him, she'd slept with him! Of course she'd known he was her fiancé, her intended husband. Because, if she hadn't known, why the hell had she slept with him? Agreed to marry him?

'Zayed…' Her face had gone pale, her lips bloodless, dawning horror in her eyes. Something was very, very wrong, and the cold fist that was clutching Zayed's heart squeezed painfully.

'And you,' he said forcefully, each word a throb of insistent intensity, 'are Princess Halina Amari.' She had to be. He'd seen photographs—blurry, yes, but he'd watched her in the palace. She'd played with her sisters; she'd gone into her bedroom. She had to be his intended bride. His wife.

But already she was shaking her head.

'No,' she whispered. 'No, I'm not Halina.'

CHAPTER FOUR

REALISATION UPON REALISATION was crashing through Olivia, filling her with more and more horror. This was Prince Zayed, her friend's fiancé, and she'd *slept* with him. And he'd thought she was Halina! He'd taken her from the palace believing her to be his bride-to-be. Had this been some sort of romantic seduction, and she'd botched it completely?

'If you're not Princess Halina,' Zayed asked through gritted teeth, his eyes narrowed to silvery slits, every muscle tensing as if for a fight, 'then who the hell *are* you?'

Olivia swallowed hard, her heart beating like a wild bird inside her chest. She clutched the blanket to her, more than ever conscious of her nakedness. 'My name is Olivia Taylor. I'm governess to the Amari Princesses.'

He stared at her for a single second and then he swore, viciously and fluently. Olivia flinched, and wondered if his solemn vow not to hurt her still stood. She had a feeling it didn't, although Zayed kept himself restrained, that pulsing fury leashed, if barely.

'Why, then,' he asked, his voice one of tightly controlled and yet clearly explosive anger, 'did you sleep with me?'

'I…' There was no excuse, no explanation. She'd lost her head, her *virginity* to a stranger. And he'd thought he was bedding his future bride! Olivia closed her eyes, wanting to blot out her shame, erase everything that had happened in the last few hours.

And yet, with the flickers of pleasure still pulsing through her body, she couldn't quite make herself regret it. In Zayed's arms she'd felt so cherished; what a joke. He hadn't even realised who she was. The knowledge of how she'd been duped, how she'd let herself be duped and talked herself into bed with a stranger, was utterly shaming.

'I…' she tried again, and then shrugged helplessly. She had no answer, except that she'd been completely swept away by the force of him, of her attraction to him, and she wasn't courageous or stupid enough to admit that. Surely it had been obvious, anyway?

Zayed whirled away from her in one abrupt movement, raking a hand through his hair. 'Didn't you know who I was?'

'No.'

'And yet you slept with me.'

'You slept with me,' Olivia fired back, finding her courage. She wasn't going to take *all* the blame. 'And obviously you didn't know who I was.'

'Obviously.' The single word was scathing. 'But I would have expected you to correct my mistake, preferably before we'd said our vows.'

'Vows?' Olivia stared at him, dread seeping into her stomach like acid. 'What do you mean—'

'Unless,' Zayed cut across her, ruthless now, any gentleness well and truly gone as his face, his body, his voice all hardened. 'You meant this to happen?'

'Meant it to happen?' Olivia stared at him in outrage. 'I meant for you to kidnap me? I planned it? Are you *insane*?' She could hardly believe she was talking to a prince this way—she, meek Olivia Taylor—but the situation was so surreal, his suggestion so ludicrous and insulting, that for a moment she forgot who she was. Where she was. And even what had happened.

Zayed had the grace to look slightly abashed for a millisecond, and then he simply looked impatient. 'No, not then, of course. But after. Perhaps you saw an opportunity and took it. You wanted to better your situation. You said you were a governess?'

Olivia shook her head. 'I have no idea what you're talking about.' She felt furious and humiliated, and she really wished she were wearing some clothes. 'And I certainly don't see how I've bettered my situation.'

Zayed's mouth twisted in something like a sneer. 'Don't you?'

'No, I really don't. But since I'm not Halina, and you're not kidnapping me for ransom or something like that, perhaps you could see fit to return me to the palace.' She spoke with as much as dignity as she could muster, considering she was naked. And near tears, which thankfully she blinked back. She would not cry in front of this man, even if she'd already wept in his arms. Even if she'd already experienced more vulnerability and pleasure, more heights and depths, than she had with any other person, ever. Just the memory of how he'd felt inside her, how she'd felt in his arms, the completeness of it, made heat scorch through her, along with something more powerful and dangerous, a longing she could not bear to name. 'I would like to go back home,' she added stiffly.

Zayed stared at her unblinkingly for several long, taut moments. 'Clearly,' he said finally, his voice clipped, 'that is impossible at this juncture.'

'Clearly?' Olivia tried for a look of disdain. 'I don't see how that is at all clear.' Holding the blanket to her, she scooted out of bed and grabbed the diaphanous robe she'd refused to wear earlier in the evening. Her more modest robe was on the other side of the bed, where Zayed had tossed it after undressing her only a short while ago—it felt like a lifetime. A terrible lifetime. She shrugged into the robe, tying the sash as tightly as she could. It wasn't much coverage, but at least it was something. She folded her arms over her breasts and lifted her chin, giving Zayed as challenging a stare as she could. 'So why exactly can't you return me to Abkar?'

Zayed's gaze was penetrating, relentless. His mouth had thinned into a hard, unforgiving line, his eyes blazing steel. Anger and animosity rolled off him in thick, choking waves. How on earth had she ever thought he was gentle? 'I don't know what game you are playing,' he said, each precise word feeling like a threat, 'but I advise that you cease immediately. This is no laughing matter, Miss Taylor. Millions of lives are at stake.'

Millions of lives? Surely that was an exaggeration, yet Olivia wasn't about to debate the point. She could see well enough how grim Zayed looked.

'I'm hardly laughing,' she answered levelly. 'You're the one who took me from the palace, Prince Zayed. You're the one who—' Her breath rushed out. *Seduced me.* She couldn't say the words. She'd been so stupidly willing, so *eager*, to be seduced. It beggared belief now, but only moments ago she'd been putty in his arms, wanting only to be moulded to whatever shape he chose. Still she met his gaze. 'I didn't ask for any of this.'

'Not at first, perhaps.' He took a step towards her, a different kind of fire in his eyes, one Olivia recognised, and it made her catch her breath. Even now, he could feel it. She could. The banked heat in his eyes flared to life and she felt its answer scorch through her. 'But later, Olivia,' he said, his voice low and menacing. 'Later you weren't asking. You were *begging*.'

She hated him. Officially, she hated him. Even as she felt the pulse of desire go through her, an insistent throb, she hated him. Damn her treacherous body. She knew Zayed saw it too, from the way his lip curled and his eyes travelled down her body, raking her in one scathing glance. A short while ago he'd made her feel cherished and important, and now he was making her feel tawdry and cheap, more than she ever had before. Everything about this was awful.

'I regret everything that happened between us this evening,' she said stiffly. 'More than you can possibly imagine.'

'You cannot regret it more than I do,' Zayed snapped. He swore again, turning away from her. 'Dear heaven, do you know what this is going to cost? Everything.' His voice choked and for a second he covered his face with his hands. *Everything.*

Watching him, Olivia saw a man in torment and she didn't fully understand it. She had a bizarre yet deep-seated urge to comfort him, to make it better. 'Is it because you—you have been unfaithful to Halina? I don't think she expects such fidelity until you're wed. You haven't even met. She'll understand.' She probably wouldn't care. She hadn't wanted to marry Zayed in the first place.

'Unfaithful?' He dropped his hands and let out a bark of humourless laughter. 'I have not merely been *unfaithful.*'

'You mean because you kidnapped me,' she said slowly, as reality caught up with her. 'And Sultan Hassan will know you meant to kidnap his daughter. He might call the engagement off.' He would be angry, she supposed, but that angry? She liked her employer, found him to be generous and carelessly affectionate, but she knew he had a strong and unwavering core of honour and dignity. She had no idea how he'd react to what Zayed had done.

'Might?' Zayed turned around to face her, his expression one of weary scorn. 'There is no *might*. He most certainly will. He will be furious that I dared to try to take his precious daughter. That I slipped through his defences.'

'How did you? Why were the gates open when we left?'

Zayed shrugged. 'A cousin of a cousin is one of the guards. He has been my spy for years. He made sure the gates were open to me.'

No, Sultan Hassan would not like that. He would be furious that someone had breached his security, and also threatened and maybe even a little scared by how seemingly easily it had been done. Unless...

'They might not even know I'm gone,' Olivia said slowly. She could hardly believe she was trying to help him, this man whom had taken so much from her, whom she had told herself she hated. Perhaps it was simply that ever-present urge she had to be helpful. Needed. Or perhaps it was the connection they shared, whether they wanted to or not. They'd been lovers. It was not something she would forget easily, or ever. 'If no one saw your men come or go...'

'How would they not know you're gone?' Zayed demanded. 'You were in the next room from the Princess. Someone would come looking for you.'

'Not necessarily.' It hurt a little to admit it, but Olivia ploughed on. 'I'm the governess, Prince Zayed, not one of the Princesses, and it was late. Princess Halina might be annoyed that I didn't say goodnight to her, but she would have assumed I'd gone to bed. No one will miss me till morning.'

Outside the tent silvery-pink light streaked the sky. It was just coming on to dawn and they were several hours' ride from the palace. 'You could return me,' she pressed, surprised and a little alarmed by the weird shaft of disappointment that went through her at that prospect. Surely this was the best solution, what she wanted? What she *had* to want? No other option made sense. 'And no one would be the wiser,' she added.

'And you wouldn't say anything?' He looked disbelieving. 'You wouldn't tell your employer of your kidnapping?'

'I do not wish people to know what has happened as much as you,' Olivia returned. The thought of Halina learning what she'd done with her fiancé… Olivia's stomach swooped. How could she have been so *stupid*? So utterly reckless? She'd never acted like that before in her life. 'Surely you can understand that?' she challenged Zayed, her voice rising a little.

'Yes, of course, but…'

For a second Zayed looked tempted. Torn. To make this all go away…they both wanted that. Of course they did. But yet again she felt that inexplicable disappointment flickering through her. Zayed shook his head. 'No, it is impossible.'

'Why?' The word burst out of Olivia and that flicker of disappointment faded away. She couldn't turn back the clock, but returning to Abkar was the next best thing, especially if her abduction hadn't yet been remarked upon. In a few hours she could be in her own bed and she could put the memory of this night completely behind her as if it had never happened…even if she knew she would never, ever forget it, or the feel of being in Zayed's arms.

'For many reasons,' Zayed said shortly. 'None of which you seem to have taken into consideration.'

'Then perhaps you could enlighten me,' Olivia snapped as her patience started to fray. She never spoke out like this, but some strange courage seemed to have taken hold of her. 'Instead of treating me like some sort of imbecile.'

* * *

Zayed stared at the woman he'd wed—his *bride*—with a mixture of frustration and despair. This was a complete disaster, one he was still reeling from. And yet, reeling as he was, a leaden weight had settled in his stomach, making him realise this could not be undone as easily as Olivia seemed to think. Of course it couldn't.

'Because too many people know. The Sultan's soldiers, my own people, the imam.' Who, at his instruction, would have shared the news throughout Kalidar that he had wedded and bedded Princess Halina. He had wanted the news to spread to strengthen his claim. He had never envisioned something like this happening.

'The imam?' She stared at him, stormy eyes narrowing. 'What imam?'

Impatience bit at him, chasing the fury and fear. 'The man who married us, of course.'

Olivia's mouth dropped open in wordless shock. '*Married?* But…'

Zayed stared at her, yet another unwelcome realisation flashing through him. 'You didn't know.' It was a statement, and one that was confirmed by the emphatic shake of her head. 'You don't speak Arabic,' he stated flatly. No wonder she had seemed so confused during their rushed wedding. He'd assumed she'd just been overwhelmed by events, but she hadn't actually known what was going on. Known that he'd been hurrying her into a binding, life-long commitment.

For the first time he felt a flash of true shame for the way he'd treated her. His instinct was to blame her for not having revealed her true identity, and it was one he couldn't let go of easily. He still suspected her motives, her ambition. Why hadn't she said anything all evening long? That part still didn't make sense.

But he'd never actually said who he was. He'd simply assumed she knew. Just as he'd assumed she'd realised they were marrying. *'Say yes,'* he'd told her, impatient to have the thing done. And so she had. An uncomfortable and unwelcome sensation of guilt trumped his suspicions for the moment.

Olivia dropped onto the bed, her robe flying out, revealing tempting glimpses of golden skin. Zayed looked away. Now was not the time for desire. 'How?' she whispered. 'How can we be married?'

'Easily. You said the vows, as did I.'

'I said yes…'

'Exactly.'

'But if I didn't know what I was doing, if I didn't *realise*, surely it can be annulled?'

Zayed gestured to the rumpled bed. 'Considering what we have just done? The entire camp knows what has transpired here tonight. Our marriage has been consummated. Most thoroughly.'

Olivia's cheeks went pink and she looked away. Zayed felt a stab of pity for her. He'd taken her innocence. She'd given it willingly enough, but still. It was a hard burden for a woman to bear, especially in this culture. And, he realised, she was not acting as if she expected to benefit from it. Surely she should be insisting he honour his vows rather than suggesting he seek an annulment? Unless she was playing a long game.

'Are you promised to someone else?' he asked, and she looked up in surprise.

'Promised?' She let out a short laugh. 'No. There's no one like that. There never has been. Obviously.' She looked away. 'You could set me aside, of course,' she said in a low voice. 'A divorce. It's done often enough by men of power.'

And would bring her even more shame. Zayed shook

his head. 'I am a man of honour.' Besides, he could not instigate a divorce without first knowing where he stood with Sultan Hassan.

'Are you?' Olivia challenged him shakily. 'Because a man of honour would not, it seems to me, abduct a woman and then take her virtue.'

Again he felt this guilt, along with a cleaner, stronger anger. 'I thought,' Zayed bit out, 'you were my *bride*.'

'And I suppose you think that makes it acceptable? I would say even less so, then.'

'I was intending to consummate a marriage that has been planned for nearly twenty years,' Zayed snapped. 'I admit, taking Princess Halina from her palace bedroom might seem like a drastic action, but I assure you, it was necessary.'

'Necessary? Why?'

He didn't really want to go into all the reasons behind the politics, not now when he was still reeling, his mind spinning, seeking answers when he feared there were none. He was married, and he'd made sure it was done in a way that was legal, binding and permanent. The trouble was, he'd married the wrong woman.

How could he have been so stupid? So rash? The events of the evening blurred in his mind; he'd been fuelled by both determination and desperation, needing to get it done, and quickly. So he had.

In one abrupt movement Zayed strode to the table and poured himself a healthy measure of arak. From behind him Olivia laughed softly.

'That's what got us into this trouble in the first place.'

'What do you mean?' He tossed it down in one burning swallow and then turned around. 'Are you saying you wouldn't have slept with me if you hadn't been drunk?' Another reason to be appalled by his own behaviour.

'I wasn't drunk.' Olivia glanced down. 'But my inhibitions were loosened, I suppose.'

Zayed thought of the way she'd arched and writhed beneath him, drawing him into her body, begging him to continue. Yes, they certainly had been loosened. And so had his. For a little while he'd lost sight of himself, and all he needed to achieve, when he'd been in Olivia's arms. When he'd felt the sweet purity of her response. It had pierced him like an arrow, it had shattered his defences, but thankfully he'd been quick to build them back up again.

And now he needed to think. He poured himself another measure of arak and sat down to drink it slowly, his mind starting to click into gear. 'Why were you in Princess Halina's bedroom, as a matter of interest?'

Olivia looked at him warily, as if suspecting a trap. Perhaps there was one. He had to know if she was hiding something. Had she known of the plot—had she positioned herself to be taken? Perhaps she'd been acting on Halina's behalf; Zayed had heard that his bride was less than enthused about their nuptials. Or maybe Olivia had seen a chance to better her seemingly small prospects and become Queen. The truth was, he knew nothing about her, and he had every reason to suspect her motives and actions. What gently reared woman fell into bed with a stranger without even asking his name or telling her own? And not a just a stranger but a man who had kidnapped her, for heaven's sake. Olivia's actions bordered on incredible in the truest sense of the word.

'I was putting her clothes away,' she said after a pause.

'You said you were a governess, not a maid.'

Olivia shrugged, her robe sliding off her shoulder. 'Lina and I were friends in school. That's how I got the position. I was in her sitting room, talking with her after she'd returned from dinner, and tidying up as I did it. Nothing unusual, really.'

'Where was Halina?'

'Sitting on the sofa. She was in the next room when you came in through the window. I could hear her humming.' Olivia shook her head slowly, her eyes wide. 'This all feels so completely surreal.'

And yet, unfortunately for both of them, it wasn't. He hadn't even seen Halina. In truth, he'd only had eyes for Olivia. Even through the blur of binoculars he'd been arrested by her slender form, her movements of efficient grace. And yet...

'You look like her.'

Olivia frowned. 'You think I look like her? No.' She shook her head. 'Not really. A pale shadow, perhaps.'

A pale shadow? It was a revealing choice of words. 'You have the same colouring,' he continued. 'Dark hair...'

'Halina is much prettier than I am,' Olivia insisted. 'Her hair is darker and wavier and...' She paused, biting her lip, and Zayed raised his eyebrows, curious now.

'And?'

'Her figure is...curvier.' Olivia flushed. 'Everyone thinks she is very beautiful.' The implication seemed to be that they thought Olivia was not. Yet Zayed had enjoyed her curves, slight as they were, and her hair—a deep, rich brown—was dark enough for him. Although, now that he was studying her properly, not blinded by the wilful determination he'd felt earlier, he saw that Olivia was right. She resembled Halina only to a small degree. Her colouring was lighter, more European, and she was a bit taller as well as slenderer. Even he could see that, having only glimpsed Halina in blurry photos. So why hadn't he realised it earlier? Because he'd been too focused. Too desperate.

'You don't speak Arabic,' he recalled slowly. 'And your name sounds English. Where were you raised?'

'All over the world. My father was British, a diplomat. We moved every few years to a new posting and then I went to boarding school with Halina in England. My mother was Spanish.'

Was. 'You are an orphan?'

Olivia nodded. 'My mother died when I was small, my father five years ago when I was seventeen. Since I was a friend of Halina's, Sultan Hassan took me under his protection. It was very kind of him.' Zayed nodded slowly. Hassan had presumably taken Olivia on as a paid employee. It wasn't quite the same, yet Olivia seemed grateful.

He took a sip of arak, needing his senses blunted even if he knew he couldn't afford the luxury. His mind moved in circles, seeking a way out of this trap he'd unwittingly made for himself, but all he felt was it tightening inexorably.

'So people know we're married,' Olivia said slowly. 'Too many people, it seems. What…what will this mean for you? And for Kalidar?'

'I don't know.' He glanced at her from beneath his lashes, suspicious all over again. She seemed too good to be true—innocent and helpful and eager to please, caring more for his situation than her own. *Was* she hoping to become the next Queen of Kalidar? Not that he could offer her that much yet. He had tents in the desert and a small cadre of loyal men. In ten years he had not left the barren desert of his country; he had not wanted to give Malouf an opportunity to seize even more power or let his men think he'd abandoned them. If Olivia was hoping for a life of luxury and ease, it would be a long time coming…but it would come. Was she banking on that? Or had she sacrificed herself for Halina's sake?

What *did* she want?

'I'm sorry,' Olivia said after a moment, her voice soft and sad, and Zayed let out a harsh huff of laughter. Now he really was suspicious. She was laying it on a bit thick, her concern for him and his country, when he'd taken her innocence and ruined her reputation.

'*You're* sorry?'

She hunched one slender shoulder. 'You have more to lose than I do. That's what you meant by "millions," isn't it? The people of Kalidar. This marriage—marriage to Halina—was important to you politically. Wasn't it?' She searched his face, her expression both guileless and compassionate. 'I don't know the details, of course.'

'You don't need to know them.'

'But what will you do if you cannot marry Halina?' Olivia's eyes were round, her hair tousled, her lips parted. Even now she looked desirable, and Zayed wanted her all over again.

He suppressed that painful stab of inconvenient desire. Was this her ploy, to get him to admit that he had to stay married to her? Because he wouldn't do it. He'd make her no promises. He'd made far too many already. 'I don't know what I will do,' Zayed said shortly. 'I have to think.' He looked away, a muscle working in his throat, a pain lodging in his chest like a cold, hard stone. This marriage had been essential. Without it...*without it*...

He *had* to get out of this marriage. He had to make it right with Sultan Hassan. Anything else would be failure, *doom* for his kingship, his country. Far too much was at stake for him to worry about the finer feelings of one forgettable woman.

Zayed rose from his seat while Olivia watched with wide eyes, apprehension visible in every taut line of her body. 'Where are you going?'

'Out,' Zayed said brusquely. 'I need to think.'

'But what…what am I meant to do?'

He raked her with one deliberately dismissive glance, determined not to care about this woman to even the smallest degree. He still suspected her. How could he not? To have fallen into bed with him… Maybe he was being judgemental, but he had to be. Too much was at stake for him to trust her an inch.

'You can do what you like,' he informed her. 'Get some sleep, stay in the tent or wander around. I wouldn't go far, though. Outside this camp there is nothing but barren desert for a hundred miles in any direction. You wouldn't last long, Miss Taylor.'

And, with that parting warning, he stalked out of the tent.

CHAPTER FIVE

OLIVIA CURLED UP on the bed, hugging her knees to her chest. She couldn't even begin to comprehend everything that had happened and, far worse, what it might mean. Married. *Married*.

She'd been an idiot for not realising, or at least not suspecting, something of what had been going on. It had been some kind of ceremony, she could see that now, and through her dazed confusion she'd managed to grasp snatches of words: *commitment...responsibility...vow*. She'd heard it, but she hadn't put it all together to realise what was actually happening. How could she have? She hadn't known her captor was Prince Zayed, or that he thought she was Princess Halina.

But even that was the pinnacle of stupidity, Olivia thought wretchedly. Why would a stranger kidnap her, the governess, a mere servant? Of course he'd thought she was someone else. Someone important.

And as for what had come afterward...as magical as it had been, she couldn't think about that. Couldn't wrap her mind around it...or what it might mean.

Through the tent flap Olivia could see a sliver of dawn sky, a pearly pink lighting up the world. Her body ached with fatigue, and her mind too. She needed to sleep, like

Zayed had suggested. And after that… Olivia couldn't even begin to think what the future held.

She stretched out on the bed, inhaling the already familiar musk of Zayed. The feather mattress still bore the indent of their entwined bodies. She closed her eyes, willing herself to sleep. Her mind seethed with remembered sensations, and she felt herself tensing up despite her best efforts to relax. She was never going to get to sleep, yet she knew she needed the rest. Desperately.

Somehow, despite the tumbled thoughts in her mind, the tension in her body, she fell into a restless doze that at some point turned into a deep, dreamless slumber. When she awoke, for a few seconds she couldn't remember what had happened, and she lay there, blinking up at the tent ceiling, her mind fuzzy and blank. Then it came back with a sickening rush, and she closed her eyes as her mind relentlessly played a montage of memories from the night before: the moment Zayed had come through the window, dark and fearsome, yet with those gentle eyes; then the dizzying fall from the window; the endless hours on horseback…and then…

Olivia let out a rush of breath. Even now she could feel Zayed's mouth on hers, moving so persuasively, his hands caressing her, knowing exactly how to touch her and make her respond. And her own utter wantonness… She hadn't even questioned herself, not really. She'd simply wanted… and taken. Or, rather, let herself be taken.

It had to be mid-morning now; the tent was baking hot, bright sunlight filtering through the entrance flap. The skimpy robe Olivia had put on last night now stuck to her body. She rolled into a sitting position, groaning as her head spun, no doubt from the alcohol she wasn't used to, as well as being dehydrated. From outside the tent she could hear the sounds of activity: men talking in shouts and laughter; a horse nickering. What, she wondered as she held her head in her hands, happened now?

A few moments later Suma came in with a tray of food and drink. She smiled at Olivia, looking pleased.

'You wear the robe,' she said in more distinct Arabic. Zayed must have told her that Olivia had trouble understanding. What else had he said? How many people knew what had transpired in this tent? Olivia had a feeling it was just about everyone in the camp, and she blushed with the shame of it.

'Yes, thank you,' she answered in her own halting Arabic. Suma put the tray down on the table.

'Come and eat,' she instructed. 'Drink.'

'Thank you.' Olivia realised she was both thirsty and hungry. She'd had little to eat and drink last night besides the arak, a few grapes and a bit of cheese. Remembering how Zayed had fed her a grape made her blush all over again. How could she have allowed him such liberties? Why hadn't she been thinking more sensibly?

'It was a good night,' Suma said with satisfaction. She beamed at Olivia as Olivia sat down at the table and began to serve herself some of the traditional Arabic dishes. There was labneh yogurt with lemon juice, fava beans with mint and fresh cucumber, as well as dates flavoured with cardamom. It all looked delicious. There was also a little brass carafe of coffee that smelled wonderful.

'A bride needs to eat,' Suma added, smiling widely. She looked homely and happy, and even through her embarrassment Olivia's heart went out to her. Did Suma not realise she wasn't the Princess? That this marriage was a complete disaster? 'Especially if there is a *nunu*.'

For a second Olivia didn't know what she meant; the phrase was colloquial and beyond her understanding. Then she saw Suma pat her stomach meaningfully and realisation rushed through Olivia. A baby. *Especially if there was a baby.* If Zayed had got her pregnant.

She stared at Suma in ill-disguised horror, but the older woman merely took it as maidenly surprise and chortled happily before leaving the tent. Olivia stared down at the plate piled high with various dishes, her mouth dry, her appetite vanished. What if she was pregnant?

It was perfectly possible, she realised with a sick feeling. Her cycle was regular and she was right in the middle of it. Even she in her virginal—or not—innocence knew that this was a peak time for fertility. She could very well be pregnant with Prince Zayed's baby.

Recrimination tore through her, worse than before. She felt like screaming, stomping her feet or, worse, sobbing. How could she have been such a besotted fool? Twenty-two years of living quietly, staying safe, and she'd risked it all in a single night with a stranger. It was as if, last night, she'd become someone else entirely.

The trouble was, she couldn't stay as that person. She wasn't that person. And now she was back to being plain Olivia Taylor, except she was married to a prince and she very well might be expecting his child. She would have laughed at the sheer lunacy of it, if there hadn't been a lump the size of a golf ball in her throat.

Somehow she managed to choke down some of the breakfast. She needed to eat and drink, *nunu* or not. She'd half finished her plate when Suma returned with fresh clothes, thankfully modest. Olivia took the loose tunic and trousers with murmured thanks.

'You wish to wash?' Suma asked, miming washing. 'The oasis has a private area. You go?'

Olivia nodded. She'd like to see something other than this tent, even if she inwardly quailed at the thought of facing a camp full of strangers. With some miming and basic directions, Suma instructed her how to get to a private inlet of the oasis.

Smiling and murmuring her thanks, Olivia took a deep breath and then ducked out of the tent.

'My Prince?'

Zayed started from his ill-humoured reverie to see Jahmal at the entrance to his private tent, a respectful but inquisitive look on his face. Did he know of his mistake? From the guarded curiosity on his aide's face, Zayed doubted it, but Jahmal could sense something was wrong.

'It...went well?' he asked cautiously.

Zayed almost laughed, except there was nothing remotely funny about this situation. Nothing at all. He'd spent the last hour pacing his tent and trying to figure a way out of this mess of his own making. Because it was of his own making, no matter what Olivia Taylor was in it for. If he'd kidnapped the right woman, he would not be here, cursing his fate as well as his own idiocy.

'It went,' he said tersely. He scrubbed his face with his hands, exhaustion crashing through him. He hadn't slept for over twenty-four hours and he didn't foresee much sleep in his future. He still had no idea what to do to fix this situation. Send an envoy to Hassan? How the hell could he explain?

'The Princess is...happy?' Jahmal ventured, his forehead creasing as his dark eyes searched Zayed's fierce expression.

This time Zayed did laugh, because what else could he do? There were no walls to punch, no way to let out the fury he felt, directed solely at himself. For ten years failure had not been an option—and yet after all the war, all the bloodshed, all the loss, grief and pain, he wondered if the last decade had been nothing but failure. And now this.

'I have no idea how the Princess feels,' he told Jahmal, 'because she's not here.'

Jahmal's frown deepened. 'My Prince? I don't understand…'

'I took the wrong woman,' Zayed explained, biting each word off and spitting it out. It was like some ridiculous farce. 'I kidnapped the governess, not Princess Halina.' Colour surged into his face just from stating it so baldly. How could he have been so stupid?

'The wrong woman…' Jahmal's face drained of colour. 'But…did she not say…?'

'No, she didn't say. She didn't protest at the wedding, either.' An hour of sitting here stewing had made suspicion solidify in Zayed. He might be to blame for taking the wrong woman, but why the hell hadn't Olivia spoken up? There had been plenty of opportunity. Why hadn't she asked who he was? He'd assumed she'd known, because she'd never said otherwise. Really, she'd been remarkably quiet, all things considered. And that made him wonder if she'd seen a good deal and decided to take it.

There was, he knew, only one way to find out. Not that it would make much difference to the outcome, but at least it would ease his conscience when he informed Olivia in no uncertain terms that he was divorcing her and marrying Halina at the earliest opportunity…and that she would help him to achieve that goal.

After Jahmal left, Zayed decided to go talk to Olivia. The sooner he could implement some damage control, the better. But when he went to the tent, it was empty, and Suma informed him that Olivia had gone down to the oasis to bathe. Fine. He would see her there.

The small camp was built around a verdant oasis,

shaped like a kidney, so there were several private inlets. Olivia had gone to one of these, well out of sight of the camp, and Zayed strode down the palm-fringed path to the private cove to find her.

He paused as he crested a gently rolling dune; Olivia was hip-deep in water and wearing absolutely nothing. The breath rushed out of Zayed's lungs as he took in her perfect slender form, the bright morning sunlight gilding her body in gold.

She held a cloth above her head, squeezing it so water dripped out, the droplets running down her shoulders and back. Desire surged through him, an irrepressible force. Zayed clenched his fists, willing it back. Lust for this woman had weakened him once. It would not do so again.

He came down the hill, the long grasses that fringed the oasis rustling as he moved, and Olivia turned, gasping as she caught sight of him. She rushed to cover herself and Zayed's mouth twisted sardonically. Her maidenly outrage was just a little too melodramatic to be convincing, especially considering what they'd been doing together mere hours ago.

'You don't need to rush,' he drawled as she waded out of the water and snatched a towel. 'I've seen it all before.'

'That doesn't mean you need to see it again.' She knotted the towel above her breasts, her hands shaking. Zayed folded his arms and surveyed her dispassionately. Never mind that she looked utterly lovely, with her dark, damp hair already starting to dry and curl in tendrils about her heart-shaped face. Never mind that her eyes looked huge and blue, and that those thick, sooty lashes drove him to distraction. *Never mind.*

'As soon as possible, I am going to send an envoy to Sultan Hassan, explaining the situation.'

Her eyes widened and Zayed thought he saw disappointment flicker in their stormy depths, vindicating his suspicions. She was in it for herself. She had to be.

'Everything about our situation?' she asked cautiously.

'Word will already have got out.'

'Even so...'

'I am not a liar.' His voice came out hard. 'I will be honest with Hassan, and so will you.'

'Me?'

'You will write him a letter that I will include as part of my correspondence, explaining what happened and how you did not correct my misinformation.'

Anger flared in her eyes and she hugged her arms to herself, hitching the towel higher. 'Correct your misinformation?' she repeated with a surprising edge of acid to her voice. 'I didn't realise it was my responsibility to make sure my abductor's kidnapping attempt went smoothly.' She planted her hands on her hips, making the towel slip and affording Zayed a tantalising glimpse of the rounded curves of her breasts. 'When should I have done that, Prince Zayed? When I was being thrown out of a window? Or when I was gagged on horseback?'

'I removed the gag.' Pain flickered at his temples as he set his jaw.

'Or when I was thrust into a tent and a marriage ceremony without having exchanged a word with you? What should I have done? Said, *Pardon me, but I think you might have the wrong woman*?'

'Surely,' Zayed gritted, 'you realised a mere employee would not be kidnapped?'

'A mere employee.' Hurt flashed in her eyes and she looked away. Zayed suppressed an unnecessary flicker of guilt. He'd only been stating the truth. It wasn't meant to be an insult. 'I'm afraid I was too overwhelmed and fearful for my life to consider the practicality of it all,' she said after a moment, her gaze still averted.

Rage billowed inside him, rage he knew shouldn't be directed at her, or at least solely at her. Yet he could not keep himself from it. 'And later? When we were in the tent alone, eating and drinking—surely you could have said something then?'

Colour washed over her cheekbones. 'What should I have said?' she asked in a suffocated voice.

'You could have said who you were! You could have asked who I was. We could have avoided consummating the marriage, which would have made things much simpler now.' Olivia didn't answer and Zayed took another step towards her. 'Unless you had no intention of revealing who you were. Or that you knew who I was.' It wasn't quite a question and her gaze swung back to him, her fine eyebrows drawn together.

'What are you implying?'

'That you took advantage of the situation,' Zayed said evenly, ignoring the flicker of unease that rippled through him. Olivia had gone very still, her blue eyes wide, her expression strangely fathomless.

'Advantage,' she said after a moment, her tone as fathomless as her face.

'Yes, advantage. As a lowly governess, essentially a servant in the royal household with few prospects, you saw the advantage in being my wife. Being Queen.'

'Queen? Of what?' Contempt rolled off every syllable. 'A huddle of tents in the desert?'

Zayed flinched under the words, although he knew they were more or less true. 'I will regain my inheritance,' he said in a near growl. 'I promise you that.'

'When? And why would I take such an enormous risk?' She hitched the towel higher, her face flushed now, her eyes bright with anger and even hurt. 'You are contempt-ible to suggest such a thing.'

'What am I supposed to think?' Zayed demanded. 'There were any number of opportunities for you to tell me who you were.'

'I didn't realise I needed to! Why should I?'

'And what about after?' Zayed took another step to-wards her; he could smell the freshness of her damp skin, almost feel her quiver. 'What about the wedding night?'

She set her jaw, although her hands shook on the towel. 'What about it?'

'You fell into my arms easily enough. Too easily, I think.'

'It is to my own shame and regret that I did.' Tears trem-bled on her lashes and she blinked them back. 'Whatever you believe.'

'What woman falls into bed with her kidnapper, with-out even knowing his name?'

'What man seduces a woman without checking who she is first?' Olivia snapped. 'I accept I was seduced, and far too easily at that. But you are the one who kidnapped me, Prince Zayed. You are the one who took me from my home and forced——'

'I did not force.' The words were low and deadly.

'Not…not that. But the wedding ceremony. You didn't even explain——'

'I thought you knew.'

'Then you made a lot of assumptions, and now you are paying the price, as am I.' With her chin held high, Olivia went to move past him, but Zayed grabbed her wrist, feel-ing the fragile bones beneath her skin.

'We are not done here.'

She whirled around to face him, fury tautening her fea-tures, the towel slipping so her breasts spilled out, golden and perfect. Despite everything, or perhaps because of it, desire arrowed through Zayed, impossible to resist. He drew her towards him and she came, willingly, her lips parting, her features already softening. It was that easy. Her instant acquiescence hardened something inside him and he dropped her wrist.

'Even now you are willing,' he said, not bothering to hide his disgust, and Olivia flushed crimson as she yanked the towel back up.

'As were you,' she choked. 'Don't deny it.'

'I am not now,' he told her coldly, and then turned away, only to still when he saw Jahmal coming over the hill. How much had his aide seen?

'My Prince.' Jahmal's gaze flicked to Olivia and then away again quickly. 'Forgive my interruption, but a message has just come through.'

'A message?' Zayed tensed, wondering if Hassan had already heard, was already angry. If he broke the betrothal... Except, of course, Zayed had already broken it by marrying another woman.

'It is Malouf.'

Olivia might not have understood the Arabic, but she clearly understood that name, for she gasped softly.

'What has he done?' Zayed demanded.

'He sent some men to raid a village two hours' ride from here. There are wounded.'

Zayed swore. Malouf wreaked his bloody war to no purpose and innocents paid the price.

'Let us depart at once.' He started to stride from the oasis when Olivia's voice stopped him.

'Wait!' she cried, and Zayed turned around impatiently. 'What is it?'

She stretched out one slender hand. 'Take me with you.'

CHAPTER SIX

OLIVIA WATCHED AS Zayed's eyes flared with both impatience and irritation and knew he would consider no such thing. She was a liability, a burden, in every possible way. He despised her, it seemed, for having given in to him... just as she despised herself.

And yet she didn't want to be abandoned. Who knew when Zayed would come back? He might leave her here to languish; conveniently forget about her while he pursed his political destiny. And, more importantly, she wanted to do something, to feel useful, rather than sit and wait and worry. If she went with Zayed, she could help.

'Take me with you,' she said again, her voice stronger now. 'I have training in first aid, and I can help if any women or children have been hurt.' She pulled the towel around her more tightly, conscious of the other man's carefully averted gaze. 'I can be of use; I know it.'

Zayed's lips thinned and his eyes narrowed. 'But you don't speak Arabic.'

'I speak enough.' Olivia lifted her chin, willing him to agree. She was afraid to be left here, alone with strangers. Zayed might hate her at the moment, but at least he knew her. He knew her all too well.

Zayed glanced at the other man, who was keeping a deliberately neutral expression. Then he gave a terse nod.

'Very well. Suma will see you have the appropriate clothes. Jahmal will fetch you in five minutes.'

He strode away from the oasis, followed by Jahmal, and Olivia's breath came out in a whoosh of both relief and trepidation. What had she just got herself into? Yet anything was better than staying here and waiting, wondering. The future seemed like so much fog, impossible to know…and yet terrifying at the same time.

Back at the tent Suma brought her some more clothes—desert boots and a headscarf to keep out the sand. Olivia finished dressing quickly, her fingers shaking as she did up the laces on her boots.

Zayed's horrid accusation ricocheted through her brain, filling her with both shame and fury. How could he think she'd somehow planned this? But what was he supposed to think, when she'd fallen into bed with him so willingly, so instantly? Olivia didn't know what was worse—Zayed thinking she was a scheming gold-digger or a wanton woman.

Exactly five minutes later Jahmal entered the tent and Olivia followed him out, her heart thudding in her chest.

Prince Zayed was waiting in front of a desert camouflage Jeep parked outside the camp, looking both fierce and royal in combat boots, loose trousers and a camouflage shirt that clung to the muscles of his chest and arms. His agate gaze swept over her, giving nothing away. With one brief nod he indicated she should get into the back of the Jeep, so Olivia did. Zayed climbed into the driver's seat and Jahmal slid in next to him.

The sky was a hard, bright blue, the unforgiving sunlight illuminating the barren desert landscape Olivia had been unable to see last night. She'd glimpsed a bit of it on the way to the oasis but now, as the Jeep started away from the camp, she grasped something of the utter isolation of their location.

Undulating sand dunes swept to the horizon, interspersed with large, jagged-looking boulders. She felt as if they were a million miles from anywhere.

The Jeep jostled over the sand and Olivia leaned back, fatigue crashing over her now that the initial adrenalin burst of her confrontation with Zayed had gone.

What was he going to do with her? He'd mentioned sending an envoy to the palace and her writing a letter. But what on earth could she write? Would Sultan Hassan even employ her after hearing that she'd slept with his daughter's fiancé? The thought of being out of a job, potentially without a reference, filled her with fear.

Even worse was the prospect of being without a home, which filled her with a worse grief. For years she'd called the palace on the outskirts of Abkar's capital city home. She'd loved Sultan Hassan's little daughters, had played with them and plaited their hair, taught them English and teased them about their future husbands. She'd felt part of a family for the first time in her life, even if it had been in a small way, as an employee. She would lose it all, she feared, when Hassan heard about what she'd done. Never mind that Zayed had abducted her; Olivia knew how these things played out in this culture. A woman would not be forgiven.

And now, in the hard, bright light of day, she wondered yet again how she had succumbed so easily. He'd been a stranger, a threat, yet when he'd touched her she hadn't cared. She'd only wanted to feel more, to experience the wonder of desiring and being desired. It was as if her common sense, usually in such abundance, had abandoned her completely. She supposed she wasn't the first woman to be in such a position, but it still smote her sorely.

Still, Zayed would annul the marriage on some obscure grounds, or else simply divorce her. They wouldn't stay married and she would hopefully be able to find another position. The thought made her feel mixed up inside, a jumble of emotions she couldn't let herself untangle quite yet.

She'd felt too much already, from the electric tingle of Zayed's touch to the churning fear when she'd first been taken, and then the overwhelming shock, like a tidal wave of numbness, when she'd realised the colossal mistake they'd both made.

Zayed glanced back at her, his expression closed, his eyes hard. 'Are you holding up?' he asked brusquely, and Olivia nodded, knowing she shouldn't be touched by such a small, simple question, yet feeling it all the same. Tears stung her eyes and she blinked them back fiercely. The last thing she wanted to do now was cry. She didn't even know what she'd be crying for—for what she was about to lose, or what she'd already lost?

They rode in silence, bumping over dunes for two hours, until they came to a huddle of Bedouin tents by a small oasis fringed with palms. Even before the Jeep came to a stop outside the circle of tents Olivia could feel the sense of desolation and despair. It hung like a mist over the camp, a darkness despite the sun that glinted diamond-bright off rock and boulders in the distance.

Zayed leapt out of the Jeep in one graceful movement and then, to Olivia's surprise, he reached behind and held out his hand for her. Olivia took it, the feel of his rough, callused palm on hers reminding her of how he'd touched her earlier, and how she'd responded to it.

It seemed incredible that she could be affected by him even now, with confusion all around them, but her body felt as if it were supernaturally attuned to his. Or was she just naïve because no man had ever paid her any attention before? Either way, she had to ignore the fizzing sensation in her stomach, the electric excitement that pulsed through her as his hand brushed hers.

'Come.' Zayed dropped her hand once she'd exited the Jeep and Olivia followed him into the camp. Men, women and children milled about in states of sadness and anxiety; after speaking to some of the leaders, Zayed told Olivia that Malouf's men had raided the camp and stolen their goats and camels, roughed up a few of their men. A few of the women and children were hurt, collateral damage, but fortunately no one had been too badly injured.

'It could have been worse,' Zayed said grimly, his expression making Olivia think that he had seen worse before, more than once.

'Let me help,' she said. 'Where are the women and children who have been hurt?'

Zayed nodded towards the tranquil pool of water the camp had been built around. 'They are washing in the oasis.'

Nodding, Olivia started towards the group of women she saw huddled by the pool. She didn't know exactly what she could do to help, only that she wanted to be of some use. Her heart ached for these people, the confusion they felt at having their home so needlessly destroyed.

The women turned as she approached, eyes narrowing with curiosity, and Olivia wondered how on earth she could explain who she was. But then, for better or worse, it turned out there was no explanation needed.

'I…help,' she said haltingly, and a child ran towards her, tackling her around the knees. Relief poured through her. Until that moment she hadn't quite realised how much she needed to feel useful. To be needed.

She spent the next few hours bandaging cuts and cleaning scrapes, communicating in a mixture of halting Arabic and miming that made the children chortle with glee.

Olivia soon realised that the way she could be the most useful was simply by listening and chatting to the women and children, distracting them from their worries. And, goodness knew, she could use some distraction as well.

When all the injuries had been seen to, they retired to one of the women's tents, drank apricot juice and nibbled on pitta bread with fresh hummus.

Before long she had a chubby baby on her hip and a toddler clinging to her legs as the women began firing questions at her, only half of which Olivia could understand, and none of which she could answer.

Who was she? Was she Zayed's bride? Had he married in secret? Were they in love? When Olivia blushed, the woman crowed with laughter, delighted by her response. Even when she said nothing, it seemed she gave something away. And, with dread curdling in her stomach, she had a feeling Zayed would be furious.

But perhaps he would be furious with her, no matter what. He seemed determined to be, just as he was determined to regain what he'd lost. She would just be collateral damage, so much jetsam to be thrown away. The thought made her throat close. It hurt to be so disregarded, even though part of her understood it. Really, what else could she expect? Prince Zayed had a country to think of. She was just one woman, an unimportant palace servant he needed to get rid of.

'Come.' One of the women smiled at her and plucked her sleeve. 'You are tired. You rest.'

She was tired, every muscle and sinew pulsing with exhaustion. With a smile of relieved gratitude, Olivia followed the woman to another tent where she could sleep... and perhaps forget, for a little while, the mess she was still hopelessly embroiled in.

* * *

It had been a strange, surreal kind of day. Zayed had been immersed in meetings with the tribal leaders, listening to their complaints, assuring them he would have vengeance on Malouf's men. He'd already sent one of his own patrols out after the raiders, in the hope of recapturing the tribe's valuable livestock. He saw the hope and, far more damning, the faith in the eyes of his people when he spoke to them and guilt cramped his stomach. How could they trust him as their leader, when he'd made such an enormous mistake? When he'd married the wrong woman and put his country's most valuable alliance at terrible risk?

Even though he barely saw her, Zayed was conscious of Olivia throughout the day. He saw her down at the oasis, washing and bandaging the children's scrapes with meticulous care. Later, when all the injuries had been seen to, he saw her laughing and playing in the water, kids crawling over her. The women seemed to have accepted her into their fold without question, which made Zayed wonder if they assumed she was his bride. Did they know she wasn't the woman he'd meant to have? He had no idea if Olivia's rudimentary Arabic was up to the task of disabusing them of any of their assumptions…or if she even would. Perhaps she was simply making herself useful so he would see what an asset she could be to him.

He shouldn't have brought her, he supposed, so he could have stemmed any questions or curiosity, but he hadn't thought the news of his bride would have spread to such a remote place. And he hadn't wanted to let Olivia out of his sight, not until he knew what he was going to do with her.

In late afternoon, as the shadows started drawing in, Zayed met with Jahmal.

'We'll stay the night,' he informed his aide. 'And leave in the morning for Rubyhan.'

Jahmal raised his eyebrows. 'Rubyhan? Is that wise?'

Zayed took a deep breath and let it out slowly. 'I need to retrench and decide what I am going to do about Olivia.' Rubyhan, the summer palace of the royal family of Kalidar, had thankfully remained in his possession throughout Malouf's reign. He used it as the seat of his provisional government and the place to which he went when he needed to regroup. And he certainly needed to regroup now.

A headache flickered at his temples and Zayed closed his eyes, fighting the pain. The last thing he needed was one of the crippling migraines he'd suffered from since receiving a head injury eight years ago in one of the battles against Malouf's men.

'My Prince?' Jahmal sounded cautious. 'Surely you can simply set her aside? She is only a servant.'

Irritation prickled his scalp and tightened his gut at the suggestion, although it was no more than what he'd already thought himself. Yet somehow he didn't like his aide saying it.

'It is not so simple,' he said tightly. 'Sultan Hassan will have realised I kidnapped his servant and, moreover, that I intended to kidnap his daughter. Our negotiations will be thrown into total disarray.' If not broken off completely. 'I need to mend things with Hassan. When I have an answer from him, I can decide what to do about Olivia.'

'Still,' Jahmal persisted. 'It can be managed. If she is only a servant...'

Only a servant.

It was true, of course. Olivia was, to all intents and purposes, expendable. So why did that thought bother him right now? It shouldn't, Zayed realised with sudden, crystalline clarity. He was letting sentiment cloud his vision, soften his determination. Despite his suspicions, he felt guilty for the way he'd treated her last night, so he was resisting the prospect of setting her aside and what it would mean for her. But he couldn't let last night change things. He couldn't let Olivia matter at all.

'I do not wish to discuss it now,' he said in a clipped voice. 'I am going to wash and then we will eat with the tribal leaders.'

'Very good, My Prince.'

Later, after he'd washed and eaten, he went in search of Olivia. He hadn't seen her for several hours, and the realisation made unease deepen within his chest, although he couldn't say why.

One of the women informed him she'd been given her own tent, which confirmed his suspicions that the tribe knew she was a woman of importance, perhaps even his bride. He really shouldn't have brought her. His judgement was being clouded again and again, it seemed. The sooner this woman was out of his life, the better.

He bent to enter her tent, the flap falling closed behind him. He straightened, glancing around at the rough furnishings, a far cry from the sumptuous luxury she'd had back at his own camp. She was sitting on a pallet covered with sheepskin, her slender fingers flying as they plaited her damp hair. Her eyes widened as she saw him come in but she said nothing, just watched him warily.

Zayed's gaze flicked over her. She wore the same nondescript tunic and trousers she'd been in earlier, hardly clothes to inflame a man, yet even now he felt that inexorable pull to her. What was it about this woman? She wasn't anything special. Yes, her eyes were lovely, and her figure was appealing, but she was just a woman. One among many, although he hadn't had a woman for a long time before Olivia. Perhaps that was it. He'd denied himself carnal pleasures for too long, in pursuit of his inheritance. His kingdom.

'Tomorrow we are travelling to Rubyhan.'

'Rubyhan?'

'The summer palace of the royal family and the seat of my government.'

She nodded slowly, finishing her plait before resting her hands in her lap. 'And then?'

'Then I will contact Sultan Hassan, and you will write the letter.'

'And when I do? What are you hoping will happen?'

'That he will understand the mistake I made and we will reopen marriage negotiations.' Anything else was intolerable, impossible. He had to have Hassan's support in fighting Malouf. For the last ten years various political leaders had tried to distance themselves from Kalidar's civil war, waiting to see the outcome. On several occasions he had been on the precipice of victory; once he'd made it to the capital city of Arjah, only to have the palace gates closed against him.

With Hassan's support, he could exert political pressure on Malouf and force him to resign. The man was old, with no heirs; his soldiers were starting to dissent, tired of the endless fighting against Zayed and his men, knowing him to be the rightful King. A bloodless coup would be the perfect victory and finally, finally, an end to all the war and loss.

Olivia nodded slowly, her head bent, her gaze on her clasped hands. Zayed could see the nape of her neck, the tender skin, the pale, curling hairs, and the sight caused a nameless feeling to clench his insides in a way he didn't like. 'And what will happen to me, do you suppose?' she asked after a moment.

'Are you hoping for a settlement?'

She looked up, eyes flashing. 'You sound so judge-mental.'

'I was merely asking a question.'

'No, you weren't.' She took a quick, shuddering breath. 'You have judged me again and again for falling into bed with you. I admit, it was a mistake. A colossal mistake. But I didn't mean to do it. If I could undo it, I would. I have no desire to be your Queen. I have never been inter-ested in power or money.' Another quick breath tore at his senses. He had a bizarre urge to comfort her, even though he knew he couldn't.

'All I've wanted,' Olivia continued more quietly, 'is a place to belong. A sense of family. A job to do. I had all that with the royal family of Abkar.'

'And so you will have it again.'

She glanced at him, scorn clear on her face, surprising him. 'Now you are the one who is naïve.'

'What do you mean?'

'It doesn't matter.'

'No, tell me.' Zayed took a step towards her. 'What do you mean? What do you think will happen to you when you return to Abkar?'

'Why do you care?' Olivia challenged. 'You have not been all that interested in my welfare, Prince Zayed.'

He stiffened with affront. 'I told you, I am a man of honour.'

'I have yet to see any evidence of that,' Olivia said qui-etly. It was her tone that got to him. She wasn't angry or accusing. No, she was merely stating a fact. And, with a rush of churning regret, he realised it was true.

'You must understand why I have to be suspicious,' he said after a pause. 'So much is at stake. There is no one I can trust.'

She arched an eyebrow. 'What do you think I am going to do? Perform some act of sabotage? I am not some spy for Malouf.'

His blood chilled to hear it so plainly. He would not put such a preposterous idea beyond the wily fiend...but he didn't think Olivia was part of such a nefarious plan. Nor, he realised, did he think she was scheming to better her position. He'd seen too much despair and shock from her to believe that any longer, even if it would have made it easier to plot his own course with no consideration of the woman before him.

'I know you are not a spy,' he said gruffly. 'But I must be careful.'

'I understand.' Now she simply sounded tired. 'And tomorrow I will write your wretched letter and hopefully all of this will go away. Or at least I will.' She glanced at him, her expression filled with weariness. 'Now I'd like to go to bed, if you don't mind.'

Zayed stared at her, wishing he'd got more answers. What would happen to her when she returned to Abkar? He could settle money on her, enough to make sure she would need nothing for a long time. Fortunately he'd been able to secure the royal family's personal investments before Malouf had taken control, which were considerable. He didn't want for money, and he could make sure Olivia didn't either.

But was it enough? And why were such things bothering him now? He glanced at her, at the slight shoulders bowed under an invisible weight, that tender nape. Her lashes swept her cheeks in sooty fans as she lowered her gaze, waiting for him to go.

But he didn't want to. Quite suddenly he could remember the exact feel and taste of her. He could recall how pliant she'd been in his arms, and how exquisite it had felt to

be sheathed inside her. Inconvenient memories that made
his body stir with insistent desire.

'Please let me know if there is anything you need,' he
said finally, shifting to ease the ache in his groin. 'I'm
sorry your accommodation is not more comfortable.'

'It's fine, and more than I expected from somewhere so
remote.' She didn't look at him, merely stretched out on
the pallet, waiting for him leave, ready for sleep.

Zayed hesitated another second. This was his bride,
whether he wanted her or not, whether he'd meant it or
not. He might set her aside as soon as possible, but for now
she was his responsibility, and he felt the weight of it with
sudden, inexplicable fierceness.

Yet at the moment she wanted nothing from him. She
refused even to look at him. And so, filled with a restless
unease, Zayed bid her goodnight and left the tent.

CHAPTER SEVEN

THEY LEFT FOR Rubyhan early the next morning. The sky was a pale, luminescent pink as Olivia climbed into the Jeep, gazing around at the harsh desert landscape transformed momentarily into softness and light as dawn broke over the dunes.

She'd spent four years in Abkar, on the edge of the desert, but she'd rarely ventured into its barren heart. If she wasn't at the palace, then she was accompanying the Princess on various holidays, mostly to Europe or the Caribbean, playgrounds of the rich and royal.

Prince Zayed was an entirely different kind of royal, she mused as she watched him swing up into the Jeep, his muscles rippling with the graceful movement. He reminded her of some ancient warrior, proud and defiant and definitely dangerous. He wasn't like the pampered aristos she'd seen on some of her travels with the royal family, partying it up, whinging about whatever they could. No, she couldn't see Prince Zayed at some Monte Carlo night club. He was too raw and primal for that, and even now she was drawn to him.

Yesterday, as she'd helped the women and children, her gaze had been drawn to him again and again. Drawn to his powerful form, and also the way he spoke and listened, the intense responsibility he felt for his people, his country. She'd had the sudden, crazy thought that, when Prince Zayed did love a woman, it would be with that same blazing focus. It just wouldn't be her.

Now his grey-green gaze caught and snared hers and Olivia looked away, afraid her thoughts would be written on her face. Why on earth was she thinking about whom he might love? Their one night together had awakened a longing inside her she'd managed to suppress until now. And she had to keep suppressing it. The last thing she wanted to do was feel something—something more—for Zayed.

She'd thought they would be taking the Jeep to Rubyhan, but after an hour's travel they reached a helipad on a flat plain, the horizon stretching out to nowhere in every direction.

'We're going by helicopter?' Olivia asked, even though she supposed it was obvious.

Zayed nodded. 'Rubyhan is unreachable by any other means. It will take an hour by helicopter.' Anything else he said was cut off by the whirring of blades as a helicopter appeared on the horizon, coming closer. Olivia put her hands over her ears as the sand kicked up and the military helicopter landed.

Zayed opened the door and held out his hand to help her climb up. She took it, conscious of the strength of his grip as he hoisted her inside. She buckled herself into one of the seats, feeling the surrealness of the situation all over again. How could she be in a helicopter in the middle of the desert with a prince? And yet she was.

Zayed climbed in after her, settling into the seat next to her, then his aide who had told him about the attack. The door closed and the craft lifted into the air, the desert dropping away beneath them.

Olivia craned her neck to look out of the window as they sped towards the horizon. From above the desert looked tranquil, the undulating dunes smooth and graceful, belying how rugged and dangerous the landscape truly could be.

After a little while a mountain range rose up in front of them, jagged peaks piercing the blue sky. The helicopter began to descend, the pilot navigating his way through the ferocious-looking peaks, making Olivia press back in her seat. Out of the window she could see snow-covered mountains adorned with shreds of cloud, almost close enough to touch.

And then the palace was in front of them, like something out of a fairy tale, its walls emerging from the rock as if they had been hewn from it, each one topped with a bright, domed minaret.

'Wow.' She breathed, and Zayed turned to her with a small smile.

'It is impressive, is it not? Built six hundred years ago by my ancestor.'

'I've never seen its equal.'

'It is called the Palace of Clouds. Rubyhan is its formal name only.'

'It is a palace of clouds,' Olivia said with a little laugh. 'I can't believe how high we are. I saw snow.'

'Yes, it will be far colder here,' Zayed warned her.

'How long will we be here?'

Zayed's mouth thinned. 'A few days only,' he answered, and Olivia's stomach did a little nervous flip. A few days... and then what?

After they landed Zayed escorted her into the palace; the interior was just as incredible as the outside: rooms with soaring windows and balconies that overlooked the stunning vista, the ground dropping away to nothing immediately beyond the walls.

'You will stay in the former harem,' he told her. 'I think you will be very comfortable.'

The harem was a suite of rooms with every luxury to hand: a huge bedroom with a king-sized bed on its own dais; an en-suite bathroom with a sunken marble tub, an infinity shower and underfloor heating. A balcony extended from the bedroom, making Olivia feel as if she was walking on thin air. She could hardly believe all the luxuries found in such a remote place—it was even more sumptuous a palace than the one she knew in Abkar.

Zayed left her there, telling her to rest and relax, and after a few moments of uncertainty Olivia decided to take him at his word. It had been a harrowing few days, and she could certainly use the opportunity to relax, especially considering how rarely she did it.

Her days at the palace in Abkar were taken up with caring for the three young Princesses—teaching them English, keeping them in line, managing their lessons, their social calendars, their wardrobes. Olivia hardly took any holiday—she never needed to. Where would she go? Besides a godmother in Paris she saw every few years, she had no one in the world.

And if she lost her position in Abkar, which she was almost certain she would, she'd have nowhere to go. But she couldn't think about that yet. She was going to take one day at a time, one hour if necessary, and right now she was going to revel in a lovely, long soak in the sunken tub, which was a far cry from the cool water of the oasis where she'd last washed, the bottom slimy with seaweed and mud.

She'd just got out of the bath, wrapping herself in the velvet-soft terry-cloth robe that had been hanging on the bathroom door, when there was a discreet knock on the door of the suite.

'Miss Taylor?' The voice was female and had a crisp English accent, which filled Olivia with relief. She'd been managing all right with Arabic, and Zayed's English was flawless, but it would be nice to have someone else to converse with in the language of her birth.

'Yes, just a moment.' She opened the door to a young woman dressed in a business suit, her dark hair pulled back in a sleek ponytail. Olivia liked the look of her instinctively. 'Hello.'

'Hello, Miss Taylor.'

'Please, call me Olivia.'

The woman smiled and nodded. 'I'm Anna, Prince Zayed's PA at Rubyhan. He's asked me to make sure you have everything you need.'

'Yes, it's been rather amazing.' Olivia let out a self-conscious laugh, aware she was in nothing but a dressing gown. 'I just got out of the bath.'

'And I hope you enjoyed it,' Anna said smoothly. 'Prince Zayed wishes your stay here to be as pleasant as possible.'

It sounded a little...formal. 'Oh. Okay.' Olivia tried for a smile. Zayed was being thoughtful for once; she should be pleased. So why did she feel uneasy, as if she was being managed? Dealt with?

'So there is nothing you need?' Anna pressed, and Olivia shook her head.

'Then Prince Zayed asks that you join him for dinner in the Blue Room in an hour. Is that acceptable to you?'

Olivia tried to suppress the flutter of nerves and, yes, excitement she felt at the prospect. 'Um, yes. Sure. Thank you.'

'Good.' Anna smiled. 'I believe that the wardrobe in your suite should hold any clothes you might need, but please do alert me if you require anything further.' She handed Olivia a pager. 'If you push that button, I'll be here in less than five minutes.'

'Oh. Wow.' Olivia had never experienced such service

before. She'd never experienced *anything* like this before. It really was out of this world. Out of her world.

'I'll leave you to it, then,' Anna said with a smile. 'When you're ready for dinner, press the pager and I'll escort you to the Blue Room.'

'Okay. Thanks.'

Anna left her alone and, feeling a mix of curiosity and trepidation, Olivia opened the louvre doors of the huge built-in wardrobe. A row of blouses, skirts and dresses in every imaginable shade and fabric greeted and amazed her.

She ran her finger along the garments, touching the sumptuous fabrics, from cotton and linen to silk and satin. Beneath the dresses were shoes of every description— high heels and sandals, court shoes and plimsolls. They all looked incredibly expensive. Olivia slid open one of the drawers built into the wardrobe and nearly gasped at the delicate garments laid out there—lingerie sets in shades of ivory and beige, scalloped with lace and as thin as gossamer. Why on earth did Zayed have all these women's clothes here? How had he got them here so quickly?

She spent an enjoyable half hour trying on different outfits, from the evening gowns to the day dresses, knowing she wouldn't dare to wear anything too extravagant or sexy. She finally settled on a simply cut sheath in royal-blue linen, pairing it with a pair of taupe court shoes. Simple, safe clothes that were still more expensive and elegant than anything she'd ever worn before.

It felt strange, to be dressed so nicely, waiting to have dinner with a man she barely knew, yet who she'd known more than any other man in her life. Strange, and more than a little bit exciting.

'There is absolutely no reason to be looking forward to this,' Olivia told her reflection as she put on the minimum of make-up—the bathroom came equipped with a dazzling array of cosmetics and toiletries. 'No reason at all. Prince Zayed no doubt just wants to talk to you about dissolving this marriage.'

The reminder was timely and squelched some of that nervy excitement. This was a business meeting, and one she certainly shouldn't be looking forward to.

Taking a deep breath, she pressed the pager. Minutes later, as promised, Anna appeared at her door and led her down several corridors with mosaic floors and Moorish arches to a room on the ground floor of the palace. She opened the door and stepped aside so Olivia could enter, which she did with her heart starting to jump around in her chest.

But she needn't have been so nervous, because the room, stunning as it was, was empty. Anna closed the doors softly behind her and Olivia looked around, taking in the pillars decorated with lapis lazuli and the gold leaf on the walls and ceiling. In the centre of the room a table for two had been set with linen and crystal and flickered with candlelight. It looked rather romantic, Olivia couldn't help but think.

Then the doors opened and Zayed stood there, freshly showered and shaven, dressed in western-fashion trousers and a matching charcoal-grey button-down shirt open at the throat. His eyes shone like pieces of agate as his gaze surveyed her. He looked absolutely devastating, and Olivia couldn't form so much as a word as she stood there like a rabbit in a snare.

Zayed closed the doors behind him with a soft click and came forward. 'Hello, Olivia,' he said.

Zayed watched the pulse flutter and leap in Olivia's throat as he walked towards her. He was reminded of their wedding night, when he'd seen how nervous she was and he'd tried to relax her. Tonight was different, though. Yes, he was trying to make her comfortable after everything she'd endured, but he had no intention of seducing her…as tempting as that prospect seemed at the moment.

'Everything in your suite was to your satisfaction?' he asked.

'Yes.' Olivia cleared her throat and gave him a nervous smile. 'It was all amazing, thank you.'

'I'm glad.' He pulled out her chair and she sat down, bending her head so he could see the nape of her neck, and just as before he was struck by the tender vulnerability of it. Struck in a way he did not wish to be.

'It's incredible, all the luxuries here,' Olivia continued as Zayed moved around to sit opposite her. 'The bath…the underfloor heating…the clothes…' She shook her head, marvelling. 'How did you get so many clothes here so quickly, and most of them in my size?'

Zayed hesitated a second too long, and realisation darkened Olivia's eyes to a deep navy. 'Oh, how stupid of me,' she said with an uneven little laugh. 'They were here already, weren't they? For Princess Halina.'

Her perception was razor-sharp and Zayed couldn't deny it. 'I was intending to bring her here afterwards,' he said. 'A honeymoon of sorts.'

'How lovely.' Olivia reached for her napkin and spread it in her lap, her head bent so he couldn't see her expression.

Annoyance and something deeper stabbed through him. He had been looking forward to this evening, even though it would have its expedient uses, of course. Now, right at the beginning, it felt spoiled somehow, which was absurd. Halina would still be his wife. She had to be. And Olivia's perception provided a timely reminder.

'I hope you were able to relax and enjoy yourself.'

'I was, thank you.' She sounded cool, and Zayed gritted his teeth. He wasn't even sure why he was so irritated.

'Have some wine,' he said, and reached for the bottle chilling in a silver bucket. Olivia lifted her gaze to his, a slightly teasing look lightening the blue of her eyes, reminding him of the sea.

'I didn't think you experienced all this luxury in your exile,' she confessed as he filled her glass. 'I thought you lived in a tent pretty much all the time.'

'Mostly I do. But Rubyhan is my official base and the seat of my government.'

'So Anna works for your government?'

'She is my personal assistant, but yes, I have a small staff living here permanently arranging correspondence, managing affairs. Although I am in exile, I am still the globally recognised leader of Kalidar. It is Malouf who is the rebel, the impostor.' A familiar pressure started in his chest.

'I know that,' Olivia said quietly. She took a sip of her wine, her lashes lowered. 'It must be very difficult to be fighting for so long.'

'I want the fighting to be over.' The ache in his chest intensified and came out in his voice. 'I want innocent people to suffer no more.'

'And your marriage to Princess Halina will help accomplish that,' Olivia finished softly.

'Yes.' He paused, feeling the need suddenly to explain to her why he was so committed. 'For ten years Fakhir Malouf has lived in my home and taken my place. But worse than that, far worse, he has implemented policies and laws that go against everything my father taught me as a ruler—justice and mercy, kindness and equality. Kalidar was one of the most forward-thinking nations in this region, and now it is one of the least, all thanks to Malouf.'

'But why doesn't someone intervene—another government?'

Zayed's fingers clenched around the stem of his wine glass and he forced himself to relax. 'We are a small if wealthy country, and no one has wanted to risk getting involved. Malouf had the support of a certain section of the military, and it gave him more clout, even if no one was willing to recognise him officially.'

'So for ten years you have been living on the fringes,' Olivia said with a little shake of her head. 'It's so terribly unfair.'

'It is an injustice I will make right, even if it costs me my life. Nothing else matters.' He held her gaze, willing her to understand. He couldn't let himself care about her finer feelings.

'I understand,' Olivia said softly, and Zayed let out a low breath, accepting her response.

He leaned back in his chair, wanting to recapture some of the enjoyment of the evening. He was sitting with a beautiful woman in candlelight, drinking smooth, velvety wine. Nothing could happen between them, for both their sakes, but they could still have a pleasant time together.

'So tell me about yourself, Olivia,' he invited as a member of his staff slipped into the room quietly to serve them the first course of lamb *sambousek* with fresh cucumber sauce.

'Tell you…?' Olivia looked startled. 'There is not much to know, I'm afraid.'

'That can't be true.' Zayed realised he was curious about her. 'You said you had been working for the royal family since you were seventeen?'

'Eighteen. Right after I finished school.'

'You went to boarding school?'

'Yes, in Switzerland. My father moved around a great deal and he wanted me to have a stable education.'

'Did you enjoy it?'

She shrugged. 'It was a finishing school for aristocrats and princesses, and I was a minor diplomat's daughter, a nobody. I was there on a scholarship,' she explained. 'And of course everyone knew it, since I didn't fly in by helicopter, or wear designer clothes on the weekends, or keep my own pony.' She let out a small laugh that sounded just a bit too sad. 'Halina was my best friend,' Olivia continued. 'She took me under her wing, made sure other people didn't tease me.' But not being teased, Zayed acknowledged silently, wasn't the same as being liked.

'That was very kind of her.'

'Yes, it was. She's a very giving person.' She took a quick breath, looking up at him uncertainly. 'I hope things are able to work out between you.'

'So do I.' Yet it felt odd in a way he couldn't elucidate to talk about Halina as his wife. He didn't want to talk about Halina right now, didn't even want to think about her. Not with Olivia sitting across from him and looking so very lovely. If that was an act of betrayal, so be it.

'This letter,' Olivia said slowly. 'What exactly do you want me to say in it?'

He didn't want to talk about the letter now, either. 'There is time for that tomorrow,' he said swiftly. 'Why don't we eat?'

Olivia nodded and took a small bite of the *sambousek*, fragrant with cinnamon and mint. 'Delicious,' she murmured. 'Better than any I've tasted before.'

'Tell me about your duties in Abkar,' Zayed suggested. He wanted to know more about her, although he knew there was no real reason to. 'You take care of the three younger Princesses?' He didn't know their names.

'Yes, Saddah, Maarit and Aisha. They are twelve, ten and eight.'

'And what do you do?'

'Everything,' Olivia answered with a small smile. 'I'm meant to teach them English, but I also look after their belongings and arrange their lessons and social events. They are quite busy girls. Dancing, riding, tennis… Saddah will go to boarding school, the same one I went to, next year.'

She lapsed into silence, her face drawn into sorrowful lines that made Zayed lean forward and touch her hand. 'What is it? Why do you look sad suddenly?'

She refocused on him with a wry smile that was still touched with sadness. 'I'll miss them, that's all.'

'But you can return to the palace in Abkar when all this is over,' Zayed insisted. 'I will make sure of it.'

'I am not sure you will be able to arrange such a thing,' Olivia answered quietly. 'Sultan Hassan has entrusted me with the care of his precious daughters. I'm meant to be an example of womanhood to them—quiet, submissive, modest womanhood.' Her lips twisted. 'No matter how discreetly things are managed, word will get back to him and to them that…' She gestured between them with one slender hand. 'I have compromised myself.'

Zayed's mouth thinned into a hard line. 'And in the letter, we can explain that it was not your fault.'

'And have you take the blame? That would jeopardise your marriage negotiations, surely?'

Yes, it would. Zayed stared at her in frustration, disliking how he'd put her in such an untenable position. After the events of the last few days, he realised how unfounded his suspicions were.

Olivia was not a scheming gold-digger, trying to get the most out of this unfortunate arrangement. It would have been easier to maintain such a fiction, but he couldn't, not when he'd seen her help the women and children at the camp; not when she'd shown so much concern for his welfare as well as that of his country.

'Still,' he persisted. 'I will give you a handsome settlement. You will want for nothing.'

'That is very generous of you, Prince Zayed.' But she didn't sound entirely pleased by the prospect, and he didn't understand why.

'You could travel,' he continued, determined that she see some benefits. 'Or start over. Work somewhere new.'

'Yes.' She laid down her fork, her appetite seemingly gone.

'Does none of that appeal to you?'

'It's only...' She sighed. 'Abkar has been my home for four years, the only home I've ever really known. Sultan Hassan is my employer, I know, but he's been kind to me, and more like a father than my own, who I barely knew. I'll miss that.'

So not only had he robbed her of her innocence and livelihood, but he'd taken her family and home as well. Guilt corroded his insides like acid. There had to be some way he could make this right.

CHAPTER EIGHT

OLIVIA TOOK IN the frown settled between Zayed's straight, dark brows and wondered what he was so worried about. What did it matter to him if she travelled or got a new job? Or was she simply a burden to his conscience, and it would be far easier for him if she quite happily toddled off into whatever future remained for her?

'I'd like to travel,' Olivia said, injecting a note of enthusiasm into her voice that she didn't quite feel. 'I'd like to go to Paris. My godmother lives there.'

'Your godmother?' Olivia saw the unmistakeable relief on Zayed's face and knew she had been right. He wanted her dealt with, taken care of.

'Yes, an old friend of my mother's. I haven't seen her in years. It will be good to see her again.' Which wasn't quite true. Her godmother was elderly and practically a stranger, and she'd welcomed Olivia during her few, brief visits with a sense of obligation rather than enthusiasm. But Olivia knew what Zayed wanted to hear, and it was her instinct, as ever, to say it. Whether it was her father having needed to be reassured that she was fine at school, or Halina that she didn't mind it when she went off with other friends, or even the little Princesses, needing to be soothed and petted, Olivia couldn't help but give people what they wanted. It was so much easier, and being useful was almost as good as being loved.

Zayed gazed at her, eyes narrowed, the relief fading from his face. 'Why are you trying to make me feel better?'

His perception surprised her. 'You don't want to worry about me. You don't have to.'

'You're my responsibility.'

'Not really.' She met his gaze levelly. 'And, as for money, I don't need any. I have savings of my own and I'd prefer not to be paid off.' Just the thought of accepting money from him after everything they'd done together made her feel cheap. Cheaper than she already felt.

Zayed shook his head. 'Like I said, I have a responsibility—'

'And I'm absolving you of it.' Olivia managed a smile even though her heart felt as though it were being wrung out like a sponge. She understood she couldn't stay with Zayed; she didn't even want to, not really. But neither did she feel confident or courageous enough to embrace the unknown future. 'At least you don't think I'm some scheming witch any more,' she said lightly, 'trying to trick you into staying married to me.'

He had the grace to look abashed. 'I'm sorry. I have come to realise that was unfair of me.'

'When did you realise that?'

'Over time,' he said slowly. 'When I saw you helping at the settlement yesterday. Or perhaps the way you seemed to care more for my situation, my people, than you did for yourself.'

His admiring words caused a warm glow to start inside her. 'You have a lot more at stake, Zayed. Plenty of people are your responsibility, so I don't need to be one of them.'

He didn't look convinced, and Olivia decided it was time to change the subject. There was only so much reassuring she could do, especially when the truth was the thought of her unknown future made her stomach churn. She didn't have that much in savings; Sultan Hassan paid her a pittance because she was also given food and board. Her employment skills were limited to being some kind of governess, but she'd hardly get a reference from the Sultan.

And what if she was pregnant?

That was a possibility she hadn't let herself dwell on. Zayed hadn't seemed to have considered it, although perhaps it was simply not of concern to him. Despite his seeming solicitude now, she knew she shouldn't entirely trust him, even if she wanted to, and she doubted he trusted her. What would he do if she *was* pregnant? She didn't even like to think about it.

'What's wrong?' Zayed asked suddenly. 'You've gone pale.'

'Nothing.' She'd been meaning to change the subject, so now she did. 'This meal is really quite delicious. What is the main course?'

'I have no idea.' Zayed pressed a pager to summon the staff. 'But we can find out.'

Moments later a member of staff came in and silently removed the dishes, returning shortly with the main course—grilled meat with rice and yoghurt sauce. Again it was delicious, and Olivia said so, but she knew she couldn't just keep talking about the food.

And Zayed, for whatever reason, seemed determined to find out more about her. 'What kind of job might you have done, if Hassan hadn't offered you the governess position?'

Olivia shook her head. 'I never really thought about it.'

'Did you consider going to university?'

'No, not really.'

Zayed frowned. 'Not even for a moment? In this day and age...an educated woman like yourself... Why not?'

She pressed her lips together. 'There wasn't the money for it.'

His frown deepened, turning almost to a scowl. 'No money? Did your father leave you nothing?'

'He died virtually bankrupt.' He'd had a penchant for gambling that Olivia hadn't known about, and there had barely been enough to cover her most basic expenses after the funeral. 'I didn't really feel like going to university,' she told him, wanting to avoid his pity. 'I didn't have a burning passion to study anything, and the truth is I'm not very adventurous.' The thought of starting over alone in a strange city had been most unappealing. She'd done that enough as a child, before she'd been sent to boarding school at age eleven.

'And what about now?' Zayed pressed. 'If you could do anything, what would you do?'

'I...' Olivia hesitated. She didn't have dreams. She hadn't let herself have them, because they'd seemed so pointless. Better to be happy pleasing other people, accepting their thanks when it came. Better to be useful than important or loved.

'Think about it,' Zayed urged. 'This could be a great opportunity for you, Olivia.'

A great opportunity? Olivia blinked, stung. She understood about putting a good face on things, heaven knew, but that was stretching it a little far.

'I'm sorry, Prince Zayed,' she said stiffly. 'But I can't quite see that from where I am.' She put her napkin next to her plate, her appetite vanished.

What was she doing here, really? Having a romantic candlelit dinner with a man who was going to put her aside so he could marry someone else? A man who had taken her innocence, her livelihood, her *home*. Did she have anything more to lose? The last thing she needed was to sit here, eating delicious food and drinking fine wine, as if they were on some sort of date. It just reminded her of all she didn't have, would never have, and, while she usually didn't let herself think like that, right now it hurt.

Because part of her wanted that—the romance, the anticipation, the seduction—with Zayed. She didn't want to feel that persistent ache of yearning, but she did. He was a powerful and devastatingly attractive man, and despite his ruthlessness she knew he could be kind. It was enough right there to half tumble her into love with him, and that she could not have.

'I'm sorry,' she said as she rose from the table. 'It's been a long day. I think I'll go to bed.'

'Olivia, wait.' Zayed rose as well, catching her arm and turning her towards him. A wave of heat, the tangy citrus of his aftershave, assaulted her senses and felt like a taunt. Even now she felt the ripples of desire spreading outwards from her centre, like a pebble had splashed into her soul, and she couldn't stand it.

She didn't want to want him. Didn't want to long for things she couldn't have, to yearn to feel those strong arms around her, pulling her against him, and more. So much more.

'I'm sorry,' Zayed said, his hand still on her arm. 'That was a poor choice of words. I'm trying to see the bright side of things for you, but I understand that there doesn't seem to be one at the moment. Please stay and finish the meal with me.'

Olivia knew she should tug her arm away from Zayed and keep walking out the door. Protect herself rather than let herself ache and yearn. But somehow she couldn't. She wasn't strong enough, and the thought of going back to her room and spending the rest of the evening alone made loneliness swamp her.

So she nodded and Zayed released her arm, a small smile flitting across his features.

'Thank you,' he murmured, and they both sat down.

It had been a stupid thing to say. Zayed saw that now. He saw it in Olivia's pale face, in how her hands were not quite steady as she spread her napkin across her lap. He'd been trying to make her feel better and it hadn't worked.

Hell, he realised, he'd been trying to make himself feel better. Because guilt was an emotion he couldn't afford to feel. If Olivia could get something out of what had happened, if she could benefit, then he'd feel better about putting her aside.

The fact that he even needed such a sop to his conscience filled him with fury—and shame. For ten years he had let himself think of nothing but duty, fuelled by grief. When he closed his eyes, he saw the tormented face of his mother, dying simply because she had no more wish to live. He saw the helicopter in flames. He heard the anguished cries and shouts of his father and brother, even though he knew that was only in his imagination. It would have been impossible to hear over the sound of the blades and the flames. The headache he'd been trying to suppress for the last forty-eight hours flickered insistently at his temples.

He could not believe how weak and sentimental he was being. Why was he trying to make this woman, who meant so little, feel better? That was why he'd brought her to Rubyhan, Zayed realised with another rush of shame. Why he'd given her the sumptuous suite, the clothes. Why he was wining and dining her tonight.

Although that wasn't quite true. No, it was worse than that—he was wining and dining her because he wanted to. Because he'd wanted to see her, be with her. Because even now, with so much at stake, he still desired this slip of a woman who should be completely forgettable to him. *Why?*

'Zayed…?' Olivia glanced at him uncertainly. 'It's late and I am sure you have many things to do tomorrow. Maybe I should go…'

She started to rise again, but Zayed stayed her with one upturned palm. He took a deep breath, willing the pain in his head to recede. 'No.'

'You seem…' She hesitated. 'Angry.'

'I am angry at myself,' Zayed confessed. Olivia gazed at him in confusion.

'You mean for marrying me by mistake?'

'Yes, that.' His mouth twisted in something like a smile. 'But also for wanting you even now, when I know I shouldn't.'

It was as if he'd stolen all the air from the room in a single breath. Olivia froze, her eyes wide and stormy, her pink lips parted.

'You do?'

'Can you not feel it, Olivia? Why do you think we fell into bed together so easily?'

Colour touched her cheeks. 'I thought… I thought it was just me.'

'I assure you, it is mutual.' Zayed sat back in his chair. He felt surprisingly glad he'd told her, that he'd acknowledged what throbbed between them. It was a relief, like lancing a wound, relieving the pressure. The trouble was, what was he going to do about it now? Again he felt the flicker of pain at his temples.

'I'm…sorry,' Olivia said after a pause, sounding unsure. Zayed let out a laugh, trying not to wince in pain.

'This is not something you need to apologise for, Olivia.' He studied her, the colour in her face, the slight upturn of her lips. Had he pleased her by acknowledging what he felt for her? Did she find it so hard to believe? 'Have I given you another new experience, to have a man desire you so openly, so strongly?'

Her pupils flared. 'You have given me many new experiences, Prince Zayed.'

'I think we are past using my royal title.'

'Are we?' She gave a little shake of her head. 'I don't know where we are.'

And nor did he. But he knew where he wanted to be. He wanted to be in her arms, sinking himself inside her. The need throbbed inside him, obliterating every other consideration, overriding the pain growing inside his head.

She must have seen the heat in his eyes, because she let out a shaky laugh and looked down. 'Why me? I'm no one special. You must have had many women, Prince Zayed.'

'Not as many as you think.' A soldier's life in the desert had prohibited prolonged affairs. 'In fact, before you I had not been with a woman for many years.'

'Many years?' Her expression of astonishment was almost comical. Zayed smiled wryly.

'There has not been much opportunity.'

'That's why, then. You probably wouldn't look at me twice otherwise.'

'Why do you put yourself down?'

'I'm not.' She looked surprised. 'Just stating a truth.'

'It is not a truth to me.' Suddenly he felt the urge to show her how beautiful she was to him. How utterly lovely. 'Trust me on that, Olivia.' He held her gaze, willing her to see the desire in them. To feel it in herself.

And he knew she did; he heard it in the quickly indrawn breath, the way she touched her lips with her tongue. Neither of them moved.

Distantly, over the roar of his own heated blood, Zayed felt the pulse of pain in his eyes and spots danced before his eyes. Damn it, now was not the time for one of his migraines to torment him. Often he could simply will the pain away, but now Zayed feared it had gone too far. Already his vision was blurring at the edges, the room going cloudy.

'Zayed...?' Olivia's voice was filled with alarm. 'Are you all right?'

So much for his seduction. Zayed tried for a laugh, but nearly retched instead. The pain came like a tidal wave now, drowning out everything else, waves thundering through his head. 'I...' He tried to speak but couldn't manage it.

'Are you in pain?' He felt Olivia's cool fingers on his cheek and breathed in her lemony scent. He closed his eyes, trying to block out the pain, but it was too late. Far too late.

'Headache,' he managed to get out through gritted teeth. Stupid of him to ignore the pain, to be so intent on seducing Olivia. If he'd gone to lie down in a dark room with a cool cloth on his head, he might have been able to avoid the worst of it. Now it would overtake him.

'A migraine,' she corrected softly. 'One of the Princesses gets them sometimes. They're terrible.'

'I just need to lie down.' He forced the words out, his teeth clenched so hard his jaw ached, cold sweat prickling on his back. He hated that Olivia was seeing him in such a weak and helpless way.

'Let me help you,' she said. 'Do you want me to call someone?'

'No.' He wanted to manage on his own, but he knew he couldn't. Still, better to keep the knowledge of his condition as closely guarded as possible. No one wanted to see their leader weak and in pain, and there was enough for his staff to worry about already.

'All right.' She placed one slender hand under his elbow. 'I'll help you to your bedroom.'

He rose unsteadily from his chair, leaning far more than he would have liked on Olivia's petite frame, yet she held his weight with surprising strength. She was slender and small, but she was not fragile. He felt the tensile strength running through her like a wire.

'It's not far,' he managed, and then stopped, because the spots dancing in his vision had coalesced into unending blackness. Standing there, Olivia's hand on his arm, her body bracing his, Zayed realised he could not see a thing. He was blind.

CHAPTER NINE

ZAYED STILLED AND Olivia sensed the shock in him, although at what she didn't know. Everything had spiralled out of control so rapidly—his admission of desire, the blatant invitation she'd seen in his eyes. If he hadn't developed a migraine, who knew what would have happened? Although Olivia could imagine it all too easily—and evocatively.

'What is it?' she asked because Zayed still hadn't moved.

'I...' His jaw bunched. 'I can't see.'

'Can't see? At all?'

'No.' The single word was a gasp of pain. A light sheen of sweat coated his pale face and his eyes were glazed.

'Let me get someone—'

'No.' The single word was like the snick of a blade. 'I don't want anyone else to see me like...this.'

'All right.' Olivia absorbed that, along with his sudden blindness. Here, at least, she could be as useful as she knew how to be. As needed. 'Then we'd better get you to your bed.'

Slowly they walked from the room, Zayed gripping her hand tightly as she put her arm around him and guided him with halting steps.

'I don't actually know where your bedroom is,' she said in a low voice when they'd reached the thankfully empty hall outside the room where they'd been dining. 'Can you direct me?'

'Yes.' Zayed drew a quick breath. 'To the right, up the stairs, and then along the hallway.'

'All right.'

Each step felt painstakingly slow, as Zayed felt his way and battled his pain. Olivia could tell from his tightly clenched jaw just how much pain he was in, and her heart ached for him.

On the upstairs hallway Zayed suddenly went still, then shrugged away from her, even though Olivia could see that it cost him.

'What...?' she began in a whisper, but Zayed shook his head, a flinch of pain crossing his face.

Then his aide, Jahmal, came down the hallway. Zayed straightened.

'My Prince,' Jahmal said. He gave Olivia a cursory, curious glance and then looked away, dismissing her. 'Is everything well? I thought you were dining downstairs.'

'I'm finished.' Zayed spoke tersely. 'I will work in my room. I don't wish to be disturbed, please.'

Jahmal glanced at Olivia again, a frown marring his forehead. 'Very well...'

'Miss Taylor is helping me with a matter.'

Jahmal's frown cleared. 'The message to Sultan Hassan?'

'Yes. Leave us now, please.'

Jahmal sketched a short bow and strode down the hallway. After a few tense seconds Zayed expelled a low breath and then leaned against Olivia again; she took his weight, wrapping her arm around his waist.

'Get me to my room,' he said through clenched teeth. 'Before I humiliate myself even further.'

'There's no shame in pain.'

'You are wrong in that, at least for me.'

They didn't talk further; all their energy was expended on making it down the hallway.

'Here,' Zayed said when they were in front of an arched door that looked like any one of the dozen others along the corridor.

'How do you...?'

'I counted.'

Olivia turned the handle and the door swung open into a room that was sparsely furnished and masculine in every detail. She led him to the king-sized bed in the centre, and then guided him down onto the soft mattress. Zayed stretched out with a groan, one arm thrown over his eyes.

'Let me get you something,' Olivia suggested quietly. 'A damp cloth? Some tablets?'

'There's medicine in the bathroom.'

'All right.' She went into the sumptuous en suite, feeling as if she were invading his private space as she rifled through his medicine cabinet looking for the painkillers. She shook two out of the bottle and then poured a glass of water from the tap. She found a flannel and dampened it, and then brought it all back to Zayed.

'Here,' she said, perching on the edge of the bed. She pressed the tablets into his hand and then guided the glass of water to his lips. He swallowed in one powerful gulp and then subsided back onto the pillows. 'And this too,' Olivia said, and she gently laid the damp cloth across his forehead.

Zayed reached out his hand and found hers, lightly squeezing her fingers. 'Thank you.'

'I wish there was more I could do.'

'This has been more than I deserve.'

Deserve? It seemed an odd turn of phrase. 'Surely

everyone deserves care when they're hurt?' Olivia said quietly.

'That depends,' Zayed murmured. Her hand was still encased in his. Olivia watched his powerful chest rise and fall in steady breaths. Outside the sun was setting, sending streaks of light sliding across the floor, the sky lit up with the most vivid pinks and purples she'd ever seen. She wondered if she should go, if Zayed wanted to be left alone.

As if sensing her uncertainty, he squeezed her fingers again. 'Stay,' he entreated in a low voice. 'Stay with me.'

Something warm and wonderful unfurled in Olivia's heart, like a hug from the inside. She realised how much she'd wanted to stay, wanted him to want her to. 'Okay,' she said softly. 'Of course I will.'

She settled herself more comfortably against the pillows and Zayed drew her hand to his chest, still in his, so she could feel the thud of his heart against her palm.

His eyes were closed, dark, spiky lashes feathering the rugged planes of his cheeks. His mouth looked surprisingly lush and mobile on that harsh face, now softened as his breathing evened out. It could have been an hour or only a few minutes, but eventually Olivia realised he was asleep.

She'd lost track of time, of herself, in watching him, taking in every beautiful detail of his face and form, along with things she hadn't noticed before—a scar on his temple, another by his ear, both now faded to pale white streaks. Beneath his button-down shirt she could see the ridges of his chest and abdomen, perfectly and powerfully muscled.

She remembered how those muscles had felt under her questing hands, and she closed her eyes, trying to banish the memories for her own sanity, even though they were so achingly sweet. She'd never felt as treasured, as important, as she had in Zayed's embrace. Which was foolish, considering how she would most likely never see him again after the next day or two. The thought brought pain when Olivia knew it shouldn't, just as she knew every moment she spent in his company was dangerous because each one bound her closer and closer to this man—a man she would come to care for, if she let herself.

She told herself he was arrogant, assumptive and impatient. Yet she could understand why, considering how much he was fighting for. How much he'd lost. He'd barely mentioned the family whom had been murdered by Malouf, but Olivia sensed the deep, dark current of pain running right through his centre and it made her ache. He was also kind, considerate and gentle, and that made her ache even more.

She should leave, Olivia thought, before she did something both dangerous and stupid and started to fall in love with him.

As quietly as she could she started to move from the bed, but the second she tried to slip her hand from his his grip tightened, and he hauled her forward so she was pressed against him. He moved again, seemingly in his sleep, so she was resting with her head on his shoulder, their hands still entwined on his chest. Once again his breathing evened out.

Olivia lay there, enjoying the feel of his powerful body pillowing her head, the steady thud of his heart under her cheek. She could smell his aftershave and feel his heat and it felt so very, very nice to lie here in Zayed's arms, the moon starting to rise, creating silver patterns on the floor. For a moment she let herself imagine having something like this every night—and the man in that far too pleasant fantasy was Zayed.

She wasn't falling in love with him. She absolutely couldn't be. And yet she longed. She couldn't deny the river of yearning that wound its way through her at this very moment, threatening to flood its banks as Zayed pulled her even closer, his other hand splayed possessively across her hip, his knee nudging in between her own.

Olivia closed her eyes, both savouring the sweetness of the moment and trying to fight its intensity. Because it would be so easy to let herself be swept away, let herself fall.

Eventually she started to relax and, with Zayed deeply asleep, she fell into a doze.

The pain in his head receded to a dull ache as Zayed drifted in and out of sleep, conscious of the softness of the bed and the even more enticing softness of the warm, pliant body next to his. Sleep still fogged his mind as he pulled the body closer, enjoying the way her breasts were pressed against his chest, her hips nudging his. Heat flared, and when she arched a little bit against him, it flared hotter and brighter.

In one smooth movement he rolled on top of her, his hands seeking and finding all the soft curves and tempting dips of her body. He slid his hand up one slender, perfect thigh to the warmth at her centre, and she moaned. The heat inside him was a pulsing need, taking over all his senses.

He pressed his knee between hers, nudging her legs apart even further, positioning his body so he could bury himself in her welcoming depths.

She arched up to meet him and Zayed braced himself on his forearms. The pain in his head flickered, a second's distraction that had him suddenly stilling. God in heaven, what was he doing? He could jeopardise everything by making love with Olivia now.

With a groan he rolled off her, his body aching, his heart thudding. It felt like the hardest thing he'd ever done.

After a taut second Olivia rolled the other way, curling her knees up to her chest. The pain thudded through Zayed's head again and he closed his eyes.

'Olivia…'

'It's all right.' Her voice was a broken whisper, a ragged breath.

'I'm sorry.'

'I know.'

'The moment… I was asleep…' He felt that nothing he said could help. 'I got carried away and I shouldn't have.'

'I got carried away too.' She spoke softly, her back to him. When he cracked an eye open he could see the tender nape of her neck, and it made guilt rush through him all over again. Enough with the guilt. He needed to get Olivia out of his life, or he needed to get out of hers, and the sooner the better. He couldn't let himself get distracted. Duty was far more important. He closed his eyes again and pictured the helicopter filled with flames. Imagined he could see his father's and brother's faces, although he hadn't been able to at the time. And then he saw himself running away, hustled by his staff to safety. Even now, ten years later, the shame of it bit deep. *Coward.* No one had ever said it to him, but he'd felt it. How he'd felt it.

'Survivor's guilt,' his advisors had told him more than once. *It happens.* And he knew, in his head, in his gut, that he'd needed to survive. He was the last of the line, the only one remaining of a dynasty that stretched back centuries, the only person who could wrest control from Malouf. But in his heart he felt the guilt, the shame, and he didn't think it would ever leave him.

Which was why he had to focus on his duty and how to atone for the past. And the only service Olivia Taylor could provide for him was going away quietly.

As if she read his thoughts, she rose from the bed in one fluid movement, shrugging off the hand he hadn't even realised he'd stretched out to her.

'I'll go,' she said quietly, smoothing her dress down and slipping on her heels. 'You need your sleep. Is the headache better?'

'A bit.'

'Good.' She gave him a fleeting smile that didn't meet her eyes.

'Thank you, Olivia. I am sorry.'

'It's fine.' She lifted her chin. 'It's fine,' she said again, and then she was gone.

The silence of the room felt endless and empty as Zayed lay on his bed, his head aching as much as his heart. He didn't care about Olivia, he told himself. He didn't care about anyone like that and never would. Caring was inviting vulnerability and pain, something he had no intention of doing. If you cared about someone, your enemies could and would use it against you. He would never allow that to happen again.

But he still felt guilty and restless, wishing things had been different. If he'd kidnapped the right woman...*then he would never have met Olivia.*

The very fact that he could think that showed him how quickly and decisively he needed to act. Tomorrow he would send the message to Sultan Hassan and make sure Olivia wrote her letter. He would set the wheels in motion for all this to be repaired.

By the time Zayed fell asleep, the pale pink streaks of dawn were lighting the sky and he didn't waken until after the noon hour. Thankfully his headache was gone, and after showering and dressing he went in search of Jahmal and then Olivia.

'Has there been any news on the Sultan?' he asked Jahmal as they sat in his office in the west wing of the palace, the arched windows open to the sky.

'Only that he is displeased,' Jahmal answered with a grimace. 'Queen Aliya has taken Princess Halina to Italy,' he added. 'To keep her from being kidnapped.'

'As if I would try the same thing twice.' Zayed rubbed his temples. 'It was a foolish plan in the first place, even if it felt necessary at the time.'

'He still might be open to a communication from you,' Jahmal offered.

'He'd better be,' Zayed returned grimly. 'I'll send a gift with the message—some of my finest Arabians.'

'The Sultan is known for his love of horses.'

'Yes.' Briefly Zayed thought about how Olivia had said she couldn't ride. Right then he should have known it wasn't the Princess. Why had he been so unbelievably blind, seeing only what he'd wanted to see?

'I need to find Miss Taylor,' he said. 'Do you know where she is?'

'She has spent the morning with some of the women,' Jahmal answered. 'In the gardens.'

Some of his staff and soldiers had wives who lived in the palace. It was an isolated but safe existence, and he knew they all longed for the day when they could return to Arjah and their normal lives. They'd all been waiting a long time for that.

Outside the sun was shining brightly, the air still holding a hint of crispness from the cold night. Zayed strolled through the gardens, enjoying the sunlight on his face. He'd forgotten how pleasant it was out here, with the orange and lemon trees, the trailing flowers, the tinkle of the many fountains.

He wandered for several minutes through various landscaped gardens, each one surrounded by its own hedge, until he came onto a small, pretty courtyard with a fountain splashing in the middle and several ornate benches around. Lahela, one of his aides' wives who had just had a baby, was laughing at something Olivia said.

And Olivia... She sat on a bench, wearing a casual sundress the exact shade of her eyes, her hair falling down her back in tumbling chestnut waves, Lahela's baby on her lap gurgling up at her. She looked so happy and natural, almost as if...

Zayed's mind suddenly screeched to a halt, freezing on one simple fact that he'd completely ignored since he'd first taken Olivia and married her. Had slept with her.

He hadn't used birth control.

Of course he hadn't. It had been his wedding night; if he'd got Halina pregnant it simply would have strengthened his cause. Since then he hadn't thought for a moment, a single second, that Olivia could be pregnant...pregnant with his child. His heir.

Her laughter drifted across the courtyard, a deep, delighted sound, and she bounced the fat, smiling baby on her knee. Then she looked up and her gaze caught Zayed's, clashing with it so he felt as if he'd come up against a brick wall.

Her eyes widened, pupils flaring, and colour touched her cheeks. She looked away, bending her head so her hair fell forward and hid her face. Zayed's chest tightened. The pain he thought he'd banished crept back.

Keeping his voice as even as he could, he greeted the other women in the courtyard before turning his attention resolutely to Olivia. She still wasn't looking at him.

'Miss Taylor,' he said. 'May I have a word?'

Olivia handed the baby back to Lahela, trying not to let her trepidation show. Her heart was thumping in her chest as she followed Zayed out of the garden, both of them silent. He seemed angry, and she could only suppose it was about last night…and what had almost happened between them.

She'd spent most of the night practically writhing in shame—and unsated desire. When Zayed had started touching her, she'd been helpless to do anything but respond. Want. Beg. Just as he'd once said. Even now the memory made her face flood with colour and she closed her eyes briefly against it. How could she be so helpless when it came to her response to this man?

Zayed walked swiftly through several corridors and then finally opened the door to a small, ornate room that looked like a private study. Olivia stood in the centre of the room, knotting her hands together so they wouldn't shake.

Zayed closed the door and then whirled around to face her. 'Could you be pregnant?' he demanded tersely.

Olivia blinked. That had not been what she was expecting at all. 'Pregnant…?'

'From our wedding night.' He ground the words out, his mouth compressing. 'I did not use birth control and, as you were a virgin, I question whether you were on it.'

'I'm not,' she confirmed quietly.

'And you have no…issues with fertility?'

Her face burned even hotter. 'None that I know of, no.'

Zayed swore under his breath and turned away from her in one abrupt movement. At least she knew how he felt about a possible pregnancy, and could she even be surprised? He was planning to divorce her. Of course he didn't want her to have his baby. Yet strangely, stupidly, Olivia felt hurt.

Zayed squared his shoulders, his taut back to her. 'So there is a chance you could be pregnant?'

'Yes, I suppose.'

He turned around. 'You suppose?'

Irritation bit. 'Yes, I suppose. I'm not omniscient, Zayed, and this is not my fault.' Her voice quavered. 'I thought you'd realised that, but it seems you're back to blaming me.'

'No, I'm sorry.' He rubbed a hand wearily over his face. 'I don't mean to blame you. I blame myself, if anyone, for being so presumptuous and rash. It's just another complication in what is already a very complicated situation. And I should have thought of it sooner.' He dropped his hand from his face, giving her a surprisingly wry and honest look. 'I'm ashamed that I did not.'

'It's understandable,' Olivia murmured. Her flush had thankfully faded but she still felt embarrassed to be talking about this at all. 'You've had a lot on your mind.'

'Yes, but...' He stared at her for a moment, his gaze hard and assessing. Olivia looked back at him warily. 'You realised,' he said, and it was a statement. 'A while ago, I think. Yet you didn't say anything.'

'What was I supposed to say?'

'That you might be pregnant?' His brows drew together in a line. 'I know it's stating the obvious, but it is clearly a potential issue, and one that we needed to discuss.'

'I suppose I didn't see the point of discussing it until it was a certainty.'

'But by that point you might have been out of my life!' Zayed took a step closer to her. 'Were you considering not telling me about my child, Olivia?'

She gazed at him in disbelief. 'Are you serious, Zayed? Are you accusing me of something that hasn't even happened yet? I may not even be pregnant. I'm probably not.'

'Probably? Why do you say that?'

She shrugged. 'I don't know, but there's a good chance I'm not.'

'But there is a chance you are. That is the point.' He gave her a long, level look. 'Would you not have told me?'

'I... I don't know. I didn't think that far ahead.' She turned away from him, hating this whole conversation, all the what-ifs that had come into her life when everything had once been so certain, so safe, if a little staid. And she hated that a conversation about their possible child was so clinical, so cold. Some part of her wished for an alternative scenario, one where they hoped for such a thing. Revelled in the miracle of it. Was she insane?

'What did you think, then?' Zayed asked.

'Why does it matter?' she demanded, whirling around again. 'Why do you always have to make me feel guilty, Zayed?'

Remorse crumpled his features for a split second. 'Is that how I always make you feel?' he asked in a low voice, and Olivia heard the sudden innuendo in it, as well as the intent.

'No, but now... I know this is a potential problem, Zayed, but it's not my fault.'

'I know it isn't.' He closed his eyes and shook his head. 'I'm sorry. I don't mean to act in such a way. When I'm around you...' He stopped, and curiosity flickered through her, along with an excitement she could hardly credit.

'When you're around me...?' she prompted.

Zayed opened his eyes and the blazing heat she saw in their depths lit a fire in her soul. 'When I'm around you I lose my head. My very self. I can think of nothing but you...of having you.'

Excitement exploded inside her; she felt dizzy with it. Dizzy with desire, the rush of it so unexpected considering they'd just been arguing. But had it ever really gone away? She'd been fighting it, in one form or another, since the moment she'd met him.

'I know it's wrong,' Zayed murmured. 'I know it's fool-ish. I know we shouldn't, and yet I want to. I crave you, Olivia. Why do I crave you so much?'

'I crave you,' Olivia whispered. She couldn't look away from his fierce face, every muscle straining as he sought to control himself. Then he couldn't, and as she watched in breathless anticipation he swallowed the space between them in a couple of strides and she was in his arms, his mouth coming down hard and demanding on hers, the dam they'd both been constructing finally broken, the de-sire rushing in.

His mouth was hard and soft, the kiss sweet and strong at the same time, both sexy and sacred. *Wonderful.* Olivia returned the kiss with all that she had, unable to stop from giving him her everything. Zayed backed her across the room and her bottom came up against a desk. He growled against her mouth as he hoisted her on top of it, papers and books spilling onto the floor with a clatter.

No sweet seduction now; the force of their desire swept them along, caught up in its tidal wave as it dragged them under. Zayed nudged her legs apart with his own and then stood between her thighs as he plundered her mouth, his hands roving possessively over her body, demanding even more from her. And she gave it. Her mind a frenzied blur of sensation, she gave it willingly, joyfully, because, no matter how impossible their situation was, this man called to something in her that she hadn't even known she had—and she called to him. That alone was a miracle, a won-derful, incredible miracle.

She felt Zayed's fingers on the edge of her underwear, pulling it down. She moaned aloud, squirming against the feel of his hand, unable to wait even a second longer for the satiation they both craved, needing it with every fibre of their beings. This. Again *this*.

Zayed fumbled with his trousers, and with one swift stroke he was inside her. Olivia's muscles clenched around him and she wrapped her legs around his waist, uniting their bodies as closely and completely as she could, glorying in the feeling of it, the pleasure as well as the unity. She felt complete again, as if everything in her had been waiting to feel this way since the last time.

Zayed began to move, each strong, sure stroke sending Olivia higher to that dizzying peak. She matched his movements, learning the rhythm, finding it naturally, as if this had always been a part of her. As if he had.

And then she reached that glittering pinnacle, a cry bursting from her like a song of joy. She buried her head against Zayed's shoulder as the spasms of pleasure shuddered through her body before receding in a lazy tide, leaving her feeling boneless and sated.

Seconds and then minutes ticked by, slowly, and then ominously. Dimly Olivia realised they'd just had unprotected sex again. And, if she wasn't already pregnant, she could be now.

Another few seconds ticked by, each one tenser than the last, then Zayed withdrew from her, cleaning himself up quickly before adjusting his trousers. His face looked as if it had been hewn from stone, his eyes dark and fathomless.

Olivia pulled her sundress down over her hips, smoothing the crumpled material, unable to look him in the eye. The wonderful, lazy feeling of sated desire was leaving her and only trepidation remained. *What now?*

'It seems,' Zayed said in a tight voice, 'I cannot control myself around you.'

Olivia moistened her lips with her tongue. 'I'm sorry.'

'*You're* sorry? I am the one who should be sorry. I am the one who should be thinking of my kingdom, my people, my duty.' His voice broke and he whirled away from her, scrubbing his eyes with the heels of his hands as if he could obliterate the memory of what they'd just done.

With a jolt Olivia realised how much of Zayed's anger was directed at himself, rooted in guilt. He'd hinted as much, but she hadn't really believed it. Now she saw a depth of pain in the tense lines of his body, in the torment so clearly written on his face.

'Zayed,' she whispered, a plea, although for what she could not say. She just wanted to offer him comfort, even though she feared she had none to give him. None he would take, except what he already had, and now they were both living with the aftermath of regret.

'You have no idea,' Zayed said in a low voice of anguish. 'No idea—and how could you? No idea of what is at stake.'

'I know your marriage to Princess Halina is very important,' Olivia offered, wanting to show him she understood. Even now, she understood.

'Important?' Zayed choked out the word. 'It isn't *important*. It's essential. To finally have a political leader publicly recognise and fight for my rightful claim…' He closed his eyes. 'But it's not even that. It's what I see every night before I go to sleep. Every time I close my eyes.'

Olivia drew a short, shocked breath. 'What did you see, Zayed?' she asked softly. 'Tell me what you see.'

Zayed knew he shouldn't say anything more. He shouldn't tell her anything. Heaven knew, he'd told her enough, done enough, already. Even now the aftershocks of their explosive lovemaking were rippling through him, reminding him how sizzlingly potent their attraction was. It frightened him, the intensity of what he felt. When she was near him it was as if he was swallowed up by a vortex of need. He forgot everything.

'Zayed.' Olivia touched his arm, her fingers as light as the wings of a butterfly. 'Please. Tell me what haunts you so much.'

He resisted, because to tell was to admit his weakness, his shame. He didn't talk of the loss of his family to anyone. Everyone knew the facts, of course; it was a matter of national history. But no one knew about his nightmares, his helplessness. Yet some contrary, shameful part of him wanted to tell Olivia. Wanted to share the burden which, considering everything he'd already put her through, seemed more than unfair.

'Tell me.' Her voice was soft, a soothing balm to his fractured spirit. Her fingers stroked his arm.

Zayed let out a shuddering sigh. 'I see my father and older brother in the helicopter. Going down. I always see them.'

'Oh, Zayed.' Olivia gave a sorrowful little gasp. 'Of course. I'm so sorry.'

She knew the facts, he realised, just as everyone else did. The bare facts—the bomb that had exploded in the helicopter, the attempt on his mother's life, his cowardly scurry to freedom. Not that anyone would say so to his face, but he knew. He knew.

'I didn't realise you'd seen it,' Olivia said quietly after a moment, her hand still on his arm, as if she could imbue him with the strength he was just beginning to realise she had. The incredible strength. 'I didn't think you were there.'

'I was. I was in the palace, watching them take off. My father and his heir.' His lips twisted. They'd been going to do their civic duty, to speak at the opening of a hospital in another city, a landmark of Kalidar's recent transition to national healthcare. Of course Malouf had taken that away. He'd taken away so much. 'Perhaps you're wondering why I didn't go with them,' he said, his voice harsh, his breathing ragged. Olivia's fingers tensed on his arm.

'No,' she said carefully. 'But perhaps you want to tell me?'

He didn't, but he would, because she deserved to know. After everything, he owed her that much. The truth he'd kept from everyone else. 'I was bored by the idea,' he said flatly. 'I'd just got back from Cambridge and I found the desert so very tedious. My father asked me to accompany them and I said no. Minutes later I watched them go down in flames.'

Olivia was silent for a moment. 'Then perhaps you should be thankful,' she said finally, 'that you were so bored.'

He drew back from her, disgusted by the suggestion. Just as he was disgusted by his own actions all those years ago. 'Thankful?' he repeated, the word a sneer. 'How can I be? I deserved to die that day!'

'And if you had Kalidar would have no rightful King.'

'Don't you think I know that?' He felt caught between fury and despair. 'Why do you think I fight so hard? Why did I try to kidnap the Princess?' He let out a harsh bark of laughter. 'Everything I do, everything, is for their memory. And for mine. Because I failed my family once, and I never will again.'

'I understand why you are so driven,' Olivia said steadily. 'But you did not plant that bomb in the helicopter, Zayed. You did not poison your mother.'

She knew that too, then. 'She died in my arms a few months later. Wasted away to nothing. But the doctors didn't even think it was the poison. She'd recovered from that. It was from grief. She had no reason to live.' He felt a spasm of pain, like a knife thrust in his gut. For a second he couldn't breathe, and he swung away from Olivia, hating that she could see this weakness exposed in him. See his need, his hurt.

'I'm sorry,' Olivia said quietly. 'I know how painful that must have been for you.'

Something in her voice made him ask, 'You do?'

Olivia was silent for a moment. 'My mother died when I was young. Cancer—very quick. I don't remember much about her, but we have photos—family photos that are so different from what I became used to as a child. Looking at them is like seeing someone else's life.'

Zayed frowned, waiting for her to go on. 'After she died, my father shut down. He hired a nanny and hardly ever saw me, and then sent me to boarding school as soon as he could. He was a stranger to me but, when I see those photos, I realise he wasn't always that way. Before my mother died, he hugged me and tickled me and read me stories at night. I have the photographic proof.' Her voice was wistful and sad. 'And it made me realise that he *chose* to be a stranger. He didn't think I was worth being something more.'

'Perhaps he couldn't be anything more, because of grief.'

'Perhaps,' she acknowledged, 'and perhaps your mother didn't have the strength to go on just for you. But it still hurts. It still feels like you failed somehow. Like you weren't enough.'

Her perception left him breathless, because he knew she was exactly right. His mother's death, the way she'd seemed to choose it over life, had been a further blow after his father and brother's death. A further and harder grief, because they could have held each other up, supported each other, been strong for each other. And she'd chosen for him to go it alone.

'I'm sorry, Zayed.' Olivia stepped closer to him, reaching up on her tiptoes to cup his cheek with her palm. Zayed closed his eyes. 'I'm so sorry.'

'You have nothing to be sorry for, Olivia,' he said. 'I know that absolutely.'

'I'm sorry all the same. For all you've endured, and for so long. I'm in awe of your strength. To keep fighting for all these years, to be so determined; I wish I possessed such courage. Such conviction.'

'You are brave,' Zayed told her, opening his eyes and giving her a small smile. 'You have shown me that.'

'Brave?' Olivia shrugged. 'I don't think so. But I try to be useful. That's something, at least.'

Useful? It sounded like so little. Did Olivia hope for more from her life? For the love of a husband, of children? She wouldn't get it from him, and yet…

'I promise I will do everything in my power to make your marriage with Princess Halina go forward,' she told him. 'I'll write that letter, whatever it takes.'

The letter, the damned letter. Zayed stared at her, a conviction growing inside him, crystallising into clarity. 'No,' he said, and Olivia's eyes widened in surprise. 'I don't want you to write a letter. I don't want to contact the Sultan, not until we know whether you're pregnant or not.'

'But…'

'And, considering what we just did, we may have to wait awhile.'

'You can't jeopardise your country's future—'

'I already have. Kidnapping you has infuriated Hassan. He's taken Halina to Italy, away from my possible clutches.' He smiled wryly. 'Not that I would try such a foolhardy and desperate act again.'

'But you will contact him? You will try to make amends?'

How could he, when he already had a wife, and one

who could very well be pregnant? Zayed shook his head. 'Like I said, not until we have ascertained your condition.'

Olivia's hand crept to her belly in a gesture as old as time. 'And if I am pregnant?' she asked.

'Then,' Zayed said, his tone brooking no argument whatsoever, 'we stay married. The child in your belly will be my heir and the future King of Kalidar.'

CHAPTER TEN

OLIVIA GAZED OUT at the mountain peaks dusted with snow, at the sun shining brilliantly, and let out a sigh that was half happy, half discontented. They'd been in Rubyhan for nearly two weeks now and it had been a surprisingly wonderful two weeks.

Olivia, as she was wont to do, had made herself useful helping out in the administrative office—as her knowledge of both French and Italian had proved useful—and also taking care of Lahela's baby so the new mother could get an occasional rest. The atmosphere in the palace was a surprisingly cheerful one, with everyone determined to work towards the same important goal. Zayed had an incredibly loyal team, and they believed in him utterly.

Which made Olivia understand why he was so private with them. He didn't share his headaches or his nightmares or any of his worries or concerns, as far as Olivia could see. He presented himself as a fortress, solid and impenetrable, because everyone was depending on him. It was, Olivia suspected, a heavy burden to bear. And it made her feel more honoured that he'd shared those things with her. As impossible as it seemed, they did have a connection, one that grew deeper on her side every day. One she could no longer deny, at least to herself.

Over the last few weeks Zayed had taken time out of his

busy days and spent it with her, and they'd shared several meals as well as a few sunny afternoons simply whiling away the hours and getting to know each other.

Olivia had treasured those stolen hours, the easy conversation, the glimpses of humour, the attraction that always, always simmered between them. She'd started to feel comfortable with him, known by him, and that made her desire and care for him all the more. Which was foolhardy in the extreme, because she knew it was all likely to come to an end when she found out she wasn't pregnant.

And if she was pregnant and Zayed kept her as his Queen? That was the possibility that brought her to both the heights of hope and the depths of fear. The more time she spent with him—the more time she saw his solicitude, his moments of humour, his care for his people and even for her—she feared she was falling in love with him. And that was something that she couldn't allow to happen. Not when she knew a marriage to Zayed would only happen for expediency's sake, not because of love. And she didn't know if that was something she could accept, not in the long term. But in any case, she might not even have a choice. If she was pregnant, Zayed would not let her walk away. And Olivia had no idea how she felt about that.

A knock sounded at the door of her bedroom, and Olivia turned from the stunning view. 'Hello?' she called in Arabic. 'Come in.'

'It's me.' Zayed appeared around the door, looking crisply attractive in a western-style business suit. When not among the tribes of the desert, he tended to wear western clothes, a preference he'd said was from his Cambridge days. Olivia had enjoyed getting to know this little detail about him, as well as countless others. He preferred coffee rather than tea, and he listened to jazz. He had glasses for reading, and a partiality for Agatha Christie, something that had made her smile.

'Hi,' she said now, trying to ignore the tumble of her heart simply at the sight of him. 'How are you?'

'Oh, fine.' He braced one shoulder against the doorway, surveying her bedroom with a distracted yet strangely purposeful air. Olivia wondered what he wanted. Although he'd made a point of seeing her every day, he'd never come to her bedroom first thing in the morning. She felt a little frisson of fear. Was this odd sort of honeymoon period over already?

'It's been two weeks,' Zayed said, and there was an intractable note in his voice. Olivia stilled, one hand resting on the stone windowsill.

'Yes,' she agreed cautiously. 'Thirteen days, to be exact.'

His agate gaze searched hers. 'You should take a pregnancy test tomorrow, then.'

'Is there one available?' Olivia asked as lightly as she could. Her heart had started to hammer just at the thought of taking such a test. And, as luxurious as their accommodation was, they were in the middle of nowhere. How would Zayed procure a pregnancy test?

'I'm having it flown in.'

She swallowed. 'Oh.'

'Better to know than not.'

Which sounded rather awful, and she couldn't tell anything from his expression. 'Yes, I suppose.'

So as soon as tomorrow this could all be over. He'd send her away and reopen negotiations with Sultan Hassan for Halina. Why, oh, why, did that thought have to hurt so much?

'I'm having dinner with a government official from France tonight,' Zayed said abruptly. Olivia looked at him in surprise.

'Here?'

'He's flying in.'

'Along with the pregnancy test?' she couldn't help but quip, and Zayed gave her a tight smile. 'On the same helicopter, as it happens, although obviously two very separate requests. I thought you could join us for dinner.'

'You—what?' Now she was really flummoxed. Although she'd enjoyed her time at Rubyhan, and had socialised and interacted with just about everyone there, she still felt as if she were being hidden away from the rest of the world, Zayed's unfortunate mistake, his dirty little secret. She'd hardly expected to be introduced to someone important, someone who expected Zayed to be married to Princess Halina and not a governess nobody.

'You speak French,' Zayed pointed out. 'You told me a few days ago.'

'Yes, but…'

'And having you there will make the dinner less formal, which is important at this stage.'

'This stage of what?'

'France might be willing to support me against Malouf,' Zayed explained. 'This is their initial approach.'

'Okay.' She didn't understand the ins and outs of the politics, but she accepted that Zayed did, and if he wanted her there, she would go. 'How…how are you going to introduce me?'

'Simply as my companion. I do not think Pierre Serrat will ask any awkward questions. He is a diplomat, after all.'

Olivia nodded, unsure how she felt about any of this. It was so unexpected, yet the last few weeks had been filled with unexpected things.

They'd been exciting, she acknowledged, and she'd known more happiness here than she ever had in the Sultan's palace, a fact which made her feel a little sad. When and if Zayed sent her away, she would do something different with her life, she vowed. She would go to Paris, get a job, live independently as she never had before. The prospect made her wilt inside. She was falling in love with him, she acknowledged despondently. With every moment, every second she spent in his company, she tumbled a little bit further. And there was nothing she could do about it.

'I'll send Anna to you later,' Zayed said. 'To prepare for tonight.' Olivia nodded, and he paused in the doorway. 'Thank you, Olivia.'

'You're welcome.' The words were squeezed out. Zayed nodded once, then he was gone. She stared at the empty doorway for a moment, wishing she knew what was in his head. Was he hoping that she wasn't pregnant, so he could get rid of her as soon as possible?

Of course he is, you ninny.

No matter how pleasant the last two weeks had been, and they'd been very pleasant for her, Zayed was a man on a mission, one he'd explained to her himself, one she understood and sympathised with. He needed Sultan Hassan's cooperation too much to jeopardise it by staying married to her.

She was so foolish, half daring to dream about a life with a baby and a husband at side. A man, she reminded herself ruthlessly, who would be there only by duty, not by desire. Far better for her as well as for Zayed if she hadn't fallen pregnant. She knew that, even if in her weaker moments she didn't feel it.

Olivia spent the morning as she had intended to, proofreading some correspondence in French. It was wordy stuff, about support for Kalidar's social programmes, and made Olivia wonder about Serrat's visit. What exactly were he and Zayed going to talk about? And why did Zayed want her there?

Anna fetched her in the afternoon and Olivia looked in surprise at her bedroom which, it seemed, had been transformed into a beauty spa.

'Prince Zayed thought you would enjoy some spa treatments,' Anna said with a smile.

Olivia spent the next few hours being pampered and massaged, tweezed and trimmed. When she finally emerged from the bathroom in a huge terry-cloth robe, she felt as if she were glowing from the inside.

Anna had laid out an evening gown, a column of deep blue, with a diamanté belt and detailing on the hem. Diamanté-studded high heels matched the outfit. It was the most gorgeous dress Olivia had ever seen.

Anna helped her slip it on and zipped up the back, then one of the beauty stylists came to do her hair in a loose chignon, a few dark tendrils slipping down artfully to frame her face.

'I feel like Cinderella,' Olivia said with a little laugh, but inside she felt a pulse of both disappointment and longing. She needed to give herself the reminder, because she *was* Cinderella. It was going to turn midnight on her very soon...if she wasn't pregnant.

And if she was...

'Come,' Anna said as she handed her a matching gauzy wrap. 'Prince Zayed and Monsieur Serrat are both waiting.'

With her heart starting to thud in anticipation, Olivia followed Anna from the bedroom to a small, private salon on the ground floor, its arched windows overlooking the back gardens that had been developed on the mountainside, surprisingly lush and green.

'Ah, here she is.' Zayed turned as she entered the candlelit room, giving her a smile that was both reassuring and devastating. He wore black tie, and the crisp white shirt and midnight tuxedo jacket suited him perfectly, the ultimate foil to his bronzed skin and ebony hair. Olivia became breathless just looking at him. 'Monsieur Serrat, please let me introduce Miss Olivia Taylor.'

Olivia turned to the second man, who looked to be in his forties, with thinning hair and a kind smile as he nodded at her. 'Pleased to meet you, *mademoiselle*.'

'And you, *monsieur*,' Olivia answered in French. 'It is a pleasure.'

Pierre Serrat's face lit up. 'You speak French.'

'Mais bien sûr,' Olivia answered with a laugh. She came further into the room, her dress swishing about her ankles. She felt so beautiful in this dress, beautiful and confident in a way she never had before. She extended her hand, and with a grin Pierre Serrat kissed it. Olivia glanced at Zayed and saw a flash of something turn his eyes silver—admiration and perhaps even pride. An answering emotion fired through her, buoying her confidence all the more.

It wasn't just the dress that made her feel this way. It was Zayed. Knowing that he'd needed her, that he wanted her here at his side...it felt like the ultimate empowerment.

The member of staff who was quietly serving them handed Olivia a glass of champagne, and the conversation flowed easily, from where Olivia had learned her French to the places she'd visited in France.

'And what do you think of Kalidar?' Serrat asked as they were seated at a small, intimate table laid for three. 'It is quite different from Europe.'

'I've been living in Abkar for several years,' Olivia replied. 'So I am used to this part of the world. And I find Kalidar to be quite beautiful, even if it is a harsh beauty.'

'Well said,' Serrat answered, raising his glass, and Olivia tilted her head in acknowledgement.

The conversation continued through five courses of a meal that could have been served in a Michelin-starred restaurant in Paris and, as Zayed had promised, Serrat did not ask any awkward questions about who she was or what she was doing there. Neither did he talk of politics or policy. Olivia suspected that would come later, when she wasn't present, if it hadn't already happened.

As she sipped her wine she let herself drift into a daydream that this was her reality—that Zayed had been restored as King and she was his Queen. That they were entertaining together, as they often would, a partnership, a team. It was such a pleasant daydream, but it also created an ache in her that was painful. It hurt to let herself imagine things that would never come to pass. Even if Zayed insisted on keeping her as his Queen, she knew instinctively that he would not want the kind of loving partnership she dreamed of. But perhaps it would come in time...

Was it foolishness to hope for such a thing? Madness? Yet she did. To her own weakness and shame, she did, because she wanted to be pregnant with Zayed's child so she could live as his Queen...whatever he felt for her.

Olivia sparkled like the most brilliant jewel. All evening Zayed had trouble keeping his eyes off her and so, he'd noticed bemusedly, did Serrat. He'd made the right decision in having Olivia attend. Serrat had relaxed, seeing the western influence in Zayed's life, speaking his own language. Their discussions that afternoon had been tenuous and wary; France was willing to support Zayed against Malouf but wanted to be reassured that Zayed would take Kalidar in a different direction—and what better way to prove that than by taking a western wife?

When Jahmal had told him that Sultan Hassan had sent Halina away and was refusing to accept his message or his gifts, Zayed had realised he needed to think seriously about an alternative. And he had, quite suddenly, realised that Olivia *was* the alternative, and a good one at that... even if she wasn't pregnant.

Admittedly, he would have preferred a wife with further-reaching connections, but Olivia's background as a diplomat's daughter, her ease with languages and the fact that she was European were all points in her favour. If she was carrying his child, so much the better.

It was after midnight when Serrat said goodnight, and left Zayed and Olivia alone in the dining room, the room flickering with shadows and candlelight. Zayed ached just to look at her, her slender body encased in the sheath-like evening gown, the diamanté details making her sparkle so she looked like a blue flame.

'You were lovely tonight,' he said in a low voice. 'Perfect.'

'I didn't do much,' Olivia answered with a little laugh. 'Just made small talk.'

'Which was exactly what was needed.' Zayed had a desperate urge to make love to her. He'd been fighting it all evening; he hadn't touched her in ten days, since that madness had overtaken them both in his study, and he'd had her on his own desk. Even now he couldn't believe how quickly and completely he'd lost control, yet it had felt so good. So right. He didn't think he'd ever tire of her—and why should he? She was his wife. And she could stay his wife.

'Do you think France will support your claim?' Olivia asked. Her eyes were wide as she looked at him and Zayed knew she felt it too. The desire twanged between them; the air felt electric. He reached forward and took her hand, her fingertips sliding along his.

'I hope so. Serrat will return to his government with a

very favourable report, I have no doubt, and in no small part thanks to you.' He drew her towards him and she came hesitantly, a question in her eyes. 'I want to make love to you, Olivia,' Zayed said, a ragged note entering his voice. His need was too great to hide it. 'I've been wanting to make love to you all evening. For ten days, in fact. I'm in agony.'

She laughed softly at that, and as her hips nudged his heat flared. 'I would hate to be the cause of your pain.'

'You are the only one who can assuage it.' His hands cupped her face, his palms sliding over her silken skin. He could never get enough of her. She tilted her face up to gaze at him, everything about her open and trusting. When he told her he intended to keep her as his Queen no matter what, pregnancy or no, she would give no objections. Of that he was certain.

Zayed lowered his head and brushed his lips against Olivia's. She tasted cool and sweet and so very lovely. He deepened the kiss, loving the feel of her softness against the hard planes of his chest and thighs.

'Zayed,' she murmured against his mouth, a protest. He stilled, surprised. Surely she would not deny him now? She wanted this as much as he did—even more. 'Someone will come in.' She gestured to the table strewn with dirty dishes. 'To clear up.'

'Not while I'm in here,' Zayed answered confidently, and started drawing her towards him again, aching to feel her mouth once more.

Olivia shook her head. 'They'll be waiting until you leave. And they'll be tired, having served us all night. Let's not make them wait any longer.'

'You are thinking of my staff?'

Olivia's eyes flashed. 'Having worked in a royal household for four years, I have some sympathy.'

'Of course.' With a smile he reached for her hand. 'You are talking sense, especially as I would much rather make love to you on a bed. My bed.'

Her cheeks went pink. 'Do you really think this is a—'

'I don't think.' Zayed cut her off before she could verbalise any concerns. 'I know. I want you, Olivia, and you want me. It's that simple.'

'Yes, but…' Shadows crept into her stormy eyes. 'What about…?'

'Shh.' He silenced her with a kiss. 'Tonight is for us. Only for us.' And, as she kissed him back, he knew he had her acquiescence. Her surrender.

Silently, holding her hand, he led her to his bedroom. The corridors were dark and shadowy, the mood singing with expectation. Her hand felt small and fragile in his.

Back in his bedroom his bed had been turned down by one his staff, the lamps turned to low, the perfect setting for seduction. Except this wasn't even a seduction; this was both of them wanting each other. Revelling in each other.

As soon as the door closed behind them Zayed turned to Olivia and she came willingly; their bodies clashed, their mouths tangled and his blood and heart both sang. He backed her towards the bed and she tripped on her dress; the fragile material tore but Zayed didn't care. He didn't care about anything but the woman in his arms.

A single tug of the zip and the torn garment slithered off her, leaving her in nothing but a sheer bra and pants. She shivered slightly and Zayed realised she was nervous. The last time they'd been together, it had been rushed and urgent, and the time before that it had been a consummation, a matter of expediency. Tonight felt different for both of them.

'You're beautiful,' he said softly as he smoothed his hand from her shoulder to her hip. 'Utterly beautiful.'

Relief flashed across her face and then, with an impish smile, she reached for the studs on his shirt. Her fingers trembled slightly as she undid the first one but then, emboldened by the throaty growl he couldn't help but give, she undid the others, the studs clattering to the ground, then pushed his shirt aside before resting her palms flat on his chest.

'You're beautiful too,' she said softly, and the blood roared through Zayed's veins. This woman enflamed him. He pulled her to him, wanting to be slow and deliberate but craving her too much, even now. Especially now.

They fell onto the bed in a tangle of limbs, hands and mouth reaching for whatever bit of skin they could access. He skimmed his hand along her inner thigh and she bucked, her response overwhelming.

Zayed reached for a condom from his bedside table. This time he would be careful. Within moments he'd buried himself inside her and, as Olivia met him thrust for thrust, he forgot about everything…everything but her.

CHAPTER ELEVEN

'HERE YOU ARE.'

Olivia took the slim rectangular box and tried not to gulp as she stared down at the lettering on its front. Zayed met her uncertain gaze evenly, his face completely bland, grey-green eyes shuttered. She'd spent all last night lost in his arms, seeking and finding pleasure after pleasure and joy after joy, but right now she had no idea what he was thinking or feeling, and she lacked the courage to ask him. A depressing thought, considering how wonderfully intimate last night had been—far more than the last two occasions they had come together.

Even now, with Zayed standing so fathomlessly in front of her, Olivia remembered how tenderly he'd held her, the Arabic endearments he'd murmured in her ear, the way he'd touched her, so reverently, as if she were a cherished treasure…and that was how she'd felt. She'd slept in his arms all night and woken in the morning with the biggest smile on her face and in her heart.

This moment was another proposition entirely.

'Should I…?' She glanced down at the rather lurid pink and blue writing on the side of the box. 'Should I take it now?'

'I don't see why not.' Zayed's voice was as bland as his face, yet in both she detected an intensity that alarmed her.

Was he dreading the possibility of her being pregnant that much? If she was pregnant, would he feel trapped, tied to her in a way he might hate?

'Right.' Her numb fingers closed around the box. 'Well, then…'

He nodded towards the en-suite bathroom. 'I'll wait here.'

Wordlessly Olivia nodded, then she turned and made for the bathroom, closing the door behind her with a final-sounding click. She laid the box on the edge of the sink, willing her heart rate to slow and her nerves to steady. She was so nervous, and she had a terrible feeling it was because she was scared she wasn't pregnant. That she'd be sent away. Or was she worried that she was pregnant and would be made to stay? The trouble was, Olivia didn't know which she felt. Everything was a churning, mixed-up jumble inside her, and Zayed's inscrutable face and tone weren't helping.

Still, there was no point analysing her emotions until she knew the truth of the matter. Taking a deep breath, Olivia opened the box.

Three minutes later she turned over the test she'd taken to read the results, her nerves and hand both surprisingly steady. Three minutes had been an agony to wait, but now that the time had come she felt calmer because she knew she wanted to know, needed to know, for her own sake, her own sanity. She couldn't take any more limbo. Even so, the single line, stark and vivid, felt like a smack in the face, a fist to the gut.

One line. Not pregnant.

Olivia sank down onto the edge of the sunken tub, her heart plummeting like a stone. Disappointment. That was what she felt now—like a tidal wave crashing over her and pulling her under. Total, sick disappointment. Tears stung her eyes and, impatient with herself, she blinked them away. This was a good thing. It had to be.

If she'd been pregnant, Zayed would have felt honour-bound to keep her as his wife, and theirs would have been a marriage of expediency and growing resentment, hardly the kind of environment in which to raise a child, never mind find her own happiness.

She took a deep breath and let it out slowly. Yes, this was better. Even if her heart now felt like a leaden weight inside her, dragging her down.

'Olivia?' Zayed rapped on the door. 'Surely you must have taken the test by now?'

'Yes.' She couldn't let the disappointment show on her face, Olivia realised with a jolt of panic. That would be far too humiliating, to have Zayed realise she'd wanted his baby. She'd wanted to stay. 'Yes, I've taken it.'

'Well?' Zayed sounded impatient, and Olivia couldn't tell if there was any other emotion underneath that, hope or fear or something else.

'I'm coming out.' She glanced at the test one last time, the single, stark line, and then threw it into the bin. As she washed her hands she gave herself a silent and stern talking-to in the mirror.

This is for the best. It really is. You know that, Olivia, in your head, if not in your heart. You wouldn't want Zayed to feel trapped. You wouldn't want to feel trapped.

'Olivia,' Zayed prompted, a definite edge to his voice. She opened the door. His narrowed gaze scanned her from head to foot, assessing. 'Well?'

'I'm not pregnant,' Olivia said quietly. Thankfully her voice was steady, as were her hands, which she folded in front of her.

'You're not?' Zayed sounded surprised. 'But...'

'But what? This was the most likely outcome, really.'

She made her mouth turn up in a smile. 'It's a relief for both of us, I'm sure.'

'Yes.' Zayed's lips pressed together in a firm line. 'Yes,' he said again.

Olivia took a deep breath, willing this moment onward. 'So,' she said, prompting him to make that painful cut she knew was necessary. Zayed simply stared at her, eyes still narrowed. 'You will resume negotiations with Sultan Hassan,' Olivia continued. 'And I will…' She paused, wondering just what she would do. Where she would go from here. The future felt like a void. 'I'll make my plans.'

Zayed's eyes narrowed further, to silvery-green slits. 'And what plans are you thinking of making?'

Olivia tilted her chin. 'That's not your concern any more, is it?'

'You're my wife. Of course it's my concern.'

'Don't, Zayed.' She didn't think she could take one of his autocratic dictates right now, never mind his playing the marriage card. 'You know I'm not your wife like that.' Never like that.

'You're my wife in every way possible at the moment,' Zayed returned. 'Or have you forgotten last night?' Heat simmered in his eyes and Olivia felt as if the very air between them had tautened.

Olivia knew she'd live with the memory of last night for the rest of her life. 'Of course I haven't.'

'Until this issue is resolved to my satisfaction, you will make no plans,' Zayed ordered.

'Your satisfaction?' Was he actually going to keep her prisoner? She didn't think she could bear it. 'And what about mine?'

'And yours,' Zayed allowed. 'I will make sure you are provided for, no matter what. But we are not finished here, Olivia. Not yet.'

'How can we not be?' His words, flatly delivered as they were, offered her a shred of hope that she knew she should refuse. Far better for him to release her, free her, so she could start to recover and heal. Staying with him would prolong the agony of wanting something she now knew she could never have. 'You need to focus on Princess Halina,' Olivia pressed on. 'And Sultan Hassan. I'm no help there, Zayed.'

'You might be. Princess Halina might want to speak with you.'

'And do you want that?' she challenged. What on earth could she say to Halina that her friend wanted to hear? The conversation would be devastating for them both.

'In any case,' Zayed said, 'Sultan Hassan has taken Halina to Italy and is refusing my messages as well as any possible meeting. I cannot resume any marriage negotiations at the moment.'

She stared at him, surprised at how unperturbed he seemed by the situation, when he'd already told her more than once how essential this marriage alliance was. 'Then…what will you do?'

Zayed stared at her for a long moment, his gaze considering. Olivia held her breath, although she wasn't even sure why. It felt as if they were on the precipice of something important, but what?

'I rather thought,' he said slowly, 'I might stay married to you.'

The words echoed through her, reverberating for several endless moments. 'You rather thought?' she repeated in numb disbelief, even as she tried to tamp down the absurd happiness spiralling inside her. 'Do I have no say in the matter, then?'

'Of course you do.' Impatience flickered across Zayed's face and then he deliberately relaxed, offered her a smile. 'That's why I'm discussing it with you now.'

Olivia blew out a breath. 'I didn't realise this was a discussion.'

'Let's not quibble about semantics.' He crossed the room to sit on a divan by the window, one leg elegantly crossed over the other. 'Let's have a reasonable, measured conversation.'

About marriage. Because, of course, this was going to be a business arrangement, just like his marriage to Halina would have been.

'All right.' Olivia moved over to the sofa flanking his and sank onto it. 'Tell me what you're considering, then.'

Zayed glanced at Olivia; she sat with her ankles crossed and her hands folded in her lap, like a nun awaiting her orders. Zayed knew he needed to handle this with both care and sensitivity. What seemed obvious and easy to him would not necessarily be so to Olivia.

'It's come to my attention that having a western wife with a background in diplomacy is no bad thing.'

'A background in diplomacy?' Her eyebrows rose. 'I'd hardly give myself so much credit. My father was a diplomat, yes, a minor one, but I never was.'

'Still, you speak several languages; you've lived in many countries. Whether you realise it or not, Olivia, you are a woman of the world.'

She looked away, colour touching her cheeks. 'With very little experience of anything.'

'You were as at ease with the tribe's women a few weeks ago as you were with Serrat last night. Your lack of worldly experience does not discredit you.'

She shook her head, her gaze still averted. 'What of the marriage alliance that was so essential to you?'

'I took a risk when I attempted to kidnap Princess Halina. A knowing risk. It hasn't worked out, so I can look elsewhere.'

'Elsewhere?'

'To France and other European countries. If they support my claim, I don't need Hassan.'

'You don't need me, either.'

'Not in the same way, perhaps,' Zayed said after a moment. Jahmal had raised the same issue when Zayed had broached his proposition a few days ago. Surely, his aide had argued, there were other, more suitable women to be the Sultan's bride? In Jahmal's eyes Olivia was still nothing but a servant, even though Zayed knew he'd come both to like and admire her over the last few weeks.

Olivia turned back to face him, resolute now. 'In what way, Zayed?' she asked quietly. 'In what way do you need me?'

It felt like a loaded question. Was she acting from the practical, pragmatic viewpoint he was determined to keep with regard to marriage, or was she asking about something more? About need…the way he'd needed her last night? Love, even? Zayed couldn't tell anything from her face; her eyes were a stormy blue, her mouth compressed.

'We are already married,' he said, knowing he was prevaricating but unsure how to deal with her in this mood. She seemed very quiet and self-contained, her head slightly bowed.

'Yes, but you were willing to set me aside before. Why not now?'

Zayed felt an uncomfortable twinge of guilt at those simply stated words. Yes, he'd been willing to put her aside. He'd had to be. But he felt differently now…and he realised he didn't particularly like Olivia asking him why.

'I've seen the advantages of our alliance,' he finally said. 'And since we are already married, and divorce or annulment is no small matter, it makes sense to stay married. Besides,' he added, watching her, 'we have a certain chemistry, do we not? That is no small thing.'

'I wouldn't know,' Olivia answered shortly.

'Nor perhaps would I,' Zayed agreed with a small smile. He longed to lighten her mood; he wanted her to be happy about this, damn it. 'Before you, Olivia, I had not been with a woman since my days at Cambridge.'

He'd surprised her with that. 'Ten years? I know you said it had been a long time…'

'As long as that.' He shrugged. 'My point is, we are good together. You are an asset to me.'

'As asset,' she repeated, and he had a feeling he'd chosen the wrong word.

'I would be honoured,' he said a bit tightly, 'to have you as my wife.'

A tiny smile curved her mouth, lightened her eyes. 'Is that a proposal?'

'After the fact, but yes.' He waited, feeling tenser than he wanted to be. Her answer mattered to him very much. He'd been hoping she was pregnant, and then there would have needed to be no discussion. The matter would have been resolved. As it was, he needed to convince her of the merits of their marriage. And if she said no? Would he let her go? The possibility caused him an unexpectedly strong wrench of feeling.

Olivia pursed her lips, her expression distant. 'What kind of marriage would we have?' she asked after a long, taut moment of waiting.

'The kind anyone has. A real marriage in every sense of the word.'

'Real?' She finally met his gaze, her own startlingly direct. 'A real marriage means a loving one.'

He recoiled a little, unable to keep himself from it. 'Is that what you want? Love?'

Her mouth twisted in a sad smile. 'I've dreamed of it, yes. I think most young girls do.'

'True.' He hesitated, wanting to appease her but knowing he could make no promises to love her. None at all.

'I know you don't love me, Zayed,' Olivia said. She almost sounded gentle. 'I'm not expecting you to proclaim your love or something like that.' She laughed softly. 'The expression on your face! You look horrified.'

Zayed tried to school his features into something more appropriate. 'I'm sorry.'

'It's all right.' She sighed and leaned back against the sofa. 'I just have to consider if it's something I'm willing to give up.'

'There are worse things than being a slave to such an emotion.'

She glanced at him curiously. 'Is that how you see it? As some form of slavery?'

Zayed shrugged. 'It traps you. Takes you hostage.'

'You've been in love, then?'

'No, not romantically. But I've lost people I've loved, and I don't want to feel that…vulnerable again.' His hands tightened into fists. He felt vulnerable enough just admitting that much.

Olivia nodded slowly. 'I suppose I can understand that.'

'Can you?' He felt a wave of relief, then a flicker of hope. 'Then…?'

'I need to think about it,' Olivia said. 'We're talking about a life decision, Zayed, not something to be decided in a moment.'

'Of course.'

'Although I understand your need to have this issue resolved as quickly as possible.'

He smiled, letting it linger. 'Your understanding is very considerate, Olivia.'

She smiled back, and there it was, the spark that always seemed to be snapping between them, kindling into flame. He wanted her all over again, and he let her see it in his eyes.

'We would be good together, Olivia. We *are* good together.'

'In that way,' she murmured, looking away. 'Yes.'

'It is not to be discounted.' He paused, wanting to convince her, to seal the deal, no matter what she said about needing to think. 'I believe I could make you happy.' He realised as he spoke the words that he meant them. He could make her happy and, moreover, he wanted to make her happy. Over the last few weeks he'd enjoyed seeing that shy smile bloom across her face. Last night he'd loved feeling her come alive in his arms. She'd lived a quiet, sheltered life, a life of restraint and shadows. He would be able to give her so much more once he was restored to his throne. And he would be restored. Soon. Very soon.

Olivia nodded, seeming lost in thought, her gaze averted from his. Zayed wished he knew what she was thinking. He wished he knew how to convince her.

'Why don't you come with me tomorrow?' he said impulsively. Olivia at least turned back to look at him.

'Come with you? Where?'

'I'm touring some nearby villages, to reassure the people.'

Olivia frowned. 'Should you really have me accompany you when it hasn't been decided?'

Probably not, but Zayed wanted her there. Wanted to show his people as well as Olivia herself that she could be his Queen. That she was his Queen.

'It would be an opportunity for you to see what your role would be, and for my people to see you.'

'And if we dissolve the marriage...?'

He shrugged. 'Then I will explain.' He leaned forward, urgent now. 'But give us a chance, Olivia. Give Kalidar a chance.'

Olivia let out a long, low breath and nodded slowly. 'All right,' she said, and it sounded like a concession rather than something she might look forward to. 'I'll go with you.'

CHAPTER TWELVE

THE WIND WHIPPED Olivia's hair away from her face as the Jeep bumped over the desert dunes. They'd touched down in a helicopter an hour ago and had been travelling steadily since then under a bright blue sky and lemon-yellow sun. After the cool alpine temperatures at Rubyhan, the desert heat felt overwhelming, like entering a furnace. At least the breeze from the open-top Jeep helped.

Besides being hot, Olivia felt bone-achingly tired. She had barely slept at all last night, her mind going round in dizzying circles as she considered Zayed's 'proposal,' unromantic and businesslike as it had been. What had she been expecting? That he'd confess he'd fallen in love with her? She'd known all along Zayed wasn't interested in that. His duty was to his country and his people and, if marriage to her helped those two things, then he would pursue it.

But would she?

That was the question she was afraid to answer. Afraid to want.

Zayed glanced back at her, a reassuring smile curving his mouth, his eyes glinting in the harsh desert light. 'We will be there soon.' He touched her hand briefly, and even that sent sparks racing along her nerve endings. No, she supposed, just as Zayed had said, their physical chemistry was not to be underestimated. But was it enough?

The Jeep continued to bump along and Olivia leaned back against the seat, closing her eyes against the stunning view and the questions that thudded relentlessly through her. She had no answers, which was why she hadn't had any sleep last night.

After another twenty minutes or so the Jeep slowed down and Olivia opened her eyes to see they were on the edge of a small village of single storey, mud-brick dwellings. Most of the village had come out to greet them, wide smiles and curious eyes for their future King and the woman accompanying him. His future Queen. Could she really be that person? Did she want to be?

Zayed got out of the Jeep first, waving at the crowd who had gathered before turning to open the door for Olivia.

'Who will they think I am?' she whispered as she took his hand and clambered out of the vehicle.

'My Queen,' Zayed said simply. 'Because that is who you are.'

'Zayed…' This was not the place to discuss the future, yet already Olivia felt trapped; a noose, tempting as it was, was tightening about her neck. Had Zayed invited her along today so it would be harder to back out? The more people who saw her as his Queen, the more she'd see herself that way? And the more people she'd disappoint if she walked away from all of this.

Such thoughts were swept away as Zayed led her to the crowd. She waved and saw the women sigh or look speculative; clearly everyone was wondering. But she couldn't let herself worry about that as the day went on and they moved from one festivity to another, inspecting a newly built school, listening to children sing, having glasses of tea with the head of the tribe.

By late afternoon Olivia was feeling tired and a bit overwhelmed, but also surprisingly happy. She had a role here, and one she was surprisingly good at. She liked chatting to people—her Arabic had improved over the last few weeks—and entering into their lives. After a lifetime spent in the shadows, she was finally, wonderfully, stepping into the light, in all sorts of ways, thanks to Zayed. Who would ever have thought a kidnapping would lead to self-awareness and fulfilment? And yet she knew now, whatever the future held, she would be a better, braver person for it...thanks to Zayed.

By nightfall she was ready to crawl into bed and sleep for hours. The women of the village had brought her to the finest house, and in it to a bedroom that was surprisingly sumptuous, considering how little the people of the village had. Olivia thanked them and then began to undress. She'd just taken off her headscarf and slipped out of the traditional kaftan she'd worn when the door to the bedroom opened.

Olivia whirled around, clutching the kaftan to her. 'Zayed...' His name came out in a surprised rush. 'What are you doing here?'

'Sleeping, as are you.'

'But...' She shook her head slowly. 'Then the people of the village know we are married?'

'It would seem so.' He seemed remarkably unperturbed.

'Did you tell them?'

'I did not tell them otherwise.'

Olivia sank onto the bed, the kaftan still clutched to her chest. 'Are you making it harder for me to say no?'

Zayed shrugged out of the linen *thobe* he wore, revealing his bronzed, muscled chest in all its perfection. 'Maybe,' he admitted, eyes glinting. 'As I've said before, Olivia, we're good together.'

'In bed.' She spoke flatly.

'In all ways. Today, for example. You were in your element out there.' His glinting gaze turned penetrating as he looked at her. 'You enjoyed it, didn't you? Talking to people, listening and learning? You've spent all of your adult life as a servant, silent and obedient, but you don't need to be like that any more.'

It was so close to what she'd been thinking earlier, so... why was she resisting? Why was she fighting what Zayed was offering, when it was so much more than she'd ever had before, ever hoped to have?

Olivia stared at him helplessly, knowing that she'd been resisting all along because she was afraid. Afraid of loving him as desperately as she knew she did while he felt only desire and perhaps affection for her.

Yet... *Would that be so bad?* Couldn't she live with it? She'd lived with less—far less—and she'd found a certain kind of happiness. She could have more of it with Zayed. He enjoyed her company, at least, and they *were* good in bed together. And when children came along and she was able to be a mother...

'Why fight it?' Zayed asked softly. 'Why fight us?'

'It's a big decision, Zayed,' Olivia answered, her voice shaky. 'And just because you've reached a certain conclusion doesn't mean I have.'

'But you are beginning to,' Zayed said, and there was certainty in his voice. 'You are.'

She opened her mouth but no words came out. She couldn't deny it. She wasn't even sure she wanted to. What was love, anyway? An ephemeral emotion, a will-o'-the-wisp, nothing you could hold onto, and perhaps nothing you could count on either. Zayed was offering her more than anyone else ever had. Why not take it? Why not grasp happiness while she could?

'Olivia,' he said, his voice full of warmth and promise. He reached for her and she came willingly, closing her eyes as their bodies brushed and collided. She leaned her head against his shoulder and they stood there, embracing, for several sweet moments.

I love you. The words came unbidden into her mind, hovered on her tongue. How had she fallen in love so quickly, so easily? Olivia closed her eyes, willing those treacherous words away. Zayed would not want to hear them. Not now, and most likely not ever.

With his arms around her, Zayed guided her towards the bed. Laughing, Olivia stumbled slightly, her leg brushing against something she assumed was the bed, but then she felt a sharp, stinging pain in her ankle. She gasped, and Zayed looked at her in surprise, but before Olivia could so much as open her mouth she felt a strange, numbing cold sweep over her body, and then she knew nothing at all.

'Olivia…?' Zayed stared at her in confusion—at her face, pale and shocked. 'What is it—'

Out of the corner of his eye he saw a movement and he jerked around to see the sinuous, black shape of a desert cobra slither across the darkened floor.

Zayed swore aloud and then he shouted for help. Already Olivia's body was going stiff, her eyes sightless. Quickly Zayed hoisted her onto the bed, looking for where she'd been bitten. He found the angry-looking fang marks on her ankle, and he tore off a strip from his *thobe* to tie around her leg and isolate the venom, praying that he wasn't too late.

Seconds later Jahmal burst into the room, followed by several of his armed guards.

'What is it? What has happened?'

'Snakebite,' Zayed said tersely. 'Do we have an antivenom injection in the Jeep?'

'I'll get it.' Jahmal left quickly, while Zayed stared down

at Olivia, her body jerking in response to the venom flowing through her system, her gaze blank and unresponsive. Cobra bites were some of the most dangerous in the world, with a high mortality rate, especially in such remote areas as this.

Damn it, why hadn't he checked for snakes? After ten years of living in the desert, he was used to doing it, but he'd been so consumed by Olivia, by the promise he'd seen in her eyes, that he'd forgotten. And now he stood here, helpless, holding her hand, her life at stake, *his* life at stake...because she was his life. The realisation cut through him cleanly, leaving him dazed and reeling.

He loved her, Zayed acknowledged with a terrible, sinking sensation, and once again he was going to have to stand by and watch as the person he loved most in the world suffered and died. It was more than he could bear. Not again. Not ever.

'Hold on, Olivia,' he whispered, trying to imbue her with his own strength. *'Hold on.'*

The next few hours passed in a blur of grief and fear. Jahmal administered the antivenom medication, and Zayed watched, utterly helpless as Olivia writhed and retched, so clearly suffering and in pain that Zayed felt as if his own body, his own heart, were being rent apart. He wished he could take her pain, longed to ease her suffering, but just as before, just as always, there was nothing he could do. And he didn't know if he could live through that again.

'Will she survive?' he asked the doctor he'd flown in from Arjah, thirty-six hours after Olivia had first been bitten. Zayed had barely left her bedside in all that time.

The doctor gave him a sorrowful smile and shrugged. 'It is impossible to say. A snakebite... As a man of the desert, Prince Zayed, you know how dangerous and even deadly these can be.'

'Yes, I know.' Zayed's hands curled into fists. 'But a person can survive if the venom hasn't spread.'

'Yes, and we will not know whether that has happened.' The doctor dared to lay a hand on his arm. 'If it is fatal, it will be soon. We will have an answer in the next day or two.'

An answer Zayed couldn't bear to think about.

Forty-eight hours after the serpent had first slithered away, Olivia stirred and then opened her eyes. She licked dry lips, her unfocused gaze moving around the room. Zayed leaned forward.

'Habibi...' The endearment slipped from his lips unthinkingly. He reached for her hand. 'You're awake.'

Slowly, as if the movement made everything in her ache, Olivia turned her head to look at him, her expression still dazed. She opened her mouth to speak but only a sigh came out.

'Don't speak,' Zayed urged her. 'Don't strain yourself, not now.' Relief broke over him like a wave on the shore, followed by a deep, unsettling unease. If she was awake, if she was cognisant, she had survived. She *would* survive. And, as grateful as Zayed was for Olivia's life, he didn't know if he had it in him to withstand something like this again. How many risks would he have to take? He'd live his whole life in jeopardy, in fear, for the one he loved. For the heart that could break.

Back in his own room, Jahmal was waiting with a grim look on his face, having just returned from Rubyhan. Zayed glanced at him, both irritated and alarmed by his aide's gloomy face.

'What?' he demanded. He hadn't slept in over two days and his mind was a haze of physical and emotional fatigue. 'Why are you looking like the walls have come crashing down?'

'Perhaps because they have, Prince Zayed.'

Zayed stilled in the action of taking off the linen *thobe* he'd worn for far too long; he hadn't bothered to change his clothes since Olivia had been hurt. 'What do you mean?'

'There was a message from Serrat back at Rubyhan. He says he is sorry, but his government is not willing to support your claim at this point.'

Zayed sat heavily on the bed and raked his hands through his hair. After the success of the dinner with Serrat, he had hoped for better. Hell, he'd expected it.

'Did he say why?'

'He gave no reason, My Prince.'

Zayed nodded slowly. 'There will be others.' But it was a blow—a big blow—that woke him from the stupor of grief and fear he'd been in for the last two days.

'You should return to Rubyhan,' Jahmal urged. 'Speak to Serrat and reach out to Sultan Hassan again, before Malouf hears of these developments and grows even bolder.'

'But Olivia...' The words died on Zayed's lips as he caught sight of his aide's face, and the flicker of something almost like contempt that went across it. He was a prince—would be the King when he could return to Arjah and be crowned. He was a leader of men, of a people, a country, and he had a duty to them, to the memory of his family...and that came before any duty he had to his mistaken bride. Besides, Olivia was getting better, and the greatest danger was past.

He gave Jahmal a terse nod. 'Be ready to leave within the hour.' Zayed did not miss the relief that broke across Jahmal's face before he turned away.

After washing and dressing in a fresh *thobe*, Zayed went in search of the doctor.

'She seems better,' he said, part-statement, part-question, and the man nodded.

'Yes, the worst is past. But it will be some days before I can discover whether there has been lasting damage.'

Zayed's stomach clenched. 'What kind of lasting damage?'

'To organs, muscles, even the brain. I am hopeful, my Prince, that the venom did not spread so far, but I can make no promises at this juncture.'

'Of course.' Dread swirled in his stomach at the thought of Olivia facing such damage…and it would be his fault. His fault for bringing her here, for kidnapping her in the first place. 'Give her the best care,' he instructed. 'And, when she is well enough, arrange for her transport back to Rubyhan.'

The man nodded. 'It will be done.'

Jahmal was waiting in the Jeep when Zayed slipped into Olivia's room for a private farewell. She was asleep, her face pale, her dark hair spread over the pillow, her lashes sweeping her cheeks. Her breathing was steady and yet so very light; she was barely a bump under the covers, her body fragile and slight.

Zayed sat next to her and took her limp hand in his. A dozen different memories ran through his mind in a bittersweet reel: that first explosive night; the way she'd cared for the women and children after Malouf's attack. Seeing her in the palace garden, Lahela's baby on her lap, looking so happy. The way she'd given herself to him, so freely and utterly. The stormy blue of her eyes, the sudden surprise of her smile. His insides twisted in an agony of indecision. Love *hurt*.

He didn't want to leave her, but he knew he had to. And perhaps it was better this way; he'd never meant to love her, never meant to open himself to that kind of pain again. If he left now, he could gain the emotional distance he needed and so could she. Yes, it was better this way. Better for both of them.

Zayed squeezed Olivia's hand gently and then brushed a kiss against her forehead. As he eased back, her eyelids flickered, but before she could open them properly she'd lapsed back into sleep.

With a wrenching pain feeling as if it were tearing him in two, Zayed backed out of the room and then headed for the Jeep, Rubyhan and the rest of his life.

CHAPTER THIRTEEN

OLIVIA WOKE SLOWLY, as if she were swimming up to the surface of the sea, the light shimmering and sparkling in the distance. Someone was speaking to her, saying her name, and she felt fingers on her wrist.

Her eyelids felt heavy, as if someone had placed weights on them. As much as she tried, she could not open them.

Olivia... Olivia...

Waves of fatigue rolled over her, making it even harder to hear that voice. Every muscle in her body ached, so she felt as if she'd been ruthlessly pummelled and punched. All she wanted to do was sleep, and so she did.

When she woke again the room was lost in twilit shadows, and although she still felt that overwhelming fatigue she was able to open her eyes. A man was sitting by her bed. In the shadowy darkness she thought it was Zayed and her heart leapt.

'Zayed...'

'No, Miss Taylor. I am Ammar Abdul, the Prince's doctor.'

'Oh.' As her eyes adjusted to the dim room, she could see the man, tall and thin, looking nothing like Zayed. 'Where...where is Zayed?'

'Prince Zayed has returned to Rubyhan.' There was a faintly repressive note to the doctor's voice that made Olivia realise her question had been presumptuous.

'I...see.' Her mouth felt terribly dry. 'Could I have a drink of water?'

'Of course.' With alacrity the doctor rose and poured her a glass of water from the pitcher on the bedside table, held it to her lips. Olivia took several grateful sips before subsiding back on the pillow, exhausted by even that small amount of activity.

'What...what has happened to me?' she asked. The last thing she remembered was Zayed taking her in his arms, telling her not to fight him. Not to fight them.

Tears pricked her eyes; her emotions felt so very raw, right up at the surface of everything. Why had he left her?

'You were bitten by a snake, Miss Taylor. A desert cobra. You are fortunate to be alive.'

A snake. Briefly, distantly, Olivia remembered the stinging pain in her ankle. 'How...how long have I been like this?'

'It has been four days since you were bitten. For some time we did not know whether you would live or die. As I said, you are very fortunate.'

'Thank you,' she murmured. 'How much longer will I be here?'

'Prince Zayed wishes you to return to Rubyhan as soon as it is safe to do so, perhaps in another day.'

Olivia nodded, and after a few moments the doctor left her to rest. She stared into the darkness, her heart a leaden weight inside her. Four days, and her life at stake. And Zayed had left. No matter why or when, she couldn't ignore that fact. She couldn't move past it.

He never promised to love you, she reminded herself. *He has a kingdom to run.*

But the fact that he wasn't here, that he'd chosen not to be here, felt like a hammer to her fragile hopes. It was a wake-up call to the reality of what she'd been about to agree to, and a much-needed one at that.

Olivia spent the day resting and trying to recover, and by the next morning Ammar Abdul deemed her well enough to be transported back to Rubyhan.

'It does not appear that you will have any lasting effects from the snakebite,' he told her after he'd checked her over. 'But you will require another complete check in a few weeks to make sure. In the meantime, rest, sleep, eat and drink.' He gave her a smile with sympathy. 'You will feel a little better each day.'

'That's good to hear.' She felt about a hundred years old at the moment, moving slowly, everything aching. The ride in the Jeep was torture, with all the bumps and jostling, and the short helicopter ride to Rubyhan was no better. By the time Olivia arrived at the Palace of Clouds, she was exhausted and aching more than ever, longing only for her bed…and Zayed.

He was not waiting at the helipad when she touched down and she didn't see him as Anna escorted her into the palace. Although she knew she probably shouldn't, Olivia couldn't keep from asking about him.

'How is Prince Zayed?'

Anna gave her a brief, inscrutable look. 'He is quite busy at the moment, dealing with various issues of diplomacy, but I will let him know that you have arrived.'

'Thank you,' Olivia murmured, fighting that bone-deep disappointment she'd felt since she'd woken up and realised that Zayed was gone. That he didn't care. Or was she being unreasonable, expecting him to sit by her bedside like some lovesick nurse? He had a country to run, duties to perform. She was being over-emotional and ridiculous, but she couldn't help herself.

It was another full day before she actually saw Zayed. She'd spent most of her time in her room, resting or sleeping, trying to manage a few meals although she had no appetite. Then, the evening of her second day back at Rubyhan, Anna fetched her.

'Prince Zayed would like to see you now,' she said, and Olivia suppressed the sarcastic reply she wanted to make: *what, now?* He beckoned and she came, apparently.

Anna led her not to one of Zayed's private, more casual rooms, but to a formal audience chamber on the ground floor, with marble pillars and walls adorned with gold leaf. Zayed stood at the far end of the room, dressed in a traditional *thobe*, embroidered with red and blue thread, and loose trousers. He could not have shown her more thoroughly that he wanted to create a distance between them.

What had changed since he'd drawn her in his arms and told her how good they were together? What had happened?

Anna quietly closed the door behind her so Olivia was alone with Zayed—Prince Zayed, because that was how this felt. He was the Prince and she was the commoner. She swallowed hard and walked slowly to one of the gilt-covered chairs at the side of the room.

'You'll have to excuse me,' she said stiffly. 'I still cannot stand for long periods.'

'Of course you must sit.' Zayed took a step forward and then stopped as Olivia sank into a chair. His gaze, as unreadable as ever, swept over her. 'You are looking far better than when I last saw you.'

'And when was that?' Olivia returned, a touch sharply. Zayed frowned and she looked away, biting her lip. There was no point in revealing her hurt feelings. It was clear they didn't matter.

'Five days ago.' Zayed's voice was cool. 'I had to return to Rubyhan on official matters.'

'Of course.' Neither of them spoke, the silence between them a heavy burden that Olivia didn't have the strength to bear. Not now, and maybe never. 'What's happened, Zayed?' she asked quietly. 'What has changed?'

'Changed?'

'Between us.' She met his gaze directly, unafraid now. How much more could he hurt her? 'I don't remember much after the snake bit me, but I remember before. I remember you telling me to fight for us and drawing me into your arms.' She swallowed. 'Then, the next thing I know, I've been desperately ill for four days and you're back in Rubyhan. I arrived yesterday morning and this is the first I've even seen you.'

Zayed's jaw was tight. 'I've been busy.'

'And when I do see you, it's as if I'm some supplicant coming to beg a favour from the king.' She gestured to the ornate reception room. 'What is this? What are you trying to tell me?'

Zayed was silent for a long moment and Olivia waited, holding her breath, because there was something. She just didn't know what it was.

'I've heard from Serrat,' Zayed said at last.

'Serrat? The French diplomat?'

'Yes.'

'And?' She searched his face, finding nothing, feeling cold. 'What did he say?'

'France is not willing to support my claim.'

'Oh. I'm sorry.' She absorbed the statement for a few seconds and then realised what it meant for her. 'You are questioning whether my credentials matter any longer,' she said slowly. Zayed didn't answer. 'Whether a western wife who can speak French and has a background in foreign service matters at all.' It was suddenly so obvious and it hurt so much. Far more than she wanted it to. She nodded slowly, accepting, because what other choice did she have? She loved him, but he didn't love her. She'd known that all along. 'So, back to plan A?' she asked with an attempt at levity that fell entirely flat.

'There's more.' Zayed bit the words off, his jaw clenched tight. 'Sultan Hassan has been in contact.'

'Ah.' She leaned back and folded her arms. 'His temper has cooled off, I suppose?'

'Something like that. He wishes to discuss my engagement to Princess Halina.'

'Right.' So it was all happening for him. She was no longer needed. And suddenly Olivia realised she was glad. No, not glad, never that, but relieved, because at least this had happened now and not in months or years, when the prospect of being set aside would have been utterly devastating. Her heart was broken, but it would mend. She would make sure of it. 'Then all that remains is for me to book my plane ticket to Paris.' Her lips trembled and she pressed them together, determined not to cry. Not to reveal one shred of heartbreak to Zayed. Not when he so clearly didn't care at all.

'I will arrange it for you,' he said after a brief, tense pause. 'But first I must ask you to do one last thing.'

'Which is?' Olivia asked, although she could guess already.

'To accompany me to Abkar. Princess Halina wishes to see you, as does Sultan Hassan.'

Olivia squeezed her eyes shut, steeling herself against the pain, and then snapped them open again. She could do this. She could survive. 'Fine,' she said, her voice as terse as Zayed's. 'When do we leave?'

This felt all wrong. Zayed gazed at Olivia's pale, heart-shaped face and wanted nothing more than to sweep her into his arms and never let her go. Seeing her walk into the room, standing, recovered, *alive*, had been almost too much to bear. The last five days had been utter hell, the news from France and Abkar overridden by his fear and concern for Olivia. He'd had hourly reports on her condition from Ammar Abdul, and he hadn't cared how it had made him look.

But he'd still arrived at this moment and brought Olivia with him. Whatever had been between them was over. He had to put his country first. His duty first. The memory of his father and brother spiralling down to their death, his mother in his arms, they came first. They had to. The news of Hassan's renewed interest on top of Serrat backing away had felt like an omen, a wake-up call. He had to stop pursuing his own pleasure, his own happiness, and do what was best for Kalidar.

'We'll leave tomorrow,' he said. 'The visit should be brief.' He paused, swallowing past the jagged lump that had formed in his throat. 'You can be in Paris in a few days.'

Zayed didn't see Olivia until they were boarding the helicopter the next morning. He'd barely slept all night, wanting only to go to her. One last night in her arms, forbidden and sweet. He didn't, because he knew it wouldn't be fair to her, or Princess Halina, for that matter. The break needed to be clean, quick and final.

They didn't speak on the helicopter ride from Rubyhan, or in the armoured car they took through the desert to Abkar. Olivia's face was turned to the window as the dunes slid by, and after several hours they arrived on the outskirts of Abkar's capital, the single-storey dwellings giving way to apartment buildings and high rises.

When the palace walls came into view, built of golden stone and interspersed with minarets, she let out a little sigh. 'It feels like a lifetime,' she said quietly.

It was a lifetime. A part of him had come to life in the

last few weeks, and then died. The grief he felt was for that part of him as much as it was for losing Olivia. He didn't want to go back to the man he'd been, closed off from emotions, an island of independence and strength. He wanted to need her but he knew he couldn't.

Staff met them as soon as the car pulled up to the palace's front entrance. Zayed had barely a glance for Olivia before she was being ushered away, and he was taken to wait on Sultan Hassan in the palace's throne room.

The Sultan came quickly into the room, unsmiling, and Zayed gave him a brief nod, one head of state to another. The two men stared at each other for a long moment and then Hassan finally spoke.

'I do not applaud your methods, Prince Zayed, but at least you got my attention.'

'For that I am glad, Your Majesty.'

'It is unfortunate that you made such a grievous error.'

Zayed inclined his head. 'Indeed.' Part of him wanted to argue about the nature of that error, for Olivia was so much more to him than that, yet he did not. He couldn't.

'Under normal circumstances, I would not even receive you,' Hassan continued. 'While I understand your reasoning, as well as your intense desire to be restored to your kingdom, Princess Halina is my daughter, and a royal in her own right, and you attempted to treat her with immense disrespect.'

'I meant none, I assure you, Your Majesty.'

'Even so.' Hassan blew out an irritated breath. 'But the fact remains that the Princess's circumstances have changed.'

'Oh?' Zayed stood alert, a new wariness charging through him. What did Hassan mean?

He made it plain soon enough. 'Her mother took her to Italy a few weeks ago, to keep her out of the drama unfolding here,' Hassan said flatly. 'And it appears in that time that she got into trouble.'

'Trouble?'

'She is no longer a virgin,' Hassan stated, his face set like stone. 'In fact, she is pregnant with another man's child.' Shock ripped through Zayed, leaving him speechless for a few seconds. Hassan smiled grimly. 'It is not what you expected, I imagine.'

'I am taken by surprise,' Zayed admitted carefully.

'She has been dishonoured and ruined. The only way for her situation to be redeemed is for you to marry her as was originally planned. The child can be passed off as yours.'

Revulsion at such a cold-blooded suggestion made Zayed nearly recoil. 'And what of the biological father? Has he no interest in his child?'

'He has no say. He doesn't know, and I have no intention of him knowing.'

'Who is he?'

'That is not your concern.'

'On the contrary, it is most certainly my concern. You are asking me to raise his child as my own and potentially, if it is a son, to be my heir.'

'That is the price you must pay for your own misdeed,' Hassan returned coldly. 'Did you think I would forgive so easily? If you want my support, if you want to reclaim your kingdom, then you will do this one thing.'

Zayed took a quick, even breath, willing his temper to stay in check. Hassan had always been autocratic, assuming more authority and power than he'd ever truly possessed. Abkar was a small country, smaller even than Kalidar, although it was rich in resources and had a stable economy. But he would not take orders from the man. 'And what does the Princess think?'

'It is of no concern.'

'Even so, I would like to know.'

Hassan shrugged. 'You may ask her yourself. I will grant you a private audience with her later today.' His eyes flashed. 'You will take no liberties, I trust, or this offer will be rescinded.'

'Of course I will take no liberties.' Zayed knew he could hardly claim the moral high ground, but he'd forgotten, since his last interview with Hassan years ago, how much he disliked the man. He could be charming when he chose, but underneath that veneer of paternal kindness ran an arrogant, self-serving strain.

Hassan gave him a cold smile. 'Then we are finished here.'

A muscle ticked in Zayed's jaw. He realised he was furious—and not because of the other man's lack of respect for his title and position, the autocratic way he spoke, or the way he talked about his daughter, as if she were nothing more than a stain on his reputation. No, he was angry at this man, furious with him, because of his complete lack of concern for Olivia. She'd considered Hassan like a father. She'd viewed the palace as her home.

'You have not asked about Miss Taylor,' Zayed said, his voice low and level.

Hassan arched an eyebrow. 'And you, it seems, think I should have?'

'She has been a member of the royal household for four years.'

'She has been a servant, yes. I assume, Prince Zayed, that you have treated her comfortably?'

'Of course I have.' Zayed glared at the man, fighting an urge to throttle him.

'In any case, Miss Taylor is no longer a member of this household. Her position has been terminated. Understandably.'

'Will you give her a reference?'

Hassan's eyes glittered. 'I think not.'

It was just as Olivia had predicted, yet Zayed hated that this man, that anyone, thought so little of her.

Including yourself?

Pushing that most uncomfortable thought away, Zayed nodded once to Hassan then turned on his heel and left the room.

CHAPTER FOURTEEN

'Olivia!'

With a startled, *'Oof!'* Olivia put her arms around Halina as her friend rushed at her, hugging her tightly the minute she entered the small sitting room where Halina had been waiting for her arrival.

'Hello, Halina.'

'Are you all right? Have you been hurt? Has—has he hurt you?' Halina leaned back, sniffing, her eyes wide and frightened.

'I'm fine.'

'But you look so pale and tired.'

'I've been ill,' Olivia said briefly. 'But I've been treated with respect at all times.' With a tired smile she extricated herself from Halina's arms. She felt so very fragile, as if she could break, and it had nothing to do with her recovery from the cobra's bite. 'How are you? You've been in Italy, I heard?'

'Yes.' Halina bit her lip. 'Olivia, I'm afraid I've made a complete mess of things.'

'How so?' Olivia couldn't imagine how Halina could make things more of a mess than they already were. 'I think Zayed was the one who messed things up,' she added with an attempt at a wry smile, but it wobbled all over the place. She'd loved him, she still did, and he'd felt nothing for her. No matter how many times she ruthlessly hammered that truth home, it still hurt, the wound as fresh and deep as ever.

'Yes, but…' Tears filled Halina's eyes before she blinked them away. 'I made it all so much worse.'

Curious and a bit alarmed, Olivia shook her head. 'I don't understand, Halina.'

'When I went to Italy…' Halina broke off, turning away towards the window that overlooked the palace's landscaped gardens. 'I was so stupid,' she muttered, rubbing her temple with her fingers. 'So stupid and so naïve.'

'Halina…' Olivia took a step towards her old schoolfriend. 'You're scaring me a bit.'

'I've scared myself.' She let out a humourless laugh. 'I can't believe…'

'What happened?' Olivia asked gently. 'You can tell me.'

Halina took a deep, shuddering breath and then, turning around, she squared her shoulders. 'Mama took me to Italy, to a hotel in Rome, to get away from Abkar. Father was worried someone might attempt to kidnap me again. He didn't realise it was Prince Zayed, at least not at first, and then of course when he did he was furious.' She reached for Olivia, squeezing her arm. 'Was it awful, Livvy?' she asked, using the nickname from their school days. 'I'm so sorry.'

'It's not your fault,' Olivia said, her voice sounding funny. 'And it wasn't awful.' Halina must have seen something in her face—she could be remarkably perceptive at times—for her eyes narrowed, light dawning in their soft brown depths.

'What do you mean?'

'You were going to tell me what happened to you,' Olivia reminded her quickly. 'In Italy.'

Halina's shoulders slumped briefly. 'Yes, although I'm

too ashamed to say. I thought I was so much more worldly than I really was—than I am. I was a *joke.*'

'What do you mean, Halina? Tell me what happened.'

'I snuck out of my hotel room,' Halina confessed, her face full of misery. 'And I slipped into a party being held downstairs. I just wanted a tiny bit of excitement, that was all. It didn't seem like so much.'

Which was what Olivia had wanted when she'd chosen to surrender to Zayed that first magical night. 'And what happened at the party?' Olivia asked in a hollow voice. She had a feeling she could guess, yet she could scarcely believe it.

'I met someone. A man. A handsome devil of a man.' Halina sniffed. 'Olivia, I spent the night with him,' she confessed in a near wail. 'I slept with him. Lost my virginity to…to a stranger! I don't know what came over me. I wasn't even thinking. I thought I could handle it all, handle him, and of course I couldn't.'

'You don't mean he—'

'Forced me?' Halina gave a bitter laugh. 'Not a bit of it. I was completely willing—eager, even—and spinning stories in my head of I don't know what.' She shook her head. 'And then one of the royal guards found us.'

'Oh, Halina,' Olivia murmured, full of sympathy for her friend, yet finding it hard to believe they'd both succumbed to the same kind of overwhelming temptation. 'I'm so sorry.'

'That's not the worst of it,' Halina returned grimly. She sank onto a sofa, her head in her hands. 'Father made me take a pregnancy test a few days ago and guess what?' She let out a sound that was half laugh, half sob. 'I'm pregnant.'

'Oh, my goodness.' Shocked, Olivia sat onto the sofa next to Halina and put her arm around her. Halina leaned her head against Olivia's shoulder, drawing in a few ragged breaths.

'He was so, so angry, and I can't even blame him,' Halina said in a tear-filled voice. 'I've made a mess of everything.'

'And what of this man in Italy? Surely he has something to do with it?'

'He doesn't even know I'm pregnant,' Halina admitted. 'And Father won't tell him.'

'Why not?'

She lifted her head, wiping the tears from her long-lashed eyes. 'Because he wants Prince Zayed to accept the child as his own,' she said. 'What is he like, Olivia? Is he a savage? To think he wanted to kidnap me.' She shuddered. 'And now I'm meant to marry him.'

Abruptly Olivia rose from the sofa and crossed to the window, not wanting Halina to see the expression on her face. Not knowing how she felt about any of it: Zayed to pass off another child as his own, and marry Halina when he didn't love her and she obviously didn't even know him. It was so awful, so unjust, but it was what Zayed had chosen. It was what he wanted. Not love, and not her.

'What is it?' Halina asked after a moment. 'You've gone all strange and silent. What are you not telling me, Olivia?'

'Nothing.' Even to her own ears Olivia's voice sounded distant and strained.

'No, there's something; I can tell. I know you, Olivia. I've known you since we were both eleven years old. What are you not telling me about Prince Zayed? Is it something terrible?'

'No, nothing like that.' Olivia dragged a breath into her lungs. 'He's…he's a good man, Halina.'

There was a tense moment of silence, and Olivia willed Halina to believe her, to be satisfied and for this conversation finally to be over, because she didn't think she could manage much more.

'You love him,' Halina said slowly. 'It's so obvious now that I can see it. You've fallen in love with him.'

'I haven't,' Olivia said, but her denial was so feeble she knew it wouldn't fool anyone, not even a child.

'You're in love with him, and he's meant to marry me!' Halina exclaimed, her voice filled with dismay. 'This is *awful.*'

'Zayed wants your marriage to go forward,' Olivia insisted. 'What I feel doesn't matter. Trust me, Halina, I know that.'

'Matter to whom?' Halina demanded. 'It matters to you, and it matters to me. And, if you love him, it should matter to Zayed.'

'It doesn't,' Olivia said wretchedly. 'He's made that clear.'

'I haven't defied my father over this because I knew I brought shame to him. But it's different now.'

'It isn't.' Alarm filled Olivia and she whirled around. 'Halina, please don't break the engagement. *Please.* Zayed needs the alliance with your country. Your father will have told him what happened in Italy and he will have accepted it. I know. Please don't do anything rash.'

'You love him,' Halina said slowly, 'and you still want him to marry me?'

'He doesn't love me,' Olivia answered flatly, 'and I don't want to be with a man who doesn't love me. So think of it this way, if you must—I'm choosing not to be with him.'

'Except it doesn't seem as if you have much choice in the matter.'

'Let things be, Halina, please.' Olivia's whole body sagged; she felt as if she could barely stand. 'I can't talk about this any more. I was ill recently, and I need to rest. But promise me you won't say anything to Zayed.'

'Anything at all?'

'About me. About what I feel.'

Halina sighed. 'I promise, if you really don't want me to. But does he know you love him, Olivia? Because—'

'Trust me, Halina, it doesn't matter.'

Halina nodded slowly. 'Then get some rest. I'll see you later.' She kissed Olivia's cheek and squeezed her hand. 'What a pair we are,' she whispered with a hint of her old dramatic impishness. 'Having such adventures.'

'Yes.' Olivia smiled wearily and walked from the room, skidding to a halt halfway down the corridor when she saw Zayed striding towards her.

'You've been with the Princess?' he asked, his agate gaze sweeping over her and revealing nothing.

'Yes.'

'She told you?'

'About her pregnancy? Yes. I'm sorry, Zayed.'

'I have no one to blame but myself. And I can hardly accuse the Princess of being impetuous when I was just as rash.' He sighed and rubbed his temple.

'Are you getting a migraine?' Olivia asked quietly.

'It will pass.' He dropped his hand and subjected her to a direct look. 'How are you? How are you holding up?'

Her heart was in pieces, and she ached everywhere it was possible to ache, but she wasn't going to tell any of that to Zayed. 'I'm fine.'

Zayed looked at her closely, as if he could chip away at the thin veneer of calm and control she'd managed to erect. 'Olivia…'

'I need some rest.' Olivia knew she couldn't withstand his apology, not now, not ever. It would be better if she never saw Zayed al bin Nur again in her life.

She tried to move past him but he caught her arm, turning her to face him. Their faces were close, their hips brushed and, despite the ache in her heart, desire rushed through her veins. She felt herself melt, knew she was utterly helpless from the moment he touched her.

'I wish...' Zayed breathed, one palm coming up to cup her cheek. 'I wish things had been different.'

'But they aren't.' She forced the words out even though it felt as if they were tearing her in two.

'I know.' Zayed's gaze became hooded as it dipped to her mouth. Olivia tensed, straining for his kiss even though she knew she should resist. He brushed his lips across hers, once, twice, before settling on them for a moment, pressing hard, as if he were sealing her memory inside him. Olivia clutched at his shoulders, accepting the brand, needing it to sustain her, and then finally she wrenched away with a gasp.

'Your fiancée is waiting,' she choked out, then hurried down the hall.

Zayed waited a moment, until his breathing and libido were both under control, before he opened the doors and stepped into the sitting room where he knew Princess Halina was waiting.

She whirled around at his entrance, her eyes widening as she realised who it was. 'Prince Zayed.'

'Princess Halina.' He gazed at her for a long moment, trying to view her objectively. Yes, she was pretty—tumbled, ebony hair, wide brown eyes, a delectably curvy figure. But she wasn't Olivia, and that was all that mattered.

'You've met with my father,' Halina said, and her voice wavered.

'Yes. He told me what happened in Italy.'

She lowered her gaze, lashes sweeping her cheeks. 'And you are willing to accept the change in circumstances?'

'It seems I have no choice.'

Halina looked up, all modesty gone as her eyes flashed.

'Of all the people in this situation, Prince Zayed, you have the most choice of all.'

Surprised, he frowned. 'How do you mean, Princess?'

'You don't have to marry me.'

'I believe you are aware of the political incentive to do so.'

'Political incentive?' To both his shock and irritation Halina looked scornful. 'Do you really think my father will support your claim to the throne?'

Zayed felt a chill spread through his body. 'Do you know something I do not, Princess Halina?'

'No, only that I have never trusted my father wholly. He isn't a cruel man, but his own reputation and comfort comes above everyone else's.'

'I suppose it is a risk I am willing to take.'

'And what of Olivia?'

Zayed tensed. 'What of her?'

Halina cocked her head, her soft brown gaze moving over him slowly. 'Does she not matter at all?'

Zayed said nothing, although everything in him wanted to protest. Shout.

She matters. Of course she matters.

'We are not here to discuss Olivia,' he answered, his tone repressive.

'No,' Halina said slowly. 'We are not.' She was still gazing at him, her expression hard and assessing. 'We are here to discuss our possible marriage.'

'Yes.'

'And the truth is, Prince Zayed, I cannot marry you. I will not.'

Zayed stared at her in shock. 'What?'

'I'm not going to marry you,' Halina stated again, shrugging. 'I'm sorry if it is a disappointment.'

'Your father...'

'My father wants me to marry you. He wants to tidy away my mistake. But he cannot force me.' She lifted her chin. 'No matter what.'

Zayed paused for a moment, aware of what a risk she was taking. Hassan would be furious; he would likely send her away to a remote palace in the desert, never to be seen in society again. He felt a reluctant admiration for the Princess, and underneath another emotion, damning in its intensity. He felt relief.

He didn't want to marry Halina. Whether she was pregnant or not, whether she was willing or not, he didn't want her. He wanted Olivia.

'May I ask why you have come to this decision?' Zayed asked.

'Yes, it is quite simple.' Halina's gaze met his with an unspoken challenge. 'I will not marry a man who is in love with someone else.'

Zayed was too shocked to hide his reaction. *In love...?* 'I don't...' he began, and then stopped. He couldn't deny it. He'd been trying to for days, cutting himself off from Olivia and all that she meant to him because it was necessary for his country. For his rule.

Now Halina tilted her head and gave him a mocking look. 'I'm glad you didn't bother denying it. That does you credit.'

Her audacity surprised and somewhat amused him. 'What I feel for Olivia has nothing to do with our potential alliance.'

'I'm afraid it does. Because, like I said, I don't wish to marry a man who is in love with someone else, especially when I am pregnant with another man's child.'

'Do you love him?' Zayed asked. He felt nothing either way for Halina and her child—no jealousy, no anger, no interest.

'No,' she answered after a pause. 'But with my child and your love of Olivia our marriage would be both a battle and a breeding ground for resentment.'

'It wouldn't have to be,' Zayed said, but even he sounded unconvinced. The picture Halina was painting was bleak. But what choice did he have?

'Do you know what I think?' Halina said, and Zayed wasn't sure he wanted to know. 'I think you're using your sense of duty as a big, fat excuse.'

'What?' The breath whooshed out of Zayed's lungs as he stared at her in mounting fury. 'My father and brother died in the war against Malouf. They were assassinated. I *watched* them die. For the last ten years—' He broke off, struggling with the tidal wave of emotion he felt. 'For the last ten years,' he resumed, 'I have dedicated my life, everything I have, to serving their country and protecting their memory.'

Halina's face softened. 'Prince Zayed, I'm not trying to diminish what happened to your family, or what you've done for them. Of course I'm not. You have suffered and worked tremendously for the good of your country, of your people.'

Zayed nodded, his jaw tight, pain flickering at his temples.

'What I'm saying,' Halina continued steadily, refusing to be cowed, 'is that I believe you are using your sense of duty as a way to get out of being with Olivia.'

'Why,' Zayed demanded, 'would I do that?'

'Because you're scared.'

He stiffened in outrage. He had never been called a coward in his life before this slip of a woman had dared to do so—and over what? *'Scared?* Of what?'

'Of love. Of risking everything for another person. Of fighting for another person, and not just a cause. Of putting yourself out there, of getting hurt.' The smile she gave him was whimsical and a little sad. 'Take your pick.'

Zayed was unable to speak…to think…because in that devastating moment he knew she was right. He *was* scared. He'd lost people he'd loved so he'd never wanted to love again. Seeing Olivia after the snake had bitten her had been utterly terrifying, and he'd done his best to distance himself from her both physically and emotionally—for his own sake. Because he was scared. Because he was a coward.

'Princess Halina, I still need your father's support.'

'I have to believe that there are other ways of getting it, or other countries who can come to your aid. Don't make that your reason, Prince Zayed, not when it is merely an excuse.'

'Plenty of rulers have chosen to marry out of duty,' Zayed snapped.

Halina smiled. 'Then don't be one of them.'

'And what about you? What will you do?'

Halina shrugged, not meeting his gaze. 'I am not your concern, Prince Zayed. Olivia is.'

Zayed's mind was in a ferment all afternoon as he paced his room at the palace, his thoughts going round in an endless, useless loop. He loved Olivia. He was afraid to love her. Afraid, too, to follow his own heart. What if it left his country in an even worse place, his people even more oppressed? Could he possibly be so selfish?

He stood at the window and watched the sun set over the desert, turning sand and sky to blazing gold. He had a sudden, piercing memory of Olivia in the desert, tending to the tribespeople, showing love and gentleness to all she encountered.

She would make a wonderful queen. She was his wife and his people had already accepted her. Why had he not been able to see that before in all its breath-taking clarity? He'd been so consumed with the alliance with Hassan, but in a sudden second of absolute certainty he realised that he should never have counted on that at all. He needed to win his people over, his country over, not depend on someone's support from the outside. Just as he needed to win Olivia.

He turned from the room, determined, desperate to see her. To tell her all that was in his heart and mind. He found his way to the staff quarters where she normally slept, saw the small, spartan chamber she'd called her own and felt his heart rend all over again. She'd had so little here, yet she'd been so grateful. And she'd asked for nothing from him...but his love.

He spun away from the room and hurried downstairs, needing to find her. 'Where is Olivia?' he asked the first member of the palace staff he came across, a startled-looking man in royal livery. 'Where is Miss Taylor?'

'Miss Taylor?' The man shook his head. 'She is gone. She took a car to the airport an hour ago.'

CHAPTER FIFTEEN

Three months later

PARIS WAS BEAUTIFUL in the autumn. From her apartment on the Ile de la Cité, Olivia could see the winding green of the river, the leaves of the trees alongside now starting to turn red and gold.

She'd been in Paris for three months, having left her heart back in Abkar with Zayed, but she was doing her best to live her life without it. Without him.

Upon arriving she'd stayed with her godmother, who had been surprisingly glad to see her. Olivia had been grateful to renew the acquaintance, and her godmother had also provided a useful contact to enable her to get a job in translation for a large corporation. Within a few weeks Olivia had both a job and an apartment and was cultivating a small group of friends from work. This was the life she had dreamed of, yet it felt so terribly empty.

She had heard nothing from Zayed, no word of an annulment or divorce, even, so bizarrely they were still married. She'd avoided tabloids and gossip magazines, not wanting to read of his resumed betrothal to Halina, and when her friend had contacted her on social media Olivia had guiltily ignored her. She wasn't ready yet. Everything still felt raw and fragile. But she would get there. The last few months, first with Zayed and now in Paris, had showed her how strong she was, and she depended on that strength now. A broken heart could mend. A shattered life could be rebuilt.

She had heard news of Kalidar; it was impossible to ignore when it made the headlines. The military had staged a coup and asked Zayed to return as their leader. Apparently, they had been growing tired of Malouf's ill treatment. Bloody skirmishes had followed, with Malouf making a desperate last stand, but a week ago Zayed had ridden into the capital city of Arjah, triumphant and regal. He'd had Malouf imprisoned and tried for war crimes as well as the murder of his family. In a few weeks he was finally going to be crowned King of Kalidar.

Olivia was happy for him. He'd finally achieved all he'd been striving for for so long. All he deserved. She wondered if his marriage to Halina would go ahead, but she knew it didn't matter anyway. Zayed hadn't loved her. Hadn't chosen her. Whether he married Halina or not was irrelevant.

And she needed to get on with her life. With a weary sigh Olivia reached for her bag and slung it over her shoulder. She enjoyed the translation work she did, but she couldn't see herself doing it for ever. The future yawned ahead of her, as bleak and endless as the desert sands.

She needed to stop thinking like that. And to stop thinking about the desert, or Kalidar, or anything to do with Zayed. Anything could trigger memories of their time together—a hard blue sky, the taste of anise, the whisper of silk. All of it brought the days and nights she'd spent with him, falling in love with him, rushing back.

Olivia walked down the four narrow flights of stairs to the street, opening the front door of her building to a crisp autumn day...and Zayed.

She stared at him in disbelief, blinking several times as if she thought he might vanish, a desert mirage right here in the middle of Paris.

'Hello, Olivia.'

Still she stared. He wore a navy-blue business suit, his dark hair brushed back from his bronzed face, his grey-green eyes sparkling as he gave her a smile that was both wry and tender.

'What…?' Her voice was hoarse. 'What are you doing here?'

'Looking for you.'

The frail hope that had been unfurling inside her withered before it had had the barest chance to bloom. 'You want a divorce,' she said woodenly. After all this time, it shouldn't hurt, but even now it felt as if he were plunging a careless fist into her chest and yanking her heart out. Her last tie to him would be cleanly severed.

'A divorce?' Zayed shook his head. 'No, Olivia, I don't want a divorce.'

'But Princess Halina…?'

'Have you not heard from her?'

Olivia bit her lip and shook her head. 'I haven't.'

'And nor have I. Princess Halina refused to marry me, back when we were both in Abkar.'

'Refused,' Olivia repeated. Her mind was whirling. 'That must have been disappointing.' Had he come to her as second best? Once she would have accepted being the runner up, a last resort. She would have been grateful. But Zayed, funnily enough, had shown her that she was worth more. That she deserved more. Too bad he hadn't realised it.

'It was surprising,' Zayed allowed. 'But not disappointing. What I felt most of all, *habibi*, was relief. Because the only woman I want to be married to is my wife.'

Olivia registered the term distantly. She still couldn't believe what he was saying, what he was implying.

'It's been three months, Zayed, and I haven't heard a word from you.'

'I know.' He took a measured breath. 'A few days after I last saw you, Malouf's military staged a coup. There was bloodshed and violence; I could not leave my country.'

'I know that. I read about it in the news. But since then…not even a message…?' She shook her head, hating that it had come to this, that part of her, even now, wanted to accept whatever he was offering. How little he was offering.

'I had to find you first,' Zayed replied steadily. 'And, the truth is, I wanted to give you some time.'

'Time?'

'To consider what you really want. I know, Olivia, that you've never really lived on your own. You never had a chance to discover what you were truly capable of. I wanted to give you that chance, as well as some emotional distance from what we experienced. So we could both discover if what we felt was real and lasting.'

'What we felt.' Olivia hitched her bag higher on her shoulder, afraid to hope. 'What is it you feel, Zayed?'

There was no hesitation in his voice as he answered. 'I love you. I've loved you for a long time now. The seeds were planted that first night.'

Why was she so afraid to believe? 'But you left me,' Olivia whispered. 'When I was so ill…'

'That's when I realised I loved you. I was terrified, Olivia, of losing you. Terrified, selfishly, for myself and the pain I would feel. That's why I started to keep my distance, because I was a coward.' He shook his head, his features pinched with regret. 'But I realised—and Princess Halina helped me—that I didn't want to be that kind of coward.

Loving you has brought out the best in me, and I want to be the kind of man who loves. Who isn't afraid to love. And I love you, quite desperately. Very deeply. But...' His gaze was steady on her, a shadow of vulnerability in his mossy eyes. 'The question is, do you love me? Will you remain as my wife, Olivia, and as my Queen?'

Olivia took a deep breath, trying to sift through all her emotions. She drew another breath and her face crumpled.

'Olivia!' Zayed exclaimed, her name torn from his lips, then she was in his arms, her face buried in his shoulder, his hands stroking her hair. '*Habibi*, I'm so sorry for hurting you. I wanted to give you your freedom, but perhaps I should have come sooner.'

'No.' Olivia took several gulping breaths before she felt able to continue. 'No, it's just... I didn't think I'd ever see you again. And I love you so much, Zayed. It felt as if it was tearing me apart.'

'I know how that feels, and I wouldn't wish it on anyone. But we are together now, Olivia, and I promise you, I swear on my life, I will never hurt you. That is my solemn vow.'

Olivia let out a little gurgle of tearful laughter as she eased away from him. 'Do you know, that was the first thing you said to me when you came through the window? That you wouldn't hurt me, and it was your solemn vow.'

'And I'm sorry for the times I did hurt you,' Zayed said seriously. 'Emotionally.'

'Oh, Zayed...'

'I meant it then and I mean it even more now,' Zayed told her. 'I love you with my life, Olivia, my soul. I want you by my side, in my bed, hand in hand through everything.'

'I want that too,' Olivia whispered, her eyes shining with tears of pure happiness. 'So much.'

A smile of both relief and joy split Zayed's face and he drew her towards him for a deep and lingering kiss.

'Then I am the happiest man on earth right now.'

'And I,' Olivia answered, kissing him back, 'am the happiest woman.'

Three months later

Bells rang throughout the capital city of Arjah in celebration of the wedding of Kalidar's new King and Queen. Zayed listened to the joyful peals and felt happiness swell in his heart. He could not ask for more from his people, from his country, from his wife.

He turned to Olivia, dressed in a white lace dress and veil, her dark hair pulled back in a low chignon. She looked radiant, her eyes sparkling with happiness, her mouth curved with laughter.

'At least I understood that ceremony,' she teased as she came towards him.

Zayed grinned back at her. 'It was only a blessing, rather than a proper marriage. We can't be married twice.'

'Once is enough for me.' She took his hand and laid her head against his shoulder. 'I couldn't ask for more.'

'I was thinking the same thing.'

The last three months of peace and prosperity in Kalidar had brought Zayed immense satisfaction. Leaders around the world had offered their support, and he'd slowly but surely set about righting ten years of wrongs, building up his city and his people. His father, his family, would have been proud, he hoped. He felt a peace deep inside him that had been absent this long decade; their memories had been honoured, their deaths avenged.

Below them, in the courtyard in front of the palace, a cry rose up.

'I think they want us to go out on the balcony,' Olivia said with a smile.

'Then so we must.' Drawing her by the hand, Zayed stepped out onto the balcony with his bride. The cheers were deafening as the people filling the square called out their approval. Zayed glanced at Olivia and saw the love that suffused her face, felt its answer in himself. No, he could not ask for more. He had absolutely everything he wanted in the woman by his side.

Zayed and Olivia waved at the crowd, both of them smiling, their hearts full of happiness as they gazed out at their shining city.

* * * * *

MARRIED FOR
THE PRINCE'S
CONVENIENCE

MAYA BLAKE

CHAPTER ONE

SHE WAS A THIEF.

A thief...

Jasmine Nichols's heart pounded the indictment through her bloodstream. She hadn't stolen anything yet, but that was beside the point. She'd travelled thousands of miles for the sole purpose of taking something that didn't belong to her.

Telling herself she had no choice didn't matter. If anything, it escalated her helplessness.

By the end of the night, she would wear the damning label as close to her skin as her black designer evening gown clung now.

Because failure wasn't an option.

Fear and shame duelled for supremacy inside her, but it was the deep knowledge that she couldn't turn her back on her family that propelled her reluctant feet up the sweeping crimson carpet towards the awe-inspiring masterpiece that housed the Contemporary Museum of Arts, perched on a cliff-side overlooking Rio de Janeiro. Even the jaw-dropping beauty of her surroundings couldn't detract her from the simple fact.

She'd come here to steal.

The smile she'd plastered on her face since alighting from the air-conditioned limo threatened to crack. To calm her nerves, she mentally recited her *to do* list.

First, she had to locate Crown Prince Reyes Vicente Navarre.

And there was her first problem.

All effective search engines had yielded no pictures of the reclusive prince, save for a grainy image taken at the funeral of his mother four years ago. Since then, no pictures of the royal family of the South American kingdom of Santo Sierra had been released to the public. They guarded their privacy with a rigour that bordered on fanaticism.

As if that weren't bad enough, according to reports, the House of Navarre's Crown Prince had left his kingdom only three times in the last three years, all his time spent caring for his gravely ill father. It was rumoured King Carlos Navarre wasn't expected to live past the summer.

Which meant Jasmine had no means of identifying Prince Reyes Navarre.

How did she get close to a man whose identity she had no idea of, distract him long enough to get her hands on what she'd come for before her mother and, more importantly, her stepfather, Stephen Nichols, the man who'd saved her life, and whose name she'd adopted, found out what she was up to?

Stephen would be heartbroken if he knew she was being blackmailed.

A nerve-destroying shudder rose up from the soles of her feet, making her clench her teeth to stop its death rattle from escaping. She smiled some more, mingled with the insanely wealthy and well heeled, and tried to reassure herself she could do this. By this time tomorrow, she'd be back home.

And most importantly, Stephen would be safe.

If everything went smoothly.

Stop it! Negative thinking was the downfall of many a plan. How many times had Stephen told her this?

She fixed her wilting smile back in place, stepped into the main hall of the museum, but she couldn't summon the enthusiasm to gawp at the stunning paintings and sculptures on display.

A waiter approached bearing a tray of champagne. Accepting the sparkling gold-filled crystal goblet, she smoothed a shaky hand over the pearl choker around her throat, ignored the nervous flutter in her belly, and made her way to the bowl-shaped terrace where the guests were congregating for pre-dinner drinks.

So far the plans set out by Joaquin Esteban—the man threatening her stepfather's life—had gone meticulously. Her name had been on the guest list as promised, alongside those of world leaders and celebrities she'd only seen on TV and in glossy magazines. For a single moment, while she'd waited for Security to check the electronic chip on her invitation, she'd secretly hoped to be caught, turned away. But the man who held her stepfather's fate in his cruel hands had seen to every last detail she needed to pull this off.

Everything except provide her with a picture of the thirty-two-year-old prince.

The first stage of the treaty signing was to take place in half an hour in the Golden Room behind her. And with the occasion coinciding with Prince Mendez of Valderra's birthday, guests had been invited onto the terrace to witness the spectacular sunset and the prince's arrival, before the signing and birthday celebrations began.

Crown Prince Reyes himself was expected at eight o'clock. A quick glance at her watch showed five minutes to the hour. With every interminable second that ticked by, Jasmine's nerves tightened another notch.

What if she was found out? Certainly, she could kiss her job as a broker and mediator goodbye. But even if she succeeded, how could she ever hold her head high again? She'd worked so very hard to put her past behind her, to tend the new leaf she'd turned over. For eight years, she'd succeeded. And now, at twenty-six, she was on the slippery slope again.

Because once a juvie princess, always a juvie princess?

No. She hadn't let that voice of her detention cellmate taunt her for years. She wasn't about to start now.

And yet, she couldn't stop the despair that mingled with anxiety as her gaze drifted over the orange-splashed water towards the stunning silhouette of Sugarloaf Mountain in the distance.

Under normal circumstances, the sights and sounds would have filled her with excitement and awe. For a girl with her past and dire upbringing, sights such as these didn't feature in her *normal*. Except these weren't normal circumstances. And fear was threatening to block out every other emotion.

Which was dangerous. She couldn't afford to fail. Yet success would bring nothing but shame. Would prove that the past really never stayed in the past.

But the reality was her stepfather had gone too far this time, hedged his bets, literally, with the wrong person.

Joaquin, with his soft voice and deadly smile, had calmly given her two choices.

Come to Rio or watch Stephen rot in jail.

Of course, Joaquin had counted on the fact that, aside from his very public humiliation of being thrown out of his Foreign Office position for gambling away government money, Stephen Nichols's devotion to his wife meant he would do anything to save her the distress of watching him suffer. As would Jasmine.

Even when Jasmine was a child, long before Stephen had entered their lives, her mother's fragility had meant she had assumed the role of the caretaker. Her mother wouldn't survive losing Stephen.

So here Jasmine was, about to step into a quagmire she wasn't sure any amount of self-affirmation would wash her clean of.

'He's here!'

She roused herself from her maudlin self-pitying. A quick glance showed it was precisely eight o'clock. Her heart double somersaulted into her throat. When her stomach threatened to follow suit, she took a hasty sip of champagne. Whatever Dutch courage she hoped to gain was sorely lacking as the butterflies in her stomach grew into vicious crows.

Following the direction of excited voices and pointing, she focused on the bottom of the cliff. A sleek speedboat approached, foaming waves billowing behind the fast-moving craft. It gathered speed as it neared the shore. Swerving at the last second, it created a huge arc of water that rushed to the shore in a giant wave before heading away from the jetty.

The pilot executed a series of daredevil manoeuvres that

brought gasps of delight from the crowd and left the other two occupants—bodyguards, judging by their bulging muscles and ill-fitting suits—clinging grim-faced to the sides.

Finally, bringing the vessel alongside the quay, the tuxedoed figure stepped boldly onto the bow of the boat and jumped lithely down onto the jetty. Smiling at the enthusiastic applause, he clasped his hands in front of him and gave a deep bow.

Jasmine released the breath trapped in her lungs. So, this was Prince Reyes Navarre. Considering his near reclusive status, she was surprised he'd chosen such a narcissistic, highly OTT entrance. She wrinkled her nose.

'You're not impressed with His Royal Highness's maritime prowess?' a deep voice enquired from behind her left shoulder.

Jasmine jumped and whirled around. She'd assumed she was alone on the terrace, everyone else having rushed down into the main hall to welcome the prince.

How had this man moved so silently behind her? She hadn't even felt his presence until he'd spoken. Jasmine's gaze raced up, and up, until it collided with dark grey eyes.

Immediately, she wanted to look away, to block the probing gaze. She had no idea why, but the urge was so overwhelming, she took a step back.

A strong hand seized her arm. 'Careful, *pequeña*. It is a long tumble from the terrace and the evening is too beautiful to mar with tragedy.'

Glancing behind her, she realised she'd stepped dangerously close to the low wall bordering the terrace.

'Oh. Thank you.' Her words twisted around her tongue. Her senses dovetailed on the warm hand that held her. She looked down at the elegant fingers on her skin and drew in a sharp breath. His bold touch transmitted an alien sensation through her blood.

As if he felt it too, his fingers tightened imperceptibly. A second later, he let go. 'So, you don't like speedboats?' He nodded over her head at the spectacle below.

She tried to pry her gaze from his face, but she only succeeded in moving her head a fraction, before becoming equally hypnotised by the alluring spectacle of his mouth.

It was just spectacularly…sensual. Like his eyes, the lines of his lips drew equal interest from her stunned senses. Without stopping to assess her reaction, she found herself raising her hand to his face.

A hair's breadth away, she saw his eyes widen. Her heart slammed with horror and embarrassment at what she'd almost done. She snatched her hand back and for a split second contemplated taking that fatal step backwards. Maybe dashing herself over the rocks at the bottom of the cliff would knock some sense into her.

'What makes you say that?' she prevaricated when it became clear he expected an answer to his question.

'You have a very expressive face.' His beautifully deep accented voice was solemn.

'Oh.' She stalled and tried to think fast. What could she say without causing offence? 'They're okay, I guess. I mean, they're not my thing. Too fast. Too…wet.' Not to mention, they reminded her of the times Stephen had taken her out on his boat very soon after she and her mother had gone to live with him. Still in her destructive phase, she'd given him a hard time about those trips. Despite his many reassurances, a part of her had remained untrusting, afraid he'd end up being like all the men her mother had fallen for in the past. Each morning, she'd woken up anxious that that would be the day Stephen tossed them out of his life. He hadn't, of course, but she still couldn't look at a boat without remembering that distressing period. 'But they're nice to look at, I suppose.' She bit her lip to stop further inanity spilling out.

The stranger's grave nod did nothing to distract her stare.

'But exhilarating, some would say. No?'

Light-headedness encroached. Exhilarating. Breath-stealing. Captivating. But all those adjectives had nothing to do with speedboats and everything to do with the man in front of her.

Belatedly, Jasmine realised she hadn't taken a single breath since she'd clapped eyes on him. Sucking in oxygen restored some much-needed brain activity. 'I wouldn't know. I've never been inclined to take a trip on one. Mainly because I get sea-sick standing on a beach.'

'That's a shame. There is a tranquillity I find on water that I haven't found anywhere else.'

The thought of this man, powerfully built, quietly commanding and confident, craving tranquillity touched a strange place inside her.

'My stepfather loves the water too.' Damn. She needed to watch her tongue.

'But something about it makes you sad?' His voice softened as his eyes grew even more solemn.

Her startled gaze flew to his. 'Why do you say that?'

'You speak with fondness but your eyes darken with unhappiness.'

His intuitiveness disturbed her, made her feel vulnerable. Wrenching her gaze from his, she looked around. The terrace was deserted, but soft lights glowed from exquisite crystal-cut chandeliers and showed the guests slowly filling the large hall.

The hall...

Where she should be. Trying to make contact with Prince Reyes Navarre.

Instead she was alone with this strangely captivating man.

A man she didn't know.

Although she'd talked herself into believing not every stranger meant her harm, she knew better than most which situations to avoid. Being alone with a man twice her size wasn't a good idea.

But rather than fear, a thrum of excitement fizzed through her veins. Her breathing constricted, her heart thumping loud in her ears as she inhaled. Almost drawn by an invisible force, her gaze returned to his face.

His black dinner jacket and crisp white shirt gave his features a vibrancy, helped in no small measure by the golden perfection of his skin. Cast in part shadow by the broad shoulders blocking the light, his taut cheekbones and strong, uncompromising jaw made her fingers tingle with the urge to explore him.

As she stared his mouth hardened into a tight line, as if he held some emotion in. The strong need to touch those lips, experience their firm texture and soothe them softer with her thumb grew. Her eyes flashed back to his to find him regarding her, waiting for a response.

'I have issues with water. Let's just leave it at that.'

He looked as if he would demand more. But he merely nodded. 'Tell me your name.' His authoritative tone demanded nothing but her compliance.

Without questioning why, she answered, 'Jasmine Nichols.'

His solemn expression altered, fleetingly replaced by a small smile that creased his lips. 'You are named after the flower that blooms in the gardens of my home, Jasmine.' His voice caressed her name in a way that made all the hairs on her body strain to life. 'It is a fragile yet sturdy flower that has soothed us with its heady fragrance for thousands of years.'

Overwhelmed by the equally heady blend of emotion swirling through her, she gave a nervous laugh. 'Blimey, I hope I don't look that old!'

'Be assured. You don't.'

His smile disappeared, but she suspected he was still amused by her. The thought created a joyous fizz in her blood. It struck her that this man, whoever he was, hadn't smiled or laughed in a long time. The urgent need to catch another glimpse of that enigmatic smile grew.

'Great. Living to a thousand sounds like fun, but I bet it becomes a nuisance after that. A few more decades will do me just fine, though. I have things to do, people to impress.'

Joy sang in her chest when he rewarded her with another fleeting smile.

'I have no doubt that you will make your mark on the world before you leave it.' His head dipped in a shallow bow. 'Enjoy the rest of your evening, Jasmine.' With graceful, long-limbed strides, he walked away from her.

His abrupt departure stunned her into stillness. She watched four figures detach themselves from the shadowed doorway and fall into step behind him. She didn't need to be told they were bodyguards.

And rightly so. He was far too lethal to walk around without armed escort.

It wasn't until he reached the bottom of the stairs that led into the main hall that she regained the power of speech.

'Holy hotness, Batman,' she muttered under her breath, still more than a little stunned.

Watching him cut a path through the assembled crowd, Jasmine realised she hadn't even asked his name. Without pausing to think, she dashed through the doors after him.

She came to a screeching halt after a few steps.

What was she doing? She hadn't come to Rio to check out its male citizens, or to fall flat on her face for the first enigmatic man who looked at her with deep, hypnotically solemn eyes.

The real reason wrenched her back to reality, making any dream she harboured glaringly impossible. Whoever the mysterious, formidable stranger was, he had nothing to do with her mission here.

A mission that should've been the one and only thing on her mind.

She slid her wrap closer to ward off the sudden chill invading her body.

How could she have lost sight of her objective so quickly? Her stepfather's well-being depended on her. Running after a man who'd made her feel so alive, so special that she would have given up all she held dear to spend another minute in his presence was out of the question.

She clutched her grey silk purse and tried to think clearly, but it was no use. His smell, the feel of his hand on her skin, the intensity of his dark gaze that seemed to see past the outer trappings of civilised conversation to her inner self, remained imprinted on her.

Her breath rushed out shakily. She tried to tell herself what she'd felt didn't matter. That wasn't her purpose here. The only thing that mattered was finding Prince Reyes, getting her hands on the treaty and making it out of here in one piece. By way of grounding herself, she recited the list once more and forced herself to move into the hall as she did so.

The first thing she noticed was that the man she'd been speaking to was now on the other side of the room. Similarly suited men surrounded him, yet he remained curiously aloof, standing out so spectacularly, everyone else faded into insignificance.

Forcing her gaze away, she looked around. In halting Portuguese, she tried to enquire discreetly from her waiter which of the men was Prince Reyes, but her query only drew a blank stare.

Her anxiety returned when she realised most of the conversation going on around her was in Portuguese. Naïvely, she'd assumed since most of the staff at her hotel spoke English, everyone in Rio did too.

But the man who'd spoken to her on the terrace had used perfect English.

So ask him.

Except she couldn't. She'd have to cross the room to get to him, and in the time she'd been dithering his audience had tripled.

Insinuating herself into his crowd would only draw attention to herself. And for what she'd come here to do, anonymity was key. Wishing she'd pressed Joaquin Esteban for more details about the prince, she cast another look around.

A bell sounded nearby, making her jump. Guests started taking their places at the long banquet table. She found her place and had just sat down when a light-haired man joined her.

He looked at her hopefully. 'Please tell me you speak English?'

Jasmine smiled with relief. 'Yes, I do.'

'Thank God! You think your Portuguese is all right until someone asks you a question. Then even the little you know flies straight out of your head. I'm Josh, by the way.'

'Jasmine,' she responded.

'Crazy, isn't it?'

Startled, Jasmine glanced sideways to him. 'Sorry?'

He nodded to the group of men taking their seats at the far end of the long banquet table. 'Unbelievable that between the two of them, those men control nearly half of the steel and precious gems in the world.'

Unwilling to disclose her ignorance, she murmured, 'Right.'

'Shame their trade relations are in a shambles, though. Hopefully once the treaty is signed, there should be some semblance of order, otherwise the chaos will only get worse.' He shook his head. 'Prince Reyes has done an outstanding job of bringing the treaty to fruition, though. Have to commend him on that.' He took a healthy gulp of champagne.

Sneaking in a breath to calm her screeching nerves, she casually asked, 'Which one is Prince Reyes?'

He looked puzzled for a second, then he shrugged. 'I understand how you might be confused. They're descended from the same bloodline, after all.' He nodded to the men. 'Mendez, the shorter one who rocked up in the speedboat, is the birthday boy celebrating the big four-oh. He's in charge of Valderra, the larger of the two kingdoms. The taller one at the head of the table, talking to the prime minster, is Reyes. Don't get me wrong, his might be the smaller of the kingdoms, but Santo Sierra is definitely the big kahuna.'

Jasmine's throat threatened to close up as she absorbed the information. Her fingers clenched around her cutlery as ice drenched her blood.

The lights went up just then and two officious-looking men stepped up to the twin podiums carrying black briefcases. Heart in her throat, she realised what she'd done.

She'd been speaking to Prince Reyes Navarre all along!

And she'd told him her name!

After a short speech, the first stage of the treaty signing was completed. Jasmine watched as the documents were placed back in the briefcases.

Clammy sweat soaked her palms. Carefully, she set down her knife and fork. Every instinct told her to get up. *Run.* Not stop until she was on the next plane back to London.

But how could she? Even if she sold her two-bedroom East London flat and somehow found the balance to pay the half a million pounds owed to Joaquin, the loan shark still possessed enough documentary evidence to bury her stepfather.

Jasmine's heart lurched at the thought. Her family was far from perfect, but Stephen Nichols had single-handedly ensured she and her mother had been given a much-needed second chance. There was no way Jasmine was going to turn her back on him now.

Nervously, she swallowed the moisture in her mouth. 'You mean, Prince Reyes is the tall one…' *with the impossibly broad shoulders, sad eyes and expressive, elegant hands*, she nearly blurted out.

'Looking our way right now,' her table companion muttered, a vein of surprise trailing his voice.

Her head jerked up and slate-grey eyes locked on hers. Even from the length of the banquet table, the stranger from the terrace loomed larger than life, his stare unwavering.

Except he wasn't an intriguing stranger any more.

He was the man she'd come to steal from.

from the table, bowing their heads. Seeing them sort of stumbling being thanked and dismissed merely after being... Suddenly the edge of her knife dug in, she wobbled...

CHAPTER TWO

SHAME SHOULD HAVE been the paramount emotion ruling Jasmine as her gaze remained trapped in Prince Reyes's stare.

Instead, the alien emotion from earlier pulsed through her again, and, impossibly, everything and everyone seemed to fade away. Even the sound of her own breathing slowed until she barely knew whether she breathed in or out.

Alarmed and more than a little unsettled, Jasmine wrenched her gaze away. All through the meal she barely tasted, she forced herself to make light conversation with Josh. But even with her focus firmly turned away from Prince Reyes, she could feel his stare, heavy and speculative, on her.

Now, realising just how precarious a position she'd put herself in, Jasmine was barely able to hold it together. Which was why she didn't hear Josh clear his throat.

Once. Twice.

Her gaze jerked up to find Prince Reyes Navarre standing next to her. Startled, she dropped the knife and cringed as it clattered onto her plate.

'Miss Nichols, was your meal satisfactory?' He glanced pointedly at her half-eaten meal.

Aware of the countless pairs of eyes on her, Jasmine wasn't sure whether to remain seated or stand and curtsy. She opted to remain seated. 'Y-yes, it was, thank you.'

'I am not interrupting, I hope?' A glance at Josh that was at once courteous and incisive.

'No, we're…just two countrymen who find themselves at the same table.' Josh laughed.

'How…fortunate,' Prince Reyes said, his gaze speculative as it rested on the other man.

Vaguely, she saw him gesture. Suddenly, the guests rose

from their places and started to mingle. Sensing some sort of etiquette being observed, Jasmine stood shakily to her feet.

Snagging the edge of her heel on her chair, she stumbled.

Prince Reyes caught her arm. She gasped at the electricity sizzling over her skin. When she straightened, he dropped his arm and just stared at her.

A block of silence fell between them. For the life of her, Jasmine couldn't form any words to ease the sudden tension. Heat crawled over her body and her dress felt suddenly very restrictive.

Josh cleared his throat a third time, glanced from one to the other, then put his glass down. 'I need to find a business acquaintance. Please excuse me, Your Highness.' He bowed quickly, then scurried away before Jasmine could draw breath.

And once again, Jasmine was trapped by a pair of compelling grey eyes.

'Are you here with him?' Prince Reyes asked.

Did she detect a hint of disapproval in his tone? She raised her chin. 'No, I'm here on my own.'

If anything, his disapproval increased.

She scrambled to continue. 'I was told Rio was safe. So far nothing's happened to make me think otherwise.'

A gleam smouldered in his eyes. 'Danger comes in all forms, Miss Nichols. Sometimes in least expected packages. I'd urge you to practise caution.'

Hearing him use her surname instead of her first name as he had on the terrace, made her realise how much she missed hearing it.

'Thank you for the advice…umm…Your Highness.' She didn't add that she wouldn't need it. She didn't plan on being here long enough to get into any more danger than she was putting herself in tonight. In fact, as soon as she'd completed the hateful task, she was heading to the airport to catch the next flight out. 'But it's really not necessary.'

He continued to regard her in that disquieting manner. A

tiny shiver shimmied along her skin; the enormity of her task hit her, sharp and forceful.

Again the instinct to *run* slammed through her and it took everything Jasmine possessed to stand her ground and continue to meet his eyes.

This man possessed her only means to save her stepfather. Instead of dismissing his concern, she should be using it. The shame welling inside her didn't matter. The fear of stepping over the line couldn't be allowed to overtake the most important thing—saving Stephen. Saving her family.

She watched, scrambling to keep her distressing thoughts from showing, as Prince Reyes held out his hand. 'Very well. Far be it from me to cause offence by suggesting one of my bodyguards accompany you to your hotel. It was a pleasure to meet you, Miss Nichols.' He turned away and she noticed said bodyguards take their protective stance behind him. One was carrying the briefcase containing the treaty.

He was leaving! Taking with him the only chance of saving her stepfather.

Gripping her purse, she cleared her throat and quickly back-pedalled. 'Actually, you're right. A strange city isn't a place for a woman to be wandering at night. I'd be grateful for your assistance.'

She heard the indrawn breath of the nearest guests, but ignored it.

Letting Prince Reyes leave was unthinkable. She'd travelled thousands of miles to make sure her stepfather didn't go to jail. Ten minutes was all she needed. Less, if she was really quick. She *had* to get her hands on that treaty. Even if it meant following a predator straight into his den.

He turned. Jasmine's breath stalled as his eyes darkened. He stared at her for what felt like an eternity before his lids descended. She sensed his withdrawal before he spoke.

'I'll arrange for my chauffeur to deliver you to your hotel.' He was already nodding to a dark-clad figure nearby.

Acute anxiety swelled inside her.

She couldn't fail. She just couldn't. Stephen might *just* survive prison but her mother wouldn't make it.

'Or I could come with you. Save your chauffeur making two trips,' she offered, cringing at the breathless tone of her voice.

He held up a hand to stop the bodyguard who stepped forward, his gaze imprisoning hers. Silence pulsed between them. A silence filled with charged signals that made the blood pulse heavily between her thighs. Every sense sprang into superawareness. She could hear every sound, smell every scent on the evening breeze, feel every whisper of air over her heating skin. Her nipples hardened and her cheeks heated at the blatant evidence of her awareness of him.

The thought that she was insanely attracted to a man whom she planned to deceive, albeit temporarily, caused hysterical laughter to bubble up.

She strained not to react. To keep the wrap draped over her arms and not use it to hide the proof of her arousal. She'd never used her feminine wiles to capture a man's attention. Doing so now made her insides clench with disgust. All the same, a small part of her gave a cry of triumph when his eyes dropped to her chest for an infinitesimal moment.

'You want to come with me? Now?' His voice had altered, his eyes narrowing with icy suspicion that warned her to tread carefully.

Jasmine couldn't afford to back away. She had too much to lose.

'Yes. Take me with you. My hotel isn't that far from here. I'll even buy you a drink as a thank you.' The single brain cell that remained shook with astonishment at her boldness. Afraid that her plea had emerged more of a command, and might perhaps cause offence, she hastily added, 'If you don't mind.'

His gaze darkened with a predatory gleam that made Jasmine swallow in trepidation. 'Perhaps it is you who should mind, Miss Nichols. Some would advise you against what you're asking.'

With deliberate slowness, she passed the tip of her tongue

over her lower lip. Stark hunger blazed in his eyes, stealing her breath as the grey depths turned almost black. A warm rush of air whispered over her skin, but even that small change caused her to gasp as if he'd physically laid his hands on her.

'Maybe, but something tells me I can trust you,' she replied, her nerves jangling with terror at the uncharted waters she found herself in. Flirting and sexual games had never been her forte. Not since her one attempt at university had ended in humiliating disaster.

Another step brought Prince Reyes within touching distance. His narrowed eyes, still holding that trace of sadness she'd glimpsed earlier, were now laced with a healthy dose of bitterness.

Jasmine didn't have time to dwell on his expression because his scent engulfed her, fuelling her already frenzied senses. She inhaled, filling her entire being with his essence. As if he sensed it too, his nostrils flared.

'You're playing a dangerous game, Jasmine,' he murmured.

'It…it's just a lift back to my h-hotel,' she croaked.

'Perhaps. Or it is something else. Something neither of us is ready for.' His voice was pitched low, for her ears alone. His gaze slid over her face, its path as forceful and yet as gentle as a silky caress.

'I'll be out of your hair in less than half an hour. Seriously, you have nothing to fear from me.' *Liar.* She tried to curb the accusing voice, thankful when it faded away under the onslaught of the heavy emotion beating in her chest.

His jaw tightened. 'I have everything to fear from you.' Again the bitterness, sharper this time. 'The curse of a beautiful woman has been my ancestors' downfall.'

She forced a laugh. *Beautiful? Her?* Well, if he could flatter, so could she. 'So prove it's not true. Deliver me to my hotel and walk away. Then you'll be free of this…curse.'

He tilted his head to one side, as if weighing her request. His hand rose again, this time to reach down to encircle her wrist. With a subtle but firm tug, he pulled her to him.

'If walking away resolved centuries-old issues, my kingdom wouldn't be in shambles.'

'I didn't mean—'

He pulled her closer. Jasmine was too mesmerised by this enigmatic man to acknowledge the curious stares of the guests beyond the protective circle of Prince Reyes's bodyguards. And he didn't seem too disturbed by their growing audience.

His stare turned into a frown. 'You intrigue me, Jasmine Nichols.'

'Is that a bad thing?'

He stepped back and he seemed to come to a decision. 'I'm not certain, but I wish to find out. Come.'

Reyes Navarre drew a deep breath.

What in *Dios's* name was he doing? Not since Anaïs had he behaved so rashly. His carefree period of picking up liaisons for a night had come to a jagged halt five years ago when he'd experienced for himself just how duplicitous women could be. His own mother had hammered that lesson home forcefully in the weeks before her death.

Overnight, Reyes had witnessed the family he'd foolishly thought he could bring together disintegrate beyond recognition. He'd watched the will to live slowly extinguish from his father's eyes until only a husk remained.

Reyes's chest tightened painfully with equal parts of remorse and bitterness. Remorse that grew each day because he knew he'd failed to grant his father, King Carlos, his one wish—an heir to the throne while he was still alive. Bitterness because his father had condemned Reyes for choosing to learn from past mistakes. What his father didn't know was that the woman Reyes had thought would be his queen had turned out to be just as conniving and as faithless as his own mother.

The double blow had made abstinence a far better prospect. One he'd embraced and pushed to the back of his mind when his father's health had worsened.

But tonight…

He glanced at the woman whose delicate scent filled every corner of the limo.

She hadn't spoken since they'd driven away from the banquet, but Reyes had caught the fleeting glances she sent his way every now and then. Just as he'd glimpsed the little darts of her tongue at the corner of mouth when her gaze fell on him.

She did it again, just then. A different sort of tightening seized his body.

Grinding his teeth, Reyes forced himself to examine why Jasmine Nichols intrigued him. Perhaps it was being away from Santo Sierra for the first time in over a year. Perhaps it was the knowledge that, after months of tough negotiations, Mendez had finally agreed to sign the trade treaty.

Or it could be that he just needed to let himself feel something other than bitterness and recrimination...to experience a moment of oblivion before the relentless pressure of his birthright settled back on his shoulders.

Whatever the reason, he didn't stop himself from pressing the intercom that connected him to the driver.

'Take us to the boat,' he instructed.

Jasmine immediately turned to him. 'You're not taking me to my hotel?' Her voice held a touch of trepidation but no hint of panic.

She knew the score.

As he should.

Except he didn't.

He was acting out of character. Had been from the moment he saw her.

His smile felt strained. 'You owe me a drink, I believe. I'm choosing to take it *before* I have you delivered to your hotel, not after.'

'Just in case I renege? You're not very trusting, are you?'

The twinge in his chest stung deeper, but he refused to acknowledge it. 'No, I'm not.'

Her eyes widened and she looked away. 'Are we really going to your boat?' she asked with a curious note in her voice.

'Yes.'

Reyes remembered she didn't like boats. Was that why he'd brought her to his yacht instead of the royal suite that awaited him at the Four Seasons? Was he hoping she would quail at the sight of the big floating palace and ask to be returned to her hotel?

Or had he brought her here for his own selfish reasons? Because, for some reason, focusing on her made his tumultuous feelings subside just a little?

All through the interminable dinner, he'd watched her, his gaze unable to stray from her for more than a few seconds because every time it had, he'd felt the darkness encroaching.

He watched her now from the corner of his eye, waiting for a reaction. But her hands remained folded in her lap, her gaze on the large vessel they'd pulled up to.

Unfortunately his thoughts and emotions suffered no such languor or calm. They churned in rhythm to the heavy pounding of his heart at what was to come.

Thoughts of sating himself on a woman had been pushed far back into the recesses of his mind, especially in the last year as he'd battled to salvage the trade treaty with Valderra. But his efforts had paid off.

He'd brought Mendez and Valderra to the treaty table, the result of which would mean a much-needed economic boost for his people.

Tomorrow they would complete the signing of the Santo-Valderra treaty. The concessions had been heavy. Mendez had made outrageous demands, like the excessively extravagant banquet held here tonight to honour his birthday. A ceremony Reyes had initially balked at attending, but had eventually given in to, because he suspected Mendez would use any excuse to postpone the final signing of the treaty.

The concessions Santo Sierra had given would be recouped with time. And, most importantly, the trade blockage had been removed.

He still faced an uphill battle in convincing his council

members to accept the changes to come. And there was also his father...

Reyes pushed thoughts of his father and grief aside and reminded himself that his father was alive.

And for one night, *this night*, Reyes intended to turn his mind to more...pleasant matters.

Jasmine sat in silence beside him, a beacon in the gloom that threatened to swallow him whole. But Reyes sensed that she was almost as reluctant as he to test the depths of awareness that zinged between them, just as he was quietly amazed by the depth of his attraction for her.

The memory of her skin when he'd held her on the balcony returned. His hand tightened next to his thigh.

He'd taken one look at Jasmine and the foundations of his self-imposed celibacy had started to shake. All through the banquet he'd been unable to take his eyes off her, a notion that had at once fascinated and irritated him. By the time the banquet was over, he'd known his resistance was severely compromised.

Yet, he'd been determined to walk away. Bitter experience and the heavy burden of duty had taught him to weigh his decisions carefully.

One-night stands weren't his *modus operandi*.

So what in the name of Dios *was he doing?*

He hadn't touched her since that last electrifying contact, and yet a storm unlike anything he'd ever known raged inside him. From the corner of his eye, he watched her fiddle with one earring. The sweet, yet provocative movement fanned the inferno of his lust.

'Are we going to get out?' Her question emerged with that same breathy, husky quality that sent shivers racing through him. Her eyes, blue like the ocean surrounding his kingdom, slid to his and the throb in his groin accelerated.

'Momentarily,' he replied, hoping for some last-minute perspective.

But the only perspective his brain was willing to consider

was the one where this enthralling woman ended up in his bed, her voluptuous body quenching his ferocious need.

She'd shown herself a worthy opponent, and yes, he considered the insane tug and pull of attraction between them a battleground. A battle from which he would emerge the victor and walk away with everything he held dear intact.

During their intriguing exchange not once had her gaze slid from his. In fact, more than once he'd seen a spark of defiance in the blue vividness of her eyes. That spark had ignited something inside him he'd long forgotten.

It had reminded him of a carefree time when life had been less fraught.

He glanced up at the lights of his yacht. He'd deliberately not moored at the same quay as Prince Mendez because he'd wanted to avoid the avid media attention Mendez courted.

Reyes preferred privacy…solitude…silence. His mother had created enough chaos in his life when she was alive.

So what are you doing bringing a total stranger on board?

He faced Jasmine.

Her gaze immediately riveted to his and heat surged through his bloodstream. She gave a nervous smile and pulled her wrap tighter around her. He frowned at the protective gesture. The interior of the car wasn't cold, in fact the night air blowing gently through the half-open windows was sultry. So there could be only one other reason for the telling gesture.

'It's not too late to change your mind.' His statement emerged harsher than he'd intended, partly, he realised, because he didn't want her to leave.

Her eyes widened and she wavered for a second before a curiously resolute look settled over her face. 'No. A deal is a deal. Although I'm not sure how to go about buying you a drink when we're boarding *your* boat.'

Relief made him exhale unsteadily. He signalled to his bodyguard, who opened the door. Reyes handed him the briefcase holding the treaty and held out his hand to Jasmine. 'We'll continue our debate on board.'

She glanced from his hand to his yacht. He held his breath. Slowly, she reached out. His grip tightened on her fingers as he stepped out of the car and helped her out. He'd taken two steps when he felt her tug at his grip.

'Wait. I can't do this.'

Disappointment curled through him. Reyes bit back a sharp retort as he dropped her hand. In the time since his last liaison, the world hadn't changed, then, he mused caustically. Women continued to tease, to engage in sexual games in the hope that playing hard to get would make them seem more attractive to the opposite sex. The bitterness he'd tried to douse welled up again.

'Save the excuses, Miss Nichols. I'm disappointed that women seem to believe creating intrigue involves mind games, but I am not willing to indulge you.' He nodded to his driver, who stepped forward. 'You'll be delivered to your hotel. Enjoy the rest of your stay in Rio.' He couldn't stem the regret that settled gut-deep inside him. Not to mention the uncomfortable arousal that tightened his groin and made thinking straight difficult.

He turned away, wanting to be far away from her, from the temptation of her voluptuous body and seductive scent that insisted on lingering in the air around him.

'Actually, that's not what I want.' She sounded hurt and a little confused. 'I didn't mean that I'd changed my mind about the drink.'

He whirled round. 'Then what did you mean, Jasmine?'

An uneasy look crossed her face. 'I told you, I don't really like boats. But I thought I'd make an exception...just this once...' She shook her head. 'Anyway, I'm not coming aboard wearing these shoes.' She gestured to her feet.

Puzzled, he frowned. 'What?'

'My step—umm, I read somewhere that heels and boats aren't a good combination.' Her shrug drew his attention to the silky curve of her shoulder. 'Of course, I don't know what sort of flooring you have on your yacht, but I don't want to ruin it.'

Laughter replaced Reyes's disappointment. It rumbled through his chest, a sensation he hadn't felt for a while.

'*My floors?* You don't want to ruin the floors on my boat?' His incredulity grew with his words and he barely stopped himself from shaking his head.

'No, I don't. Plus, my feet are seriously killing me. So if you don't mind?' She held out her hand for him to take. 'It'll only take a minute.'

Caught in the surreal moment, Reyes took her hand. He felt the rough ridge of scarred tissue and looked at the thin line crossing her palm. About to ask what had caused it, he was stalled by the sight of one graceful leg, lifted, one ankle strap unbuckled before the process was repeated with the other shoe.

His gaze dropped to her feet. They were small but perfectly formed with pink tips. The sight only aroused him further, tweaked his already dangerously heightened senses.

'Good idea,' he murmured inanely, his voice curiously hoarse.

She nodded and fell into step beside him. 'I think it's only fair to warn you, though, the last time I rode a dinghy, I ended up falling overboard. I hope you'll rescue me if that happens again?'

A smile tugged at his lips. 'As you can see, my boat is slightly bigger than your dinghy. It'll take a lot of effort to accidentally go overboard. But be assured, I'll come to your aid should the worst happen.'

'Well, if you put it that way, then I have nothing to worry about,' she said with a smile.

Reyes smiled, feeling less burdened than he had in a long time. He took her shoes as they approached the gangplank and followed her up the stairs onto the deck and through into the large, open salon. He watched her take in her surroundings, her mouth parting to inhale sharply at the opulence that embraced her.

Reyes had seen different reactions to his yacht, some openly covetous and some hidden behind careful indifference. Jasmine's eyes widened in something close to childlike, uninhibited awe as she took in the polished wood panels, gold ornamentation and monogrammed accessories in royal Santo Sierran blue he'd commissioned for the vessel.

'Wow!' She turned full circle and found him watching her. A faint blush touched her cheeks and she walked over to the large sofa and perched on the edge. 'Sorry, I didn't mean to gush.'

'A genuine reaction is better than artificial indifference.' He walked over to her and placed her shoes next to her.

'Seriously? Who would be indifferent to this?' She waved her hand around the deck.

'People with ulterior motives they prefer to hide?' The last female on this boat had been Anaïs. She'd been in full playing-hard-to-get mode, which had swiftly crumbled when Reyes had threatened to walk away. Of course, she'd had other aces up her sleeve. 'In my experience, people are rarely what they seem at first blush.'

'Oh, right.' Jasmine's eyes darted to his and slid away, and she seemed lost for words. Her tongue darted out to lick the corner of her lip.

Reyes's heart beat just that little bit faster. His fingers tightened as anticipation fizzed faster through his veins.

Her skin, creamy with the barest hint of tan, glowed under the soft lights of his deck. His fingers itched to touch, to caress. But he held back.

There would be time for that later. He had no doubt he was about to indulge in something he'd never indulged in before—a one-night stand; this could be nothing more than that—but he didn't want to rush it.

Morning would come soon enough. The treaty would be signed. He would ensure Santo Sierra's continued economic prosperity. And he would return to his father's bedside to continue his vigil.

But for now... 'I think it's time for that drink, yes?'

* * *

Jasmine swallowed her relief as the heated look in Prince Reyes's eyes abated. For a moment there, he'd looked as if he wanted to devour her where she stood.

And as much as that had sent a bolt of excitement through her, part of her had quailed at the look.

Hastily, she nodded. 'Yes, thank you.'

She watched him walk towards an extensive, gleaming wood-panelled bar. A steward approached, but he waved him away. Opening a chiller, he grabbed a bottle of wine and expertly uncorked it. Rounding the bar, he handed her a glass and indicated a row of low, luxurious sofas.

Taking the seat next to her, he lowered his long body into it, driving the breath straight out of her lungs.

'What shall we drink to?' he asked in a low, deep voice, his stare focused solely on her.

Jasmine's mouth dried. 'Um, how about congratulations on the progress you've made with the treaty so far?' Talking about the treaty helped keep her grounded, reminded her why she was here.

His smile held more than a hint of pride. *'Gracias.'*

'Did you achieve what you set out for?'

Against his usual guarded judgement he found himself sharing with her. 'It was a long, hard battle, but we're almost there. By this time tomorrow, a solid trade agreement will exist between our two kingdoms, something my people have needed for a long time.'

Jasmine's heart thudded loudly in her ears. Her hands started to shake and she hastily put her glass down. Sensing him following the movement, she flexed her fingers and smoothed them over her dress.

'You should be back there, then, at the museum, celebrating. Why did you leave early?'

'I don't like crowds,' he declared. His eyes widened, as if he'd let something slip he hadn't meant to. A moment later, his expression shuttered.

Something inside her softened. 'I don't like crowds, either.'

His head snapped up, his gaze searching hers. At her small smile, his tense jaw relaxed.

'I mean, who does, aside from rock stars and, well, crowd lovers?' she joked. She wasn't making much sense, but at the moment Jasmine would've kept babbling just to keep that smile on his face.

A small, enigmatic smile twitched his lips before he took a sip of his wine. 'So what brings you to Rio alone?' he asked. 'Carnival was last month.'

She forced herself not to tense. For a wild moment Jasmine wondered if he could see through her to the truth of her presence in his life.

Clearing her throat, she shrugged and struck for the half-truth she'd practised in her head. 'I haven't had a holiday in years. An unexpected gap opened up in my schedule, and I took it.'

His eyes slowly narrowed, his fingers stilling around his wine glass. 'And you just happened to gain the most sought-after invitation to the Prince of Valderra's birthday party?' Mild disbelief rang through his voice.

'No. Of course not. My trip isn't all play. The brokerage firm I work for have been following the Santo-Valderra negotiations for some time. When one of my…clients offered me the invitation, I thought it would be good experience to learn more about it.'

'And have you?'

Jasmine shook her head. 'Only what's been released to the press, which is plenty interesting. I mean, from a brokerage point of view, it's mind-blowing what you've achieved—'

Jaw tightening, he set his glass down with a sharp click. 'And you want to know more? To gain first-hand information? Is that why you're here?'

CHAPTER THREE

JASMINE SWALLOWED, TREPIDATION jangling her nerves. 'I am interested, yes. But no, it's not why I'm here.' She spoke through the shame-coated lie.

His gaze dropped to her mouth. Heat rose in her belly, slowly engulfing her chest, her throat.

She fought to breathe as the feral, dangerously hungry look once more stole over his face, permeating the air with thick, saturated lust.

He reached out a hand, caught a lock of hair in his fingers and slowly caressed it. 'Why exactly are you here, Jasmine Nichols? Why did you not demand to be returned to your hotel?'

'I meant what I said. I'm intrigued by the treaty.' That much was true. 'From what I've been able to learn about it—'

He frowned. 'What you've been able to learn? Are you a spy?'

'No!' she replied hurriedly. Hoping she wasn't digging herself into an even deeper hole, she continued. 'The firm I work for brokers deals like these all the time, on a much smaller scale…and I was just wondering if what I'd heard was right.'

'What did you hear?'

'That the treaty heavily favours Valderra…' Her voice drifted away as a dark look blanketed his face.

God, what was she doing?

She wouldn't be surprised if he threw her off the boat for prying.

'Concessions were made prior to my handling of the negotiations that I have no choice but to honour.' He didn't sound happy about it. Just resigned.

She nodded. His fingers grazed her cheek. She only had to

turn her head a fraction and she'd feel more of his touch. Her every sense craved that touch.

He drew closer, slowly, his fingers winding around a lock of her hair; his eyes not leaving hers. 'Why do I get the feeling that you're holding something back from me, Jasmine?' he asked again, softly this time, his breath fanning over her lips. 'Tell me why I'm fighting my instincts when I should be heeding them?'

Her insides quaked with fear...and anticipation. 'I guess I could tell you that you're not the only one feeling that way. There's something about you. Something overpowering, that makes me...'

'Makes you what?'

Shaking her head, she surged to her feet and stumbled to the railing. Frustrated tears stung her eyes as she stared into the dark waters.

She couldn't do this.

She'd come too far, clawed herself back from a destructive, chaotic past. Going through with Joaquin's plan, giving in to the thug's demands would mean stepping back into that dark tunnel.

But walking away meant Stephen's destruction. A broken mother.

She gulped down the sob that threatened.

And jumped when his lips touched the back of her neck. A mere graze. But it pushed back her dark despair, lit her up like a bonfire on a sultry summer's night. As if galvanised by that simple touch, she came alive.

He grabbed her to him, one hand sliding around her shoulder while the other gripped her waist. He kissed the delicate skin below her ear, imprinting himself on her so vividly, every atom in her body screeched in delight.

He spun her in his arms and kissed her.

Jasmine had been kissed before. But not like this. Never like this. The fiery tingle started from her toes, spread through her body like wildfire, stinging her nerve endings. He tasted of wine, of dark, strong coffee, of heady pleasure that made her heart hammer as he drew her even closer.

Her breasts crushed into his chest. The imprint of his muscled torso against hers caused her fingers to tighten on his nape. He growled something under his breath, but the words were crushed between their lips as they both moved to deepen the kiss.

Somewhere deep within, a voice cautioned her against what she was doing. She tried to heed it, tried to pull back. Vaguely she sensed him move towards a doorway in the saloon.

Her good sense kicked in. 'Wait...'

He carried on walking, his lips now straying to the astonishingly sensitive skin just below her ear. She shuddered, a melting deep inside that threatened to drown her.

'Umm...' She paused as she realised she didn't know what to call him. What was the etiquette when you were snogging the face off a South American Crown Prince? 'Your Highness... wait...'

His deep laugh made her blush. 'When we are alone, you may call me Reyes. After all, you can hardly call me Your Highness when I'm deep inside you,' he murmured into her ear. 'Although that does present interesting possibilities...'

Her shocked gasp brought another laugh and Jasmine had to scramble to hang on to her sanity. 'Please...Reyes, put me down,' she pleaded.

Sensing her agitation, he slowly lowered her down before capturing her hands in his. 'What is it, Jasmine?'

For one absurd moment, she wanted to blurt out her guilt, but bit her tongue at the last minute. 'I haven't...I mean, this isn't something I normally do,' she babbled instead.

Raising both her hands, he pressed kisses onto her knuckles, his stunning eyes cooling. 'I understand. This is where you establish ground rules? Where I let you name your price because I'm too lust-hazed to see straight?' he asked cynically.

The ground rocked beneath her. Somewhere along the line, life had dealt this man serious blows. The depths of his sadness, suspicion and cynicism weren't traits he'd picked up by chance. And she should know. Life could be cruel beyond measure. Especially with men like Joaquin calling the shots.

But they only win if you let them...

The rebellious teenager whose antics had landed her in juvenile detention threatened to break through. Reminding herself just what was at stake here, she swallowed. 'Is it too much to believe that I'm nervous and a little bit overwhelmed?'

He lowered her hands. His eyes narrowed, probed and assessed. Jasmine understood how it was that Reyes Navarre had negotiated the sometimes almost insurmountable treaty with Valderra.

'So you don't want anything from me?' he asked.

Only the gritty determination that had seen her stand up to dangerous men twice her size kept her gaze from falling. 'Honestly, I would like to see the treaty. But I won't be sleeping with you because of that...' She realised what she was saying and stopped. A scalding blush suffused her face. 'I mean, nothing happens here that won't be my choice—'

He stopped her with a finger to her mouth.

'Understood. But remember this, too. Whatever happens between us will not go beyond tonight. It cannot,' he stated imperiously. 'My desire for you is finite.'

Hearing the words so starkly drew a cold shiver from her in spite of passion's flames arcing between them. He felt it and immediately captured her shoulders. 'But make no mistake. This desire burns bright and strong and I promise to make the experience—should you *choose* to stay for it—pleasurable for you.'

His accent had thickened, his words burning away the cold as if it had never existed. He lowered his head and brushed his lips over hers.

Jasmine swallowed as his words echoed in her head. A powerful aphrodisiac intent on eroding rational thought.

Walk away. Now!

She groaned and pulled away. 'I can't. I know you probably think I'm a tease, but I promise, I'm not. I'm not in the habit of jumping into bed with a man I just met. I hope you understand?'

Her mind made up, she took another step back and picked up her clutch. She couldn't go through with it. She would find another way to save her stepfather. Whatever the repercussions, Jasmine would find a way to help Stephen and her mother deal with it.

But not this.

Whatever Joaquin needed the copy of the treaty for no longer mattered to her. The man who stood in front of her, who'd battled whatever demons haunted him to achieve this treaty for his kingdom, didn't deserve what she'd planned tonight. *She* would never be able to live with herself if she went through with it; if she took a step back to that dark place she'd sworn never to revisit again.

Her heart lifted, lightened, filled with relief.

She looked up at Reyes and experienced a little thrill at the stark shock and disappointment on his face. She had reduced a powerful, virile man to...what had he called himself before? Lust-crazed?

Slightly heady with the feeling, she took another stumbling step back before she succumbed to temptation.

She was in an exotic country, in the presence of a charismatic man who seemed to set her very soul on fire. Jasmine knew that if she gave in—*and she wouldn't!*—the experience with Reyes would be unique and would remain with her for ever.

After several more moments staring at her, he finally nodded. 'Very well. I'll summon my driver.'

Acute loss scythed through her. 'That would be great, thank you.'

She watched him walk to the intercom next to the bar, holding her breath to keep from blurting for him to stop.

About to press the black button, he paused and looked over

at her. 'It's not every day that I'm surprised, but you've succeeded in pulling the rug from beneath my feet,' he said.

'Umm…thanks. But why are you surprised?'

That reserved smile made another appearance and he
turned. 'You want me, but you're walking away. I may not
know why, but I admire the strong principle behind your decision. Perhaps you deserve a prize after all.'

'Oh?' Renewed excitement fizzed beneath her skin.

He retraced his steps and held out his hand. 'If you still want
to see it, I'll show you the treaty.'

Oh. Jasmine wanted to refuse. Wanted to demand another
prize, one that involved his mouth on hers. But that opportunity had passed. She'd refused Prince Reyes. A man like that
wouldn't place himself in a position to be spurned twice.

But neither could she resist the chance to glimpse a piece
of Santo-Valderran history.

He led her down several flights of stairs into the heart of the
yacht. Images of soft, mellow wood and rich chrome touched
the edge of her consciousness. There seemed to be a lot of
gold—chandeliers, paintings frames, doorknobs—but Jasmine
was too caught up in Reyes Navarre's magnificence and the
electric awareness where his hand held hers for details of the
décor to register.

She finally regained her senses when he released her upon
entering his study. The space was masculine, the furniture
rich antique. Expensive books on diplomacy, economics and
culture lined one wall. First-edition literary works lined the
other. Behind his desk, a Renaissance painting that would've
had museum curators salivating graced the wall.

He smiled at her and skirted his desk. He pressed a lever
beneath the painting and it swung back to reveal a safe. He entered a code and pressed his thumb against a digital scanner.

Jasmine held her breath as he slid out an expensive leather
folder and came to stand beside her. Very conscious of the
breadth of his shoulders and the heat emanating from his whip-
cord body, she struggled to focus on the treaty.

When the terms finally registered, she frowned. 'Why would you agree to this?'

'The terms aren't up for discussion. I need to make the best of this situation.'

Puzzled, she stared at him. His gaze captured hers before dropping to her mouth. Awareness crackled through the air. Sucking in a breath, she refocused on reading the final pages. She noticed that various preliminary terms had been agreed every year for the past three years, the first signed by his father. Prince Mendez had played a cunning game, increasing his demands with each passing year.

She started to turn the last page. Reyes put his hand over hers. 'The remaining terms are confidential.'

The effect of his hand on hers again made her pulse jump. 'And what? You don't trust me?' she joked, hoping to inject a little lightness to ease the thick tension filling the room.

His hand trailed up her arm to slide around her nape. Tilting her head, he looked deep into her eyes. 'Trust doesn't come easy to me, but I've trusted you with more tonight than I have anyone in a long time, Jasmine.'

Her breath squeezed through the lump clogging her throat. 'Why?'

He shrugged. 'Perhaps I'm learning to trust my instincts again. Perhaps because you're the only one who didn't enjoy Mendez's antics earlier.' He smiled again.

Despite his attempt at a joke, Jasmine remained fiercely glad of her decision not to give in to Joaquin's threat; she blinked back hot tears and smiled. 'You have no idea how much that means to me.'

The lightness evaporated. He stepped closer, an almost desperate hunger screaming from his body. 'I still want you, Jasmine. Very badly.'

Throwing caution to the wind shouldn't have come so easily, shouldn't have felt so freeing. Because she'd learned very early that everything came at a cost.

But she replied, 'Take me,' before she registered the enormity of the plunge she was taking.

The sensation of luxurious covers beneath her back was the first inkling that they'd left his study. The equally luxurious feel of him as he lowered himself on top of her confirmed that thought.

Crushed by his delicious weight, she couldn't mistake the imprint of his impressive arousal pushing against her. Hot sensation pierced her, settling low in her belly as he deepened the kiss. His tongue delved into her mouth, commencing a bold exploration that left her reeling and struggling to hold on to the last of her sanity.

His hands slid down her sides, creating a path of heat wherever he touched. Locating her side zip, he eased it down.

At the touch of fingers on her skin, Jasmine gasped.

He raised his head, his dark grey eyes spiking into hers. 'Your skin is so soft, so silky,' he murmured huskily.

'Thank you,' she responded, then cringed, feeling suddenly gauche and awkward. The first time she'd done this, it had ended badly. *Beyond badly.* The second time had been worse. What if third time *wasn't* lucky…?

She lost her train of thought as he gripped her hip. His heat penetrated the silk material to her skin, fanning the flame already building inside her. Wanting to experience even more of his warmth, she raised her head and traced his mouth with her tongue.

Her action drew a gasp from him, his eyes darkening even further as heat scoured over his taut cheekbones. 'I hope you'll forgive me,' he murmured distractedly as he nuzzled her jaw, planting feverish kisses that caused her heart to pound harder.

'What for?' she managed to squeeze out.

He settled firmer against her. 'It's been a while for me. I will want to take my time.'

A wave of heat engulfed her face. 'Oh. Yes…well, it's been a while for me, too.'

A look crossed his face, almost of relief. Jasmine's heart

swelled, her hand finally unclasping itself from his neck to caress his cheek. He planted an open-mouthed kiss in her palm. That intimate caress drew another gasp from her. Pleased by her reaction, he traced his mouth over her wrist, down her arm to the curve of her elbow, and licked the pulse.

Fire erupted in her pelvis so fierce and sweet, she moaned.

Galvanised by her response, he levered himself off her and stood beside the bed.

Jasmine had never imagined watching a man undress would trigger anything but embarrassment. But watching Reyes shed his clothes became another heady experience. Enthralled, she watched him ease his tuxedo jacket off his broad shoulders before releasing the studs of his shirt. Her mouth watered as his deeply bronzed chest was revealed. Her fingers itched to touch, to explore. Curling them into the covers, she held still and adored his beauty with her eyes.

'The look in your eyes threatens to unman me, *querida*,' he rasped. His fingers went to the button on his trousers.

Embarrassed that she'd done something wrong, Jasmine started to look away.

'No. Don't look away,' he commanded.

Her eyes flew to his. 'But you said—'

'*Sí*, I know, but I hate the thought of being deprived of your attention.' With an impatient shove, he kicked the rest of his clothes away and stood before her, gloriously, powerfully naked.

Jasmine silently thanked him for giving her permission to look. Because she couldn't have looked away now if her life depended on it.

He was spectacular! He stepped closer and she watched, fascinated, as the clearly delineated muscles moved beneath his skin.

Her stomach clenched with renewed arousal when he reclined next to her. 'I want you naked.'

She wanted to find fault with his imperious tone, but Jasmine would've been a hypocrite if she didn't acknowledge that every word that fell from his lips only further increased her excitement. Lending action to his words, he brushed aside her hair, slid one hand under her dress's thin strap and eased it off her shoulder.

He feasted his eyes on her, scouring every inch of her breasts as if committing them to memory. With a firm tug on her bra, he bared one nipple, a guttural groan rumbling from his chest as he lowered his head and sucked her flesh into his mouth. He teased, he tormented. His fingers traced, paused over a scar on her shoulder, a remnant from her shady past.

She held her breath, her fingers convulsed in his hair, holding him to his task even as she tensed in anticipation of a query. His touch moved on. When he turned his attention to her other breast, Jasmine whimpered in delight and relief.

Dazed, she felt him tug her dress off. Her panties and bra followed, discarded by urgent hands that caressed her skin with masterful strokes.

Wet heat pooled between her legs, a fact Reyes's exploratory fingers didn't miss when one possessive hand cupped her feminine core.

Raising his head from her tight, wet nipple, he speared her with a fiery gaze. 'Maybe I won't go slow after all. I have to have you now,' he rasped.

The next few seconds whizzed by in a blur, the sound of the condom wrapper tearing open barely impinging on her heated senses. He gathered her to him before she could draw breath. Placing himself between her thighs, he speared his hands in her hair and angled her face to his.

Eyes the colour of gunmetal held her prisoner.

He thrust inside her fast, hard, then immediately set a blistering pace that stripped her of every thought.

Their coupling was furious. Heady in ways she'd never dreamed sex could be. She screamed as the first, fierce climax hit her. He kissed away her shocked cries, almost greedy in his possession of her mouth, then slowed his pace just long enough for her spasms to ease.

Then he surged to his knees, placed her in front of him and entered her from behind. Guttural, indecipherable Spanish words spilled from him as he thrust over and over inside her, one strong arm clamped around her waist. Her throat clogged with emotion, her heart pounding wildly in her chest as tears gathered in her eyes at the magic she hadn't come looking for, but had miraculously found.

Reaching up behind her, she clasped his nape, turned her head and met his lips with hers. They stayed like that, their sweat-slicked bodies rocking back and forth until he tensed, a harsh groan rumbling through his chest, followed by convulsions that triggered her second, deeper orgasm.

His arm remained locked around her as he eased them back onto the bed, their harsh breaths gentling. He brushed away the damp hair from her face before placing a gentle kiss on her temple.

'This wasn't how I foresaw my evening ending when I arrived at the museum tonight.'

Jasmine tensed, the thought that he could be regretting what happened sending a vein of ice through her chest. Some otherworldly, more experienced woman would've found a sophisticated answer to his comment. But no such words rose to her mind, so she clamped her eyes shut and held her breath.

'Nor mine,' she murmured.

'You were amazing,' he muttered, his tone hushed.

The breath whooshed from her lungs, joy making her lips curve in a smile that seemed to emerge from her very heart. 'You weren't so bad, yourself.'

He laughed, a low, husky sound she'd begun to seriously like. With a kiss on her shoulder, he eased himself from her body and stood up.

'Come.' Again his tone was more command than request.

Again, Jasmine found she didn't mind. 'Where are we going?'

'I have a sudden need to see your body slick with water.'

He tugged her off the bed and led her into a luxurious

shower room. After adjusting various dials and testing the water with his fingers, he turned.

He dropped a kiss at the juncture between her neck and shoulder. With swift, efficient motions he secured her hair on top of her head.

Grasping her shoulders, he walked her into the misty cubicle and proceeded to wring every last ounce of pleasure from her body.

Afterwards, wrapped in a warm, fluffy towel, Jasmine watched Reyes, his lean, masculine body stealing her breath once again.

'I'm glad I met you tonight.' The words spilled out before she could stop them.

Their eyes connected, held. 'I feel the same,' he said simply. They both looked away at the same time.

In silence he led her back to his bed. And this time, their lovemaking was slow, languid, an unhurried union that brought an alien tightness to her chest and tears to her eyes. Before their heartbeats had slowed, Reyes had fallen asleep.

The low buzz of her phone woke her. Squinting in the dark, she saw the light from her smartphone illuminate the inside of her small clutch purse. The call could only be from England. And since her boss knew she was on holiday and was unlikely to disturb her, it could only be her parents…or Joaquin.

Her heart jumped into her throat.

Reyes had eased his tight hold of her during the night and now lay on his stomach, his head turned away from her.

Quickly, she slid out of bed and retrieved the phone. Seeing the name displayed on the screen, her heart plummeted. 'Hello.'

'Jasmine!' Her mother's frantic voice rang in her ears. 'Where are you? They took him. Oh, God, they broke his arm…and then they took him away!'

Walking on tiptoe to the door, Jasmine slipped out and hurried down the hallway to Reyes's study. 'Mum, take a deep breath and tell me what happened,' Jasmine said, even though deep down she suspected the answer.

'Some men broke into the house and they took Stephen!'

'*What?* When?'

'About an hour ago. They wouldn't say where they were going. But they hurt him, Jasmine. What if they…they kill him?' Her voice broke in a strangled sob.

Ice slithered down Jasmine's spine. She clutched the phone to her ear to stem the shaking in her hand. 'It's okay, Mum. I'm sure they won't. Did they…what did they say?' She tried to steady her voice so her mother's panic didn't escalate.

'They left a number…asked me to give it to you to call. Jasmine, I don't know what I'll do if anything happens to Stephen— *Oh, God!*'

Knowing how adversity had affected her mother before Stephen came into their lives, Jasmine clutched the phone harder, unwilling to contemplate the worst. Her earlier bravado began to wither before her eyes.

She took a deep breath. 'Well, stop worrying.' Jasmine tried to infuse as much optimism into her voice as she could. 'Text me the number. I'll sort this out, I promise.'

Her mother's teary, panic-laced goodbye wrenched at Jasmine's heart. Hands shaking, she started to dial the number her mother had sent through when her phone buzzed with another incoming text.

Jasmine read it. Once. Twice. Her fingers went numb.

The message itself was innocuous enough. But the meaning hit her square in the chest.

One hour. Rio Hilton. Room 419. A simple exchange. Good luck.

She returned to the bedroom on leaden feet and froze as Reyes shifted in the bed, exhaled heavily before settling back into deep sleep. Moonlight filtering through the open windows silhouetted him in soft light, his glorious body bare from the

waist up. Momentarily, she stared, recalling the way he'd unleashed all that potent power on her, his generosity in showering her with pleasure.

Her insides quivered as harsh reality hit her in the face.

She had no choice.

She'd been willing to abort her despicable mission even if
it meant exposing her stepfather's misdeeds and possible incarceration to the authorities.

But she couldn't stand by and do nothing while Stephen
was being physically harmed. Or worse. She would never be
able to live with herself.

As for Reyes…

She bit her lip and forced her gaze from the man lying on
the bed.

Numbness invading every atom of her being, Jasmine
stealthily pulled her clothes on and went back into the study.
Reyes hadn't had the chance to place the treaty back in the safe.

Insides clenched in shame, she walked to the desk, opened
the folder and lifted the heavily embossed papers.

Her hands shook as she lifted the treaty and held it in her
hands.

*'I am merely a concerned citizen of Santo Sierra, wishing
to reassure myself my crown prince's actions are altruistic,
Miss Nichols. That is all…'*

Joaquin's words reverberated in her head and she clenched
her teeth. She might only have known him for a few hours,
but Jasmine didn't doubt that Crown Prince Reyes Navarre
cared deeply about his people and held only their best inter-
ests at heart.

It was Joaquin's motives that were highly suspect.

Whatever happened, Jasmine didn't have any intention of
letting the document out of her sight.

Taking a deep breath, she folded the treaty, slipped into the
hallway and made her way to the deck to retrieve her shoes.
Clutching them to her chest, she made her way down the steps
towards the gangplank.

The bodyguard materialised in front of her, large and threatening. His searching eyes stalled her breath.

With every last ounce of strength, she straightened and lifted her chin, all at once ashamed and thankful that her old skills were coming to the fore.

Never show fear, never show fear. 'Can I get a taxi, please?' she asked, praying he spoke enough English to understand her request.

For several seconds, he didn't respond. Finally, he nodded and indicated the exit.

Despite the pre-dawn hour, people and cars rushed past on the road beyond the quay, the post-Carnival Rio nightlife as vibrant as it had been during the festival a month ago. Another set of bodyguards guarded the gangplank and exchanged words with her escort, who shrugged and said something that made the others chuckle. Jasmine tried to remain calm, regulate her breathing as she walked beside him.

Twenty minutes later, she stumbled into the foyer of the Rio Hilton. The night receptionist directed her to the bank of lifts without batting an eyelash.

When she reached the room, Joaquin Esteban's burly sidekick held the door open for her. She entered. The diminutive man rose from a cream-coloured sofa, his hands outstretched in false greeting. Jasmine sidestepped him, her fists clenched.

'What did you do with my stepfather?' she demanded.

Joaquin paused, his hard eyes glittering before his sleazy smile slid back into place. 'Why, nothing, Miss Nichols. He's fine and currently enjoying the best hospitality at my home in London until our business is concluded.'

'You broke his arm!'

'Ah, that was rather unfortunate. My men merely wanted to make sure everyone understood what moves needed to be made. But he got a little…excited.'

Rage built inside her. 'So you broke his arm? God, you're nothing but a thug!'

'I would caution against name-calling. You were on the

prince's yacht for over five hours. And from the looks of it you weren't there against your will.'

Her skin crawled. 'You were having me watched?'

'I'm very vested in our deal. It's imperative that you understand that.' His eyes slid from her face to her handbag, the question in them undeniable.

For a wild second, Jasmine wanted to tell him she'd failed.

She wanted to turn back the clock; to return the treaty, return to the bed and the magnificent, captivating man she'd left in it. A man whose haunted eyes made her yearn to comfort him.

Even now she craved one more look, one more touch...

But it was too late. Defying Joaquin would be condemning her stepfather to a horrific fate.

And yet, she couldn't just hand the document over.

'You're not merely a concerned citizen of Santo Sierra, are you?'

Joaquin shrugged. 'No. Valderra is my home.'

Her mouth dropped open in shock. What on earth had she got herself into? 'Why are you doing this?' she whispered. Just then another possibility dawned, cold and unwelcoming. 'Do you work for Prince Mendez?'

'Enough questions. The document, please,' Joaquin said coldly.

'No.' Jasmine shook her head and eyed the door. 'I won't give it to you.'

She whirled about and was confronted with the thick wall of muscle in the shape of the bodyguard. His beady eyes narrowed before he snatched the clutch out of her frozen grasp and removed the treaty from it.

Jasmine had been in enough fights to know which ones she stood a chance in and which ones were hopeless.

Joaquin's eyes glittered as he perused the sheets, before rolling up the document.

'Thank you, Miss Nichols. I think this concludes our business together.' He started to turn away.

Sick with self-loathing, she stepped forward. 'Wait! Please tell me you'll return the treaty to Prince Reyes before tomorrow?'

'You don't need to trouble yourself about that,' Joaquin answered. 'I'll make sure it reaches the right hands.'

Sweat coated her palms. 'But if the document isn't returned tonight, Rey…the prince will know I stole it.'

'And what does that matter? It's highly unlikely you and the prince will ever cross paths again, is it not? Besides, going on past experience, I wouldn't have imagined you would be bothered by something as trivial as your reputation,' he scoffed.

'I'm not that person any more. I've turned my life around.'

'So you say. But once a thief, always a thief. You reverted to type quite easily.'

Pain frayed the outer edges of her heart. Holding her head high, she stood her ground. 'I don't need to prove myself to you.' Anxiety churned through her stomach. 'What about Stephen?'

'He'll be home for breakfast. Goodbye, Miss Nichols.' He walked out of the room.

Jasmine wanted to chase after him, rip the document from his hands.

As if guessing her intentions, the bodyguard cleared his throat.

Jasmine didn't flinch. She'd dealt with brutes like him before, taken down one or two, even. But she knew she wouldn't win this battle. She'd been damned from the very start.

Nevertheless, the enormity of what she'd done settled like a heavy mantle on her shoulders. Ice flowed through her veins as she clenched her fists.

'Taxi?' the bodyguard snarled.

'No, thank you. I'll find my own way.'

The first rays of dawn slashed across the sky as Jasmine returned to her hotel. With disjointed movements, she wheeled her suitcase out of the closet and stuffed her belongings into it. Forcing herself not to think, not to feel, she undressed and entered the shower.

But tears, scalding hotter than the scouring spray, coursed down her cheeks as she desperately scrubbed her skin.

Tonight she'd sunk to a despicable low. She'd lied. She'd stolen.

She'd let herself down spectacularly.

And in the blink of an eye, stripped back the years and reverted to her old self.

CHAPTER FOUR

One month later

APRIL HAD BROUGHT an abrupt end to the cold snap and incessant rain that had engulfed London and most of the country for months.

Jasmine stepped out of Temple tube station into brilliant sunshine and stumbled past a group of tourists debating which attraction to visit. Their excited conversation barely touched her consciousness. Arms folded around her middle, she struck a path through the crowd towards the building that housed her office, clinging to the near fugue state she'd inhabited since returning from Rio. A blank mind meant she didn't have to think. Didn't have to feel.

Didn't have to remember Reyes.

Or what she'd done.

Most of all, she didn't have to acknowledge the fact that the past she'd thought she'd left behind was still with her, buried underneath her skin, ready to rear its ugly head and reveal itself in all its glory.

Naïve. She'd been so naïve. To imagine that she could escape unharmed.

A lance of pain shot through her chest. By now Reyes Navarre would know her for what she was. And despise her for it.

Despite the thousands of miles separating them, Jasmine could almost feel the weight of his disappointment.

'I've trusted you with more tonight than I have anyone in a long time.'

A moan rose in her throat. With a shake of her head, she ruthlessly suppressed it, sucking in a deep breath as she neared her office building.

Her boss had been sending her anxious looks over the past few days. Twice this week, she'd forgotten it was her turn to get the coffee and muffins.

Yesterday she'd returned from a hurried trip to the coffee shop with a serious case of nausea. One she hadn't been able to shake since.

Numbness and absent-mindedness when she was alone was fine...welcome in fact. But she couldn't afford to let it affect her work—

Her thoughts scattered as a body slammed into her.

Jasmine grasped the nearest solid thing to break her fall, but it was too late. She slid sideways, taking with her half of the contents of the small newsstand as she stumbled.

'For goodness' sake, miss, watch where you were going! Now look what you've done!'

Glaring at the retreating back of the man who'd barrelled into her, Jasmine regained her feet and started gathering the magazines. 'I'm so sorry,' she muttered.

'It'll take me ages to sort out the newspapers,' the kiosk owner grumbled.

'It's fine. I'll pay for—' Jasmine's words dried in her throat.

From the numbed state she'd lived in for the past four weeks, the fiery bolt of electricity that smashed through her body made her reel. Her heart thundered, sending a rush of blood roaring through her veins so she didn't hear the concerned voices around her as she grabbed the newspaper, her gaze riveted on the picture on the front page.

Reyes!

Her fingers shook, wildly fluttering the paper as she stared. Reyes...the reclusive crown prince...on the front page of an English newspaper. The why slammed into her brain a split second before her eyes sought the headlines.

Santo-Valderra Trade Treaty In Chaos... Economy Threatened!

An anguished moan scoured her throat, her heart lurching so painfully she had visions of it stopping altogether.

'Miss, are you all right?' the kiosk owner's voice finally impinged.

Trembling, she dug into her bag and paid for the newspaper, mumbling at the seller to keep the change to pay for the damage she'd caused.

Clutching the paper, she darted through the crowd, breaking into a full run as fevered urgency flooded her bloodstream.

In her office, she sank into her seat, her shaking fingers spreading open the newspaper.

She blinked eyes that stung, forced back her panic and focused on the words of the story.

The Santo-Valderra talks had broken down after Prince Reyes Navarre had been unable to produce his part of the treaty. Prince Mendez of Valderra had agreed to continue treaty talks on condition his further demands were met.

Mendez had walked away from the negotiation table when his demands had been refused. Now both kingdoms were at an economic stand-off.

Acid churned through her gut as she turned over the pages to find the rest of the story. But things only got worse.

Unable to keep the bile down, Jasmine stumbled from her desk and barely made the toilet before she emptied the meagre contents of her stomach.

Oh, God, this was all her fault!

Shakily, she returned to her desk, read the story one more time, and fished out her phone. The small part of her brain that could function sent a small prayer of thanks that her boss had left last night for an overseas assignment.

After sending a quick email taking the day off, she entered a search into her computer. Locating Santo Sierra's embassy in London, she jotted down the address, slipped it into her bag and left her office.

By the time the taxi delivered her outside the embassy in Kensington, her shaking had abated. Her insides still trembled, but outwardly she projected the picture of calm she'd strived so hard to achieve over the last few years.

Striding into the opulent reception, she made a beeline for the receptionist. Jasmine wasn't sure exactly what her game plan was, but she had to do *something*.

Maybe she could speak to the ambassador, convince someone to let her try to fix the chaos she'd created…

God, she was grasping at straws. But she couldn't cower away—

'Can I help you?'

She focused on the receptionist. 'Yes.' She stopped and cleared her throat. 'Can I see the ambassador, please?'

The receptionist's eyebrows rose. 'Do you have an appointment?'

'No…but I…this is important…' Jasmine ventured, her voice trailing off when the neatly dressed woman shook her head.

'Perhaps you'd like to leave your name and the reason for your visit and I'll arrange an appointment…?'

Jasmine smothered a grimace. 'My name is Jasmine Nichols. And it's about the Santo-Valderra treaty.'

The other woman's eyes narrowed suspiciously. 'What about it?'

'I just read in the paper about it breaking down. I wanted to offer my help in any way I can…?'

The receptionist stared at her in silence, her scepticism turning to downright incredulity as the seconds ticked by. The phone rang. She picked it up. The conversation in rapid Spanish flew over Jasmine's head.

She focused when the receptionist gasped. *'Sí. Sí. Su Alteza.'*

Her eyes widened as she replaced the handset. 'Please take a seat, Miss Nichols. Someone will be with you shortly.'

The flood of relief that surged through Jasmine nearly crippled her. Reaching out, she gripped the edge of the desk. 'Oh, thank you. I know he's busy, but I really appreciate it.' She started to walk towards the plush seats, then froze when her stomach heaved.

Swallowing, she turned. 'Can I use your bathroom?' she asked, alarm rising when her stomach roiled harder.

The receptionist was still staring at her as if she'd grown extra limbs, but Jasmine was too desperate not to heave onto the polished floor to decipher why. Eyes wide, the other woman pointed down a small hallway. 'Through those doors.'

Nodding, she rushed into the bathroom and locked the stall. Five minutes of wretched heaving later, she stared at her reflection in the mirror and groaned.

How did she expect anyone to take her seriously when she looked like an electrified corpse? She dampened another roll of hand tissues and pressed them to her cheeks. Whatever was ailing her would have to be investigated later.

Drying her hands, she pinned a confident smile on her face, exited the bathroom. And came face to face with Prince Reyes Navarre.

The pounding in Reyes's head when he'd learned that Jasmine Nichols was in his embassy had subsided to a dull throb.

For a single moment his rage had been total. All-encompassing. The feeling had been followed closely by shock at her sheer audacity.

It'd been several moments before he'd realised the ambassador was about to turn her away. His countermand had raised several eyebrows around the conference table where he'd been conducting his meeting. He hadn't explained his reason.

He didn't need to.

His plan for retribution where Jasmine Nichols's betrayal was concerned was no one's business but his.

He watched with satisfaction as she paled. That prim little smile on her face disappeared and her eyes rounded.

'Reye—Prince Navarre!'

Was that a tremble of fear? Good.

'You will address the prince as Your Highness.' His ambassador spoke sharply from beside him.

Jasmine's gaze swung from him to the short, fatherly figure, and back to him. Noting for the first time that they had an audience, she blinked. Reyes noted her drawn features.

If she had a conscience, he hoped it was eating away at her. But he knew women like her possessed no conscience. They seduced and betrayed with no thought for anyone else but themselves.

His jaw tightened as her lashes swept down in a false gesture of apology.

'Of course. My apologies, Your Highness. I wasn't... expecting you here.' Her hand shook as she clutched her handbag. When she bit her lip, Reyes smothered the memories threatening to awaken.

Turning to where his bodyguards hovered, he waved one forward. 'I have confidential business with Miss Nichols. Take her down to the basement. Until I say so, she's not allowed to contact anyone or leave the premises under any circumstances.'

'*What?* You can't do that!' She'd paled further and her breaths jerked out in shallow pants.

Reyes smiled. 'You're on Santo Sierran soil. I can do whatever I please with you.'

'But I came here to help. *Please*, Reyes—Your Highness!' she screeched as Reyes stepped back. Her fear was very real.

Reyes steeled himself against it and walked away. Never again.

He'd failed his people because of this woman.

Remembering brought a burn of pure white rage that obliterated any lingering mercy.

Even before he'd come fully awake the next morning on the yacht, he'd known something was wrong. The silence had been deafening. Complete. Where he should have heard the soft breathing and felt the warm, supple body of the lover he'd taken to his bed, there'd been a cold, empty space.

His instinct hadn't failed him. Even faced with the discovery of the theft, he'd hoped he was hallucinating. For endless minutes, he hadn't believed what he'd let happen. How much he'd let his guard down.

How spectacularly he'd failed in his duty to protect his people. That was what made the burn sting that much deeper. The full realisation that he'd taken a stranger to bed, a stranger who'd turned out to be a thief, had pointed to a singular lack of judgement, preyed on his mind like acid on metal for the last four weeks.

In the time since then Reyes could've hired a team of investigators to find and bring her to justice. But that would've served no purpose besides granting him personal satisfaction. Seeking personal vengeance, although tempting, had been relegated very low on his list. Rescuing the trade talks with Valderra had been paramount.

Of course, Mendez, handed the perfect opportunity to sink his hands deeper into the Santo Sierran coffers, had sought to do exactly that.

Relentless greed had threatened to destabilise the economy. Jasmine Nichols's actions had accelerated the process as surely as if she'd lit a fuse to a bomb.

Reyes breathed in and out, forced himself to focus through the rage and bitterness eating at him. There was no time for recriminations. For the sake of his father, for the sake of his people, he had to put personal feelings aside.

First, he would salvage the economy.

Then he would deal with Jasmine Nichols.

Jasmine pushed away the tray of tea and sandwiches. The thought of eating or even taking the smallest sip of tea made her stomach churn. She took a deep breath, folded her hands in her lap and silently prayed for strength.

The room she'd been brought to was comfortable enough. Sumptuous sofas were grouped in one corner, centred round a low antique coffee table. A conference table took up a larger space and, mounted on the far end of the wall, a large screen TV and a camera.

The red light blinked, telling her she was being observed. The memory of Reyes's cold rage slammed into her mind. Unable to sit, she jumped up. She'd been shown into this room two hours ago. Luckily, her nausea had abated but her shock and anxiety had risen in direct proportion as the realisation of what she'd walked into ate at her.

She paced, twisting her hands together. Reyes was angry and disappointed with her. No doubt about that.

She'd foolishly thought she, a junior mediator in a small-sized firm, could help rectify the situation she'd caused. Make amends for what she'd done...

Jasmine's heart lurched, a feeling of helplessness sliding over her. Reyes was probably laughing his head off at her audacity. And for all she knew, he could've already left London. The newspaper article had mentioned he was visiting several European countries to garner economic support for Santo Sierra.

If he'd truly left her to be dealt with to the fullest extent of the law, she would probably be prosecuted for treason and thrown in a Santo Sierran jail.

Her legs threatened to give way, but she forced herself to walk towards the camera. Swallowing, she looked up at the black globe.

'Can I speak to His Highness, please? I won't take up much of his time, I promise. I just... I need five minutes. Please...'

The light blinked at her.

Feeling foolish, she whirled about and paced some more. Another hour passed. Then another.

Jasmine was ready to climb the walls when the door swung open. Breath stalling, she rushed towards it. Only to stop when confronted by yet another bodyguard bearing a tray.

It held several tapas dishes, fragrant rice and a tall carafe of pomegranate juice.

'Your lunch,' the guard said in heavily accented English.

As violent as the nausea had been, the hunger cloying through her now, when the appetising smells hit her nostrils, was equally vicious. But she forced herself to shake her head. 'No. I won't eat until I speak to His Highness.'

The thickset guard blinked. Pressing home her advantage just in case she was being watched on camera, she pushed the tray away, sat on the far end of the sofa, and crossed her legs.

The door shut behind the guard. Hearing the lock turn, her insides congealed. Another half an hour passed in excruciating slowness before the handle turned again.

Reyes stood in the doorway.

The shock of seeing him again slammed into her. But she took advantage of the wider distance between them to observe him.

His face had grown haggard since Rio; perhaps it was the short designer beard he sported, his hair a little longer, shaggier. But his body was just as masculine and breathtaking as before, or even more so with the added angle of danger thrown in.

Or she could be going out of her mind, dwelling on superficial things when there was so much at stake.

'You wanted to see me.' He stepped into the room and the door shut behind him.

Now that he was here, Jasmine wasn't sure where to start. *I'm sorry* seemed so very inadequate.

So she nodded, struggling to hide the guilt eating her up inside. 'Yes. I think I can help with your…situation.'

He sucked in a sharp breath. His fingers opened and closed in a gesture of restrained control. '*Help!* You don't think you've helped enough?' he snarled.

'Please, I'm trying to make things right any way I can. Please tell me what I can do and I'll do it, Reyes—'

His eyes turned to dark pools of ice. 'You will address me as Your Highness. Addressing me by my first name was a one-time privilege. One you abused with the coarsest atrocity. And Miss Nichols?'

'Yes?'

'I suggest you eat. You won't be enjoying luxuries such as three-course meals for very much longer.'

CHAPTER FIVE

JASMINE'S BREATH SNAGGED in her throat. 'What do you mean by that?'

'I mean your situation is precarious. Once I apprise the ambassador and my council members of your crimes, your destiny will be sealed.'

'But you haven't done it yet. And you…you said earlier that the matter between us was personal.'

'I only meant I have more important matters to attend to.' His mouth compressed in a grim smile. 'You will get what's coming to you. My intention was to deal with you at a later date. I didn't think you would be foolish enough to cross my radar of your own accord just yet. So perhaps I'll watch you suffer for a long time.' His gaze went to the tray of cold food and his jaw clenched. 'You'll be brought another tray. Eat.'

He stepped towards the door.

'Wait. Please.'

'What?'

She cleared her throat. 'Will you join me for lunch? That is, if you haven't eaten yet? I can tell you why I came here while you eat? Please.'

The icy incredulity in his eyes didn't recede as he shook his head. 'You're brazen and audacious, I'll give you that. But your offer is declined, Miss Nichols,' he replied sarcastically. 'Was there anything else?'

She squeezed her eyes shut for a second. 'Please tell me what I can do to make things right. I'll do anything.'

He raised an eyebrow at her. 'I don't trust a single word out of your mouth. So I suggest you save your breath.'

She licked her lower lip and tried anyway. 'You can't leave me here for ever.'

'Can't I?' The smile that curved his lips could not in any way be described as affectionate, warm, or even cordial. The starkness of it struck pure terror in Jasmine's heart.

'I...I guess you can. But, please don't.' Her nausea was rising again. She didn't think she could stand being cooped up in here for another minute, let alone hours on end.

His shark-like smile widened, the growth of beard emphasising the feral whiteness of his teeth. A dark shiver swept over her.

'Never fear, *querida*, your sins will be addressed in due course. This subject is closed. For now.'

She'd been dismissed. Just like that. Jasmine wasn't sure which emotion—despair or trepidation—churned greater in her stomach as she watched Reyes leave. She couldn't force him to listen to the apology she'd practised for a month now. From his blatant hatred of her, she'd have to abandon any hope of asking for his forgiveness.

For now she had no recourse but to stay a prisoner.

Despair cloying through her, she paced for another hour before exhaustion deadened her limbs.

Kicking off her shoes, she sank onto the sofa. Despite the creature comforts, there were no windows in the basement. The remote for the TV had been removed. She had no idea exactly how much time had passed because her bag and phone had been taken away. The second tray Reyes had ordered delivered had also gone cold, its arrival coinciding with another case of severe nausea.

That, coupled with the exhaustion, convinced Jasmine she'd definitely picked up a bug of some sort.

Stretching out, she shivered and tried to tuck her skirt down to cover her legs as much as possible. Then, closing her eyes, she succumbed to the darkness tugging at her consciousness.

'Jasmine, wake up!'

'Mnnnh.' Her tongue felt too thick to convey the *no* she'd been attempting. She tried to burrow into the blanket some-

one had draped on her, but a sharp shake of her shoulder stopped her.

'Wake up!'

She groaned at the effort it took to pry her eyes open. 'What?'

A man, presumably a doctor from the stethoscope clinging to his neck, hovered above her. She squirmed and started to raise her hand as he shone a light in her eyes.

Sharp pain shot up her arm. 'Ouch.'

'Lie still. You have an intravenous needle in your arm.'

Reyes's deep voice was unmistakeable. Her attention swung to him as he barked at whoever else was in the room. When the volley of Spanish ceased, he was holding out a glass of water with a straw to her lips, and someone was pressing a soft pillow beneath her head.

Questions swirled in her fuzzy brain. 'Reyes...what...?'

'Don't try and speak,' he said, his eyes narrowed on her face as he addressed the doctor in Spanish.

The doctor nodded repeatedly and patted Jasmine's shoulder.

'What's he saying? What happened to me? And why do I have a needle in my arm?'

Reyes glared at her, but she saw shadows lurking in his eyes. 'You fell asleep but you didn't respond when I tried to wake you.'

The doctor spoke to Reyes. Reyes turned to her. 'Are you on any medication?'

Frowning, she shook her head. Then noticed her new surroundings for the first time. 'Where am I?'

'You're in my suite in the guest wing of the ambassador's residence.'

About to ask why she'd been relocated, she paused as the doctor addressed Reyes again. After a few minutes, the thin man bowed and left the room.

'Should I be worried that the doctor didn't want to speak to me, his patient?'

'You don't speak Spanish. And you're not a patient. You're a prisoner.'

Jasmine's temper twitched despite the knowledge that she deserved his caustic tone. She glanced at the pole next to the bed holding the IV bag. 'I know. But I'd still like to know what's wrong with me, if it's not too much trouble?' she muttered.

Reyes's mouth firmed. 'You're severely dehydrated and a touch malnourished. The fluids should do the trick. And I've ordered more food to be prepared for you. When was the last time you had a healthy meal?' he asked with a dark frown.

Her eyelids dragged heavily as she blinked. 'You mean the last time before I was incarcerated in your basement?'

'Answer the question, Jasmine.'

Her heart shouldn't have jumped at the sound of her name on his lips. But it did. 'I don't know. Yesterday afternoon, I think. I haven't had much of an appetite lately.'

Her eyes met his. Stayed. A piercing awareness lanced between them.

Reyes lunged to his feet and uttered a sharp command in Spanish. A bodyguard entered, glanced her way and nodded. She didn't need a translator to know she was the subject of the discussion. Feelings of vulnerability rose along with the hairs on her nape. 'What's going on now?'

Reyes didn't answer. He merely turned on his heel and walked through a door to a connecting room.

'His Highness requires me to attend your home…bring you a few things before we leave,' the bodyguard delivered in halting English.

Surprise froze Jasmine for all of ten seconds before her head swivelled towards the door Reyes had just walked out of. 'Leave? I'm not going anywhere.'

'You misunderstand. This is not a request from His Highness. It is a summons.'

'A what?' she asked dumbly, unable to immediately compute the words.

'You are required to pack a bag, *señorita*. We leave tomorrow.'

'You have your orders, I understand. But perhaps I can talk about it with *His Highness* when he has a minute?' Her words were delivered loud in the hope that Reyes would hear her from wherever he'd disappeared to. She didn't want to create any more waves, but neither could she let Reyes take over her life.

Silence descended in the room, the bodyguard eyeing her as if she'd gone insane.

Reyes re-entered the room. With a nod, he dismissed the security detail, waiting until they'd shut the door behind them before addressing her.

'I think during your exchange with my men something may have become lost in translation. My *request* was actually a command. There was nothing of a suggestion about it. When I leave here in the morning, you're coming with me.'

Despite her hammering pulse and the exhaustion sapping at her, she found the strength to speak. 'I understand that I'm your prisoner, but even prisoners get advance warning of their fate,' she implored.

One dark eyebrow rose. 'You forget you have no rights here. I hold all the cards. You go where I wish you to go.'

Jasmine's mouth dried up. The back of her hand itched and she yearned to rip the needle out, grab her shoes and handbag and run as fast as her legs could carry her. But she knew, even if her conscience allowed her, she wouldn't make it to the door.

Desperation made her blurt out, 'I have a life, a job to return to.'

'You will resign tomorrow.'

A death knell sounded somewhere in her head. 'Please, don't do this, Reyes.'

His eyes narrowed. 'Resign. Or I'll take pleasure in informing your superiors of the true depths of your character. *After* I hand you over to the authorities.'

'Are you saying that if I resign you won't tell them I'm—' She stopped, unable to speak the hated word that sealed her guilt. But he already knew she was guilty. His eyes narrowed scornfully.

'Afraid to say it out loud? *A thief*, Jasmine Nichols, that's what you are,' he condemned through clenched teeth. 'You not only stole from me, you stole from my people. You single-handedly set back years of trade negotiations.' His eyes blazed at her, grey fire that stripped her to the bone.

Her heart lurched as her sins were laid bare in front of her. The heat of shame burned through her, from the soles of her feet up through her body until the acrid taste of it flooded her mouth.

'Rey—I'm sorry. What happened wasn't supposed to happen.'

His laughter mocked her. 'You mean the sex was supposed to addle my brain so much I'd suspect someone else of the theft?' he snarled.

'No. I mean I shouldn't have taken the treaty in the first place.' Jasmine couldn't contain the sob that rose in her throat. Tears flooded her eyes. To hide it, she turned away and plugged a fist to her mouth.

But he heard it. Of course he heard it. 'Tears, Miss Nichols?' he taunted. 'How original. Almost as original as your pick-up line in Rio.'

Her sob emerged, thick and broken. Desperately, she tried to gulp it down.

His scorn reached her from across the room. 'Spare me the histrionics. You cry as if your heart is breaking. Which cannot be because you don't have a heart.'

Her head whipped round at the cruel assertion. He stood against the window, his hands shoved deep into his pockets. She deserved every accusation he threw at her, but she needed him to see she wasn't all bad.

'What I did was wrong, I know that. And I have a heart, or I wouldn't be here, trying to make amends.'

A cruel smile curved his lips. 'Well, that's a shame and a curse for you. Because I aim to make you pay for your betrayal.

And by the time I'm finished with you, you'll feel that heart you claim to possess ripped from your chest!'

Reyes watched her eyes widen. The same eyes had gazed adoringly up at him that night on his yacht, then darkened as passion had gripped them both. Eyes he'd drowned in as he'd sunk deep inside her.

Deceptive, duplicitous eyes that had taken his lust and turned it against him. Played him as a virtuoso plucked at willing strings. Deep down in a place he rarely liked to visit, it still burned him that he'd never seen it coming. That he'd been so completely and utterly duped for the second time in his life.

Duped by a woman who'd proclaimed to be one thing and turned out to be another.

And this time, the consequences threatened to be worse.

Anaïs had ruined one life, devastated one family. Jasmine's actions threatened thousands.

He'd been willing to bide his time. But he'd never been one to miss an opportunity. And while he hadn't expected the opportunity to arise so soon, he was perfectly willing to take his revenge now.

Jasmine Nichols had walked into his life, brazen and unrepentant. He had every intention of making her pay for her sins. Seeing the tears on her face only strengthened his resolve.

Reyes didn't doubt they were genuine, but he knew they were born of self-preservation rather than a show of repentance. He'd witnessed it many times before. From Anaïs. From his mother.

One hand came up and scrubbed at her face. In the blink of an eye her tears were wiped clean. As if they'd never been there. Just like in Rio. She'd charmed her way into his bed for long enough to get her hands on what she'd wanted. Then she'd vanished like a spent tornado, leaving devastation behind.

His jaw tightened. 'Who hired you to steal the treaty?' He hadn't meant to question her here, like this. But the need to know burned fiercely inside him. 'Was it Mendez?'

'No. I didn't…no one hired me.'

'So it was merely an opportunistic theft? The moment presented itself and you thought, *why not*? To what end, though? Blackmail?'

He caught her wince and felt a sliver of satisfaction. At least it showed she wasn't as unfeeling as he'd thought. Or maybe she didn't like her flaws pointed out to her. Tough. Before he was done, her every flaw would be exposed to the light of day.

She lifted a hand, as if to beseech him. 'No… Yes, it was blackmail, but you don't understand—'

He snorted. 'Theft is theft, Miss Nichols. It can't be explained away.'

The knock on the door made her jump. Reyes barked out an order and a member of staff walked in with a tray.

He took it and walked to the bed. Waiting until Jasmine sat up against the pillows, he set it down across her lap.

'I will force-feed you if necessary, but you will eat this meal, understood?' He didn't want to look at her, see how pale she was. Or remember his gut-churning anxiety when he'd been unable to wake her earlier.

Her head bowed as she looked down at the tray. 'No force-feeding necessary. I seem to have my appetite back.' Her stomach rumbled and one corner of her lush mouth lifted.

Reyes looked away and stepped back.

'Your things are being collected from your home. My plane will be ready to leave in the morning. Make sure you're packed and ready to leave.'

He headed for the door before he was tempted to do something idiotic. Like watch her eat.

CHAPTER SIX

'IS THERE REALLY no other way for me to make amends?'

Reyes took the empty tray and handed it to the member of staff hovering nearby.

'No.'

He glimpsed a touch of rebellion in her eyes and something fizzed through his blood, almost an anticipation of his battle with her. Which was curious. And ridiculous. All he was interested in was making her pay for her actions. 'You'll come with me—'

'Or you'll report me to the authorities? Have me thrown in jail?' Her fingers twisted in her lap. 'I know. Maybe that's a better option than...'

'Facing my brand of justice? You know, I think that's the first sensible decision you've made since we met. But seriously, do you want to take your chances locked in the basement again? You didn't last half a day. The bureaucracy before you're brought to trial alone would take months, if not years. On the other hand, a Santo Sierran prison is so much better. We deliver justice swiftly. If nothing else, you'll have wall-to-wall sunshine all year round; you can acquire a permanent tan during your lifelong incarceration.'

Fear clenched her heart. 'Is that where we—you're going?'

'Eventually. You have until morning to decide. Then I abandon you to the ambassador's mercy.'

She paled further. 'I've suffered worse, I'm sure. But I really don't think it needs to come to that.'

Surprise sparked through Reyes at her reply, then he berated himself for his reaction. Obviously his wasn't the first threat of punishment Jasmine Nichols had received in her life. Curious, he regarded her. How many other men had she tricked with her body, then stolen from? How many others had fallen for her sensual beauty? Been duped by the promise of her *bed-me* eyes and silken skin?

Anger rose inside him.

The need to deliver his own brand of justice grew stronger. Needing to turn up the heat, he stalked closer. 'You mentioned your family,' he started conversationally. 'Do they know you're a thief?'

Her colour receded a little more, her full lips firming just a tiny fraction. Satisfaction coursed through him.

'Will they be prepared to lose everything they have in order to make reparations to the Santo Sierran people?'

She drew in a sharp breath. 'This has *nothing* to do with my family.'

'That's where you're wrong, Jasmine. You wronged *my people*, my *family*. It is only right that you *and* your family make the appropriate amends.'

'No! Please—'

'A simple phone call is all it would take to round them all up. Santo Sierra has extradition treaties with the United Kingdom—'

'No. I meant what I said. It doesn't have to come to that.'

'So you would prefer me to leave your family out of this?'

Her lips worked for several tense seconds, which stretched to a full minute. Then a sigh of defeat escaped her parted lips. 'Is it worth me saying anything else but that I would like you to leave my family alone?'

He took a deep breath. And smiled. 'No.'

'Then I'll…come with you…wherever you want me to.'

He turned and walked out of the room. Jasmine set her cutlery down and tried to think through the roller-coaster speed of her thoughts. In the end, she could only hope she'd made the right decision.

Sunset bathed the hills in orange and red as their car climbed the roads leading to Reyes's Spanish hacienda. Jasmine had long given up any hope of trying to memorise her where-abouts. All she knew was that they were somewhere deep in Northern Spain.

They'd long left behind the tourist traps and sandy beaches of Barcelona. Here the houses were few and far between, with occasional villages flashing past before she could take mean-ingful note of where she was.

Reyes sat beside her but he might as well have been thou-sands of miles away. A pair of designer sunglasses shielded his eyes from her and the phone he'd commandeered since board-ing his plane remained glued to one ear.

From the snatches of conversation she'd heard, he was plan-ning several more meetings with government ministers and his own council here in Spain.

Looking carefully, she could see the signs of strain around his mouth and the skin pulled taut over his cheekbones, but he was very much a man in command.

Sensing her scrutiny, he swivelled his head in her direction. A second later, he ended his call.

'Where exactly are we going?' she enquired.

'To my estate in Zaragoza,' he replied in a clipped tone.

'And…how long will we be staying there?'

'As long as it takes. If you have any aspirations of escape, kill them now.'

She clasped her hand in her lap, refusing to rise to his bait-ing. 'My family will be worried if I don't let them know how long I'll be away,' she tried to reason with him.

Her mother had been confused when she'd called to say she was taking a holiday and had no idea when she would be returning. Stephen had been even more difficult to convince. Jasmine had been avoiding him since her return from Rio, but she knew her stepfather suspected she'd had something to do with him being suddenly free of debt and the prospect of jail.

'And you always strive to maintain the appearance of a du-tiful daughter, do you?' Scorn poured from Reyes, the naked censure in his voice stinging her skin. 'Obviously, you've succeeded in pulling the wool over their eyes all these years.'

Jasmine bit back her retort to the contrary. It *was* because of her past that her mother worried when she didn't hear from her daughter. The past she'd tried so hard to escape from but had stepped firmly back into with her one wrong decision in Rio.

Finding no adequate words to defend herself, she kept silent. With an impatient movement, Reyes ripped the glasses from his eyes and caught her chin in his hand. Jasmine found herself locked into his intense gaze.

'Are you going to speak or do you intend to play mute?' he asked.

'I don't really have anything to say to you.'

He folded the glasses and slipped them into his shirt pocket. 'Your father, Stephen Nichols, works for the British government, does he not?'

His announcement startled her. His eyes held rigid ice that threatened to stop the blood flow in her veins. 'He's my stepfather, but how…what does that have to do with anything?' Her instinct warned she wouldn't like the path this conversation was taking.

'I'm merely trying to form a picture in my head. And your mother…what does she do?'

Jasmine licked dry lips, her thoughts churning as she debated the wisdom of evading his questions. In the end, she decided withholding the information would serve no useful purpose. 'She's his PA.'

'So to all intents and purposes, they're both upstanding citizens?' he asked, one dark eyebrow raised.

Her pulse increased as her gaze followed the graceful arch of his brow. Even when her eyes dropped to encounter his frozen regard, her pulse still thundered. Because deep inside, Jasmine knew his questions weren't as innocuous as he'd couched them.

She tried not to let him see how much he riled her. 'If you have a point, please state it.'

'I'm just wondering how come you've strayed so far from the righteous path.'

She flinched. 'I beg your pardon?'

His teeth bared in a semblance of a smile, but all it did was send a wave of dread over her. 'I'm trying to understand you, *querida*. How a woman such as you, with a seemingly stable background and upbringing, ends up being a thief.'

'You know nothing about me, except for an impression you think you got from us spending a few hours together. I can understand how what I did would colour your judgement, but that's far from the whole picture.'

His face hardened. 'I *know* you were instrumental in demolishing my country's trade treaty. You don't think that's enough?' he finished on a snarl.

Remembering how she'd felt when she saw the headline announcing the breakdown of talks, Jasmine slid her gaze from his. 'I'm sorry. But technically, Mendez is also responsible—'

'And since all evidence points to you working for Mendez, isn't the conclusion the same?' he sneered.

Her head snapped round to his. '*No!* You're wrong. I don't work for Mendez. I've never even met the man!'

'Really? You work as a broker and a mediator, do you not?'

Puzzled, she nodded.

'And over the past three years, your specialty has been in brokering agreements in Latin American companies?'

Her frown deepened in direct proportion to the escalation of her dread. 'How do you know all this?'

He continued as if she hadn't spoken. 'When we met you told me you'd been watching the Santo-Valderran talks *with interest*.'

Jasmine found his reasoning difficult to comprehend. 'And you think by interest I meant to sabotage it? For what purpose?'

'What other purpose could there be aside from financial?'

'Feel free to search my finances. You'd be surprised to find I'm not as flush as you think I am.'

'You're too intelligent to display the fruits of your duplicity. Are you so confident that I won't find the evidence I need if I cast my net a little wider, like, say, your parents?'

Jasmine felt the blood drain from her face. Despite her bravado, the last thing she wanted was for Reyes to start digging into Stephen's affairs. The evidence of his gambling, misappropriation and connection to people like Joaquin Esteban would become public knowledge if Reyes took that route.

Her stepfather had been visibly shaken by his ordeal at the hands of Joaquin's men, enough to induce an angina attack that had laid him up in hospital for a week.

Unfortunately, it had taken that experience to wake him up to his dangerous addiction. He had just started a programme to help overcome his gambling problem; the last thing she wanted was for his life to be thrown into turmoil by Reyes.

Watching him struggle to overcome his weakness, she'd been reminded of what Stephen himself had said to her years earlier.

Nobody was perfect.

She'd reminded herself of that over and over again in the last four weeks. Except she was sure, when it came to Prince Reyes Navarre, that belief wouldn't hold water.

She tried to remain calm as Reyes, sensing her turmoil, tilted her face up to his.

'I see I've stumbled onto something. Who were the beneficiaries if not your parents?' His fingers tightened. 'Your lover?'

With excruciating effort, she wrenched herself free. 'What does it matter? I did it,' she admitted, not seeing the point in prolonging the agony.

Beside her, he tensed. Her fingers clenched in her lap, the rush of memories threatening to eat her alive. Desperately, she tried to push them away, but they pushed back. Hard.

I did it. This wasn't the first time she'd said those words. But she'd hoped back then it would be the last. How wrong she'd been.

Squeezing her eyes shut for a single heartbeat, she took a deep breath, opened them and tried to plead with Reyes.

'I did it. I'm willing to take the consequences. Just tell me what I need to do.' Because the earlier she could make reparations, the earlier she could put him behind her.

CHAPTER SEVEN

REYES FOUND HIMSELF riveted by the frank admission, unable to look away from the open candour in Jasmine's face as she looked back at him. For the first time in his life, he found himself speechless.

I did it.

In all the imagined scenarios when he'd dreamed of exacting his revenge, not once had he entertained the notion that she would admit her guilt so readily.

He wondered why he was surprised. Weren't her audacity, her sheer bolshiness what had attracted him a month ago in Rio? Yet even now, Reyes could see that her reaction, while mostly convincing, was just a front. But a front that hid what? What was Jasmine Nichols keeping from him?

He continued to stare at her. She stared back, her gaze unflinching. Against his will, he felt his blood firing up, his heartbeat quicken. Shifting in his seat, he sat back, took a deep breath.

Jasmine had made things easy for him. He now didn't need to bother with interrogating her. She'd admitted her guilt and he had her confession. Her punishment would wait until he'd dealt with more important matters.

'*Gracias,*' he murmured, breaking eye contact. The strange sense of loss he felt was immediately pushed aside.

'What are you thanking me for?' she asked.

'Saving me the time and energy of interrogating you. Who did you give the treaty to?'

She shook her head. 'I can't tell you that.'

'You're wrong. When the time is right you'll give me a name. Every person responsible for this chaos will be brought to justice.'

Despite the fire in her eyes, she swallowed and looked away.

His car swung into the last stretch of road leading to his estate and a sense of satisfaction stole over him. In London, he'd felt at a slight loss; that control wasn't totally within his grasp. Within touching distance of the place he called his second home, his control returned.

San Estrela was his mother's birthplace and where she had married his father. Reyes had maybe one or two fairly happy holidays here as a child…until everything had turned sour. He wouldn't be creating any more happy memories by bringing his prisoner here, but he had no choice.

As much as it burned him to admit it, he couldn't yet return to Santo Sierra. He needed to rally economic support in order to get the talks with Valderra back on track. Plus, at present, he wasn't entirely sure whom he could trust in his own council.

His insides clenched as he thought of his father. Ruthlessly, he pushed the feeling aside. If he was to achieve what he was aiming for, he needed to clear his mind of his grief; of making things right with the father he'd lost for so long. Ironically, it was his own downfall with Jasmine Nichols that had made Reyes see his father in a different light. To not judge the old man so harshly for his own mistakes.

He would return to his father's bedside soon enough. Make amends. Hopefully before it was too late.

He alighted from the car and automatically held out his hand. Jasmine took it and straightened beside him a second later. He dropped her hand, not wanting to acknowledge how her skin felt against his.

A frown crossed her face before she masked it.

Reyes didn't know what to do with that look. On the one hand, she remained stoic in the face of her guilt, yet on the other she looked at him with contrition. The enigma unsettled and irritated him.

Pushing aside the feeling, he mounted the stairs as the door swung open to reveal his major-domo, Armando. The man wore the same anxious look he'd seen on so many Santo Sierran faces.

Reminded that his people were living in a state of constant worry made Reyes's chest tighten.

Knowing the cause of all this turmoil stood two steps behind him made his blood simmer as he greeted Armando.

'This is Miss Jasmine Nichols. She'll be my guest for the duration of my stay. She is, however, not permitted to leave the house or grounds under any circumstances. If she attempts to leave, use all means necessary to prevent her,' he instructed.

'You don't need to do that. I know why I'm here. You have my word that I won't run away.'

'You'll forgive me if I don't find your *word* reassuring?'

She inhaled sharply. 'I suppose I deserve that,' she murmured.

Reyes frowned at the hurt in her voice.

Armando, his usual capable, unruffled self, barely blinked at the exchange. 'I will put her in the Valencia Suite, Your Highness.'

'No, the Leon Suite next to mine will suffice.'

'Very well, Your Highness.'

Reyes turned down the hall towards his study and had barely taken half a dozen steps when he heard the click of heels racing after him.

He stopped. 'Did you want something?'

She looked pale, her face creased in concern as her eyes fell. When she began to visibly tremble, Reyes frowned. She hadn't been well yesterday, but she'd reassured the doctor this morning that she was fine.

'What do you mean by any means necessary?' she asked.

'Stay in the house and within the grounds and you'll never have to find out. Understood?'

A tinge of relief brought colour to her cheeks. Reyes didn't realise how disconcerting her paleness was until she regained her composure.

She shook her head. 'I can't just do nothing. I'll go out of my mind.'

'That's your punishment for now. Do otherwise and I'll have to revise my decision.'

She sighed. 'Rey—I mean, Your Highness.' Her hand lifted, as if to touch him. 'Can I have my phone back? Please, I need to let my parents know where I am. My mother will send the cavalry out in full force if I don't, and, trust me, you don't want that.' A small, wistful smile touched her lips.

The idea of her delusional mother, sitting snug in her home, worrying about her perfect daughter, made his teeth clench. No doubt Jasmine had succeeded in pulling the wool over her parents' eyes the way she'd done with him. And yet the thought of the perfect family picture all that *togetherness* presented sent a dart of something very close to jealousy through him.

He'd never had a parent worry over him like that. His mother had been too caught up in trying to turn his father's existence into a living hell to worry about the two children who'd needed her attention. And his father had been too busy turning himself inside out for a faithless woman. Reyes had been a young boy when he'd realised there wouldn't be any scrap of attention from either of his parents.

It was the reason boarding school had been a relief. It was the reason he'd chosen not to form attachments to any woman. Sex for the sake of it had been his mantra.

Until Anaïs. Until his mother's death.

After that even sex hadn't mattered.

Nothing had mattered. Nothing but duty.

Feeling the bitterness encroach, Reyes whirled and stalked towards his study. 'See Armando. He'll show you where the phone is. But one call is all you get. Make it count.'

Jasmine ended the call to her mother and put the phone down in the seriously gorgeous solarium Armando had shown her into. She took a calming breath and looked around her. Outside, a carpet of rich green grass rolled away towards a stand of cypress trees at the bottom of the valley they'd climbed out of. To the right, a more cultivated garden, hedged with roses, bougainvillea and hyacinths grew beyond a sun-washed terrace. She stood for a moment, letting the sun and stunning surroundings wash over her.

As prisons went, this one wasn't so bad, she mused. Although if she had to compare jailors, she would've preferred one who didn't make her pulse jump, who didn't make her wish her path to this place had been different.

In the car earlier, she'd refused to give Joaquin's name, partly because of what it would mean for her stepfather. But she'd also shied away from the conversation because she'd been afraid Reyes would find out about her past. That he'd discover that the woman he'd taken to bed had grown up in a council estate and been nearly initiated into a drug-dealing gang. That she had a juvenile record she'd never be able to erase.

He might detest her now, but that was far better than his repulsion, his scorn.

The chirp of a bird steered her from another unwanted trip down memory lane. She'd been taking those trips far too often these last weeks. Ever since that night in Rio, in fact. She needed to snap out of it. Put it behind her.

She would face whatever punishment Reyes chose to dole out on her, but the past belonged in the past.

A sound from behind her made her turn.

Armando entered, pushing a trolley laden with food. 'I do not know the *señorita's* preference, so I have brought a selection.'

She'd missed breakfast again because she hadn't been able to stomach any of the food the embassy had laid out for them this morning. Lately, any thought of food made her stomach roil. So she approached the trolley cautiously. And breathed easier once she could look at the mouthwatering selection of *tapas* without turning green.

Perhaps telling the doctor she was fine this morning had been a mistake…

Thanking Armando, she heaped her plate with bread, ham, and a green salad and took a seat at the dining area near the window. She polished off the food in record time and went back for seconds, adding plump olives marinated in chilli oil.

She was about to pick up her cutlery when Reyes strolled in. Without a word, he selected his own food, then pulled up a chair opposite her.

In low tones, he dismissed Armando and shook out his napkin.

'So,' he started conversationally, 'you told your mother I was your boyfriend.' It wasn't a question. It was an observation, marred with thick layers of distaste.

Jasmine's appetite fled. Her cutlery dropped noisily onto the table. 'How did you know that?'

One sleek brow arched. 'Did I not mention it? All incoming and outgoing calls from San Estrela are monitored. And yes, I have a zero-trust policy where you're concerned.'

Despite the heat engulfing her face at the pointed remark, she met his gaze head-on. 'If you were listening then you would've heard that my mother *assumed* you were my boyfriend. I didn't—'

'Correct that assumption. You've been caught in yet another lie, Miss Nichols. It's quite astonishing how they trip so easily from your lips.' His gaze dropped to her lips and she felt a guilty tingle as if he'd branded her mouth with just that one look.

'I could hardly tell her I was being held prisoner somewhere in Northern Spain!'

He ripped a piece of bread in half, dipped it in his olive oil and took a healthy bite. 'Maybe you should have. For her own good, she needs to know she doesn't have the perfect daughter she seems to think she does.'

'You don't know me and you don't know my mother, so don't presume to judge us. Besides, what makes you think she believes I'm perfect?'

'She must do. She seemed to eat up all the lies you fed her without question.'

Jasmine was tempted to tell Reyes of her mother's one fatal flaw—she refused to see the bad in anyone. Her blindly trusting nature had seen her duped out of her money over and over by ruthless men. It was that nature that had landed them where Jasmine had been forced down a path of near permanent ruin.

It was a place Jasmine didn't like to remind her mother of, or ever revisit herself, if she could help it.

'It's easier for my mother to take things at face value.' Her words emerged with much more bitter introspection than she'd intended. Aware of just how much she'd let slip, Jasmine clamped her jaw shut and tried not to even breathe. But it was too late.

Reyes's head cocked to the side in the now oh-so-familiar way. 'Interesting. She knows and she accepts you just the way you are?' The way he said it, almost wistfully, drew her gaze to him.

He was staring at her and yet she got the feeling his mind was somewhere else altogether. Somewhere he didn't want to relive, but couldn't seem to help.

She picked up her fork and speared an olive. A quick whiff of it had her setting it down again. She tried a piece of ham and chewed that instead. After swallowing, she answered, 'Yes, she does. She likes to think that people change. So do I, incidentally.'

As if snapping out of whatever place he'd been, he sharpened his gaze. 'No, they don't. They like to pretend they do. Some do their best to present a different face to the world, but people inherently remain the same underneath.'

'I don't believe that.'

'Why, because *you've* changed? You've somehow seen some mystic light and repented all your sins?'

She swallowed. 'Yes.'

'We both know that's not true, don't we, Jasmine? Otherwise you wouldn't have stolen from me.'

'I had no choice.'

His jaw tightened. 'You had a choice. You made the wrong one.'

After a moment, she nodded. 'Yes, maybe you're right.'

Her answer silenced him for several moments, his speculative gaze on her face. 'And how many times have you made the wrong choice in the past?'

'My past is none of your business.' And not a place she chose to willingly visit. The stigma of being judged was one she'd learned from when her college boyfriend had treated her like a pariah when she'd confessed her past. 'I'm more concerned about the future. If you're going to hand me over to the authorities, I'd prefer it to be sooner rather than later.'

His face slowly hardened into the mask she detested, but had unfortunately become very familiar with. 'Don't push me, Jasmine. If you didn't steal from me for yourself, tell me who you did it for.'

Her heart lurched. 'I can't. Punish me, if you need to, but leave anyone else out of it.'

'Why?'

'Because the person I did it for is important to me.'

'How important?' he flung back.

'He…saved me. He didn't have to, but he did. I'm sorry, Re—Your Highness, but I won't let him pay for my mistakes.'

'So this person saved you, but decided it was okay to set you back on a destructive path to suit his purposes?'

'No, it wasn't like that.'

His hand slammed down. 'That was exactly what it was, Jasmine. To trap me so you could steal from me. From my people. To throw years of hard work into utter chaos and endanger the livelihood of millions, all for the sake of one person.'

'Yes, I know it seems irrational but that's what happened. Believe me, I'll do anything to make things right.'

He relaxed in his seat with the grace of a born predator, his long, rangy frame seeming to go on for ever. His smile held no mirth, only cynicism. 'How bravely you embrace your sins. It's almost admirable.'

She set her fork down. 'Stop toying with me and just get this over and done with.'

His smile widened, his teeth stark against the darkness of his beard. For some reason, the sight made her belly flip over. Whether it was from fear or another emotion, Jasmine didn't want to examine too closely.

'You're not in a position to dictate terms to me, Miss Nichols. Remember, you're *my* prisoner. *I* will choose the time of your trial. And the terms of your punishment. Push me and you'll like the consequences of either even less.'

Over the next four days she barely saw Reyes. She caught glimpses of him—as he paced the terrace just before the midday sun hit full blast, or as Armando took a tray into his study. Once she looked down from her window early in the morning and saw him swimming, his powerful strokes carrying him from one end of the enormous pool to the other.

Voyeuristically, she watched him, unable to look away from his magnificent, streamlined body. When he heaved himself out of the pool and scrubbed a towel through his wet hair, desire settled low and heavy in her belly.

As she lay in bed now, remembering how that body had felt up close against hers in Rio drenched her whole body in sensation. Ashamed, she flipped over, punched her frustration into a pillow and pulled the covers over herself as if her actions would block out the feelings.

But being in bed only reminded her of another bed, where their bodies had writhed, strained into each other as they'd ridden the storm of passion breaking over them.

Unnerved by the sheer depth of her riotous feelings, Jasmine threw back the covers and jumped out of bed.

Too late, she remembered that, lately, her mornings were best approached gingerly. Rushing to the bathroom, she vomited until her eyes stung.

Afterwards, clutching the sink, her fingers dug into the cold porcelain as she calculated dates and tried not to panic. She'd had her period two weeks ago, albeit a lighter than usual one.

And Reyes had used condoms in Rio. Hadn't he?

No, it was all in her head. Being cooped up in San Estrela was making her stir-crazy!

Today she was going to offer Reyes whatever input she thought would help with salvaging the treaty. Failing that, she'd ask him what he intended to do with her. This suspended limbo was sending her imagination into overdrive.

Why else would she think she could be pregnant with Reyes's baby? The very thought made her tremble.

Quickly showering, she dressed in a light blue sleeveless linen dress with a tan belt and slipped her feet into tan heels. Brushing her hair and tying it loosely at her nape, she massaged a small amount of sun protection into her skin and face and left her suite.

Carmelita, the housekeeper, was carrying a large bale of towels towards the guest suites in the west wing when Jasmine reached the top of the stairs. About to ask the whereabouts of Reyes, Jasmine paused at the sound of male voices in the hallway.

Reyes strolled into view, accompanied by four men. The first thing she noticed was that his beard was gone. A tiny, completely unprepared and shocking part of her mourned that she'd never got to experience the rasp of his facial hair against her skin.

The second thing she noticed was that all the men wore suits. And that she was the sole focus of their attention as she stood, poised, at the top of the stairs.

A block of silence passed.

Reyes turned to the men, his voice low. Without glancing her way, he led them to his study and shut the door with a firm click.

Jasmine stood rooted to the step, unable to move. She wasn't sure why she was so hurt that she'd been dismissed like a piece of trash.

What did she expect?

She was a prisoner here. Barely worth the food or accommodation she took up. Did she really expect Reyes to introduce her as his guest?

With leaden feet, she came down the stairs and went onto the terrace, where she usually breakfasted.

Carmelita brought her fresh coffee. She helped herself to a slice of toast and a plump orange, but her mind churned. When Carmelita emerged again to clear away the dishes, Jasmine's curiosity got the better of her.

'Who are those men with His Highness?' she asked casually.

The housekeeper looked uncomfortable for a moment, then she replied, 'One is the Santo Sierra *embajador* to France. Other men are from Santo Sierra.'

'How long have they been here?'

'They came late last night.' She bustled about, hurriedly gathering the used tableware.

Unwilling to question her any further, Jasmine left her in peace. Clearly, her meeting with Reyes would have to take a backseat to his meeting with his ambassador and council. But she needed something, *anything* to stop her thinking of what her past week's morning sickness meant.

Because if her suspicions were true...then...*oh, God!*

Going back to fetch her sunglasses, Jasmine came downstairs and let herself out through the solarium.

She bypassed the gardens and headed for the trees. In a distant past, she'd harboured a secret wish to be a gardener. That was before another one of her mother's liaisons had run off with her savings and they'd ended up in a tower block, where the only green in sight had been from the bile-coloured paint on the walls.

Jasmine had been only six at the time, but she'd vowed never to let her emotions blind her the way her mother did. In fact she'd killed off all her emotions...until Stephen had forced her to face them. To choose a better life than the one she'd been contemplating at seventeen.

She trailed her fingers over the expertly pruned foliage and imagined herself tending the plants and trees all year round.

Spotting a greenhouse at the end of a row of hedges, Jasmine veered towards it.

Before she could turn the handle, heavy footsteps pounded the ground behind her. In a heartbeat, Armando and two of Reyes's bodyguards had surrounded her. One bodyguard took her by the arm and marched her towards the villa.

'What are you doing? Let go of me!'

He didn't respond. Back indoors, she managed to rip herself from the guard's grasp as the door to the study flew open.

Jasmine stared at a fuming Reyes, refusing to cower under his oppressive stare.

'I thought we had an agreement.' His grey eyes flashed with barely suppressed anger.

She massaged her stinging elbow. 'The agreement still holds. I haven't run away, have I?'

'You left the house without permission.'

'To go to the garden! I'm going insane cooped up in your gilded prison. How did you know I'd left the house anyway?'

'Every time a door is opened in the house, an alarm goes off in the security suite. My men alerted me.' His gaze dropped to where she was nursing her elbow. His face grew darker. 'Why are you rubbing your elbow? Are you hurt?'

'Do you care?'

He glared at her for several seconds. Then, turning to his bodyguard, he murmured a few words.

Jasmine's heart twisted, then thundered in outrage when she saw what was being handed to Reyes.

'No! If you dare come near me with that thing, I'll—'

'You'll what? Scream? Go ahead. Give it your best shot.' He stepped closer, the handcuffs gleaming in his hands.

Memories, the worst kind of memories, crowded her mind,

pushing fear up through her belly into her chest. Her breath shortened. 'No, Reyes— No, don't. Please!'

Hyperventilating, she tried to step back. Her feet wouldn't move. The blood drained out of her head as she fought to breathe. Her head grew woozy with fog. She started to sway.

'If you insist on disobeying me, this is your only—Jasmine?'

His voice wove in and out. She blinked, fighting the light-headedness. Damn, either she really was unwell, or she was turning into a pathetic shadow of herself around this man.

Either way, it had to stop!

CHAPTER EIGHT

'JASMINE!'

Reyes caught her by the arms and watched her pull herself together. She'd gone deathly pale at the sight of the handcuffs and for a moment he'd thought she would pass out.

She continued to stare at the restraints as if they were poisonous serpents ready to strike at her.

She willingly admitted to being a criminal yet the sight of handcuffs terrified her. Surely she was used to them by now?

Puzzled, he slipped the cuffs into his back pocket and dismissed his bodyguard. Her trembling had increased and even though she tried to hide it, he caught the haunted look in her eyes.

Dios, something had happened to her.

'Jasmine.'

She didn't move. Didn't react. It was almost as if she hadn't heard him. Stepping closer, he gripped her tighter. Felt her tremble. An unwelcome emotion shifted through his chest.

'You will respond when I address you.'

Her reaction was immediate. She wrenched herself from him, almost violently. Eyes wide, she glared at him, but he was sure her consciousness was elsewhere.

'No! I won't let you use those things on me!'

'It's fine. It's okay,' he murmured, brushing her soft, silky cheek. He realised what he was doing and removed his hand, puzzled and annoyed with himself for offering comfort where he should be doling out punishment.

She stared at the hand suspended between them. Then she searched for the handcuffs before her wide, frightened eyes darted back to his face.

'Do you want to tell me what just happened?' he asked.

She sucked in a shaky breath and gathered herself with that strength of will he couldn't help but admire. 'I have no idea what you're talking about.'

A cold hand clamped around Reyes's neck. How many times had he heard his mother utter those same words? When he'd demanded to know what she was doing in the papers being photographed in the arms of a man other than his father...when Reyes had confronted her about the alcohol on her breath or the hazy look in her eyes, she'd always uttered those words.

I have no idea what you're talking about, Reyes. Don't be so fanciful, Reyes.

'So you deny that the sight of the restraints disturbed you? Then you won't mind if I use—'

She tried to snatch her hands away. 'No. Don't use it. I promise...I won't leave the villa.'

He was dying to know what had happened to her. But not so badly that he wanted to be lied to. He might have tried to fool himself into believing that it didn't matter, but Jasmine's untruths somehow managed to get under his skin. Sting that little harder.

'Your promises are worthless to me—surely you know that by now? So I'm afraid you'll have to do more than that.'

She swallowed. 'What do you mean?'

Reyes stepped back and indicated the door to his study. 'You'll stay where I can keep an eye on you.'

'So I guess a request for a trip into town is out of the question?'

Reyes let his cool stare speak for him.

She rolled her eyes before her gaze dropped to his pockets, where the cuffs were hidden out of sight. 'Fine. I'll go and find a book to read.'

For some reason, Reyes couldn't suppress a smile as she firmed her lips and sent him a glance of pure loathing.

He stopped her as she stepped past him. 'Wait.'

Surprised, she looked up. Then frowned. 'What now?'

Reyes grasped her elbow and examined where she'd rubbed

it before. Faint marks marred her skin. A touch of fury flared within him. He would be having words with his bodyguard later. 'You didn't tell me whether you were hurt or not?' he repeated his earlier question. *Why was that so important to him?* He stemmed the mocking voice and waited for her answer.

'It's nothing I haven't endured before.' As if realising her slip, she bit her lip.

The memory of doing the same to those lips, and much more, slammed into him. His groin stirred to life. Smashing it down, he concentrated on her words.

'You've been manhandled before?' The very thought made something tug hard in his chest.

'Not without fighting back, I can assure you.' The blaze of defiance and determination flared higher in her eyes.

He wasn't reassured. Intrigued, he stared at her for a long time before he could form the words. 'You will not be treated like that under my roof. Be assured of that.'

'So what do you call using those handcuffs tucked away in your pocket? An early Christmas present?'

His mouth twisted. 'Perhaps I should rephrase that. No one but I will be allowed to touch you while you're under my roof.'

'Well, that makes me feel heaps better.' Despite the bravado in her voice, a dart of apprehension crossed her eyes.

About to reassure her again that she would come to no harm, he stopped himself. Reminded himself of what this woman had done. To him. To his country.

Right at this moment, he had members of Santo Sierra's council in his study, trying to find a way out of their current predicament. So far they seemed to be agreed on only one course of action. One that Reyes was determined not to give in to.

Meanwhile, here he was trying to placate the woman responsible for causing the turbulence in his kingdom.

Twisting on his heel, he barked, 'Come.'

'You want me at your meeting?'

'I want you where I can keep an eye on you.'

He heard her footsteps behind him as he entered his study. Two of his advisors gaped at his guest. The third, most senior of them, frowned as Reyes shut the door and directed Jasmine into the seat in the corner of the room.

His senior advisor shifted in his seat. 'Your Highness, what we're discussing is highly confidential. I hardly think it appropriate to have a stranger—'

'Miss Nichols is here as my guest. She won't divulge anything we say in this room.' He looked at her. She read the clear warning and nodded.

He sat down but not before his gaze caught her bare legs as she crossed them. Again heat lanced his groin. Those legs had curled around his waist, urged him on as he'd thrust inside her.

Inside her duplicitous body...

He cleared his throat and shifted in his seat. 'You said you know how many people were thinking of backing the new treaty?' he addressed his senior advisor.

Costanzo Alvarez nodded. 'It is currently seven to nine, Your Highness. With each day that passes, the older members are being swayed to the idea of the original treaty your father agreed to sign.'

Reyes's hackles rose. 'Those terms are no longer on the table. The new treaty will create at least another five thousand jobs.'

Alvarez shook his head. 'Mendez won't sign the new treaty, and Santo Sierra needs economic stability sooner rather than later. Any delay in providing that stability is a delay we can't afford.'

His second advisor leaned forward. 'As Costanzo said, stability is what will steer the people into calmer waters. I think Santo Sierrans are more afraid than anything else of what the future holds—'

'Make your point,' Reyes cut across him.

'Should you marry and produce an heir quickly, it'll restore the people's faith in—'

'Are you seriously suggesting that the only way to please

the people is to marry? I'm supposed to be garnering economic support for Santo Sierra, not hunting Europe for a bride.'

'Santo Sierra has always thrived in direct proportion to how well its monarchy is thriving. With your father's health in rapid decline, the people are worried about their future, yes, but they're also worried about you.'

Reyes frowned. 'So I'm to conjure up a bride out of thin air, marry her and produce an heir instead of pursuing our economic growth?'

Alvarez tented his fingers. 'No reason why you can't do both. But we suggest you do it more…visibly. You've always been a private person, Your Highness. Even when you're in Santo Sierra you're hardly seen. Besides the council, most people believe you've been at the King's bedside for the past few weeks. Only a handful of people know differently.'

Reyes shook his head. 'Even if I agree to this plan, even if I calm my people for a while, we still need to bring Mendez to the table to sign another treaty.'

He heard a muffled sound and glanced at Jasmine. Her eyes met his and he read the bleak apology in them.

He wanted to believe her. Wanted to believe she was anywhere near sorry for the wrongs she'd done. But he'd let himself be fooled in the past. Let his guard down enough to believe his mother's lies.

Each time, she'd stabbed him with savage lies and callous indifference. She'd done the same to his father. Reyes and his sister had watched their father, the King of Santo Sierra, wither with each deception, each act of adultery.

And yet, if Jasmine was to believed, she'd done it not for personal gain, but to save someone she cared about. She'd sacrificed her safety, her reputation for the sake of another…

The curious tug at his chest made him tense. There was no redemption in what Jasmine had done. He was a fool to look for any.

* * *

Jasmine bit her lip as Reyes turned away. His whole body bristled in rejection of her silent apology.

She looked down at the file she'd picked up as the men talked. She refused to acknowledge that dart of discomfort that had lodged itself in her heart when the idea of Reyes marrying had been brought up.

It had nothing to do with her. She had no claim on him. She never would. She was only in this room because Reyes didn't trust her to wander his house without making a run for it.

Once he'd decided what her punishment was to be, she would serve it and be done. The fate of his country was his to deal with as he saw fit.

And yet…

Reyes…married to a princess befitting his station. An equal who would complement his heritage, who would have his babies and be gifted the privilege of waking up next to him for the rest of her life.

Her throat tightened. This time the bile that rose had nothing to do with nausea and everything to do with blind, raging jealousy.

Gripping the file, she forced herself to read the copy of the trade treaty that she'd handed to Joaquin.

Each kingdom had agreed to supply resources to one another. On execution, the two kingdoms would have combined power equivalent to the United Arab Emirates' control of the world's oil and steel. Despite Santo Sierra being the smaller kingdom, it held the richer resource. No wonder Mendez had his greedy eyes set on it.

Jasmine finished reading and closed the file.

This was what she'd wrecked.

The trade agreement would have created thousands of jobs, made countless lives better. She'd jeopardised all those lives to save one.

Caught between the fresh vice of guilt and the loyalty that

wouldn't be snuffed out, she wrapped her arms around herself. Then, unable to sit still, she jumped up.

'Let me help. Please…'

Four sets of eyes slashed to her. Condemnation. Bitterness. Curiosity. Contemptuous dismissal. All expressions she'd seen before displayed through varied gazes when she was growing up.

Seeing most of those in Reyes's eyes, she felt a lance of hurt pierce her heart.

What had she expected? That he would simply forget that she was the reason he was here, now, instead of back in his kingdom?

She cleared her throat as their gazes continued to sear her. 'I've assisted in a few international brokerage deals that—'

'Excuse me, Miss…?' Costanzo Alvarez glared at her.

She bit back a retort and breathed deep. 'Jasmine Nichols,' she replied.

He gave a curt nod. He looked at the youngest advisor at the table. The man gave a subtle nod and started tapping the tablet keyboard in front of him.

'What we're dealing with here isn't a petty squabble between two fashion houses. Or a divorce settlement where you decide who gets to keep the prized goldfish. We're dealing with—'

'I know what you're dealing with,' she retorted.

'Then perhaps you should sit down and—'

'Let her speak.' A low, terse command from Reyes.

Jasmine looked at him. His eyes were narrowed, displeasure weaving through the grey depths. But he wasn't displeased enough to instruct her to be quiet, which was a small blessing. Or perhaps he was waiting for her to make a fool of herself so he could mock her some more?

She licked her lips.

His gaze followed the movement. Electricity zapped her spine as she recalled how the potency of his kisses, the expert way he'd ravaged her, made her yearn for more.

'Have you changed your mind? Or do you wish for a dictionary to find the right words?'

She snapped herself free of the mesmerising, surely overblown, memory and struggled to focus. If she managed to prove her worth, maybe redeem herself a little in this room, she could begin to right the wrong she'd done.

'The previous treaty was skewed in favour of Valderra, we all know that. And yet Mendez never went through with it.'

'He didn't go through with it because the only copy of the Santo Sierran version, which had been witnessed by the King and legalised by each member of the council, went missing. To this day we do not know what happened to it.'

Jasmine's gaze snapped to Reyes.

The clear warning in his eyes stilled any words she'd been thinking of speaking. Fighting to keep her composure, she faced the council as Alvarez continued. 'And also because he's propelled by greed, but at the moment he holds all the cards.'

Jasmine shook her head. 'He holds all the cards because you choose to hide away in the dark.'

'Excuse me?' Reyes rasped.

An icy shiver raced across her skin but she persevered.

'Why don't you just call his bluff?'

'I won't gamble my kingdom's economic future on a bluff, Jasmine. If the choice were mine to make, I'd cut him off at the knees. But I can't do that. Not yet.'

The sound of her name on his lips produced another shiver. One that stalled her breath and made her lose her train of thought.

Jasmine frowned. 'So…what's the alternative?'

Silence descended on the table. The hairs on her nape stood up and Jasmine had a sense of foreboding so strong, she stumbled back and sank into her chair.

Reyes locked eyes with each member of his council before linking his fingers together. Poised, regal, his profile was so captivating, she couldn't have looked away if she'd tried. But she still knew she didn't want to hear what he was about to say.

'Unless another solution is forthcoming, or a new treaty is negotiated in the next few weeks, it seems my solution is to buy time by finding myself a bride.'

CHAPTER NINE

'BUT…THERE HAS to be another way!'

Reyes stared at Jasmine. Her lips were pressed together after her outburst.

'Miss Nichols—'

Reyes held up his hand to stop his second advisor. 'Go on,' he said to Jasmine. His curiosity was getting the better of him by the minute. If what she was proposing was better than the idea of marrying a faceless stranger in order to maintain peace, he was all for it.

His one attempt to marry had left harrowing scars that he would never forget. Until his sister, Isabella, had dissolved her engagement recently, Reyes had accepted that he would rule Santo Sierra in his lifetime, then let his sister's heirs inherit the throne.

But once again, the mantle was firmly on his shoulders.

'What if we can prove that he was behind the treaty going missing?'

Reyes surged to his feet, knocking the chair over. 'Gentlemen, give me the room.'

His men continued to stare at Jasmine with varying degrees of astonishment and suspicion. He slammed his hand on the table. 'Now!'

They scrambled up and hurried out.

'What the hell do you think you're doing?'

She jumped back at his bellow. 'I'm trying to help.'

He speared a hand through his hair. 'By putting yourself in the crosshairs of a dangerous man?' he demanded.

'But this is your council…'

'Some of whom are set in their ways and don't welcome

the sort of changes I hope to implement when I ascend to the throne.'

She frowned. 'And you think if they know...?' She stopped and gulped.

'Until I know who I can trust, I'm not prepared to take that risk with your life.' The knowledge that she'd almost given herself away greatly agitated him. He paced in front of her, trying to decipher why protecting her meant so much to him.

From the corner of his eye, he watched her reach out.

'Reyes—'

'No, don't defy me on this, Jasmine. I won't change my mind. I can't have another destroyed life on my conscience.' The words tumbled out.

They both froze. He saw the shock rocking through him reflected on her face.

'What...what do you mean?' Her voice was whisper-thin, puzzled.

He chopped off her question with a flick of his hand. 'It doesn't matter.' He took a deep breath to regain the balance he seemed to lose so easily around her. 'I'm calling the council back. You'll refrain from mentioning what happened in Rio. Am I clear?'

For the first time since he'd known her, she nodded readily.

He strode to the door, shock still rocking his system. His men came back. They tossed ideas around half-heartedly, until he clenched his fist.

'Gentlemen, we need to discuss the subject of my bride.'

Jasmine made a rough noise of disagreement. He ignored her. Looking at her would remind him of what he'd let slip. Remind him how easily she got under his skin.

'Well, in a way your current trade visits are a good way of introducing any prospective brides to the people. But...' Alvarez cleared his throat '...you need to be a little less closed off, Your Highness.'

'Excuse me?'

'I think any further visits should be less clandestine. The

people need to see their prince embracing life a little. Remind them that you're flesh and blood, and not a fairy-tale figure locked away in an ivory tower.'

Reyes pinched the bridge of his nose. 'Are you saying my discretion is a flaw?'

'I'm saying the people don't really know you. You brought Santo Sierra right up to the treaty table after your father fell ill, but the fact remains that the finish line was never crossed. And Santo Sierrans aren't quite sure how to take that. You don't want to estrange yourself from the people.'

Fury bubbled beneath his skin. Beside him, Jasmine's tension slammed into him. Her face was clouded with a mixture of displeasure and misery. When her eyes met his, he glimpsed regret in them.

'So you're saying whatever I do, the people won't be satisfied until they have me pressing the flesh, kissing babies with a promise of a royal wedding and an heir to swoon over?' Reyes couldn't suppress his sneer. The thought of putting himself out there, to be prodded and gawped over by the media, turned his stomach.

Alvarez knew Reyes's personal history and how he felt about the media. But his councillor nodded warily. 'That would be one way to reassure the people, yes.'

Gathering his fraying control, he turned back to his men. 'And there's no chance of presenting them with a royal wedding via Isabella?' He tried for one last ounce of a reprieve. 'Perhaps we can still rescue the situation with her ex-betrothed if we move fast enough…'

He stopped when Costanzo shook his head. 'Her fiancé declared he didn't want anything to do with Her Highness any longer after she broke things off. We had to pay his family reparations for the cancelled engagement. They won't reconsider Her Highness as a suitor.'

Dios! He looked at Jasmine, his blood boiling.

That look was still on her face—worry, regret. He looked

past that. To the luscious mouth that was parted slightly as her chest rose and fell in shallow breaths.

He wanted to forget that she was responsible for all this. Forget that the more he spoke to her, the more he doubted that her character was as black as he'd first thought. Reyes just wanted to forget. And in that moment, he wanted to use the most elemental way possible to achieve oblivion.

Her.

That stirring grew until his whole body thrummed with a carnal demand he couldn't deny.

What was wrong with him?

His youngest advisor cleared his throat. 'If Your Highness prefers, we can pursue this as a short-term union. Only until the economic situation in the kingdom stabilises.' He tapped a few keys on his tablet.

Reyes drummed his fingers on the table as he waited.

Finally, the advisor looked up. 'And I think Miss Nichols may be right. She's suitably placed to help.'

'She hasn't brought up any new solutions to Santo Sierra's problems that we haven't already considered.'

'No, but she could be the right person to broker a temporary marriage for you.'

'Excuse me?'

Reyes's eyes narrowed at her outraged tone.

His advisor glanced at her, then back at his tablet. 'According to the information I have here, you brokered the marriage between a US senator and his mistress once you arranged a discreet divorce from his wife of thirty years.'

Jasmine's mouth dropped open. 'That's supposed to be confidential.'

A douse of cold water cooled Reyes's raging temperature. 'Seems there's no end to your dubious talent,' he murmured.

Her face flushed. 'I wasn't responsible for him leaving his wife, nor was I responsible for finding the mistress, if that's what you're implying. I only assisted with the financial arrangements and ensured each party walked away happy.'

Her gaze swung to the men at the end of the table. How was it possible that one look from her commanded their silence? Reyes watched, intrigued, as she crossed her arms and narrowed her eyes for emphasis.

'That's not what you're asking me to do, surely? For what you need for Re...His Highness, you require an elite professional matchmaker. That's not what I specialise in. When I said I'd help I meant with the *economic* issues facing the kingdom.'

'This is an issue facing the kingdom. And one that has to be addressed sooner rather than later. With Isabella's marriage off the table, we need to give the people something to sustain their faith,' Alvarez said.

Pressure built at Reyes's temple. He wanted to deny what his council were saying. But deep down he couldn't dismiss that his people needed a healthy dose of bolstering news. Reyes had dashed their hopes of a royal wedding once before, five years ago, when he'd thrown Anaïs out of his life.

With his mother's subsequent death four years ago behind the wheel of her lover's car, and his father's illness soon afterwards, the only good news the Santo Sierran people had been given was the signing of the treaty and Isabella's wedding.

Both had failed to materialise. In the meantime, Mendez was pushing his greedy fingers into Santo Sierran affairs. It needed to end.

But marriage...

The only template he'd witnessed had been one mired in deception, misery and acrimony. It wasn't something he wanted to reproduce. If he was to take this road, it needed to be permanent. With both sides clear in their role and with no room for misunderstanding.

He looked down the table. Clenching his jaw, he nodded. 'The marriage will be a permanent one, not a short-term try-it-and-see-what-happens. My life isn't a scripted reality show to peddle to the people.'

Costanzo beamed with pleasure. 'Of course, Your Highness. That's a very wise decision. We'll set the ball rolling straight away—'

Reyes held up his hand. 'No, we'll reconvene in three days.'

The smile turned into a frown. 'But, Your Highness—'

'Arrange for the royal press secretary to include an addendum to my Paris itinerary. They can sell it as an investment-stroke-leisure trip.' He turned to Jasmine, noting that she'd gone pale again. 'Miss Nichols will be responsible for finding me five suitable candidates. Fly them to Paris for interviews after my investment meetings.'

'You're going ahead with it?' Her face was deliberately blank, but her eyes were pools of shock.

Somehow that bothered him. He shook himself out of the curious feeling. 'For my people's sake, yes.'

She drew in a shaky breath and looked down at her linked hands.

He surged to his feet, not liking the feeling that he'd been judged and found guilty. Nor did he like the sensation of a noose closing around his neck.

'Three days, gentlemen.'

'Yes, Your Highness.

In that moment, Reyes hated his title. Hated the responsibility weighing down on his shoulders. But despite the mixed emotions, there was one solemn vow he couldn't deny. He owed his people a better life than they'd enjoyed so far. And he intended to do whatever it took to make right his mistakes.

'You know you could've been done with me much quicker if you'd told them.' Questions had been swirling in her mind since Reyes's councilmen had left hours ago. But the one she'd wanted to ask wouldn't form, so she was trying a different route.

Reyes turned from the view to stare at her. 'Told them what?'

'What my role was in…'

'The treaty's disappearance?'

Jasmine jerked her head, still surprised he'd joined her for dinner and even more so that he'd stayed after they'd shared a delicious Spanish tapas meal on the terrace. Although the meal had gone by in near total silence, she couldn't help but feel a little less apprehensive of her fate.

She cradled the as yet untouched glass of red wine in her hands, watching the sun set on the horizon. Trying not to stare at Reyes Navarre's stunning profile as he leaned against the large pillar, facing the garden.

'Because if I had you'd be on your way to a maximum security prison in Santo Sierra. Your crime would be condemned as treason in my kingdom.'

Her heart stopped and her palms grew clammy. 'Aren't I headed there anyway? Something about getting a permanent tan?'

'Perhaps. But you might want to do something about delaying your arrival there. Before I came to Rio, I was in the process of enforcing a law that prohibited male and female prisoners being housed in the same penitentiary. That law hasn't passed yet.'

She inhaled sharply. 'You mean men and women are kept in the same prison?'

He shrugged. 'The old council deemed all criminals to be worthless regardless of their gender.'

Ice cascaded down her spine. 'But…that's barbaric!'

'They didn't care that they were potentially turning criminals who could be rehabilitated into irredeemable monsters. So do you regret my silence on your behalf?'

She slowly shook her head. 'No, I don't.' Her eyes met his. Whatever he saw in hers made him lift an eyebrow. Jasmine looked away quickly. 'I… Thank you.'

His mouth compressed. 'I neither want nor accept your gratitude. Retribution is still coming your way, one way or the other.'

The warning sent further chills dancing over her skin. While a part of her wanted him to spell out her fate and get her punishment over and done with, another part of her wanted to plead with him for mercy. She'd wronged him. Wronged his country. And he'd still saved her, albeit temporarily, from whatever the consequences were for her acts.

Reminding herself that this was the man who was contemplating marrying to please his people, she took a fortifying breath.

'My stepfather was kidnapped.'

His head whipped towards her. 'Excuse me?'

'First he was blackmailed through me, then kidnapped. He has...or had a gambling problem. He's been battling with it for almost twenty years. He embezzled government funds. And I'm not talking pennies. It was serious money. Getting caught would've meant a long prison sentence for him. So he borrowed money from a loan shark.'

'Who then turned the tables on him and demanded even more?'

She nodded. 'He said unless I brought him the treaty, he would harm my stepfather.'

Chilled grey eyes narrowed. 'Who was the loan shark?'

'His name was Joaquin Esteban. I don't know whether that's his real name or not—'

'Don't worry, I'll find him. So he took your stepfather?' he asked.

She nodded. 'In the middle of the night, right in front of my mother. They roughed him up. Broke his arm.' She shivered and he straightened from the wall.

'Did they hurt you?' His was voice was grave, intense.

'No. It happened when I was...with you, on your boat.'

His eyes narrowed. 'I don't recall you receiving a call.'

'You were asleep. My mother called. She was beside herself. I didn't want to do it, Reyes, please believe me, but I couldn't leave him in the hands of those men.'

If she'd expected sympathy, she was to be sorely disappointed. But for a heartbeat, his expression altered. Softened a touch.

'So where is this moralistic gambler of a stepfather, then? Still in his comfy government position?'

Irritation snapped along her nerves. 'Yes. But he's seeking help.'

'How noble of him.'

'He doesn't know what I did. He suspects but I don't want him to know. He'll be devastated. We can't all be perfect role models. Some of us try to put unfortunate deeds behind us and seek better lives.'

'And some of you fail miserably at it.'

Turning sideways, she set her glass down on the table. 'You have a right to condemn me. Believe me, I've condemned myself countless times. But I wanted you to understand why I did what I did. Obviously I was wasting my breath.'

Reyes twirled his wine glass, one broad shoulder still leaning against the white pillar. Dressed in a white shirt and casual trousers, he looked sinfully breathtaking. Until she glimpsed the shadows in his eyes.

Her heart lurched as his words once again swirled in her mind. *I can't have another destroyed life on my conscience.*

Her eyes rose back to his face. He was watching her with that incisive look that seemed to see right into her soul. He took a slow sip, savouring the wine before swallowing.

'Contain your righteous indignation. You'll have to fall on your sword a hell of a lot more times before you breach the surface of my mercy. But I have a few minutes to spare, so please…carry on.'

She sighed. 'I'm sorry. I never intended for you to…for anyone to suffer for what I did.' Her gaze dropped to his midriff. His mouth tightened. 'If you could find it in your heart—'

His mocking laughter stopped her painful pleas. 'My *heart*?'

She gripped the edge of the table. 'I don't see the funny side to what I just said.'

'My heart is the last organ you should be attempting to appease.'

'I don't… I'm afraid you've lost me.'

His smile held that hint of sadness she'd glimpsed at their first meeting in Rio. 'You'd be wasting your time trying to appeal to something that doesn't exist.'

CHAPTER TEN

JASMINE STARED AT HIM, trying to work out if he was mocking her or not. He wasn't. That bleak look was deepening and his breathing was growing shallow and choppy as if he was caught in a distressing memory.

Before she could stop herself, she reached out and touched his arm.

He flinched. Brows clamped together, he stared down at her. 'What are you doing?'

'You seem a little...lost.'

One corner of his mouth lifted. 'And you thought you'd rescue me?' he bit out.

'Yes. Obviously, I was wrong to do so.' She turned away, unable to stomach the wildly volatile moods she experienced around this man. One minute she wanted to hurt him for his mockery, the next she wanted to ease whatever emotional pain haunted him.

And it was clear he was suffering. As for his reference to his non-existent heart, the lengths he was willing to go to for his people proved otherwise.

'You were talking about your stepfather?'

She frowned. 'I'm not sure that I want to any more.'

'Because I'm not whimpering with sympathy?'

'Because you pretend you're devoid of empathy, but I know that's not true.'

'Your dubious powers of deduction at work again?'

She perched on the edge of the table and folded her arms before the temptation to touch him spiralled out of control. Far from being cold as he tried to portray, Reyes was warm, passionate.

Any woman would be lucky to have him as her husband...

Her thoughts screeched to a halt. The stone that had lodged itself in her belly since his announcement in his study grew larger.

Which was ludicrous. All they'd shared was a one-night stand. An incredible one for her, but a brief, meaningless one nonetheless.

She had no right to experience this ongoing bewildering pain in her heart when she thought of what he planned to do. And the idea that he wasn't looking to marry for the short term, but for ever, shouldn't make her world darken with despair.

She had no claim on Reyes...

Jasmine started when he lifted his glass and abruptly drained his wine. She jerked upright when he lifted an imperious hand and summoned a guard, who'd been somewhere tucked out of her sight.

'What are you doing?'

'Since you're unwilling to carry on even the semblance of conversation, I'm having you escorted to your suite. We'll meet at noon tomorrow and you'll present me with a list of suitable candidates.'

Her fingers curled around the edge of the table at the thought of the task she'd been set. She wanted to refuse; wanted to tell him she'd rather rot in jail than help him find the next woman to warm his bed.

But how could she go back on her word to do whatever was needed to right her wrong?

One of his bodyguards approached. He wasn't the one who'd accosted her in the gardens this morning. In fact, from being a constant shadow, that other guard seemed to have disappeared.

This guard nodded at whatever Reyes was saying to him.

'Wait!'

Reyes lifted a bored brow at her.

'It's still early.' At his continued indolent look, she pursed her lips. 'Fine, I'll talk. My stepfather is perfect in every sense, except when it comes to his gambling.'

She looked from Reyes to the bodyguard. After several

heartbeats, Reyes dismissed the guard with a sharp nod. Walking past where she remained perched, he grabbed the half-finished bottle of wine, frowned at her untouched glass and refilled his own. He sat down, crossing his legs, so his thighs were dangerously close to her knee.

Jasmine pulled stronger on her runaway composure. 'He's a kind, gentle man and he cares deeply for my mother.'

A look passed through his eyes, but was gone before she could work out what it meant.

'Where does your biological father fit into this scenario?'

His voice lacked mockery, a fact for which she was thankful. 'He left when I was barely out of nappies. And he was the first in a long line of "fathers",' she quoted, 'who came and went before I was a teenager.'

Reyes sipped his wine. Said nothing.

'I know what you're thinking,' she ventured when the silence stretched.

His eyes gleamed. 'I sincerely doubt that.'

She shrugged. 'Well, whether you're thinking it or not, my past shaped me. I was angry with the world and with a mother who couldn't see how hopeless the men she dated were. By the time my stepfather came along, I was…in a bad way.'

'How bad?'

Jasmine didn't want to tell him. Didn't want to see the contempt in his eyes, or relive the bleakest point in her life. She'd been there, done that, and wore the shame underneath her skin and physical scars on her body.

She didn't want to go there, but Reyes's steady gaze demanded an answer.

'A spell in juvenile detention when I was sixteen,' she found herself confessing.

He froze. *'Dios…'* he murmured.

Thick mortification crept over her. Struggling to cover it, she laughed. 'Now you know my deepest, darkest secret. I'm guessing you'll be holding this over my head, too—'

'Stop talking, Jasmine.'

She clamped her mouth shut. He watched her with a curious expression, his gaze intensely assessing.

'How long were you in detention?'

Strangely she couldn't read any judgement in his tone. She reminded herself that as a prince he was skilled in hiding his true emotion. But then, he hadn't held back so far—

'Answer me,' he bit out roughly.

'Nine months.'

'What for?'

She grimaced. 'I *accidentally* set fire to a drug dealer's warehouse.'

'Is that experience why you found the handcuffs distressing?'

'You mean there are people who love being handcuffed?' she threw back.

One brow spiked.

Heat stained her cheeks. 'Yes, well, I didn't like it at the time. Still don't. Those days were the most traumatic of my life. Please don't force me to relive them.'

He put his glass down and leaned forward, elbows on his knees. His intensity increased a thousandfold. As did the intoxicating scent of his aftershave and warm skin. Jasmine clenched her thighs to keep from moving closer.

'What happened after you were released?'

'My stepfather. And yes, it may sound like a fairy tale, but he saved us. And even with his flaws, he turned out to be better than any man out there, even the man whose blood runs through my veins.'

Grey eyes snagged hers. Still no condemnation in them, just a stark curiosity.

'But the gambling became a problem, obviously,' he said.

She nodded. 'He was married before, but his wife died. That's when the problem escalated for him. He stopped for a while when he and my mother were dating, but after they married he started again. No matter how much we tried, we couldn't convince him to give it up. It made me sad. I know it worried him, too, that he couldn't beat it. But I couldn't condemn him. No matter what, he was the best father I knew. When Joaquin sank his claws into him, I had no choice. I couldn't let Stephen suffer.'

'Where was your mother in all of this?' The question was framed so tersely, with a bitter underlay that grazed sharply over her senses.

She looked at him. Whatever emotion he was holding had triggered tension in his body, like a predator ready to unleash its base nature should its prey fall within his grasp. Despite her nape tingling in warning, she wanted to move closer, experience that overwhelming danger.

Clearing her throat, she answered, 'My mother is what a psychologist would term wilfully blind. She means the world to me, but doesn't see what's right in front of her. Or she chooses to ignore it in favour of burying her head in the sand.'

The misery that her mother's attitude to life had brought her before Stephen had fallen in love with her had been a stark warning for Jasmine not to travel down the same path. She understood her mother better now, but it didn't make the pain of her late teens go away.

She glanced at Reyes and saw grudging understanding. But the look was wiped clean a moment later.

'Understanding the motive doesn't negate the crime.'

The unexpected surge of tears shocked Jasmine.

What was wrong with her? He'd told her he didn't have a heart. If she chose to disbelieve him, any hurt she felt was her own fault.

Blinking rapidly, she started to rise. 'No, but a little forgiveness goes a long way.'

He clamped a hand on her thigh.

Her heart took a dive, then picked itself up and banged hard against her ribs.

Reyes questioned his sanity. Except the voice was quickly smothered beneath the headier emotions swimming in his head.

His hand was halfway down her thigh, the soft cotton of her sundress crushing beneath his fingers. He moved his hand lower.

She gasped as they connected, skin to skin. Hers was soft, smooth like the fur of his sister's pet cat. And as with Sheba's pelt, he wanted to keep on stroking her.

He watched her struggle, knew the emotions she fought were the same as the ones he battled with. The chemistry that had gripped them the first time he'd set eyes on her flared high, spiking through his blood until he didn't bother to deny its existence any longer.

'You dislike me for stating the truth?'

'I dislike the brutality of it. And the complete absence of sympathy.'

Knowing he'd done a good job of hiding his feelings should've pleased Reyes. If his feelings weren't apparent, they couldn't be manipulated, used against him. So why did the thought that he'd succeeded send a pulse of discontentment through him? Why did he want to wipe that hurt look from her face? 'I warned you not to search for feelings that don't exist—'

'And I told you I don't believe that emotion doesn't exist inside you.'

He surged to his feet. 'I've never met anyone like you,' he said, not sure whether his agitation stemmed from the Tempranillo he'd consumed or the fact that she challenged him at every turn where no else dared to.

She sucked in a breath and her eyes stayed on his. Daring. Searching. Apprehensive. 'Nor I you. So this should be fun.'

A reluctant smile tugged at his lips. *Fun...*

Another word he'd associated with her that first time. A word he hadn't let into his life for a very long time.

He started to draw back from the brink of whatever fever gripped him.

She stepped closer. Her hands slid around his waist, holding him in place.

Again her daring floored him...excited him. The women

he'd dated in his distant past had been either too overawed with his status to show much spine, or had been so eager to prove they were worthy of his time, they'd overreached. Either way, he'd tended to lose interest long before they were done in the bedroom.

Jasmine Nichols made his senses jump without uttering a word. And when she did speak, he found himself held rapt.

In the last hour, the woman she'd revealed herself to be intrigued him even more. She'd experienced adversity of the worst kind, and come through it.

And with her hand on him and her parted lips so close, all he could see, smell, *anticipate*, was her.

Drawn into a web he couldn't shake, he angled his head. 'I don't do fun, Jasmine.'

Her back arched, bringing her closer. Her mouth brushed his. He jerked at the zap of electricity. Her hands tightened around him. 'Sure you do. You just don't like to admit it.'

The sound that rumbled from inside him emerged harsh and bewildered. *'Dios...'*

He spiked his hand through her hair and kissed her. Hard. Roughly.

He palmed her breasts, gloried in their fullness, and swallowed her jagged gasp of pleasure when his thumb grazed her nipple. The sight and taste of them flashed through his mind. He squeezed the bud. Harder. She made a rougher sound. More demanding. More receptive.

His blood thrummed faster.

Capturing her waist, he pulled her into his body. Her hands drifted up from his torso, up to his shoulders. Every nerve yearned for closer contact. The ultimate contact.

He was fast reaching the point where he would be unable to deny the need to take, the need to reprise the headiness of their encounter in Rio.

Her mouth parted wider, her tongue caressing his. Reyes drove in, tasting her with deep, hungry kisses that robbed them both of breath.

His erection throbbed. Demanded satisfaction.

Dios, this was crazy. Making the same mistake twice was unconscionable. He needed to pull back.

But he couldn't. His thumb angled her jaw and he claimed another kiss. He didn't realise he'd bent her backwards until her elbows propped on the table to support herself.

Needing to breathe, he took a beat. Looked at her, spread before him like a banquet.

A tempting, *forbidden* banquet. He'd given in once and the resulting chaos still echoed through his life. Perhaps he understood her motivations a little now. Perhaps he would even contemplate forgiveness at some distant point in the future.

But he couldn't revisit the eye of the storm.

Sucking in a deep breath, he stepped back, smashing down on his body's insistence that he finish what he'd started.

He denied his body, denied his mind. It would've been easy to take what he wanted; what he craved. But he knew it would come at a price. A price he couldn't afford to pay.

CHAPTER ELEVEN

'So, just so we're clear, you want me to enquire whether she's a good kisser, or should I go the whole hog and ask her if she's dynamite in bed, too?' Jasmine folded her arms and drummed her fingers against her elbows.

She knew her foul mood stemmed from the tossing and turning she'd done last night. And her triple vomiting session this morning. She knew *why* she'd tossed and turned. Just as she feared her suspicions on why she was throwing up would be confirmed, as soon as she found a way to visit a chemist. She wasn't afraid to admit she was terrified of what the results of a pregnancy test would show. And not just for herself. She'd already thrown Reyes's world into chaos once. How would he react *if* it turned out she was carrying his child?

She'd debated through the night whether to tell him of her suspicions, and had elected to wait. There was no point stirring the hornet's nest even harder until she had concrete proof.

Feeling weak and more than a little apprehensive of what fate held in store for her, she'd have given her right arm not to perform the task of finding Reyes Navarre a bride.

He leaned back in his chair, his gaze coolly assessing. 'The latter qualities I will discover for myself long before our wedding night. Once you've tackled the more important characteristics of loyalty, trust and dependability, of course.'

'I'd never consider anyone who didn't possess those qualities. But how on earth am I supposed to know whether she's a good kisser or not?'

His eyebrow quirked and she had a feeling he was toying with her. 'Aren't you supposed to be good at your job?'

'Brokering deals and calming anxious parties before multinational mergers, yes. Judging whether a woman is a good kisser based on her pedigree, not so much.'

'So you're admitting failure before you've even started?' he asked.

She looked away, afraid he'd see the depth of the anguish she couldn't will away, no matter how much she tried. 'I'm not afraid to admit I'm not the right person for this job. We slept together, Reyes—' she saw him tense, but she forced herself to continue '—and despite everything that happened afterwards, it wasn't a casual thing for me. I can't just brush it off...' She stopped before she dug herself into a hole she'd never be able to emerge from.

'Are you saying you can't stay objective in this task?'

She forced herself to meet his gaze. 'I'm saying I have feelings. I'll do it if you want me to but I don't have to like it.'

A look crossed his face, but his expression shuttered before she could read it. 'Understood.'

Jasmine forced herself to glance down at the shortlist she'd compiled at four a.m. when she'd finally conceded sleep was a pipe dream. She rattled off the names, watching his face for a reaction. His features remained blank.

'I'm going to call their representatives. Arrange for us to meet them in Paris next week. Shall I arrange to send your private jet for them or do you want them to fly commercial?'

'I don't micromanage. Liaise with my head of security on modes of transport. And we're not flying to Paris next week. We're leaving tomorrow, and then on to Santo Sierra at the end of the week.' He slid his chair closer to his desk and opened a file.

'What?' Her heart thumped harder with a mixture of desolation and anxiety. 'I'm good at my job, but I can't find you a bride in twenty-four hours, *Your Highness*.' Pressure built in her head with the knowledge that she needed to find out once and for all whether she carried his child.

'Have you seen the news today?' he enquired.

'No. Should I have?'

His fists tightened on the desk for a moment before he relaxed. 'There was a riot in San Domenica last night.'

'Santo Sierra's capital?'

He nodded. 'Several people were hurt, including women and children, in the main square. Thankfully, no one was killed. My people are growing restless. Their anxiety is being fuelled, no doubt by Mendez's people. I have to return soon or things will get worse.'

The throb of worry in his voice was unmistakeable. For the first time she accepted that his councillors were right. Santo Sierra needed a good news story to bolster the people's confidence in its monarchy.

Caught in the quandary of having her feelings ravaged in the process of finding Reyes a wife, while suspecting she was carrying his child, and doing what she could to fix the damage she'd caused, Jasmine took a deep breath and gathered her composure.

'I'll make sure the candidates are in Paris for when we arrive.' She picked up her tablet and headed for the door.

'Jasmine?'

Her heart stuttered at the use of her first name.

'Yes?' Her answer emerged shakier than she would've wished.

'Cross Petra Nikolova off your list. We dated briefly once. She's been known to take certain banned substances on occasion. The last thing I intend to foist on my subjects is a drug-dabbling queen. And you can also delete Sienna Hamilton.'

Every single good intention fled out of her head. Her anxiety ramped up, along with a buzzing in her head and a sick feeling in her stomach she shockingly diagnosed as writhing jealousy. Coupled with the suspected extra hormones raging through her body, Jasmine had to lock her knees and count to ten before she could speak.

'What's wrong with Miss Hamilton?' Her voice trembled in a way she detested.

When his eyes locked on hers, his expression was far from mocking. 'She's a serial cheater. She's discreet about it, but I prefer not to wonder in who else's bed my wife has been when I return home at night.'

She stared at him, dying to ask why pain clouded his eyes when he talked about adultery. But, unwilling to drive the knife that seemed to be wedged in her chest further, she wiped the question from her mind. Realising she hadn't taken a breath since Reyes mentioned kissing other women, Jasmine forced herself to breathe.

'You realise that leaves me with just three candidates?' she said around the knot in her throat. It was three more than she wanted to deal with, but she couldn't see any way around this harrowing task.

He cracked a hard, sad smile. 'Then you need to make doubly sure they are right for the job.' His tone said she was dismissed.

Which was good because Jasmine couldn't get out of there fast enough. Except she couldn't leave just yet.

Reyes raised his head when she retraced her steps to his desk. 'Can I help you with something else?'

'I need to go into town this morning.'

He frowned. 'Why?'

Because I need to know whether my life is about to change for ever.

'I need stuff.'

He looked down his nose at her. Waited.

A blush warmed her cheeks. 'Women's stuff.'

Her tiny hope for him to feel a little bit of her embarrassment died a quick death when he returned his attention to his papers.

'Reyes? Can I get one of your men to drive me into town?'

'No,' he replied.

'Come on—'

'I'll drive you myself. We'll go after lunch.'

No, no, no!

* * *

Entering the solarium, she sank into the nearest lounger, clenched her fingers around the tablet to stop them shaking.

She tried to reason with herself. The likelihood that a crown prince would be caught shopping for feminine products in a chemist was very minimal.

But then so had the likelihood of her ending up in his bed in Rio. The odds that she could be pregnant with Reyes's child were one in a million, but she knew to her cost that fate was vested in singling her out for her parlour tricks.

She could be worrying over nothing. The tenderness in her breasts could be the result of her imagination. Or the residual effect of Reyes caressing them last night...

She forced herself to look at the list of candidates she needed to contact...and flung the tablet away. Covering her face with her hands, she caught a low moan before it escaped.

What was wrong with her? One night of sex and one heavy-kissing session with Reyes Navarre and she couldn't handle the idea of him with another woman? No, she couldn't deny that her feelings were more to do with the fact that she might be carrying his baby. And the growing sense that she couldn't stand the thought of him being married to someone else whether his child was growing inside her or not.

Would Reyes go ahead with marrying someone else if she was carrying his child, or would he consider another option? Like her...

Hope rose up inside her. She pushed it away.

She was going crazy...

He would never consider her in a million years. Her heart lurched. Shaking her head, she focused on the names.

One young duchess. One daughter of a media mogul. One self-made millionaire with an extensive philanthropic background.

On paper any one of the remaining three could be crown princess material and would no doubt do whatever it took to secure the attention, if not the heart, of a man like Reyes Navarre.

So get a move on...

The quicker she got this over with, the quicker she could return to her life. Forget all about Reyes and the feel of his mouth on hers, his strong arms around her.

By the time Reyes strode into the solarium, Jasmine had secured the enthusiastic agreement of all three and had arranged for their travel to Paris.

'Something's come up. I can't take you into town. Make a list of what you need. I'll have Carmelita get them for you.'

Her stomach lurched in a queasy roll. Having Reyes find out what she suspected before she knew for sure was out of the question. 'Umm…I'd rather get them myself. If you're busy, it can wait till we get to Paris.'

He frowned, but nodded and walked away.

Jasmine wasn't proud of taking the coward's way out, buying herself some more time before she had to face whatever fate had in store for her. So when the tears stung her eyes, she raced up the stairs to her room and let them fall.

'You'll be dining with the duchess at the Paris Ultime this evening at eight. I've reserved a private dining room for you and once you review the menu I can provide it to the private chef who'll be catering for you. The duchess is allergic to shellfish. Oh, and she doesn't eat carbs after six, so she requests that a bread basket not be served. She can't resist the temptation, apparently.' Jasmine made her voice crisp, businesslike, so the pain of the vice tightening around her heart wouldn't bleed through her voice.

Reyes raised an eyebrow at her as their limo left the private airport and drove towards the French capital.

'You think it's a good sign that the woman who's to bring hope to my people can't resist a simple bread basket?'

Jasmine shrugged. 'We all have our faults. If hers is a simple carbs issue, then you're all set.' She tried to keep her voice light, but the stone wedged in her belly made even thought difficult.

The last thing she wanted to discuss was the eating habits of Reyes's future queen.

'Do you resist bread baskets after six, Jasmine?'

God, why couldn't she stop her heart from flipping over each time he said her name like that? 'Nope. Bread is a vice I happily embrace.'

The moment the words were out of her mouth, she regretted it. A chill permeated the atmosphere. Reyes stared at her, tight jawed. Jasmine wondered whether to apologise, but then dismissed it. She'd apologised enough. She was here, making amends. Even if it involved doing a job every fibre of her being rejected.

After several minutes, she cleared her throat. 'Liliana Simpson will have lunch with you tomorrow, and I've scheduled Berenice Holden for an early dinner. Once you make your decision, I'll liaise with your royal press secretary about making an announcement. I've also arranged for a few photographers to take some pictures...' She stopped when his jaw clenched harder. 'What?'

'One camera, one photograph, one photographer.' His tone was acid.

'But I thought you wanted the world to see that you're alive and dating? You can't hide away for ever. You need to get in front of the people. Show them that you care about them. That you're excited to lead them. And that you're also not a eunuch.'

'Excuse me?'

She attempted a shrug that fell short of the mark. 'One photograph isn't going to do the job.'

'You forget there was a riot in my kingdom less than twenty-four hours ago. I can't be seen living it up in Paris, proving my manhood, while my people are suffering. The article will stress heavily that I'm on my way home, possibly with a potential bride in tow. The intention is to take their minds off their anxiety without making it seem like I've forgotten about them, is it not?'

'Yes, of course. I'll take care of it.'

As she made unnecessary notes in her tablet her mind raced. She could feel the waves of tension coming off his body, and knew Reyes would rather be in Santo Sierra, seeing to his people, than here in Paris vetting potential brides.

While the thought perplexingly lifted her heart, she couldn't help but be concerned for him.

'Have you thought about what you'll do about Mendez?' she asked.

His mouth compressed. Wedging his elbow on the armrest, he glanced at her. 'Once the wedding is done and I've elected a new council, I'll make him a take-it-or-leave-it offer. The time for pandering to his whim is over.'

She nodded. When he turned to look out of the window, she stared at his profile. The question she'd been avoiding hovered on the tip of her tongue.

'Can I ask you a question?' she blurted.

Grey eyes narrowed on her. 'Go ahead.'

'Why are there no pictures of you taken since your mother died?'

A chilled look entered his eyes. 'Because I don't court publicity. Not like…' He stopped and exhaled harshly.

Her heart clenched at the bleakness in his eyes. 'Like your mother? I know she liked to…that she was a media darling.'

'Less of a darling, more of a whore,' he countered mercilessly.

Jasmine flinched. 'I'm sorry.'

'Why? We finally have something in common. Mothers who would've been better off remaining childless.'

'I wouldn't go as far as that. After all, if that had happened, neither you or I would be here.'

His gaze raked her face, as if he were trying to burrow under her skin, see inside her soul again. 'And our night in Rio would never have happened,' he murmured.

Her breath stalled. 'No…I guess not.'

'Do you regret that, Jasmine?' he rasped.

'I like it when you call me Jasmine. Miss Nichols makes me sound like a kindergarten teacher.'

A low, deep laugh broke from his lips, but he continued to stare at her. Then he lifted his hand and traced a finger down her cheek. 'You haven't answered my question, Jasmine.'

'Do I regret Rio?' The truth wasn't difficult to admit. But she feared the can of worms she would be opening by admitting it, even to herself. She licked her dry bottom lip. 'The first part, not at all. It was the most memorable night of my life.'

His eyes darkened and his nostrils flared. 'And the second part?' he demanded.

'The second part...very, very much. I would do anything to take it back.'

He said nothing, but he nodded after several seconds. And she dared to hope that he believed her.

CHAPTER TWELVE

THE DINNER JACKET he wore felt tight, restrictive. And someone had turned up the temperature in the private dining room. Or had it been turned down?

Dios...

Reyes passed a finger underneath his collar and moved the food around on his plate.

'I would need to fly to Europe at least twice a month. I have a standing appointment for full works at my favourite spa in Switzerland.' Carefully styled blond hair curtained to one side as the duchess tilted her head. 'That won't be a problem, will it?'

The bread basket. Suddenly, Reyes needed it more than he needed to breathe.

'Reyes...you don't mind me calling you Reyes, do you? Or do you prefer Rey?' She smiled.

Perfect teeth. Perfect hair. Perfect manicure.

No character-forming scars on her body. As Jasmine had across her palm. Or that thin two-inch scar on her shoulder.

He growled under his breath. He was sitting opposite a beautiful, poised woman who was warm enough for his people to fall in love with. Visually, the duchess was the antithesis of his mother and Anaïs, and that alone would sway his people, who'd hated Queen Isolde Navarre, towards her.

And yet he couldn't stop thinking about the reluctant thief with the body that called to his like a siren to a sailor.

He forced himself to focus on his dinner companion. After another minute, he threw down his napkin, stood and smiled down at the duchess.

'We won't need to worry about what you'll call me. After tonight we'll most likely never meet again.'

He entered his suite twenty minutes later. It was barely nine o'clock so he knew Jasmine would still be up. He told himself he was searching for her to give her a piece of his mind about how appallingly his evening had gone.

He had a right to, after all.

When the living room proved empty, he contemplated leaving the dressing-down till morning. Going to the bar, he poured himself a cognac and walked out onto the penthouse terrace.

He heard the splash of her swimming before he rounded the corner to where the private pool was located.

Despite warning himself that he needed to stay away, he couldn't stop his feet propelling him forward until he was standing on the edge of the aqua-tiled pool, staring at her stunning figure as she swam underwater.

Her arms and legs kicked in a graceful flow, the sight of her scantily clad figure robbing him of breath and sanity. That feeling of skating on the edge of his control escalated to the point where he was in a foul mood by the time she broke the surface.

'You failed.' His snarl was deep and ruthless enough to make him inwardly grimace.

Nevertheless, he felt a measure of cheap satisfaction when she whirled to face him. 'Actually, I was winning. Twenty laps without stopping is an achievement for me.'

'I don't mean your swim. I mean you failed with the duchess.'

A single frown line marred her perfect skin. 'Okay. I guess that's why you're back early? What happened?'

Her legs continued to swirl lazily underwater as she stared up at him. Reyes's groin pounded hard as he followed the sexy movement.

When she raised her eyebrows, he dragged his gaze away, tried to find words to enumerate the duchess's faults. None came to mind. 'She lacked the qualities I need.'

Jasmine's eyes shadowed. She glanced away, then back at him. 'You did the kissing test?' An odd note in her voice made something jerk in his chest. He didn't have time to examine it because she kicked away from the edge. Her breasts bounced, and he nearly swallowed his tongue as flames spiked into his groin.

'I didn't need to. I knew she would fail.'

'Wow, you're psychic now?' Her tone had returned to normal. She swam towards the steps.

He followed, mesmerised by the curve of her spine and the roundness of her behind. He watched her rise from the pool and pluck a towel from the chair. His fingers tightened around his glass when she patted the towel over her body.

Focus! 'Perhaps you need to be reminded of my earlier statement. You *failed*.'

'You have two more candidates. Maybe you'll strike it lucky second time round. If not, three times will be the charm.'

The restlessness that prowled through him intensified. 'You'll come with me tomorrow.'

She froze and stared at him with wide, wounded eyes. 'I'd rather not, Reyes. I'm not the one marrying these women!'

He exhaled harshly. Ploughing a hand through his hair, he glared at her. 'I...need you.'

Her eyes widened further. He kicked himself for uttering words he had no business saying. 'No, you don't. I've done my bit. It's time to do yours.'

'*Dios!* Have you always been this infuriating?'

Her face fell. 'You think I'm infuriating?'

Reyes was overcome with a desire to placate her. Take that look off her face. Replace it with one of those stunning smiles that lit up his insides.

He pondered the feeling, adding extreme puzzlement to the many emotions he felt around this woman.

This woman should be in jail somewhere dark and harrowing, not enjoying the luxury of a Parisian emperor suite, wearing a sexy bikini, and swimming in his pool.

'Yes. You're infuriating. And you're also supposed to be good at your job. So far you're doing a pathetically poor attempt. Were you in my permanent employ I'd have fired you a long time ago.'

She looked down at the floor for several seconds, before she glanced back up. 'Wow, you don't hold back when you really get going, do you?'

He dragged a hand through his hair. 'I had a call on my way back. My father had a better health day today than the doctors have seen in the last six months. I missed it, Jasmine. I missed it because I'm attending dinners and vetting potential brides just so my people's faith in me can be restored. You think I should go easy on you for that?'

She'd grown paler as he spoke, and tears filled her eyes by the time he finished.

Reyes felt like a toad for upsetting her. He cursed silently when her mouth trembled.

'I wasn't going to apologise again. I think saying sorry loses its power after the first dozen times. But once again, please know that I never wished for this to happen to you, Reyes. I was protecting those I love and misjudged the consequences. But what's happening with your father is good news. You weren't there to witness it but that doesn't take away from the fact that he's better.'

About to denounce her for her unwanted optimism, he paused in surprise when she leaned in close and kissed his cheek.

His breath punched out as her alluring scent engulfed him. Too soon, she stepped back and he fought down a keen sense of loss.

Rocking back on his heels, Reyes eyed her. 'Why did you do that?' He was shocked enough for his voice to emerge flat. At every turn this woman threw him for a loop.

'You looked like you needed it. You'll be back home soon enough and in control of things. And Santo Sierra will get better with you in charge. I'm certain of it.'

She secured the towel around her, grabbed another one and

proceeded to dry her hair. He found himself transfixed, unable to take his eyes off her.

When she sat cross-legged on the lounger, Reyes fought to avert his gaze from her bare thighs. Seeing another scar on her knee, he frowned. From what he knew about her, he was aware her childhood hadn't been a bed of roses. But the physical marks caused him to wonder exactly what had happened to her.

'Did this happen to you in juvie?' he asked tersely as he sat opposite her.

She followed his gaze and shook her head. 'No. It was yet another product of my misspent youth.'

His fist clenched. 'That's not an answer, Jasmine.'

Her throat moved in a small swallow. 'I was pinned between two gangs during a turf war on the council estate where I lived. This is the result of flying glass from a shattered window.'

He forced himself to release his hold on the glass before it broke in his fist. 'Shattered glass from…?'

'Bullets.'

Icy fury washed over him. 'Your mother let you live in such a dangerous place?' His voice sounded gruff and almost alien in his ears.

'We had nowhere else to go.' No self-pity, just a statement of fact. And yet he knew that the situation must have been gruelling. Why else would she have fought to never return to a place like that again?

Overwhelmed by the protective instinct that continued to build inside him, Reyes looked at her knee. He barely resisted the urge to run his hand over the jagged scar. Just as he fought to ask whether there were more signs of her traumatic childhood on her body.

It wasn't his business. She was a transient presence in his life. He wasn't even interested in punishing her for the theft of his treaty any more. Her life had been a difficult one. She'd made choices she wasn't proud of, but she'd made those choices out of loyalty, a need to survive.

As much as he wanted to damn her for the turmoil she'd

left behind, deep down he knew that, faced with the same choice, he would choose the same path. How many times had he shielded his own father from his mother's misdeeds? Lied to protect his father's feelings? Even knowing what his mother had been doing the day she died, he'd tried to keep the truth from his father for as long as possible.

Except Reyes didn't want to let Jasmine go...not just yet.

What he wanted was to assuage the alarming, visceral need to flatten her on the nearest surface and rediscover the heady pleasures of her body.

His eyes rose to her face.

Awareness throbbed between them. Then she glanced away to the view of Paris at night.

'I was about to order room service. Do you want some food?' Her voice was husky, warm and sexy in that way that reminded him of their encounter in the darkened bedroom on his yacht.

He forced his gaze from her sensual mouth, and nodded. '*Sí*. I'm starving. Make sure you order an extra-large bread basket.'

She picked up the phone to make the call to his chef. Reyes traced the seductive line of her neck, and resisted the urge to jump into the pool to cool down his out-of-control libido.

Reyes dismissed the second candidate after a mere twenty minutes.

'What was wrong with her?' Jasmine asked, despite the heady pool of relief building inside her. Taking pains not to examine the feeling too closely, she hurried after him as he strode away from the restaurant on the Champs-Élysées.

'Your notes said she had nothing to do with her father's media business. That turned out not to be true.' He rounded on her once they were in the car and driving away. 'In case I haven't made it quite clear, I detest the media. They made my and my sister's lives a living hell when we were growing up, thanks to their insatiable interest in my mother and her infidelities.' His mouth was pinched and the lines around it deep and pale.

'I didn't know that about your mother. I'm sorry.'

He inhaled deeply and loosened the blue-striped tie he'd worn with a pristine white shirt and a dark grey suit. A muscle twitched in his jaw as he exhaled. '*Gracias*. Perhaps I did you a disservice by not giving you enough time to prepare for this.'

It was the closest he'd come to an apology for the unreasonable demands he'd made for her assignment. But even though she nodded her acceptance, Jasmine couldn't shift from his statement about his mother.

'Did your subjects know…about your mother?' she asked.

He wrenched at his top buttons and pulled his tie free. 'Yes, they knew. They thought my father weak for not divorcing her and by the time she died in her lover's car, she was very much a hated figure.'

'So by definition…'

'*Sí*, the whole House of Navarre hasn't endeared itself to the people.'

The question she'd been trying to avoid asking ricocheted through her head.

Ask. This is your chance.

'Back in Spain you said something about not wanting another destroyed life on your conscience. Did something else happen with your mother?'

His features froze and he remained silent for so long, she was certain he wouldn't answer.

'Five years ago, I almost got engaged.'

It was the last response she'd expected. Her mind blanked for a second. 'What?'

His laugh was bitter. 'You wanted to know why marrying wasn't my first choice, so…' He stopped and his face contorted with bitter recollection. Jasmine wanted to tell him to stop, wanted to wipe whatever wretched memory was causing the distress on his face. He spoke before she could form the appropriate words.

'Anaïs Perdot and I met the last time I was here in Paris. It was my first diplomatic tour. Her father was doing a lot of business in Santo Sierra and Anaïs and I grew...close.'

Jasmine didn't want to guess what memory was making his jaw clench. She held her breath as he continued. 'Her parents were eager for a match. I suppose on paper we were an ideal couple. She was young and exciting. For a while she made me forget that I was the son of a queen who didn't feel any remorse about dragging the family name through the mud with her infidelities. Hell, she even helped me to forge an easier relationship with the father I detested because I thought him weak for not stopping my mother's behaviour.' His chest heaved on a deep exhale.

'For a while?' she ventured.

His lips firmed. 'Her parents thought Anaïs should live in Santo Sierra for a while before we announced our engagement. Within weeks, my mother got her claws into her.'

'How?'

He shrugged. 'It started off as lunches and shopping sprees while I was busy with matters of state. Then they turned into late-night parties when she wouldn't return to the palace until the early hours, and then not at all.'

Jasmine frowned. 'Behaviour not exactly befitting a future queen, but European royalty have been known to indulge in much worse antics.'

His eyes turned arctic. 'Really? How many female members of your royal family have been photographed having sex with another man the week before their engagement was announced?'

Her hand flew to her mouth. 'Oh, my God! What did you do?'

Reyes stared at her for several more seconds before he shook his head. 'I handed over an obscene amount of money to the camera-wielding blackmailer to prevent the pictures hitting the papers. And I set back my relationship with my father by having our biggest fight yet when he refused to lift a finger against my mother for her part in Anaïs's behaviour.'

'I'm so sorry, Reyes.' She laid a hand on his arm and felt his palpable tension.

'That wasn't the worst of it. The day I told Anaïs it was over, she went to my mother. My mother convinced her that I was merely throwing a tantrum; that I would get over it. And then she talked Anaïs into partying one more night. On their way back from the club, they were involved in a hit-and-run accident. Anaïs claimed my mother was driving. My mother claimed the opposite. The result was that a teenager was left paralysed for life, his plans to become a doctor shattered.'

'And still your father did nothing?'

Reyes pinched the bridge of his nose. 'After I threw Anaïs and her family out of my life, she decided to share her version of her time in Santo Sierra with the media. My father finally tried to do some damage control, but it was too late. We were vilified in the media. My mother's behaviour spiralled out of control. A few months later, she was dead. That's when the first ramblings of unrest began.'

'And your father's illness just compounded the problems.'

That sadness she'd glimpsed on his face that first night in Rio appeared again. 'I never really got a chance to tell him that I regretted our fight. Last night would've been a good opportunity, had I been home.'

'You'll be home in a matter of days. You'll get your chance.'

He fell silent for a stretch of time, then he sent her an intense glance. The imperious ruler of one of the world's richest kingdoms was back. And despite the determined look on his face now, Jasmine couldn't help but feel desperate heartache for what he'd suffered. She realised her hand was still on his arm and lowered it to her lap.

'You understand now why finding the right candidate is imperative?' he asked.

Despite her heart taking a cliff-dive, she nodded. 'Yes, I do.'

Again her heart wrenched at the thought that weeks from

now he would be a married man. It would be a marriage of convenience, of course, but one he intended to commit to for a lifetime.

He would be out of reach for ever.

Last night, sharing a relaxing dinner with him, she'd wondered what it would've been like if they'd met under different circumstances. Then she'd kicked herself for the absurd thought.

Their backgrounds were too diverse for that to have happened in any lifetime. As she'd thought in Rio, they were two ships passing in the night, never to meet again.

But they'd met once…and again. Right at this moment, they could share a lifetime connection.

Because of Reyes's tight schedule and his edict that she wasn't allowed anywhere on her own, she hadn't been able to get her hands on the pregnancy test yet.

Instead she'd ordered it online and was expecting it to be delivered to the hotel today.

Until it arrived and she was forced to confront whatever consequences it brought, she would concentrate on carrying on as normal. Reality would come soon enough. Certainly before Reyes left for Santo Sierra.

And if her suspicions were right and she really was pregnant…

Reyes's door opened, and the driver bowed. 'Your Highness.'

Her heart lurched as she watched him struggle to suppress painful memories behind a bland façade. Again, the need to comfort him grew until she gripped her handbag to stop herself reaching for him.

Jasmine prayed the last candidate would be what Reyes wanted, while studiously ignoring the spear of pain that lanced her heart.

CHAPTER THIRTEEN

'WELL, I THINK we've discussed everything that needs to be discussed. I hope I've proven that I can be trusted and that I will be discreet, especially in matters of media liaisons.' Berenice Holden smiled at Reyes.

'You're comfortable with this arrangement being permanent? Or at the very least a long-term proposition?' Reyes asked.

'Of course. I like to think I'm bringing a lot to the table, but I'm aware I have much more to gain by ensuring any union between us works.'

Jasmine tried to keep her composure as the cold-blooded negotiations flew between Reyes and Berenice. They'd been hammering out terms for the last hour. And Jasmine had felt her heart wither each time they'd reached a compatible agreement.

She watched Reyes cross off the last item on his list, set his pen down and reach for his cutlery.

'Excuse me.' She rose and stumbled from the table. From the corner of her eye, she saw Reyes jerk to his feet, but she didn't stop until she slammed and locked the toilet door behind her. Shaking, she collapsed onto the closed lid.

Breathe...

This would be over soon. The test kits had arrived. Her attempt to take the test had been thwarted when Reyes had summoned her to grill her about Berenice before his meeting with her, and then insisted Jasmine accompany him.

Breathe...

In just over an hour she would know. Among other things, she didn't think it was healthy, if she was pregnant, to reside in this perpetual state of anxiety.

Her fingers trembled as the thought took root. She… pregnant…with Reyes's baby.

She closed her eyes and forced herself to breathe through her anxiety. Waiting until it was impolite to linger any longer, she returned to the table, sat through the last course. Tried to stop herself from trembling each time Berenice looked at Reyes.

Vaguely she noticed Reyes stand. 'Jasmine?'

She raised her head, met his probing glance. 'Yes?'

'Are you okay?' he asked.

Her head hurt when she nodded. He touched her arm to get her attention. All of a sudden, each of her senses zinged to life.

She looked round. Berenice had left. Jasmine was alone with Reyes again.

'Are you ready to leave? Or would you like dessert since you hardly touched your food?' He frowned down at her plate.

'I'm fine. I wasn't that hungry.' She rose and followed him out to the waiting limo. Heart in her throat, she slid in beside him. Silence throbbed in the car for several minutes, until she couldn't take it any more.

'So, you think she's the one?' Jasmine realised she'd stopped breathing as she waited for him to answer.

After a few moments, he shrugged. '*Sí*, she ticks all the boxes. I'll call a meeting of the council when we get back to Santo Sierra tomorrow. Tell them to start planning my wedding.'

She was pregnant.

Three sticks had confirmed it. Several online translations of the word *enceinte* along with three thick blue lines had sealed her fate.

Setting the tablet down on the bedcovers, Jasmine lay back on the bed and spread shaky fingers over her stomach.

Several emotions eddied through her, but gradually the fear, the anxiety, the complete and utter paralyzing notion that she was in no way equipped to be a mother, fell away to be replaced by one paramount sensation.

Joy.

She had a child growing inside her. Not just any child. Reyes's baby. The situation was completely messed up, but if fate had requested in a normal world that she choose the father of her child, Reyes Navarre would've been her first, her only choice.

Reyes...

She closed her eyes and inhaled deeply. She had to tell him. No question about that. The pain of never having known her father was one she'd smothered away during her childhood and teenage years. And although Stephen had filled the desolate hole left by her father's rejection, the dull ache remained.

She would never dream of subjecting her child to the same fate by choice. But then this wasn't just any child...

The enormity of what this pregnancy entailed burned through her joy.

God, she was pregnant with the future heir of the Santo Sierran throne. And its father was getting married to someone else in a matter of weeks.

Jasmine rolled to her side and hugged a pillow to her chest. Her eyes stung. She blinked rapidly. When her vision continued to blur, she dashed her fingers across her eyes, cursing the hormones running riot through her veins.

Think! She'd faced the worst dilemmas, protected herself and her mother from the most vicious thugs. She'd even faced bullies in juvie and emerged victorious. Stronger for it.

But did she possess the right skills to be a mother to a future king or queen? She squeezed her eyes shut and tried to ignore the tears. She wasn't a crier. Never had been...

She just needed a minute to absorb the life-changing news before—

'Jasmine!'

She started and opened her eyes to see Reyes crossing the vast suite towards her bed.

Sitting up, she eyed the tablet, breathing a sigh of relief to notice it'd gone dark. The actual pregnancy tests were safely tucked beneath her pillow.

'Have you heard of knocking?' she demanded. Her heart slammed into her ribs with its usual state of excitement at the sight of Reyes. But this time there was an added urgency. He was the father of her child. Which meant, one way or the other, they would be connected to each other for ever.

'I knocked. Several times. I entered because I was concerned. Are you okay?' He frowned down at her, those hawkish grey eyes tracking her face.

Too late, Jasmine remembered she'd been crying and probably had dried marks on her face. She dashed her hand across her cheeks.

'I'm…fine. Just a little tired.'

His frown didn't dissipate. Mouth dry, she slid her legs to the side of the bed and stood up. 'Did you want something?'

'You were supposed to supply my press secretary with Miss Holden's details. He hasn't received them yet.' His eyes narrowed further. 'Are you sure you're okay? You look pale.' He started to move forward, one hand raised to touch her.

She jerked out of reach, propelled solely by self-preservation. Her emotions were on enough of a roller coaster for her to risk disturbing them further by letting Reyes touch her. She needed to formulate her thoughts rationally before she broke the news to him. And Reyes touching her had never triggered rational thinking.

She risked a glance at him. His jaw was tense and his hand suspended mid-air. A look of hurt passed over his face before it was quickly veiled. She sucked in another breath. 'I'm fine. Really. I'll send the details now.'

He nodded tersely. Expecting him to leave, she gasped when he stepped closer and cupped her cheeks. 'You've been crying. Tell me what's wrong.'

'Reyes—'

'Don't tell me it's nothing. *Something* is wrong with you.

You've been jumpy lately. The chef tells me you hardly touched your breakfast and I know you didn't eat more than two mouthfuls at lunch. If you insist you're not sick, then it must be something else. Are you worried about what will happen to you when we get to Santo Sierra?'

'Should I be?' Honestly, she'd been too preoccupied with whether she was carrying his child to worry about whether Reyes would throw the book at her once they arrived at his homeland.

'I don't condone what you did, but I understand the motives behind it.'

She searched his gaze, and only saw steady reassurance. 'You do?'

He nodded. 'You were boxed into a corner, trying to save what was precious to you. It felt wrong when I chose to pay the blackmailers for those compromising photos of Anaïs instead of turning the whole thing over to the police but—'

'You were trying to protect your father from the pain of finding out.'

'*Sí.* And also myself to some extent.' His thumbs brushed her cheeks, traced the corner of her mouth. She locked her knees to keep them from giving way. 'You did what you had to do to protect your family. I can't condemn you for that.'

She swallowed hard as a lump rose in her throat. 'Thank you.'

His gaze drifted from her eyes to her mouth. In that moment, Jasmine didn't think she'd craved anything as she craved a kiss from him.

Her gaze caressed his mouth, and every nerve in her body screeched with delight. Then reality crashed. She couldn't kiss him. Would never be able to touch him again. He was marrying someone else.

Resolutely, she stepped back. 'I need to send the email. So if there's nothing else…?'

He tensed. Then, without a word, he left her room.

Jasmine collapsed on the bed, her hands fisted at her sides.

Ten minutes passed as she stared into space. Reyes had forgiven her for what she did in Rio. Which meant, she could leave
once she'd finalised the task he'd set her. And once she'd told
him about the baby.

She had to leave. The longer she stayed around him, the
more she yearned for things she had no business yearning for.
As for the baby, parents hashed out living arrangements every
day. She was sure they could come up with an arrangement
that suited them both.

So why the hell were her eyes brimming again at the thought
of returning to London on her own?

Shaking her head, she forced her thoughts aside and dealt
with the email to Reyes's royal press secretary. Once it was
done, she went to the bathroom, washed her face and brushed
her hair. Taking a little bit of pride in her appearance bolstered
her confidence. And for what she was about to do, she needed
all the armour she could muster.

Her knock on his suite next door received a deep-voiced
response to enter. She'd never seen the inside of Reyes's suite
and stopped a few steps after entering.

Decorated in bold swathes of black and white, the luxurious space was dominated by a king-sized bed with four solid
posts made of cast iron.

The carpet was stark white and contrasted stunningly with
the black velvet curtains. The design was bold, masculine and
oozed quiet sophistication.

'Did you come to admire the décor?' Reyes said from where
he stood at the window, gazing at the Parisian skyline.

Once her eyes fell on him, she couldn't look away. Dear
God, she was like a crazed moth, obsessed with this particular flame. A flame that didn't belong to her.

She cleared her throat. 'There's something I...need to tell
you.' Her voice was little above a whisper.

He tensed. Then slowly turned and strode to where she'd
stopped in the room. His hands remained in his pockets as

his gaze raked her from head to toe. 'So speak.' His tone was rough, terse.

'I don't know how else to say this so I'm just going to spill it,' she said.

He stared at her. Silence stretched. He quirked an eyebrow.

Heart hammering, Jasmine closed her eyes for a split second and gathered her courage. 'I...we...'

'Jasmine?' he snapped.

'Yes?'

'Take a breath and find the words.'

'I'm pregnant.'

He was a crown prince. He was allowed a gamut of emotions. Courage under fire. Pride. Anger. Even bewilderment at times.

But Reyes was certain that somewhere in his kingdom's constitution, there was a clause that said he couldn't feel blind panic.

And yet that was the emotion that clawed through him once he convinced himself he hadn't misheard her. Panic and intense, debilitating jealousy.

Stop, he admonished himself. *Think for a moment.*

But he couldn't think beyond the naked fact that she'd slept with someone else, was pregnant with another man's child. That in the very near future she would no longer be in his life. She would belong to someone else.

He turned abruptly and headed for the living room adjoining his bedroom. 'Come with me.'

She followed. When they reached the set of sofas, he jerked his chin at the nearest one.

'Sit down.'

'I don't need to—'

'Sit down, Jasmine. Please.'

She sat, crossed her ankles, and folded her hands in her lap. He tried not to stare at the silky fall of her hair. The perfection of her face.

She belonged to someone else.

A piercing pain lanced his chest. He paced to the window, as if the different view would provide cold perspective.

'Obviously this changes things. You wish me to release you from your obligations?' The words felt thick and unnatural. Not at all what he wanted to be asking her.

When she remained silent, he turned. Her mouth was parted in surprise. And shock?

'Umm, eventually, yes. But I'm not doing anything that would risk the baby's health, so I can see this task through.' She stopped and bit her lip. 'If you want me to, that is.'

Did he want a woman he'd made love to, who was now carrying another man's child, completing her task of seeing him wed another woman?

Dios. When had his life turned into a three-ring circus?

'Who is he?' he bit out before the words had fully formed in his mind.

Realising the panic had been totally annihilated by jealousy didn't please him. Nor did he welcome her confusion.

'Who is who?'

'The father of your baby.' Why did the words burn his throat so badly?

Her eyes widened. 'The father? You mean you think…' She shook her head. 'It's you, Reyes. You're the father of my baby.'

He willed the cymbals crashing through his head to stop. *'What did you say?'*

'I said this baby is yours. Ours.'

Panic. Bewilderment. Panic. Pride.

Elation. Pride. Anger.

'Mine. Do you take me for a fool?' he rasped.

'No, of course not. Reyes—'

'Or did you think you'd wait until I'd forgiven you before you sprang this *happy surprise* on me?'

'I really don't know what you're talking about,' she replied. Her bafflement was almost convincing.

'You know exactly what I'm talking about. Was that the

plan all along? To innocently run into me at the embassy in London and plot your way to a higher payday?'

She shook her head. 'Plans and plots? Next you'll be accusing me of mind-controlling you into forgetting to use a condom in the shower back in Rio.'

The bolt of shock rocked him backwards. Frantically, he searched his memory.

The shower...no condom...Madre di Dios...

He stared at her, rooting for the truth. 'The child is mine?' he croaked.

Her eyes met his. Bold and fierce. 'Yes. I know my credibility isn't worth much to you, but believe me when I say that I'd never stoop to such deplorable deception. No matter what.'

He nodded, still reeling. He believed her. But the inherent need to seek the absolute truth pounded through him. The past still had a stranglehold on him he couldn't easily let go of. 'You weren't on the pill?'

'No. I didn't need to be.'

He paced in a tight circle. 'When did you find out?' he asked.

'I did the tests an hour ago.'

She pulled three pink-and-white sticks from her jeans pocket and held them up.

Reyes forced himself to move. He took them, examined them. And slid them into his own pocket.

Somehow their presence finally hammered reality home.

He was going to be a father.

Jasmine wasn't carrying another man's child. She was carrying *his*.

Elation. A strange, undeniable possessiveness.

'I'll arrange for the doctor to see you. We need to address that poor appetite of yours.'

Jasmine licked her lips. 'There's no hurry. It can wait—'

'No, it cannot wait. Nothing can wait. Not any more.'

'What does that mean?' she enquired.

'It means everything has changed.' Reaching down, he

stroked her cheek. He wasn't sure why it hadn't occurred to him before. Jasmine wasn't the perfect candidate but she was miles better than anyone he knew. There would be no false proclamations of love to confuse issues. They were compatible in bed.

And she was carrying his child...

Her silky skin made his pulse jump. Or was it his own senses jumping from the situation presented so perfectly before him? So perfect, he wanted to kiss her!

Walking away before he was tempted to give in to the hunger churning through him, Reyes strode to the polished teak desk.

'Reyes, you're not making much sense.'

They both stopped at the knock on the door. 'Yes?'

His young aide entered. 'The council is here. I've put them in the conference room, as you requested.'

Reyes nodded. '*Gracias*, Antonio. I'll be there shortly.'

Antonio retreated and Reyes rounded the desk. There was so much he wanted to say, and yet he couldn't find the right words to say it. In the end, he crouched in front of Jasmine and took both her hands in his.

'This was as much my responsibility as yours. I failed in my duty to protect you, and for that I apologise. I got carried away...but I can assure you I don't have any adverse health issues you should worry about.'

'Neither have I,' she blurted.

He nodded. 'Good. I hope you're agreeable to what needs to happen next, too.'

She frowned. 'I'm not sure I follow.'

'It means I'm calling off next week's wedding. And I'm getting married in three days instead.'

Jasmine felt the blood drain from her head. It was a good thing he was holding on to her because she was sure she would've collapsed in an agonising, pathetic heap.

'I... Okay. Leave it with me. I'll call Miss Holden and arrange for her to fly to Santo Sierra,' she replied through numb lips. Her whole body was going numb and she really needed to sit down before she fell.

Reyes's brows bunched. 'Why would you be calling her?'

'Because you're marrying her?'

'You misunderstand, Jasmine. The wedding is for you. *I intend to marry no one else but you.*'

As proposals went, it wasn't the most romantic she'd heard. But even through the shock engulfing her, she realised there would be nothing resembling romance, or love, in whatever Reyes planned for them.

good humour had dissipated, she'd known for a certainty that... the heated medical conversation currently raging... The reading on DNA... the quiet voice of that doctor on the... phone...

CHAPTER FOURTEEN

THE PICTURES JASMINE had seen of Santo Sierra didn't do it justice even in the slightest.

As the royal jet circled majestic green mountains and turquoise waters in preparation for landing, she could barely contain her awe.

'Now I get a reaction from you. I thought I'd have to surgically remove you from that tablet.'

She turned sharply from her avid landscape gazing. 'I'm sorry?'

'You've hardly spoken a word since we took off.' He frowned. 'In fact, you seem to have lost the ability to speak the last twenty-four hours.' His gaze raked her face. 'Are you feeling unwell?'

She struggled to keep her features composed and not show how much turmoil she'd been in since he'd announced *she* was his choice of bride.

Her bewildered 'Why?' had been met with incredulity.

'Are you serious?'

'Of course, I'm serious. You have your perfect candidate already picked out.'

'And you are carrying my baby. My heir.' His brows had clamped together. *'What did you think was going to happen when you told me?'* he'd asked with a heavy dose of astonishment.

And there their discussion had ended.

The council had been waiting. He'd summoned Antonio to call the doctor, who'd arrived just as the council meeting had ended.

Reyes had peppered him with questions and he'd listened with an intensity that had terrified Jasmine. Even before the poor doctor had been dismissed, she'd known Reyes was heavily vested in his baby's welfare. And that she wouldn't be returning to London to raise her child as a single parent.

She was going to Santo Sierra to marry Prince Reyes Navarre.

She, a juvenile delinquent with a chequered past, was going to be crowned Princess in just over forty-eight hours.

And if that weren't terrifying enough, the realisation of what she was trying desperately to deny had finally hit her in the face this morning. She was developing potentially heart-risking feelings for Reyes. Ironically, her mother had called this morning just as she was busy denying her feelings.

Jasmine would never have thought in a million years that she would adopt her mother's head-in-the-sand approach to life one day.

'Jasmine?'

God, the Latin intonation to the way he said her name...

'No, I'm just a little nervous.'

He waved her nerves away. 'Don't be. The palace staff will cater to your every need. And my sister, Isabella, will also be on hand should you need a female perspective on any concerns.' He smiled.

Her breath caught.

Scared he'd read any unwanted emotion on her face, she looked out of the window again, towards the mountain she'd learned was called Montana Navarre. Set on the highest peak, it was where the Royal House of Navarre had been born and where Reyes's ancestors had ruled Santo Sierra for several centuries. Airplanes were restricted from flying directly over the palace, but the aerial view she'd seen of it had taken her breath away.

With supreme effort, she looked at him. 'Are you sure we're not rushing this? I'm sure there must be special protocols to royal weddings that I need to learn first?'

His eyelids descended and his nostrils flared slightly before he pierced her with that incisive grey gaze once more. 'You're carrying my child, Jasmine. Everything else ceases to matter in light of that reality.'

She couldn't read anything into that thick emotion in his voice. It was just shock.

Recalling how his councilmen had beamed at her when they'd emerged from their meeting, Jasmine added another reason as to why Reyes was pleased about the turn of events.

Next to a royal wedding, a royal baby was the most joyous celebration for any country. Reyes was returning home not just with his future bride, but with his future heir, although the formal announcement of her pregnancy wouldn't be made for another few weeks.

Coupled with his economic plans for Santo Sierra, those two events would surely regain him his people's love and devotion.

A part of her felt relieved and thankful that her actions wouldn't leave permanent damage on Santo Sierra. The other, selfish part of her couldn't hide the pain of feeling like collateral damage.

'You're still troubled,' Reyes observed.

She'd forgotten how well he could read her. Clearing her throat, she passed restless fingers through her hair. 'It's my problem. I'll deal with it.'

His face darkened. 'You're no longer an individual, fighting against the masses on your own. And I prefer not to start our marriage with secrets between us.'

She shook her head. 'Trust me, Reyes, you don't really want to know what's going on in my head right now. I'm hormonal and perhaps conveniently irrational.'

Firm, sensual lips pursed. 'I want to hear it, Jasmine.'

The voice of caution probed, and was promptly ignored. 'Fine, if you insist. I was right in front of you, Reyes. And yet you never considered me as a bride. So excuse me if I'm feeling a pauper's sloppy seconds.'

* * *

Oh, God. Why on earth did I say that?

Jasmine was still reeling hours after they'd landed and she'd been delivered to her suite in the palace.

Despite her opulent surroundings and the rich history etched into every arched wall, mosaic-tiled floor, and ancestral painting, she couldn't see, couldn't think beyond the stark, soul-baring words she'd uttered moments before the plane had touched down.

How utterly pathetic she'd sounded.

The shock on Reyes's face alone had convinced her she'd stepped way over the line. No wonder he'd beat a hasty retreat the moment they'd reached the palace.

She rose from the beautifully carved brocade love seat by the window in her vast bedroom and entered the bathroom.

The marble-lined tub had already been filled with scented water and huge fluffy towels laid within arm's length by the palace staff assigned to cater to her needs.

She'd been lost for words when she'd walked into a closet filled with designer clothes and accessories. And even more stunned when the member of staff had told her they'd been provided for her.

Shrugging off the silk robe, she sank into the enveloping warmth. She'd been summoned to dine with Reyes and his sister this evening, no doubt to be checked out by her future sister-in-law.

Jasmine looked out of the wide tub-to-ceiling trellised bathroom window and her breath caught all over again. With nothing to mar the mountaintop view she could see the kingdom for miles.

The bustling, vibrant capital of San Domenica was spread below her. Whitewashed churches vied with modern architecture, green parks and historical buildings.

As they'd driven through it on the way to the palace she'd glimpsed the look of pride and worry in Reyes's eyes. They'd also driven past the square and his fingers had tightened on the armrest when he'd seen a woman crying next to a broken statue.

Her insides had clenched for him. But he'd relaxed against the seat, his face averted from her as they'd climbed up the highway leading to the palace.

The moment they'd been escorted inside, he'd made his excuses and strode off.

And she'd been left grappling with her mangled feelings. Feelings she still hadn't been able to resolve by the time she dressed in a long sweeping gown in emerald green with a coloured-stone-embroidered bodice that had made her gasp when she'd spied herself in the mirror.

Sweeping her hair up into a bun, she secured it with several hairpins and slipped her feet into black slingbacks.

Fernanda, the staff member appointed to shepherd her to the dining room, left her with a smile and walked away after delivering Jasmine to the high-ceilinged room displaying ancient Mediterranean frescos.

Jasmine was busy admiring it when she heard voices outside the dining room.

Going to the door, she followed the sound down a long hallway, hurrying closer to where the raised voices came from. Rounding the corner, she came upon Reyes and a tall, slim woman in the middle of a heated argument.

He wore a thunderous look as he glared down at the stunning woman. A stunning woman who was giving as good as she got, her voice rising higher as she gestured wildly and responded in Spanish.

Jasmine thought of retreating. But they both turned as they sensed her presence.

For a moment, Reyes appeared frozen at the sight of her. His hooded eyes raked her from head to toe. Then he exhaled, his massive chest drawing her eyes to his impressively broad shoulders. His black shirt moulded his lean torso and washboard stomach before disappearing into dark grey tailored trousers that caressed his powerful thighs. His hair looked damp from a recent shower. He slicked it back now as he spiked his fingers through it.

Jasmine forced herself not to remember how those strands felt beneath her fingers.

'Hi,' she ventured. The breathlessness in her voice made her cringe.

Reyes's mouth compressed before he turned to the woman. 'Isabella, meet Jasmine Nichols, my future wife. Jasmine, this is my sister, Princess Isabella. She'll escort you to the terrace for drinks. I'll join you shortly.' Without waiting for a response, he stalked off down the opposite end of the hallway.

Isabella watched him leave, her expression hurt and angry. She looked spectacular in a cream gown laced with gold and black thread. The satin material fitted her svelte figure and complemented her golden, flawless skin.

Turning to Jasmine, she shook her head in frustration. 'Apparently, I was wrong to call off a wedding to a man I did not love.'

Jasmine's insides clenched. 'Duty is very important to your brother.' She tried a diplomatic approach.

Isabella threw up her hands in despair. 'Well, duty doesn't keep you warm. From the examples we've both had, you'd think he'd know that marriage is hard enough without going into it with a cold heart. I told him if I had to wait a thousand years for a man who makes me happy, I would.'

A spurt of laughter erupted from Jasmine's throat. 'Bet he didn't take that lightly.'

Isabella smiled. 'As you saw, storming off was his reaction.' She released an exasperated breath, then eyed Jasmine. 'Or maybe it was something else?' One perfectly shaped eyebrow rose.

'I'm not sure what you mean,' Jasmine replied.

'You'll find out soon enough how difficult it is to keep a secret in this place. You are not the woman my brother's press office was gearing up to announce as his bride two days ago.

Which makes me wonder if whatever's irking him has nothing to do with me and everything to do with you?'

Jasmine licked her lips, uncomfortable about having this conversation with Isabella when she was unsure what her role entailed in this marriage of convenience. She'd have to pick it up with Reyes. Once he could have a conversation with her again without that look of consternation.

'Please, can we drop the subject?'

The other woman wrapped her hand around Jasmine's arm. 'Of course, I didn't mean to upset you. *Dios*, I can't seem to breathe for causing upset today.'

'No, please. Think nothing of it.' She flashed a smile.

Isabella's shrewd gaze rested on her for a moment before she nodded. 'Fine. Come, we'll enjoy some cocktails before dinner. If Reyes gets over his tantrum, he can join us. Otherwise it's his loss.'

Jasmine followed her down the hallway to a large, skylit room with wide doors that led onto a wide terrace. Soft lights glinted through the space dotted with large, potted ficus trees. In the centre an extensive bar had been built, manned by two servants.

One came forward with a tray holding an array of gaily coloured drinks. Isabella pointed to the iced green one.

'Try that one. It's made with guava and a local fruit called *santosanda*.'

'It's not alcoholic, is it?' Seeing the instant speculation in Isabella's eyes, she hurriedly added, 'I'll never get over the jet lag if I add alcohol to the mix.'

Isabella shook her head. 'It doesn't contain any alcohol.'

Jasmine picked up the drink and took a sip. Different textures exploded on her tongue, the dominant one a tangy sweetness that sent a delicious chill down her spine. 'Wow.'

Isabella smiled and sipped her own peach-tinged drink. She drifted out onto the terrace, and she stood staring at the horizon.

Lights came on as darkness fell and her thoughtful gaze

rested over the view of San Domenica. 'In case you're wondering, I'm really pleased about your wedding to my brother. The council is right. We need a boost of good news. We've lived with doom and gloom since Mamá died.' She shook her head. 'I know I followed my heart in not marrying Alessandro, but I had been wondering lately if I took the selfish route.'

Jasmine shook her head. 'You would've caused each other too much pain in the end. Once the rose shades come off, relationships are an uphill struggle of hard work.' *Especially without love.*

'Are you speaking from experience?'

Despite her subtle probing, Jasmine warmed to Isabella. The princess had an open, honest face that went with her take-no-prisoners attitude.

'I watched my mother turn herself inside out for men who didn't deserve her love.'

Isabella's mouth pursed. 'My mother had all the love a man could give a woman, yet she went searching for more. Over and over, and in the wrong places. My father has never overcome the knowledge that he wasn't enough for her.'

'One-sided love is just as hard to keep up as no love at all.' Her heart lurched as she said the words, but Jasmine refused to examine why too deeply. She was too scared to find out. She went to take another sip and realised she'd finished the cocktail. The servant stepped forward with another. She smiled her thanks, took it, and turned back to the view.

'How is your father?'

Isabella looked towards the south wing of the palace, and sadness cloaked her face. 'He's hanging in there. I don't mean to sound callous and it'll break my heart when it happens, but I just wish he'd let go. I want him to find peace—'

'Isabella!'

She jumped at the admonishing voice.

Reyes stood behind them, his face more thunderous than it had been before.

'I'm...sorry, *mi hermano*, but you know I'm right.'

Reyes's fists bunched. 'If those are the sorts of views you choose to share with Jasmine, then perhaps you should consider eating dinner on your own.'

Eyes widening, Isabella gulped. Then her face closed with rebellion. 'Fine. I think I will.'

Before Jasmine could draw breath, the princess had stormed off.

Her gaze collided with Reyes's. 'Upsetting women seems to be your speciality. Are you sure you don't want to relocate to a faraway monastery and live the rest of your life as a monk?'

His expression lightened a touch. Grey eyes surveyed her from top to toe before they lingered at the drink in her hand. 'The silence I can probably handle. The chastity would unfortunately be a deal-breaker. How many of those have you had?' He nodded to her drink.

'This is my second one. Isabella recommended it. That local fruit…*santosanda*? It's delicious.'

'It is, but did she mention that, once fermented, it's also a powerful aphrodisiac?' he asked silkily.

CHAPTER FIFTEEN

REYES WATCHED HER eyes widen in shock, before a flush of awareness reddened her cheeks. She glanced at the drink, then back to him.

'No, she didn't!' Her voice had grown huskier. She blinked slowly as she passed her tongue over her plump lower lip.

Dios, had she even noticed the effects taking hold of her?

She'd been languidly caressing the lip of her glass for the last several minutes. And her nipples were hard and clearly outlined beneath her dress.

Reyes swallowed. 'I think you've had enough,' he rasped. He took the half-empty glass and handed it to the hovering waiter. Picking up two glasses of water, he thrust one into her hand.

'Umm…thanks.'

He nodded tersely.

Walking onto the terrace, he'd been hit between the eyes again by her stunning beauty. So much so, he'd stood frozen while her conversation with Isabella had unravelled.

It wasn't until his sister's utterance that he'd shaken off the red haze of lust that seemed to enclose him when he was around Jasmine.

Watching her now, he recalled what she'd said to him before they'd landed in Santo Sierra.

And the resulting tailspin his emotions had been flung in. Once he'd been able to draw breath, he'd tried to analyse his reaction. Yes, the knowledge of Jasmine's pregnancy had been the catalyst that had driven everything forward. But he could just as easily have maintained the initial date of his wedding. He was a modern enough man to admit the distance between his wedding day and his heir's birthday didn't bother him. And he was sure it didn't bother Jasmine.

So why had he been intent on rushing her to the altar?

He'd tried and failed to convince himself it was because of his need to make his people happy. A week's difference wouldn't have mattered. Neither did it matter that Jasmine's past would be an issue once it became public knowledge. Unlike his mother's behaviour, Jasmine's reasons for her unfortunate past were a result of trying to survive her horrific circumstances. He was sure his people would forgive once they knew.

Just as he'd forgiven her? Just as he suspected his reasons for marrying were more selfish than he wanted to admit to himself?

Reyes thrust his balled fists into his pocket, willed the confusing emotions away, but they returned stronger. More demanding.

He didn't do feelings. Hadn't let any in, except maybe for his father, since he'd thrown Anaïs out of his life, and then stood at his mother's graveside mere months later.

But Jasmine was making him feel. Making him want... no, *need*. As for the thought that his child was growing in her belly...it pounded him with terrifyingly powerful emotions every time it blazed across his mind.

Would the mistakes that he'd made with his own father affect his child? Was failure emblazoned in his blood for ever?

More and more he'd found himself wanting to take Jasmine's example. She had found a way out of the barren wasteland of not having anyone to lean on, anyone to trust. But she'd let herself trust, allowed her faith in the goodness of humanity to be restored. Despite the harrowing experience of juvenile detention and a mother who clearly wasn't equipped for the job, she'd found herself back on a road Reyes himself was struggling to find.

He couldn't deny it. She compelled him to be a better

man. Would raising their child together make him a better father, too?

Swallowing his blind panic, he glanced at her.

Her eyes were on him, her fingers curled around the glass. 'I feel funny.'

Unaccustomed laughter rumbled out of his chest. 'You need fresh air. Dinner won't be for another hour. Come, I'll show you the grounds.'

She peered down at her feet. 'I don't think these shoes will go well with walking the grounds. They're already pinching something fierce.'

'You won't need to walk further than the bottom of these steps.' Golf buggies were housed at various points around the palace for ease of movement around the extensive grounds.

He guided her down and waited till she was seated on the buggy. Reyes wasn't at all surprised when she kicked off her shoes and sighed with relief.

The sight of her dainty feet gripped his attention. Mesmerised, he watched her rub her big toe along her other instep. Heat flared through his gut and pooled in his groin. Pulling himself out of the daze, he reversed the buggy and stepped on the accelerator.

Floodlights illuminated their path as he drove towards the northernmost point of the palace. Beside him, Jasmine oohed and aahed at the elaborate fountain his great-grandfather had built for his children to splash in, the huge lake containing white majestic swans gliding serenely in the rising moonlight, and ruins of an amphitheatre set into a cliff.

Jasmine pointed to the spotlights strung along the outer edge of the theatre. 'Do you still use it?'

He nodded. 'Isabella holds a children's Christmas concert every year.'

'That's so cool. Everything about Santo Sierra is so cool,' she amended with a husky chuckle. Then she glanced at him. 'But snapping at Isabella like that? Not cool.'

Reyes's fingers tightened around the wheel, but his reaction was more to do with her laugh and less to do with his sister.

He brought the buggy to a stop on the grassy landscape and helped her out. She started to put on her shoes.

'Leave them. You won't need them where we're going.'

With a happy smile, she dropped them.

Hiking up her dress to keep the hem off the grass, she stepped out.

Reyes tried not to stare at her feet. 'We have a temperamental relationship, Bella and I. She'll have calmed down by now.'

Jasmine frowned. 'But you won't apologise? I think you should.'

'*Sí*, I will apologise. In the morning, when I'm convinced she won't bite my head off.'

She laughed.

He stopped in his tracks as the intoxicating sound transfixed him.

When she realised he'd stopped moving, she froze. 'What?'

He cleared his throat to dislodge the uncomfortable knot. 'You should laugh more. It's an entrancing sound.'

She blushed as her eyes rounded, then her expression turned gloomy. 'I haven't had much to laugh about. Not since...' She stopped and bit her lip.

He held his breath. 'Since?'

'Since Rio,' she muttered. 'And especially since I found out what my actions caused.'

The sincerity in her voice shook the foundation of his armour. He searched her face. Her eyes met his with frank appraisal and in that moment he was sure she'd never been more sincere.

He held out his hand, his breath lodged in his chest.

She hesitated, and his hand wavered. Looking down, she indicated her dress. 'I don't want to let go in case I get grass stains on it.'

His breath punched out. 'It's just a dress, Jasmine. I'll buy you a hundred more. Let go.'

She made a face. 'Yes, Your Bossiness.' She released her grip on the dress and slid her hand into his. Warm. Firm. Almost trusting...

A simple gesture. And yet he couldn't stop thinking about it as he walked her twenty yards up the small hill.

'Where are we going?' she asked breathlessly.

He realised he'd been marching and slowed his pace. 'Up there.' He pointed.

She stopped and gazed at the stone monument planted in the earth. 'What is it?'

'You need to get closer to see it.'

She followed him. When she tried to free their linked fingers, he held on, unwilling to let her go. Smiling at him over her shoulder, she stepped closer to the stone and ran her fingers over the ancient markings set into the rough surface.

Still clinging to her fingers, Reyes walked her round the stone, then led her to the jagged crevice.

'Oh, my God,' she whispered. Reyes watched the wonder on her face as she peered into the black three-foot-wide crack scorched into the earth. 'How deep is it?'

Stepping behind, he let go of her hand and wrapped his arms around her waist. 'No one knows. All past rulers of Santo Sierra have forbidden the site from being explored.'

She leaned back in his arms and stared up at him. 'But how did it get here?'

He bent his head, and his lips brushed the top of her ear. 'Legend has it that the original Crown Prince of Santo Sierra ran off with the betrothed of the Prince of Valderra the day before they were to be married. The jilted prince hunted them down and caught up with the lovers at this spot. They fought to the death and both lost their lives. The day after they were buried, the subjects woke up to find the fissure here. The two kingdoms have been separated ever since.'

Her arms folded over his and she rested her head on his shoulder. She rocked slowly from side to side in a silent dance.

'That's tragic, but I bet it can all be resolved with a good mediation.'

He laughed, found himself moving along with her, swaying to her inner music. 'You believe you can succeed where countless others have failed?'

'Mediation is about breaking things down to the basest level and routing out what each party needs the most. Once it's clear, most people will settle for their innermost desires instead of what their greed dictates they need.' Her voice had softened to an introspective murmur.

Reyes stared down at her sweet face, her perfect nose and gorgeous mouth. Something moved within him. Not his libido, even though it was awake and alert to any imminent action.

His innermost desire included kissing her, making her his. Permanently...

He realised she was growing drowsy from the drink and visibly forced his gaze away from temptation. 'What are your innermost desires, Jasmine?' he asked before he could stop himself.

'World peace. Or barring that a magical carriage to whisk me back down this hill so I don't have to walk.' She giggled, and a smile cracked across his face again.

Dios, he was in danger of slipping deeper into her web. Maybe this trip hadn't been such a good idea.

Or maybe he just needed to take a leaf out of his sister's book and follow his heart rather than his head for once. He and Jasmine might have arrived at this arrangement unconventionally, but fate had gifted them a compatibility that he would be foolish to ignore.

Tomorrow morning, there would be a vote to elect a new council, after which he'd be named Prince Regent. The palace press had already announced his impending wedding. His father's doctors had assured him that the King's health was holding for the moment and he'd seen a slight improvement in his father's condition when he'd visited him today.

As for Mendez, the Valderran prince knew something was

up. He'd been putting out feelers as to Santo Sierra's position on the old treaty. Reyes had ignored him so far. Let him stew for a while.

For now, Reyes intended to enjoy an evening free of guilt and anxiety. With the woman who would become his in less than forty-eight hours.

The woman who was carrying his child.

He paused as a bolt of satisfaction lanced through him. Reyes realised having Jasmine and their child in his life was a prospect that didn't terrify him as much as it had this time yesterday. Yesterday, he'd convinced himself it was duty driving him.

Today, his feelings were more of...elation.

Bending, he swung Jasmine into his arms. She gave another giggle and curled her arms around his neck. Her nose brushed his jaw and his belly tightened.

Sí, a worry-free few hours were just what he needed.

'We don't have a carriage, but I have something in mind that might please you.' He strode to the top of the hill, turned ninety degrees and nudged her with his chin. 'There,' he murmured in her ear.

Jasmine pried her gaze from Reyes's breath-stoppingly gorgeous face and jawline and glanced where he'd indicated.

She was aware her mouth had dropped open. Again.

Could she help it when Santo Sierra had so far delivered one stunning surprise after another?

'It looks like a giant, gorgeous wedding cake,' she whispered.

'Because it was designed as a present for a bride's wedding day. But it's actually a summer house.'

'Set into the hillside so it looks like layers. It's perfect.'

The smile that had flashed on and off for the last half hour curved back into sight. Again her heart beat wildly, sending her blood roaring in her ears.

Although she was thankful he wasn't growling at her or

walking away from her as if she didn't exist, she was terrified at seeing this new, relaxed side of Reyes. This Reyes was too much for her senses. Too breathtaking. Too charming. Too... close.

But not too much that she wanted to get away. Or return to her lonely palace suite. She tightened her arms when he started towards the utterly splendid structure.

If she'd truly believed in fairy tales, this would've been her dream house. But she didn't, so it was just as well that the effects of the punch had worn off enough for her to realise this was nothing but a short interlude in time for both of them.

He climbed the stairs to the surprisingly large square structure and the wooden shuttered doors slid back. Jasmine's gaze slid from the love seat on the porch to the interior.

Bypassing the simple, lamplit living room furnished with more love seats and twin sofas festooned with cushions, Reyes walked her into the bathroom and set her down on a pedestal next to a wide porcelain sink.

He stepped back and turned on the tap in the extra-wide bath.

'Umm...is one of us taking a bath?'

His mouth tilted. 'I thought you might want to wash your feet since you've been walking in the grass.'

Jasmine looked down at her feet. 'Oh, I guess that's a good idea, what with the wall-to-wall white carpeting.'

She started to step down from her perch. He stayed her with a hand on her waist and leaned over to add bath salts to the warm water.

This close, his scent assailed her, claimed her senses. When he breathed his body moved against hers.

This was getting out of hand...

Despite the thought trailing through her head, she stayed where she was.

Once the water reached a quarter way, he turned to her. 'Lift up your dress.'

She tugged the material up her hips. He picked her up and

sat her on the edge of the tub. Expecting him to leave her to it, she gave a small gasp when he dropped to his knees beside her.

Grabbing a washcloth, Reyes dipped it in the scented water and started to clean her feet.

The punch of feeling through her chest made her jerk. He looked up, took her arm and slid it around his shoulders. 'Hold on to me if you think you're slipping.'

Nodding dumbly, she held on. Traced her fingers over the strands of hair at his nape. Her fingers brushed his skin. A rough sound escaped his throat. The soothing cloth cleansed her feet.

Jasmine looked from Reyes's arresting profile to what he was doing. She, Jasmine Nichols, originally from one of the roughest neighbourhoods in London, had a bona fide prince washing her feet.

The moment couldn't get more surreal than this. And yet she didn't want it to end.

'You have the most perfect feet,' Reyes murmured.

'Thank you.' Her voice emerged as shaky as she felt inside.

He raised his head and pierced her with eyes wild with raw, predatory hunger. 'The most perfect legs.' His wet hands cupped her ankles, drifted up over her calves.

Jasmine forgot to breathe. Her hand gripped his nape, her only stability in a world careening out of control.

'The most perfect thighs.'

'Reyes…'

His gaze dropped to her lips. Her heartbeat spiked a second before his mouth claimed hers.

Groaning, she fell into the kiss, wrapped both arms around his neck when he lifted her out of the tub and out of the bathroom. He returned to the living room and lowered her in front of the fireplace.

Lowering his body on top of hers, he deepened the kiss, ravaged her mouth with an appetite that grew sharper, rougher by the minute. His hand trailed up her leg, her thigh, to close over her bottom.

They both groaned when he squeezed her flesh. '*Dios*, you're perfect,' he breathed into the side of her neck when he let her up for air.

But she didn't want breathing room, didn't want even the slightest doubt to mar this incredible moment.

Catching his jaw between her hands, she raised her mouth to his. 'Kiss me, Reyes. Please.'

He swore again, the sound ragged. Scooping her against his chest, he rolled them over. Firm hands lowered her zip and tugged down her dress and flung it away. Then he reversed their position again. 'Now I can kiss you properly. Everywhere.'

He devoured her lips, her throat, the tops of her breasts.

Her moans grew louder as he rolled her nipple in his mouth before sucking in a hot pull. Jasmine's back arched, her fingers digging into his hair to keep him there, pleasuring her, torturing her. A sharp cry erupted from her lips when his teeth nipped her skin just above her panties. Rising up on her elbows, she stared down at him, drunk on the sight of what he was doing to her.

'Reyes…'

He glanced up. The look on his face threatened to send her over the edge.

'Do you want this, *querida*?' he enquired thickly.

'More than anything,' she whispered.

She smothered the voice that cautioned her as to what she was doing. Her first time with this man had ended in disaster. Granted, it'd been one of her own making. But now she knew it was more than her body involved. Her heart was at risk, too.

She was in danger of falling in love with a man who would never love her.

'I can hear you thinking.' He paused in the line of kisses he was dotting along her pantyline. 'Tell me what's on your mind.'

'I don't want anything we do here today to…confuse issues.'

His eyes narrowed. 'Shouldn't that be my line?'

Unwilling to help herself, she cupped his shadowed cheek.

'You may be a crown prince, but I believe in equal opportunities when it comes to the bedroom.'

He turned his head, kissed her palm and raised both her hands above her head. 'Well, this is my opportunity. You get your turn later.'

He took her mouth in a hard kiss, then raised his head. 'In answer to your question, there is no issue to confuse. We already know we're compatible in bed. Whether we say our vows tomorrow or the next day, we both want this, now. *Sí?*' His eyes probed hers.

Her heart lurched. 'Yes.'

CHAPTER SIXTEEN

REYES WATCHED HER expression turn from hesitant to erotically pleased as he cupped her breast and teased the hard nub.

The voice that told him he wasn't giving her room to change her mind was ruthlessly squashed. His hunger for her had flamed higher than every other need. And just as he'd taken her in Rio, he intended to let nothing stand in the way of his claiming her tonight.

He resumed his exploration of her body. Much to his very male satisfaction she arched her back and purred. And grew increasingly, pleasingly demanding.

She grabbed at his clothes and he hurriedly undressed. He yanked away her panties and positioned himself between her legs.

'Yes. Please…now,' she cried hoarsely.

Reyes surged inside her with a guttural roar. Sensation exploded all over his body at her wetness, her tight heat. She embraced him, rolled her hips in helpless abandon as pleasure overtook her.

He established a passionate rhythm she matched with enthusiasm. Much too soon, he was following her into bliss, shouting his ecstasy as he emptied himself inside her.

He watched her as they caught their breaths. Her face glowed with the flushed aftermath of sex. Reyes had never seen a more beautiful woman. His groin stirred. Her eyes slowly widened.

Smiling, he pressed a kiss against her heated cheek. 'You have that effect on me.' He pulled out of her. They both groaned at the sizzle of electricity.

Tucking her against his side, he caught her free hand in his, kissed her soft palm. Almost inevitably, his hand slid over her flat stomach. He heard her breath catch and searched her face.

A look of wonder, much like what he was experiencing at that very moment at the thought of his child growing inside her, passed over her face. For several heartbeats, he held her gaze. Then she blinked.

'Reyes?'

'*Sí?*'

'I know you're a prince and all, but please tell me you're as terrified as I am at the thought of getting it wrong with this baby.'

'I will not discuss my silent mental breakdown with you, except to mention that it's very acute. And very unsexy.'

She laughed. The sound filled his chest with pleasure so strong, he forgot to breathe for a minute.

When he had it under control he moved his hand, explored some more. When he grazed a scar, he glanced down at her.

'Tell me what happened here.'

She tensed and he pressed his mouth against her palm again. 'Everything, Jasmine. I want to know everything. Before and after Stephen.'

Indecision blazed in her eyes for several seconds before she exhaled.

'Have you heard the saying that some people are just born bad?'

She shook her head at his frown and continued. 'For a long time I believed I was one of them. You know how my mother handled our situation. I just kept rebelling whenever I could. I think I wanted my mother to *see* me, deal with me. When she pretended like I didn't exist, I turned truant at a young age. Fell in with the wrong crowd.'

'What happened?'

'I just…spiralled out of control for a long time.'

'You were trying to get yourself heard the best way you could.'

'That's no excuse. I was a brat with a mother who didn't care whether she lived or died and I lashed out.'

'That's not the end of your story though, obviously.' He trailed his mouth over her palm again.

'No.' She shivered in his arms. He reached for a cashmere throw next to the fireplace and settled it over them. She snuggled into him and that alien feeling in his chest expanded wider. 'You remember that turf war I told you about?'

Reyes nodded.

'*I* was the turf they were fighting over. It happened a few months after I came out of juvie. Each side wanted me to join their gang. I seriously considered it. But I knew I would be burying my pain with destruction. So I refused, and all hell broke loose.'

He reared up and stared down at her. '*Dios.* How did you get out of that?'

'I let myself be arrested again. I reckoned the police station was a safer place than the street. It was where I met Stephen. He was an MP then, touring the police station and I...' She stopped and grimaced.

'You what?'

A dull flush crept up her cheeks. 'I may have tripped him up when he walked past me.'

He couldn't help his smile. She answered with one of her own. Unable to resist, Reyes kissed her. When he lifted his head, she was breathless and her delicious mouth was swollen. 'I presume that got his attention?'

She nodded. 'He could've filed charges against me for assault. Instead bailed me out and he took me out for a coffee. We talked for hours. He delivered me home and met my mother. Then he started visiting us every week. A few months later I started taking on the gangs myself. But instead of knives and guns, I used words. I managed to mediate a truce between them and even extracted a promise from the leaders not to recruit children to run drugs for them.'

'That's where you got your passion for mediation from?' he asked.

'Yes. I returned to school, made good grades and got my

first job at twenty-one. Stephen married my mother, and I guess the rest is history.' Her eyes met his and shifted away. 'Until Rio, that is. I'm so sorry about that, Reyes.'

Catching her chin with his finger, he tilted her face. 'I know you are. I forgive you. I judged you harshly before I knew the truth behind your actions. You tried to protect your family the only way you knew how.'

'But I ended up making things worse for you and your people.'

'You're here now, helping to fix it. That matters to me. With a new council in place, Mendez will no longer be able to play his games. The route may have been unfortunate, but perhaps it achieved something positive in the end. So from now on, we'll consider Rio another lesson we'll both learn from. Agreed?'

'Agreed,' she replied tremulously.

He brushed away the tears forming in her eyes. His head swimming with sensations he could barely grapple with, Reyes slanted his mouth over hers. When he was kissing her like this, he didn't have to think. Didn't have to wonder why he craved her even more with each kiss, each heartbeat.

He didn't have to wonder why he wished they were already married and this were their honeymoon.

A stomach growled. He raised his head. 'I believe that was you.'

She grimaced. 'Jet lag kept me asleep through lunch, and I think we missed dinner.'

Reyes reached for his discarded trousers and took out his phone. He sent his chef the appropriate instructions and hung up.

'Dinner is coming to us?' A smile that seemed to grow more breathtaking each time curved her lips.

'*Sí.* The perks of being a prince. You will command equal power once you're my princess.'

A shadow passed over her face. He wanted to demand to know the reason behind it. Something stopped him.

Her fingers drifted over his brow and down to his cheek. 'What will we do after we eat?'

'I will bathe you and you will let me explore the rest of your scars.'

Jasmine woke in the middle of night. Although the bedroom in the wedding-cake house where they'd relocated to boasted a fire, Reyes hadn't lit it when he'd carried her in. They'd had more urgent things in mind.

Now the room had cooled and she shivered. Glancing down, she realised why. The covers had slipped to the floor and the only things keeping her warm were Reyes's muscular thigh and arm. Which left the rest of her body chilled.

Carefully sliding away, she picked up the nearest sheet and walked into the bathroom.

After using it, she came back to the bed.

Reyes was snoring softly, his face even more relaxed in sleep than it'd been this evening. A lock of hair had fallen over his brow and she itched to smooth it away but stopped herself.

Over and over tonight, her heart had filled to bursting when he'd made love to her. Somewhere around midnight, she'd finally admitted that she'd fallen in love with the Crown Prince of Santo Sierra.

She loved a man who had had his heart broken, not just by one woman, but by two. And while Anaïs's betrayal had been short-term, his mother's had gone on for years.

Her heart stuttered and tears prickled her eyes. He stirred in his sleep.

She turned away and walked quickly out of the bedroom before he woke. She couldn't risk him seeing her expression. He'd been too adept at reading her moods lately. She couldn't afford to let him see that, while she was certain he'd love their baby, she could foresee herself yearning for a love he could never give her.

Going to the window, she gazed out at the twinkling lights

of San Domenica. This place was now her home, for better or worse.

She intended to do everything in her power to make sure it was the better.

She was going from delinquent to princess. Was she being selfish in asking for the icing on the cake?

Yes! She wanted it all.

Tears slipped down her cheeks before she could stop them.

'You're crying. Tell me why.'

She whirled around.

Reyes stood a few feet away, dressed in only his boxers, intense eyes scouring her face.

'I wasn't crying.'

One eyebrow was raised at her wet cheeks. 'Unless it's raining in here and I'm not aware of it, I beg to differ.'

'I never cry. Tears are for the weak.'

His eyes narrowed. 'Who told you that?'

'A gang leader years ago.' She shook her head. 'I'm sorry. That whole trip down memory lane has dredged up things I'd rather forget.'

He stepped closer, cupped her cheeks. 'And that's what woke you?'

About to nod and let that assumption hold, she hesitated. And spoke the words that scrapped up from her shredding heart. 'Are you sure you're making the right choice, Reyes? Not for your people, but for you?'

His eyes grew wary. 'Why the sudden introspection?'

'I know we're only doing this primarily for the baby, and for your people. But we'll be in this marriage, too.'

Jaw clenching, he paced in tight circles in front of her. 'What are you saying?'

'That you need to be sure before we take a step we can't retrace.'

He froze. His nostrils flared as he jerked his fingers through his hair. 'What's going on, Jasmine? Why are you crying? Are you having second thoughts?'

She swiped at her cheeks and grappled with what to say. Settling on a half truth, she met his gaze. Slowly, she nodded. 'Yes, and I think deep down you probably are, too.'

His brows clamped together. 'Don't put words in my mouth.'

Jasmine would've given anything not to utter the words. 'Then tell me in your own words.'

He stared at her for a long time. Then shook his head. 'I don't have the luxury of being whimsical about this situation. It is what it is.'

The vice tightened around her heart. 'What about love, Reyes? Surely you have a view on whether you want love in your life or not?'

His hand slashed through the air. 'My father married for love. Look where that got him.'

'Are you saying if you fell in love and were loved back, it wouldn't be enough for you?'

'I'm saying love is never equal, no matter what anyone says. Someone always loves more, and that person has the most to lose.' Shadows flickered in his eyes before he turned to pace the room again.

Her beautiful eyes clouded. 'You really believe that, don't you?'

Striding to her, he grabbed her arms. 'I don't believe in fairy tales. And my reality speaks for itself.'

She pushed out of his arms and padded to the window. Tugging the sheet closer, she wrapped her arms around herself.

Reyes watched her, the action both angering and disturbing him. 'Jasmine?'

After a moment, she turned. 'How is your father?'

He frowned, struggling to keep up with everything she was throwing at him.

Waking up to find her gone, he'd had a chilling sense of déjà vu, before he'd remembered he was back home, in a place where Jasmine wouldn't be able to escape him easily. Except she was trying now. The woman he'd gone to sleep certain of spending the rest of his life with was having second thoughts.

And probing subjects he didn't want to discuss. Yet he found himself answering. 'As well as he can be considering his heart and organs are days away from failing.' The throb of pain the thought brought made his breath catch. His father had had a good day today. Straight after his council meeting, Reyes had gone to see him. They'd talked for a full hour, during which Reyes had stumbled over himself in his plea for his father's forgiveness for treating him so harshly.

His father had merely smiled and said, 'Finally, you love,' before he'd fallen asleep.

'Can he speak?' Jasmine asked.

He shoved a hand through his hair. 'A few words when the medication isn't strong enough to make him sleepy.'

She nodded. 'Can you do me a favour? The next time you see him, ask him if he'd do it all over again. Love your mother with unconditional love.'

His insides clenched and he exhaled. 'I don't need to ask him. I know he would.'

'Do you think that's foolish? Those brief moments of happiness to balance the pain and the betrayal?'

'Jasmine—'

'Just humour me. You have no idea how many times I wished for my mother to just tell me she loved me, or for her to remember it was my birthday without the shopkeeper down the road having to remind her. Was it always that bad between your parents?'

Reyes thought back to birthdays, skiing holidays, family gatherings. His mother had made an effort on those rare occasions. Those were the happiest he'd seen his father. But as with all things, the happy moments were fleeting, the painful moments lingering the longest.

He shook his head. 'It wasn't, no. But it was a life...so-called *love*...without trust and respect. And to me that's no life at all. Do you not agree?'

Her shoulders slumped. A flare of panic lit his insides.

'It doesn't really matter what I think, does it? You've made up your mind. We have a wedding to plan and a baby to look forward to.'

She was staying. The panic should've abated, yet it escalated. 'We can make this work, Jasmine.'

Her dejection grew even more palpable. 'Reyes—'

He cupped her shoulders. 'We *will* make it work. That is my edict.'

Her chin rose and although her eyes filled with more tears, they didn't spill. But they spiked her lashes and clung like tiny diamonds.

'I know you're the Crown Prince, possibly soon to be King, but I'm really tired of you ordering me around like I'm some type of minion. Get over yourself already.'

She flung away from him, trailed the sheet to the bedroom and then reversed her trajectory back to the living room to snatch up her gown.

Watching her try to manoeuvre the dress on while keeping hold of the sheet tugged a reluctant smile from his lips, despite his churning feelings.

She saw it and glared at him. 'You think this is funny?'

'Firstly, I don't think I've ever been told to get over myself before. Secondly, I suggest you stop hopping around like that before you fall over and break a bone. Or worse.'

'*Firstly*, I think it's high time someone told you to get over yourself. Secondly—' She yanked the dress up, dropped the sheet, and tripped over her feet. He lunged forward, all mirth gone from the situation, and caught her in his arms.

'You can let me go now. I'm done putting my dress on.'

His chest tightened again, harder than before. 'And where do you propose going at three in the morning?'

'Back to the palace, of course.'

'No. If you're upset we'll talk about it now.'

That look of inevitable acceptance of defeat crossed her face again. *Dios*, what was going on? 'You can't will something into place that doesn't exist, Reyes.'

'What are you talking about?'

'We're only marrying because of the baby. I think we should focus on that and not fool ourselves into thinking this can ever be something more, okay?'

Something more. A part of him wanted that. The part that wanted to say *to hell with everything* and jump in blind. But he couldn't afford to do that. This time the stakes were much too high. 'Jasmine, I can't give you what—'

She held up her hand and shook her head. 'I know. I'm not what you wanted. You don't need to spell it out.' She turned away. 'I'd really like to return to the palace now, please.'

He dressed. Made sure she was warm enough in the pre-dawn air as he settled her into the buggy. All the while feeling terrified that he had lost the most important battle of his life.

CHAPTER SEVENTEEN

THEY WERE MARRIED two days later in the largest cathedral in Santo Sierra. Church bells tolled at the strike of midday and white doves were released in commemoration of the historic event. Quite how the palace staff had managed to gather and accommodate world leaders and royalty in such a short space of time would've blown Jasmine's mind, had she not been in a continued state of numb shock.

Stephen and her mother had flown in this morning on Reyes's jet, and, although Jasmine had had a hard time managing her mother's questions and tearful exclamations of how beautiful Jasmine looked, she was thankful for their presence. They were literally two familiar faces in a multitude of strangers.

Her mother was riding in the second car with Isabella, while Jasmine rode to the cathedral in the back of a Rolls-Royce Phantom. Beside her, Stephen enumerated the many luxuries of the car. Jasmine nodded absently, too preoccupied with not throwing up over her astonishingly beautiful gown to answer.

All too soon, they arrived at the church. A dozen ten-year-old pageboys lined either side of the royal-blue carpet that led to the aisle, each one holding up a jewelled-hilted sword that signified the twelve generations since Reyes's ancestors had ruled Santo Sierra.

Jasmine gripped Stephen's arm as her stepfather led her down the aisle. She tried to pin a smile on her face as the sea of faces on either side of the aisle gawped at her with unbridled curiosity.

The surprise wedding and unconfirmed reports of a possible pregnancy had sent the world's media wild. The press office's *no comment* on the subject had been taken as tacit confirmation.

'Almost there, my darling,' Stephen murmured. His reassurance calmed her nerves, helping her to focus on her destination.

The top of the aisle, where Reyes waited. She couldn't see his face clearly through her lace veil, but his imposing figure was hard to miss. Dressed in formal military regalia complete with shoulder tassels, sash and sword, he looked more dashing than any man had the right to look.

The butterflies in her stomach multiplied.

Since their night at the wedding-cake house, she'd seen him for less than a handful of minutes. Each time, he'd been reserved to the point of being curt. At their last meeting, he'd presented her with an engagement ring belonging to his grandmother. The stunning baguette diamond ring she now wore on her right hand, according to protocol, was flanked by two further teardrop diamonds and completed in a platinum band.

Reyes had stopped only to ask whether she liked it before, after her startled nod, he'd walked away.

She couldn't help but think that her probing questions about love had twigged him to her feelings for him. Feelings he didn't welcome.

All through the many fittings and wedding protocol, she hadn't been able to dismiss the knowledge that Reyes would never love her, no matter how much she tried. Again and again she recalled the look on his face when she'd blurted out that damning statement on the plane. A statement he hadn't so far denied.

Stephen eased her hand from his arm, and she realised they'd reached the steps of the altar. Eyes damp, her stepfather gazed down at her. 'I'm so proud of, my dear. So very proud,' he murmured. 'You're the daughter I wished for, and I hope you'll forgive me for not always being the father I could've been.'

She knew he was referring to the business with Joaquin.

Her throat clogged and she blinked back her own tears. 'There's nothing to forgive. Absolutely nothing,' she whispered back.

His own eyes brimming with tears, Stephen placed her hand on the gloved hand Reyes held out.

She searched Reyes's face, and her heart dropped. Nothing in his demeanour showed he was happy to be here. He flinched when a muted roar sounded from outside where the crowd was watching the ceremony on giant screens.

Intent on discovering a hint of emotion that would abate the fear beating beneath her breast, she stepped closer to him.

A discreet cough sounded half a step behind her. She turned to find a teenage usher holding out a polished silver tray. Flustered, Jasmine placed her bouquet on it, and tried to ignore the hushed murmuring behind her.

Reyes squeezed her hand. Heart lifting, she glanced at him. But he was staring straight ahead, his chiselled profile holding no signs of tenderness.

They exchanged vows in Spanish and English, with the sermon and following register signing also conducted in both languages.

When the priest urged Reyes to kiss his bride, his lips barely warmed hers for a moment before he stepped back.

Through it all, Jasmine smiled, and felt her heart break into tiny pieces. She'd fallen in love with a man who she had a soul-deep suspicion would never love her back.

A cheer from the thousands of subjects lining the streets roused Jasmine from her dazed state. Her hand tightened on Reyes's arm as he helped her into the gilt-framed glass carriage.

'Smile, *querida*. Anyone would think you were attending a funeral, not your own wedding.'

Plastering a smile on her face, she waved to the crowd. 'I haven't seen anything of you in the past two days,' she muttered from the side of her lips.

Reyes lifted his hand in acknowledgement of the crowd.

'And neither will you be seeing me for the coming weeks. I'm going to be very busy. I assume you saw Mendez among the guests?'

The heart that had squeezed painfully at his first words lurched in anxiety at the reference to Mendez. 'Yes, I did.'

'I sent the opening salvo yesterday. He's desperate to re-commence talks.'

She continued to wave as she'd been instructed and glanced at Reyes from the corner of her eye. 'What about the new council? Will they back you?'

'Yes, I have people in place I trust. I don't intend to stop until a new treaty is signed.'

She nodded, feeling miserable inside. Trust was important. Would he ever trust her enough to let himself feel more for her?

Not likely.

Her hand drooped. Thankfully, they were going through a long archway that connected San Domenica to the palace, where the wedding banquet was being held.

'Are you all right?'

Her breath huffed out before she could stop it. 'I'm an ex-juvenile delinquent who's just been crowned Princess of one of the most influential kingdoms in the world. I'm very, very far from all right.'

She startled as he picked up her free hand and placed it on his thigh. 'You've overcome the adversities thrust at you many times before. You'll rise to the challenge this time, too.'

Her limbs weakened and, against her better judgement, hope sprang in her chest. It bloomed when he picked up her hand and kissed the back of it.

The roar vibrated against the glass, and she became painfully aware of the reason for the gesture. Pain slammed into her. She couldn't pull away, not without thousands of eyes witnessing the withdrawal.

She kept the smile on her face until she feared her jaw would crack. 'So the honeymoon is over even before the ink has dried on the marriage certificate?' she demanded waspishly.

His eyes gleamed. 'I'm sure you'll agree that ours hasn't been a straightforward route to the altar.'

If it hadn't been for the baby, they wouldn't have found themselves in front of an altar at all. 'No. I guess not.'

His lips pursed, an infinitesimal motion no one else would've caught. But she saw it.

'Can I suggest, however, that we make the best of it?'

When his gaze dropped to her stomach, and an intense emotion passed over his face, Jasmine's world greyed further.

'Of course.'

She tried to breathe, but there was little room in her wedding dress for such frivolities. The lace-and-satin gown cupped her breast and torso and dropped to flare in a long dress and train. Isabella had called every fashion house in Europe and had started a bidding war on who would design the Crown Princess's wedding gown. The two-day deadline hadn't daunted even one of them.

Jasmine had finally settled on a Milanese couturier who'd worked magic with fabric right before her eyes. The material was heavy without being oppressive and the lace provided her with means of keeping cool in the hot Santo Sierran sun.

Now her crown was a different story. It weighed a ton, decorated as it was with ninety-nine diamonds, rubies and emeralds.

She touched it, felt the sharp bumps of precious gems beneath her fingers, and hysterical laughter bubbled from her throat. 'Is it true the crown designer stopped at ninety-nine because the palace decreed at the time that a hundred was too ostentatious?'

One corner of his mouth lifted. 'You've been learning Santo Sierra history.'

'I thought I should, seeing as I have no choice now.'

His smile dimmed. '*Sí*, we all have our crosses to bear.'

* * *

The wedding banquet carried on much like the wedding. Except where several priests muttered homilies, Jasmine had to sit through several speeches from well-wishers from around the world.

Numerous toasts were also raised in honour of the absent king, whom she'd met for the first time that morning.

So very like his son in stature, but with a defeated look in his eyes that made him seem...*less*. He'd haltingly given them their blessing before his medication had kicked in again.

She'd watched Reyes kiss his father's forehead with tears trapped in her throat. The love between father and son had been palpable, and Jasmine could just imagine what the turbulent period had done to them.

The clear love in his eyes when he gazed down at his father had given her a little more hope. Hope that was very quickly dwindling as the distance between them grew with each hour.

She smiled for a solid hour. Then smiled some more. Finally, she couldn't stand it any more. They'd finished with the formalities and those guests who wished it were getting into the dancing session of the evening.

Jasmine rose.

'I'm going to bed.'

Reyes glanced up from where he'd been in deep conversation with one of his advisors. Rising, too, he tucked her arm through his.

'I'll escort you.'

She shook her head. 'You don't need to—'

'*Sí*, I do.' The implacable dominance behind the words shut her up.

As they mounted the stairs her heart began to flutter.

Everything had gone at such a fast and furious pace, she hadn't thought to the wedding night.

Liar.

She'd thought of nothing *but* the wedding night since she

woke this morning, and terrified herself with different scenarios, most of which had ended with her going to bed alone.

Now, as she walked beside Reyes...her *husband*...she allowed herself to believe everything would be all right.

They reached their door and he raised her hand to his mouth, kissed the back of it. 'I've arranged for two of the servants to help you with your gown. Sleep well, *querida*.'

CHAPTER EIGHTEEN

One month later...

JASMINE WAS EXHAUSTED. Her feet ached and a headache throbbed behind her left ear. Relaxing in the air-conditioned car that was taking her back to the palace, she massaged her nape.

The four hours she'd been scheduled to teach her mediation class at Santo Sierra's municipal college had stretched to six. Not because her students were dying to learn everything she could teach them about mediation.

No. She'd been delayed because her young students had been fascinated about what it was like to be Queen.

Hysteria rose in her chest. She'd been Crown Princess for a pathetically short time before the King's sudden decline in health and subsequent death had propelled Reyes onto the throne and her into being Queen.

Beyond that, nothing had changed in her world. Jasmine had wanted to rip the rose-coloured glasses from her students' eyes. Tell them to find and settle for unconditional love and nothing else.

They wouldn't have believed her, though, even if she'd managed to utter the words. They all believed she'd captured the world's most eligible man and brought him to his knees after a whirlwind romance. Just as she, Reyes and his councillors had planned in San Estrela what felt like a lifetime ago.

What they didn't know was that she hadn't seen her husband for two weeks and she hadn't shared his bed since the night they'd spent at the wedding-cake house.

He'd spent the days leading up to his father's death in a vigil by King Carlos's bed with Isabella. Jasmine had berated herself for feeling left out.

Then, after the King's passing, they'd had to deal with the arduous protocol of the coronation. Reyes had accepted his duties as King with gravity and pride, but the result had been an even greater distance between them as he'd dived headlong into securing economic ties he'd fought so hard for.

Jasmine understood the duties that being King demanded. And yet she couldn't help but think her husband was using them as a perfect excuse to stay away from her.

She had woken up one night two weeks ago to find him in bed with her, his hand spread over her flat belly. Choking back tears, she'd placed her hand over his and gone back to sleep, her heart lifting with the hope that maybe they'd turned a corner.

She'd awakened hours later to an empty, cold half of the bed.

Jasmine hadn't thought a heart could shatter into tinier pieces until that moment.

The limo turned onto the mile-long drive leading to the palace.

Unable to face the palace and her lonely suite, she pressed the intercom on the armrest that connected to the driver. 'Can you take me round to the other house, please?'

Her driver glanced sharply at her. 'But, Your Majesty, it's Thursday today, not Friday.'

Jasmine nodded. 'I know, Raul. Take me there anyway.'

'Of course. As you wish, Your Majesty,' he replied deferentially.

She'd started going to the small house every Friday and staying the night. If she'd had a choice, Jasmine would've moved into the adorable little house. But considering she needed an armed escort wherever she went, she couldn't subject her guards to nightly patrols in the cold. So she'd restricted her visits to once a week. But this week, she might make it two nights...

Reyes was off hammering out the last terms of the new trade treaty, and Isabella had left for Milan this morning to consult over her autumn/winter wardrobe.

She'd urged Jasmine to go along with her, but she hadn't

been in the mood. Besides, by the time winter rolled around she would be in the late stages of pregnancy.

Leaning her head back, she rubbed her hand over her belly. The morning sickness had finally waned and, according to the team of doctors tending her, both she and the baby were healthy.

In a way, she understood how anyone on the outside would believe her world was rosy. She had everything her heart could wish for...

Except a husband who loved her even a fraction as hopelessly as she loved him.

They arrived at the house. Her door opened and Raul helped her out. She smiled and stepped out. 'Don't worry about informing the palace. I'll let them know when I get inside.'

'Yes, Your Majesty.'

She wanted to ask him to call her Jasmine. But protocol was protocol. She could go inside her little house, pretend she was at her flat in London for a while, but the palace, the Santo Sierran people who'd welcomed her wholeheartedly, and her absentee husband would still be her reality when she stepped out again.

Jasmine climbed the steps into the house and shut the door behind her. Ten minutes later, clutching a bowl of warm popcorn and a bottle of water, she plopped herself down in front of the TV and activated the chess game she'd started last week.

She was in the middle of checkmating *GrandChessMaster231* when the door burst open.

Her heart somersaulted, then banged against her ribs. 'Reyes!'

'Do you know how long the staff have been looking for you?' he burst out.

She rose on shaky feet, the unexpected sight of him rendering her senses stupid. 'But I...Raul knew where I was. I told him...' She stopped and grimaced.

'You told him what?' he demanded.

'I told him not to bother telling the palace staff where I was because I would ring them. I forgot.'

He kicked the door shut and clawed both hands through his hair. 'Raul discovered a slow puncture after he dropped you off so he went straight to the garage without stopping at the palace. The staff have been searching for you for the past four hours, Jasmine.'

'I'm sorry, I didn't think... I just wanted to be on my own for a little while.'

He dropped his hands, took a good look around the room, before he zeroed in on her again. This time, his gaze travelled from her head to her toes and back again. His hands slowly curled and uncurled at his sides.

'I've been told you spend a lot of time in here.'

She shrugged and considered sitting back down before her weak knees gave way. But sitting down would make Reyes's presence more overwhelming. So she settled for propping herself on the armrest.

'When did you get back?'

'This afternoon.'

They stared at each other a full minute before she managed to tear her gaze away. 'How was your trip?'

He scowled. 'I don't want to talk about my trip. Why have you not been sleeping in our bed?'

The bitter laugh escaped before she could stop it. 'It's not *our* bed, Reyes. I sleep in it alone, even when you're in Santo Sierra...even when we're under the same roof, I sleep alone. I'm sorry I worried the staff but you know where I am now, so you can go back to...wherever you came from.'

He looked stunned at her outburst. Jasmine wanted to laugh again, but she couldn't trust that it wouldn't emerge a sob.

She plopped herself down on the sofa and released the pause button.

After several minutes, he sat down beside her. Awareness of him crawled all over her body. But she didn't dare look at him or she was afraid she'd beg him to stay. Beg him to love her. While she wasn't afraid of begging, she was terrified of the rejection.

Was it her imagination or had he moved closer?

'Jasmine, we need to talk.'

Her hands shook. 'So talk.'

He shifted his gaze from her face to the screen. Or so she thought until his breath caressed her ear. 'Can I make a wager, *por favor*?' he asked, his tone rough.

'Can I stop you?'

'Ditch *GrandChessMaster231*. Play me. For every game I win, you stop and listen to me for three minutes.'

Her pulse tripped over itself. Her head started to turn, but she snapped her gaze back to the screen. 'Okay.'

He beat her at the first game in less than five minutes.

'What did you—'

His lips took hers. It was thorough, hungry, incandescent. Even as her mind reeled Jasmine's lips clung to his, already desperate for the pleasure only he could provide. The pleasure she'd missed more than breathing. Her nerveless fingers let go when he tugged the control from her grasp and dropped it on the floor, all without taking his mouth from hers.

He pulled away from her, his breathing ragged. 'I have two minutes remaining. Why do you not sleep in our bed, *mi corazón*?' he rasped.

'Because...because you're not in it,' she choked out. 'It's cold and lonely without you, and I can't stand it.'

He nodded solemnly, then captured her lips in another scorching kiss. Freeing her when his time was up, he picked up the control and handed it back to her.

He won the next game, too. Another bone-melting kiss, followed by a long look into her eyes. 'If I told you I missed you every day I was away from you, would you believe me?' His voice was low, deep. Almost prayerful.

'No.'

The hand in her hair trembled. 'I deserve that. I know I've behaved badly, have approached things the wrong way—'

'Your time's up.' She handed him his control.

She had burning questions of her own, so Jasmine put all her effort into winning the next level.

Her control fell from her fingers. 'You scheduled sex with your other candidates. But you left me, your wife—'

'My queen,' he growled.

'Your queen, to sleep in our marriage bed alone. Why? Am I so unlovable?'

He squeezed his eyes shut for a split second. 'You are far from unlovable, *querida*. It was me. I was afraid.'

She looked at him, stunned. 'Afraid of what?'

'The last time we were in this house together, you tried to get out of marrying me. I was afraid you'd change your mind about staying with me. We didn't have to get married in three days. I rushed it because I didn't want to let you go. I couldn't see past the fact that you'd woken up in the middle of the night determined to leave me. I'd already jumped on the pregnancy to make you my bride—'

She gasped. 'You wanted to marry me before you knew I was pregnant?'

'I dismissed perfectly good candidates because they were not you. I didn't want to admit it to myself, but I couldn't see any of them as my wife. None of them touched me the way you did. When the pregnancy presented itself as an option for me keeping you, I took it.'

The timer on the screen beeped. They both ignored it.

Tears filled her eyes. He brushed them away with his fingers.

'I thought you were only with me because of the baby.'

He looked down at her belly, then back at her. 'I love our child more than I can adequately put into words. I was overwhelmed with terror that you'd wake up in the middle of the night and ask for your freedom.'

Her mouth wobbled before she pursed her lips. 'And the night you came to me?'

'I came to tell you that Joaquin Esteban had been arrested.'

She gasped. 'What?'

'Mendez handed him over as part of our agreement. If I have anything to do with it, Esteban won't see the light of day again.'

Tears threatened. She blinked them away. 'So you came to tell me…and?'

'You looked so beautiful. I couldn't stay away. I missed you so much I couldn't breathe, never mind sleep. I planned to leave a note and be gone before you realised I was there. Leaving you ripped me apart. After that I didn't want to put myself through it again…so I used my duties as an excuse to stay away.'

A deep tremble shook her. 'Oh, Reyes.'

The timer beeped again.

She asked the question burning its way through her heart. 'Why are you here now, Reyes?'

'Because staying away from you is killing me. I need to be with you. With our baby. Loving you, protecting you both.' He started to reach for her.

She pulled back. 'Loving me?'

He closed his eyes. '*Dios.* This wasn't how I intended it to go—'

'Stop trying to wrap everything perfectly and just tell me how you feel!'

'I love you.' He exhaled, then struggled to catch his breath again. 'You blew me away that first night in Rio. I went to sleep thinking I could have found the one, even though I wasn't looking for you or even dreaming that the overwhelming feelings I felt for you existed. I let how I felt about my mother and Anaïs cloud my judgement so I could hate you for what you did. Even after I understood your motivation I was too scared to let you in.

'But you wormed your way in anyway. I admire your courage, your intelligence. My people love you already and it's been mere weeks since you entered their lives.'

Jasmine smiled. 'I love Santo Sierra. I've loved your home and its people since I stepped off the plane, Reyes. And I adore its king. When he's not breaking my heart by staying away from me for weeks on end.'

He caught her to him and smothered her with long, breath-stealing kisses. 'Your king is back. He will never leave your side again.' He spread his hand over her belly again the way he'd done, painfully briefly, weeks ago. 'He will never leave either of you. Ever again.'

With a flick of his finger, he turned the screen off. When he pulled his shirt over his head, she could barely keep from crying with joy. 'Reyes...'

'I'm here, *querida*,' he rasped.

Strong hands reached for her, lifting her up and carrying her into the bedroom. About to kiss him back, she paused. 'Did you bring any guards with you?'

A look, almost of regret, passed over his face. '*Sí*, it's protocol. But they know not to disturb us, even when you scream with passion. Now, where was I?'

The look in his eyes set off spirals of excitement through her. Feeling almost wanton, she slowly licked her tongue over her upper lip. 'Somewhere here, I think.'

She expected his customary growl, a sound she'd become accustomed to when he was fully aroused. Not this time. His eyes fixed on hers, he slowly inhaled, taking in her scent, imprinting her on his senses.

Jasmine found that even more enthralling than his growl and she watched, fascinated, as his chest expanded on his breath. Slowly he breathed out. 'I don't know what it is about you, Jasmine Navarre, but you captivate me. I might even go as far as to say I'm completely obsessed by you.'

Her breath stalled in her throat. 'Stay that way, and we won't have a problem at all.'

'I love you, my queen.'

'I love you, Reyes.'

His eyes misted. Then he cleared his throat. 'No more talking.'

His kiss was hard, possessive, sucking out every last ounce

of sanity from her as he unleashed the raw power of his arousal. He broke from her mouth to let her inhale a mere breath before he was back again, demanding. And receiving the unfettered response she couldn't hide.

Jasmine touched. Stroked. Nearly wept with delight at the sheer pleasure touching Reyes brought her. And everywhere she touched his skin seemed to react, to heat, bunch and flex, as if his every nerve ending was attuned to her.

That thought only served to increase her bliss. He pulled away for a moment. 'I know you'll berate me if I ruin your precious shirt, so I'll let you take it off.'

She wanted to tell him she didn't care if he ripped her shirt to shreds! But no way would she be able to articulate those words, not when her brain was too busy devouring the solid, sculpted lines of his naked torso. With shaking fingers, she divested herself of her shirt, letting it fall to the ground unheeded.

She arched her back, reached for her bra.

He growled low in his throat.

'I love that sound.'

'I growl only for you, *mi amor*. Always and for ever.'

* * * * *

HER HIGHNESS AND
THE BODYGUARD

CHRISTINE RIMMER

For my parents,
Tom and Auralee Smith,
who shared sixty-five amazing years together
and taught me what true love can do.

Chapter One

How could this have happened?

Rhiannon Bravo-Calabretti, princess of Montedoro, could not believe it. Honestly. What were the odds?

One in ten, maybe? One in twenty? She supposed that it could have just been the luck of the draw. After all, her country was a small one and there were only so many rigorously trained bodyguards to be assigned to the members of the princely family.

However, when you added in the fact that Marcus Desmarais wanted nothing to do with her ever again, reasonable odds became pretty much no-way-no-how. Because he would have said no.

So why hadn't he?

A moment later, she realized she knew why: because if he refused the assignment, his superiors might ask questions. Suspicion and curiosity could be roused and he wouldn't have wanted that.

Stop.

Rhia sat very still in the old wooden pew with her hands folded tightly in her lap.

What did it matter, why or how this had happened? The point was it *had* happened.

Enough. Done. She was simply not going to think about it—about *him*—anymore.

The wedding Mass was in English and the priest was concluding the homily drawn from scripture on the subject of Christian marriage. Rhia stared resolutely forward, trying to focus on the words. On the spare beauty of this little Catholic church in the small town of Elk Creek, Montana, where her sister was getting married.

The white-frame Church of the Immaculate Conception was simple and charming, as white inside as out. It smelled of candle wax and lemon furniture polish, with a faint echo of damp outerwear and old incense. The worn pews were of oak and all of them were full. Those who hadn't found seats stood at the back and along the sides.

He would be standing. In back somewhere by the doors, silent. And unobtrusive. Just like the other security people. Her shoulders ached from the tension, from the certainty that he was watching her, those eerily level, oh-so-serious, almost-green eyes staring twin holes into the back of her head.

It doesn't matter. Forget about it, about him.

What mattered was Belle.

Sweet, dignified, big-hearted Belle, all in white and positively radiant, standing at the plain altar before the communion rail with a tall, rugged American rancher named Preston McCade. It was a double ceremony. Belle's longtime companion, Lady Charlotte of the notorious Mornay branch of the family, was also getting married—to Preston McCade's father, a handsome old charmer named Silas.

"All rise," said the priest.

Rhia stood up with everyone else. The priest made a little speech about the rite of marriage and proceeded to question both the brides and the grooms about their intentions—their freedom of choice and faithfulness, their willingness to accept God's great gift of children.

And Rhia couldn't help it. Her mind relentlessly circled back to the subject of Marcus.

It just made no sense, she kept thinking. He wanted nothing to do with her. He wouldn't have chosen this.

So then, who *had* made the choice? Did someone else know about what had once happened between them, about those magical, unforgettable weeks so far in the past? Rhia had told one person. Only one. And that person was someone she trusted absolutely to say nothing. Marcus would have told no one. Which meant that no one else could possibly know.

Could they? A cold shiver slid down her spine. Was that what had happened here? Somehow, someone else did know and had decided to throw them together like this for some completely incomprehensible reason?

No. That made no sense. The very idea was ridiculous. What possible benefit could there be to anyone in forcing proximity upon them?

And besides, who else could know? It had been so long ago—eight years. Which was three years before her brother Alex had been kidnapped in Afghanistan, back when her family wasn't so terribly security conscious.

At the time, Rhia had been a freshman at UCLA. Once she was settled in her dorm and going to classes, she'd had no one watching over her. She'd enjoyed being just another student, like all the other students. Her private life at that time had been simply that: private. After all, she was sixth in line to the throne, with four brothers and Belle ahead of her. Plus, Rhia had always been a well-behaved sort of person. Between her good-girl reputation and the extreme unlikelihood that she would ever end up on Montedoro's throne, she'd been of little interest to the scandal sheets.

Which was why she still believed that no one else knew.

At the altar, the ceremony had progressed to the exchange of vows. Rhia stood a little straighter and tried to concentrate on the beautiful, familiar words.

"I, Preston, take you, Arabella, for my lawful wife, to have and to hold, from this day forward…"

Rhia knew she was making too much of this. She should just…let it go. Let it be. Marcus wasn't going to bother her. He was all about duty and keeping to his "place," just as he'd always been. He'd hardly spoken three words to her since yesterday, when they boarded the family jet at Nice and she learned he would provide her security during this trip.

Why he'd been assigned to her didn't matter. He was there to protect her, period. And she only had to get through this one day and the evening. Tomorrow, she would fly home again.

And be free of him.

Forever.

Rhia released a slow sigh. Yes. It would be all right. She smiled a little, watching her beautiful sister. Belle was saying her vows now, her eyes only for her groom, her fine-boned face seeming to glow from within. "I, Arabella, take you, Preston…"

In the front pew, Benjamin, Preston's toddler, let out a happy trill of laughter and called, "Belle, Dada, Shar-Shar, Pawpaw!" The guests laughed, too, as Belle, her groom, Charlotte and *her* groom paused to turn and wave at the little one, who sat on the lap of a sturdy-looking older lady.

A moment later, Belle began her vows all over again.

Yes. Truly. It was only for one more day, Rhia reminded herself, her heavy mood lightened by the laughter of the little boy.

She could bear anything for a single day—a day that was already halfway through. It had been a shock, that was all. And now she was past it.

She would simply ignore him. How hard could that be?

Really hard.

Harder by the hour, by the minute. By the second, for heaven's sake.

After the ceremony, the brides, the grooms and Belle and Rhia's parents, Her Sovereign Highness Adrienne and His Serene Highness Evan, held a receiving line in the vestibule. Rhia got to hug Belle and Charlotte and wish them all the love and happiness in the world, and to congratulate the two grooms.

Then there were pictures. Rhia had to stay for those. Belle and Charlotte had chosen to forgo attendants and there were no groomsmen, but Belle wanted her family— her parents and sisters and brothers—in the photographs. So that took more than an hour. Outside the sun hovered just above the craggy, snowcapped mountaintops and the temperature was dropping.

The whole time they lingered at the church, Marcus lurked just beyond Rhia's line of sight. He had a knack for staying out of the way and yet, somehow, always remaining nearby, for keeping her constantly in his view. His expression, whenever she made the mistake of sliding a nervous glance in his direction, was as still and unreadable as a bottomless pool in some secret, hidden place.

She did try to ignore him, something so easily done with any other man. She tried so very hard not to turn her head his way, not to look at him.

But it was no good. He seemed to be everywhere—and nowhere—at once. And she needed so strongly to pick him out of the crowd, to pin him in space, to know for certain where, exactly, he was.

The photographer was posing a shot of Belle and Charlotte holding the beaming Benjamin between them, when Silas and Preston McCade came toward her. At first, Rhia thought the two men intended to speak with her. But then, with matching nods and smiles and a couple of murmured greetings in her direction, they moved on by.

She turned to watch them step right up to Marcus.

Marcus nodded at father and son. "Gentlemen." His voice so deep and solemn and contained. "Congratulations."

Silas laughed and held out his hand. "Good to see you, Marcus. Place ain't the same without you."

Marcus took the older man's offered hand and spoke again, quietly enough that Rhia couldn't make out the words. Silas and Preston both chuckled.

And Rhia was left turning, lurching away. Stunned. Stricken, that Marcus could be almost friendly with the McCade men while behaving like a bleak and watchful stranger around her. Yes, she already knew that he'd been assigned to Belle when Belle came to America to nurse her terminally ill friend, Anne, who was Benjamin's mother. But that he'd remained with Belle when Belle brought Benjamin to Montana? She'd had no idea, not until just now when the McCade men had greeted him.

Dear God, Rhia hated all the secrecy. All the lies. She was not in any way ashamed of having loved Marcus. She didn't want to keep the secrets and she didn't want to tell the lies. Marcus wanted all that. And all those years ago, she'd foolishly promised him that they would do it his way.

Thus, she had only become aware that Marcus had previously been assigned to Belle when she flew to North Carolina for Anne's funeral. She'd seen him there, guarding Belle, and been as hollowed-out and desolate at the sight of him as she was right now.

Except that now was worse because today he was watching *her* and there was no escaping him.

Rhia slipped through the wide-open oak doors to the vestibule, driven to get away from him, though she knew it was hopeless. He would only have to follow her.

In the vestibule, her sister Alice appeared at her side, all dimples and laughing eyes, her brown hair a wild mass of loose curls to her shoulders. She wrapped an arm around Rhia and whispered, "How are you managing?"

"Don't ask."

Alice chuckled. "Oops. Sorry. I already did."

Rhia loved, admired and trusted all four of her sisters. But with Alice, the bond went even deeper. They were not only siblings, they were best friends. They told each other everything. And they had sworn from childhood to protect and respect each others' confidences. Rhia needed one person in her life to whom she could say anything. Alice was that person. And Rhia told her everything. Alice was the one who knew about Marcus.

Marcus stepped through the open doors into the vestibule. Spotting her instantly, he slid back into the shadows along the wall, where he was out of the way yet could keep her in sight.

"This is ridiculous," Rhia muttered out of the side of her mouth. "I can't get away from him and it's driving me insane. I'm pathetic. How can I possibly care this much?"

Alice moved in front of Rhia, facing her, blocking Marcus's view of her. Now they could talk without the unpleasant possibility that Marcus would overhear them or read their words from their lips.

"If it's so unbearable," Alice suggested low, "talk to Alex. Tell him you want someone else." Their brother Alexander had created the elite fighting force called the Covert Command Unit, or CCU, in which Marcus served. Right now, Alex was back in the chapel with his wife, Her Royal Highness Liliana of Alagonia, and their three-month-old twins, Melodie and Phillipe.

"If I go to Alex, it will only look bad for Marcus. Plus, it could make Alex wonder if there's something between us."

Alice made a snorty sound—but when she spoke, she did it very quietly. "So what? Deny it."

"It would still reflect negatively on Marcus, you know that."

"Too bad."

Rhia suppressed a sigh and tried to explain in a near whisper, without moving her lips too much. "Haven't we been through this?" She darted glances from side to side. No one seemed to be the least interested in their conversation. "Marcus sees himself as beneath me. He couldn't stand for Alex or anyone else to suspect that there might have been something between us once, that we were..." She let the words trail off. No need to be overly specific. Alice knew, anyway.

Her sister reached out and cupped the side of her face with a soothing hand. "You really must get past all this. You know that, don't you?"

"I'm trying." And she had been trying for eight endless years. During that time she'd had two fiancés. Both good men, each supremely suitable: an internationally known artist from a fine family and a generous duke who worked diligently for a number of worthy charities. Somehow, she hadn't managed to bring herself to marry either of those men. And they had both eventually realized that her heart wasn't in it. The relationships had died. She remained on friendly terms with both of her former fiancés, a fact that made her failure with them all the more wretched. As though both men had realized that there hadn't been enough to what they'd shared in the first place to be bitter or angry over losing it.

"Try harder," Alice suggested with a sigh.

"I know you're right. And I do need to get over it. And I am completely and utterly fed up with myself, with my silly broken heart and my inability to get past something that happened years ago. I want to scream, Allie. I want to scream really, really loud."

"Just hold it together. Just a little while longer." Alice tipped her head in the direction of the open doors to the chapel. "They're finishing up. We'll be leaving for the ranch soon." The reception was to be held in the main house at the McCade family ranch, which was half an hour's drive away. Alice reached out again, still aiming to soothe. She gently stroked Rhia's pinned-up hair. "Just breathe, all right? Stay calm." She lifted her other hand, where she held the keyless ignition remote to the shiny red pickup she'd rented that morning. "You can ride to the ranch with me and the bodyguards can follow us. And after we put in our time there, we'll bust out. You'll have fun and forget all your troubles, I promise you."

Rhia gave her a wary look. "Excuse me. Bust out?"

"It's cowboy country. We'll go wild."

"No, Alice. Seriously."

Allie patted her shoulder. "Trust me. Busting out is the answer. I haven't exactly worked out the logistics yet. But it is going to be good."

Rhia should have nixed the busting out right then and there. It was a bad idea. But she was just upset enough and feeling trapped enough to think that doing something risky and wild wouldn't be half bad. *Anything* to get her mind off the bodyguard she could never quite seem to forget.

She did ride with Alice to the ranch. Marcus, along with Allie's bodyguard, a giant named Altus, followed them in one of the black luxury SUVs that the family had leased for the visit.

Alice kept up a steady stream of cheerful chatter during the ride. She was excited about the electronic key. You carried it on your person and the doors and ignition responded to the touch of your hand. "Amazing, isn't it, the things they come up with these days?"

Rhia tried to appreciate her efforts to brighten the mood. Still, it felt like the drive went on forever. Rhia stared out the windshield at the endless sky that was darkening steadily toward nighttime, at the craggy, shadowed peaks in the distance, and the rolling, open land dotted here and there with patches of leftover snow. She gazed glumly at the patient, hulking shapes of grazing cattle. Alice kept saying how beautiful it all was.

Rhia agreed with her. Montana was stark and beautiful and a little forbidding to a woman raised in a palace on the Mediterranean. It brought to mind the great Western artist, Charles Russell—or at least it did for Rhia, who had studied Russell's work in her History of American Art class when she was at UCLA.

The McCade ranch house was two stories high, made of wood and stone. They'd hired cowboys to act as valets. Allie turned over her electronic key to a tall, lean fellow in a white hat and they went up the wide front steps.

At the door, the two brides and their grooms greeted the guests with hugs and handshakes and happy smiles. There was plenty of good food—what the Americans called home cooking—laid out on the big table in the formal dining room. Guests loaded up plates and sat wherever they could find a chair, in the living room, the family room or the kitchen. Many simply stood in the foyer holding their plates, chatting about the beauty of the simple wedding, about the weather, about the quarter horses the McCade ranch was known for.

Alice, whose life revolved around the fabulous Akhal-Teke horses she bred and trained at home, was on her way out the door to visit the McCade stables the minute she'd finished with the greetings. Before she went, she whispered to Rhia, "Do you have your international driving permit?"

"It's in my clutch bag. The housekeeper took it upstairs with my coat."

"Go up and get it. Just the permit. If you get your bag and coat, you-know-who will guess that something's up."

"What exactly are you planning?"

"I told you. Escape." That was all Alice would say. She turned and went out the door, Altus behind her.

Rhia would have gone, too, but it was cold outside and she cared more than Alice did about preserving her shoes—in this case, a gorgeous pair of blue satin Manolo Blahniks with four-inch heels. And then there was Marcus, who would only follow her out there, which meant that she wouldn't be able to complain further to her sister about the awfulness of the situation, anyway.

So she went upstairs and into the bedroom where all the coats were piled. She found her bag and got her permit and put it in the concealed inner pocket of her silk suit jacket, taking a minute after that to smooth her hair and apply fresh lip gloss so that when she exited the bedroom, Marcus would assume she'd only gone in to freshen up.

He was waiting right there in the upstairs hall when she emerged. Her heart lurched alarmingly at the sight of him. She took care not to make eye contact with him as she turned for the stairs.

Once on the first floor, she proceeded to the dining room, where she piled some food onto a pretty gold-trimmed china plate, grabbed a flute of champagne and mingled with her family and the neighbors and friends that the McCades had known all their lives. She worked hard to keep her spirits up, and she knew she was talking a little too loudly and laughing too much, trying to show both herself and the silent, ever-present bodyguard that she was having a great time and didn't really even notice he was there.

It was exhausting. Her neck ached from keeping her back so straight and holding her chin high. And then there was the tension headache pounding at her temples, battering at the base of her skull. She only wanted to return to Elk Creek, to the motor inn where her family had booked every room, to take a long bath, gulp down some aspirin and climb into bed.

However, if she left now, before Allie returned to rescue her with that big red pickup she'd rented, Marcus would be driving her. She did not want to be trapped alone in a vehicle with Marcus for the ride back.

So she stayed.

"You're scrunching up your forehead," Alice whispered in her ear. She smelled of hay and fresh air.

"I have a splitting headache. Did you just come back inside?"

"I did. Preston and Silas have my complete respect and admiration. The stables are clean and open and well-lighted with excellent turnout into large, grassy pastures. The horses are happy and healthy and beautiful. It's a fine operation. I would love to get a chance to ride while we're here. Too bad we're leaving tomorrow and I failed to bring riding clothes from the Drop On Inn."

"Oh, Allie. You got mud on those fabulous Jimmy Choos."

Alice shrugged. "It was worth it. Did you get the permit?"

"Yes."

"Excellent. I have come up with a plan for you, for *both* of us."

"Uh-oh."

Allie poked her in the ribs. "Don't *uh-oh* me. It's a brilliant plan."

"Like the time you crashed that big BMW motorcycle you borrowed into that poor fruit seller's stand at the open-air market?" The open-air market was a Saturday tradition in Montedoro. Rows of street vendors set up stands and sold fresh produce, meats, baked goods and sundries on the Rue St. Georges.

"That was not a plan." Allie spoke sternly. But her eyes were gleaming. "That was an accident."

"Exactly my point."

Allie leaned closer. "Do you want to get away from him or not?"

Against her better judgment, Rhia slid him a glance. Those eyes that were both cool and smoldering at once gazed back at her. Knowing. Ever watchful. She let out a weary sigh. "You know that I do."

"Then let's go. We'll find some thrilling American bar where they play songs about lost love. We can dance with cowboys and drink tequila and you can forget all your troubles."

"You know he'll only follow us. It *is* his job—and what about *your* bodyguard?" Rhia tipped her head in Altus's direction. Like Marcus, he was close by.

"We'll wait till they both turn away and then we'll duck out."

"But Marcus *never* turns away."

Allie took her hand and dragged her into the dining room. Before the bodyguards could follow, she pressed the truck's electronic key into her palm, closing her fingers around it. "The pickup is right out in front, ready to go. I had the valet bring it up before I came inside."

Rhia opened her palm and saw that the key wasn't the only thing Allie had handed her. "Condoms." There were two of them. "You're not serious."

"Stop looking at your hand. He'll see."

Rhia closed her fist and dropped it to her side. "What could I possibly need condoms for? I'm not going to have sex with a stranger."

"Be prepared, I always say."

"But, Allie, you know me better than that."

"Stop arguing. Get near the front door so you can duck out fast. I'll create a distraction." Her eyes were bright with mischief and excitement.

"Then he'll follow *you*—and you'll lead him to me."

"No, I won't. That's why I gave *you* the key. Because on second thought, I'll stay right here. You're on your own. If you want to get away, do it."

It was a wild and stupid idea and Rhia knew she should simply say no. She wasn't like Allie. Except for that one time with Marcus eight years ago and that other crushing, humiliating event two years after that, Rhia never stepped outside the rules. She inevitably behaved in a manner both dignified and agreeable, as the daughter of an ancient and noble house should. She had a lovely career overseeing acquisitions and restorations at her country's National Museum, a career that was more of an avocation, really, as befitted a princess of Montedoro. She lived a quiet, respectable life in a beautiful little villa with a fine view of the sea.

And look where all that exemplariness had gotten her. Twice engaged to "suitable" men she'd never managed to actually love. Still pretending that she wasn't pining for a man who had made it more than clear that it was long over between them and would forever remain that way.

The man in question was standing in the doorway to the foyer. Watching. Tall, wide-shouldered and beautifully male, with those distant eyes she wanted to drown in and that fine, sculpted mouth she only longed to kiss again....

Fair enough. Maybe Alice had the right idea. Perhaps it *was* time she shook things up a little. "I'll get my coat." She turned for the stairs and the bedroom up there that had been designated as a coat room.

Allie grabbed her hand, yanked her back and whispered in her ear, "You are no good at being bad." Patiently, she explained again, "Remember? If you get your coat, he'll know you're leaving."

"But it's cold out there."

"Believe it or not, the pickup has a heater. And so will the cowboy honky-tonk bar."

"A honky-tonk bar? Where am I supposed to find one of those?"

Allie puffed out her cheeks and crossed her eyes. "Just keep driving until you see one."

"What if I never see one?"

"You will—and you're stalling."

"Am not."

"Are so. Do you want to get away or not?"

"I... If I run away, Marcus could be in trouble for losing track of me."

"That's his problem."

"But I..."

"Rhia. Make up your mind. Are you doing this or not?"

She sucked in a fortifying breath. "I am. Yes. Definitely."

"Then wander over near the front door and wait for me to distract him."

"How will you do that?"

"You'll see."

"Oh, wait. I get it. You don't *know* how you'll do it."

"I will figure out something."

"Allie, I really don't think..."

But her sister was already turning away. And not looking back.

Rhia watched her go and told herself to stop being a coward. She was busting out. It was better to make a move—even a *bad* move—than to go on like this, moping around dear Belle's wedding reception, wishing she could be anywhere but here.

So she slid around the end of a heavy china cabinet where, for a moment or two, Marcus couldn't see as she slipped the car remote and the unnecessary condoms into the pocket of her suit jacket next to her driving permit. Turning, she smoothed her hair and grabbed a bottle of water from the flower-bedecked beverage table. Sipping the water, doing her best to act as though she wasn't going anywhere but a different room, she wandered out into the living room and stood and chatted for a bit with her brother Rule and his wife, Sydney. She cooed over Sydney and Rule's new baby, Ellie, who was the same age as Alex and Lili's twins. She even got a shy kiss from the adorable Trevor, Rule and Sydney's three-year-old.

Eventually, sipping her water and playing it ultracasual, she meandered toward the foyer, pausing to share a few words with anyone who happened to make eye contact with her along the way. In the foyer near the stairs, she chatted up an older couple who were very active in the church where Belle had just gotten married, and then circled around until, at last, she was standing in front of the door.

By then, she was actually having a little fun. Preparing to do something she probably shouldn't wasn't as bad as she'd imagined it might be.

Would Allie be ready to provide the distraction—whatever it was?

And where was Allie, anyway?

No need to ask. Right then, her sister made her move. A sudden shriek had heads whipping toward the door to the living room, where Marcus just happened to be standing—though off to the side a bit. Carrying a plate mounded with food from the buffet table and a tall glass of what appeared to be iced tea, Allie tripped over her slightly muddy Jimmy Choos and lost her balance as Marcus whirled her way and caught her before she ended up facedown on the hardwood floor.

What he didn't catch was the plate of home cooking or the big glass of ice and tea. It all went flying. The food hit him in the face and the tea splashed down the front of his handsome dress uniform.

Rhia didn't stick around to see what happened next. While all eyes were on Alice and the food-and-tea-drenched bodyguard, she opened the front door and slipped through.

Chapter Two

The big red pickup, shining in the light of the moon, was waiting at the foot of the wide front steps, just as Allie had promised. Breathless and giggling, feeling wild and rather wonderful, Rhia raced down the steps and around to the driver's side.

She was up behind the wheel in a split second. Her hands were steady as she pushed the ignition button. She put the truck in gear and off she went, the tires squealing a little, fishtailing, too, making her feel thrillingly disruptive and undisciplined as she took off down the long driveway that led to the highway.

Halfway to the little town of Elk Creek, driving way too fast, with no one behind her, she threw back her head and laughed out loud. The cab was toasty warm from the pickup's excellent heater and she was on her way somewhere with cowboys and country-western music. She turned on the radio. Wouldn't you know it was set to a country station?

A duet. A man and a woman singing about the hot and dangerous love they once had and how they wanted that again. Rhia turned the sound up good and loud and let the music fill the cab.

She left it up loud. Through that song and the song after that and the ones that followed, too.

When she reached Elk Creek, she slowed down and drove through the town at the speed limit, her eyes scanning the street to either side, looking for that cowboy bar her sister had been so sure she was bound to find.

She saw a steak house called the Bull's Eye and a corner bar called Charlie's Place, but both of them looked way too quiet. Not the kind of establishments where exciting things involving cowboys, tequila shots and line dancing might be going on.

Elk Creek was in her rearview mirror before she even realized she'd driven through and was leaving town. She kept going, the almost-full moon leading her on, her designer shoe pressing the accelerator again. Eventually, Marcus would be coming after her. She needed to be far enough ahead that he wouldn't find her that night.

She should probably turn off the highway, take some other road to throw him off her trail. But if she did that, Lord knew where she'd end up.

Then it occurred to her that she ought to just use the GPS. She pulled off onto the shoulder and fiddled with it until she figured out how to ask it for bars in the vicinity.

What do you know?

Twenty-point-six miles straight ahead. Rowdy's Roadhouse. Music, liquor, pool tables, video poker—and dancing nightly. Just what Allie had promised she'd find if she only went looking.

Humming along to a song about a man who was hard to love, Rhia swung out onto the empty highway again, headed for Rowdy's.

Captain Marcus Desmarais lived to serve his country.

And right now he was doing one craptastic job of it— as the Americans might say.

He drove the black SUV faster than he should have, hardly slowing as he went through Elk Creek, eyes scanning the street, on one side and then the other, looking for a shiny red pickup or a beautiful dark-haired woman dressed in a blue silk suit with a snug jacket and a short, slim skirt that showed off her fine, long legs.

He didn't see either—the woman or the pickup.

That had better mean she was up ahead of him.

She had better not have turned off the main highway. If she'd done that, he might never find her until she was damn good and ready to be found.

But no. He was going to find her and he wasn't allowing himself to think otherwise. He would find her. Or she would come back on her own within the next few hours. He would consider no other possibility. He ground his teeth together, stepped harder on the gas and focused on the road ahead.

An hour. That was how long His Highness Alexander had given him to track her down solo and solve the problem simply, without all the unpleasantness of sounding the alarm. If he couldn't do that, the prince would be calling in reinforcements, which would terrify her family, cast a pall on what should have been a day of joy and celebration and provide fodder for the scandal sheets.

An hour—twenty-five minutes of which were already gone.

Why was she doing this? What could she possibly hope

to prove by endangering herself in this foolish, reckless, pointless way?

The questions didn't even bear asking. He knew very well why. And he knew what she hoped to gain by running: she only wanted to get away from *him.*

He should never have accepted this assignment. He'd known what it meant, that she would hate having him as her protector. Staying well clear of her was essential and had been since those eight unforgettable weeks they'd been together nearly a decade ago. So he should have spoken up, asked to be removed, no matter what the higher-ups made of it. If they'd refused him, at least he would have done what he could.

But he was too proud. And too ambitious. And he didn't want *her* hurt, either—at least, no more than he'd already hurt her. He didn't want anyone wondering why he would refuse such an assignment, didn't want them digging around in the past and maybe, against all odds, learning what had happened so long ago.

So he hadn't spoken up. He hadn't requested a different assignment. He'd left her to turn to her impetuous younger sister to find a way to escape him.

The town vanished behind him. The dark highway lay ahead, growing darker as clouds crept across the face of the moon and obscured the thick wash of bright stars. He pressed the gas harder, adjusted the Bluetooth device in his ear and kept going.

On the radio, a lonely cowboy begged his girl to come over. By then, Rhia had it turned to full volume.

A moment later, Rowdy's Roadhouse appeared up ahead, a wash of lovely, garish light on the dark horizon. "Arriving at your destination in point-two miles," said the GPS. Rhia turned it off.

She slowed as she reached the entrance to the great big parking lot lighted with bright streetlamps on tall poles and chock full of muddy pickups and enormous sport utility vehicles. Rowdy's itself was a gray-shingled square building in the center of the lot, complete with giant neon sign over the door proclaiming it Rowdy's Roadhouse and Motor Inn. The sign had two arrows. One pointed at the door below it, the other straight up—presumably indicating the long, low building at the back of the lot, which had its own neon sign advertising rooms for rent.

Rhia found a space when a big green quad cab pulled out. She parked and patted her pocket with the permit in it. In the USA, bartenders were usually careful to check the age of their patrons.

About then it occurred to her that she had no money. It was going to be difficult to get a beer and a tequila shot without cash or a credit card. But then she shrugged and climbed down from the pickup, anyway. Even without the tequila, she could still dance with a cowboy if one would only cooperate and ask her.

Or maybe she would simply have to be truly bold and do the asking herself.

It was a dirt parking lot. Not good for her satin shoes. Too bad. She'd come this far and she wasn't turning back now, not even at the risk of ruining her favorite Manolos. She locked up the pickup and turned toward the music and neon lights.

Overhead, the sky was a solid sheet of darkness now. Clouds had rolled in and obscured the moon and stars. She wrapped her arms around herself, shivering a little because the night was so cold. There were cowboys leaning against the long rail on the wide front porch of the roadhouse. They watched her come toward them.

One of them let out a long whistle. "Oh, darlin'. Hot and

classy. Just how I like 'em." He was tall and very lean. He grinned at her and she saw he had a wide space between his front teeth.

A red-haired woman in a rhinestone shirt and studded jeans smacked his big hat off his head. "Mind your manners, Bobby Dale, or I won't be responsible for what happens next."

Bobby Dale bent and scooped up his hat. "Be nice, Mona. I was only jokin' around."

Mona made a humphing sound and aimed a wide, friendly smile at Rhia. "Come on in. The music's great and the company is passable."

As it turned out, Mona was the head bartender at Rowdy's. She took Rhia inside and got her a beer and a shot of tequila on the house. At the sight of Rhia's driving permit, which gave her full name but none of her titles, Mona asked, "From Montedoro, huh? You here for Pres McCade's wedding to our princess?"

Our princess. Rhia found it rather charming, that already the people of Belle's new community thought of her as "theirs." "I am," she said. "It was a beautiful wedding."

"I knew it would be. We're all mighty fond of Pres, and of Silas. Makes us happy to see two good men find what they've been lookin' for."

The band started up again and a cowboy tapped Rhia on the shoulder. She took a sip of her beer, gave Mona a conspiratorial wink, and off she went to learn a cowboy dance called the two-step.

Twenty minutes later, she'd danced with three more cowboys, each as polite and gentlemanly as the one before. She was having an absolutely perfect time and thinking that maybe she would borrow a phone and make a call or two, see if she could reach Allie to tell her where she was and not to worry and say she would be staying out until midnight or maybe later.

Also, it would be a chance to make sure that no one was too terribly concerned about her having slipped away. She could make it very clear that she was safe and warm and had only had one beer and one tequila shot and would return to the ranch as soon as Rowdy's Roadhouse closed its doors for the night.

Mona was pouring drinks at the other end of the bar. Rowdy's was a busy place that Saturday night and the customers were thirsty. Rhia climbed onto her stool, drained the last of her beer and waited for Mona to glance her way.

She sensed a manly presence behind her. Smiling, she turned to face the cowboy she knew would be standing there, planning to tell him she would be happy to dance with him as soon as she'd made a phone call.

Her heart jumped into her throat and got stuck there, cutting off her air, when she saw that it wasn't a cowboy at all.

It was Marcus.

Chapter Three

Someone must have come up with a change of clothes for him after his close encounter with all that home cooking on Allie's plate.

He was wearing old jeans and rawhide boots, a dark sweatshirt and a heavy canvas jacket. He smelled of the cold mountain air outside and he looked more dangerous and exciting and wonderful than any of the handsome cowboys she'd danced with so far. His expression, however, was even bleaker than usual.

"Time to go, ma'am." His voice sent the usual infuriating warm shivers cascading through her.

She swallowed her silly heart back down into its proper place and remained on her stool. "No, thank you. I'm having a lovely time and I'm not ready to leave yet."

He frowned rather thunderously and then touched the device in his ear, listening. After a moment, he said, "Yes, sir. All is well, sir. Although Her Highness expresses reluctance to leave."

Rhia groaned. "Is that my brother?"

Marcus granted her a put-upon glance as he spoke again—but not to her. "Yes, sir. I will. Thank you, sir."

The call appeared to have been concluded, so she asked a second time, "My brother?"

He scowled, an expression both dismissive and chockfull of exasperation. "That was His Highness Alexander, yes. Are you ready to go now, ma'am?"

Ma'am. He was such a stickler for protocol. You would think he had never seen her naked. She wanted to toss her drink in his face. Unfortunately, it was empty. "No. I am *not* ready to go. If you insist on staying here until I *am* ready, please move away from me." She flung out a hand in the direction of the far wall. "Go over there and lurk in the shadows somewhere. No one will ask me to dance with you standing right next to me, glowering."

He told her again, as if he hadn't already said it twice, "Ma'am, we have to leave."

"No, *we* most certainly do not. Go if you want to. I'm staying."

He stood even straighter—if that was possible. "Ma'am, there's a storm coming."

She answered with excruciating pleasantness. "If you call me *ma'am* one more time, I am going to throw back my head and scream."

He tried again, without expression or vocal inflection—and without saying *ma'am,* either. "There is a snowstorm coming. It could be a bad one. It is imperative that we return to Elk Creek and the safety of the motor lodge."

"What are you talking about? There was no storm predicted."

"I noticed the clouds gathering and I listened to the

weather channel," he explained slowly and patiently, as one would speak to an idiot or a very young child. "There *is* a snowstorm coming. Please take my word for it."

"But it's April. I don't believe you. And even if there is a little snow on the way, look at all these people." She held out her hands, palms out, indicating the large, busy bar and everyone in it. "If the weather is going to be dangerous, why aren't they leaving?"

"It often snows in Montana in April."

"Oh, because *you're* such an expert."

"These people live here. They are accustomed to snowstorms. They have proper outerwear and the right vehicles, which they know how to drive."

"I have the right vehicle. And I can drive it perfectly well. And as to my lack of outerwear, the pickup I drove here has a heater. What do you think about that?"

"Rhiannon. It's time to go."

She blinked at him. "You must be upset. You just called me by my first name."

He stared at her for several seconds and then said, too softly, "Please."

She felt herself wavering, starting to feel like a spoiled, misbehaving child.

But no. She wasn't going to slink out of here just because Marcus Desmarais wanted her to. She didn't believe him about the weather. He was just saying that to get her to go.

The facts were simple. She wasn't doing anything wrong. The clock over the bar said it was just ten-thirty and she had every right to stay a little longer if she wanted to. Especially now that he'd tracked her down. Now that he was here, doing his precious duty, protecting her, if for any reason she happened to need protection—which she had not at any point thus far.

Her brother Alex knew where she was and that her bodyguard was with her and that meant no one at the Mc-Cade Ranch was worried about what might happen to her. There was no real reason she couldn't stay for just a bit.

"Marcus. Go and stand by the wall. I want to dance some more. I will let you know when I am ready to leave."

His face remained carved in stone while his eyes burned with green fury. He glared at her for a slow count of five and she became a little concerned that he would actually touch her, that he would manacle her arm with that big hand of his and drag her bodily from the premises. Sparks chased themselves beneath her skin at the very idea.

But he had iron control. In the end, he only turned sharply on his heel and went where she'd told him to go.

Marcus watched her.

It was all he was allowed to do, all she had permitted him to do.

Watch. As she danced with another cowboy. And another after that.

Frustration built. He wanted to grab her and throw her over his shoulder and carry her out of there bodily. But he could never do any such thing. She was his princess and he lived to serve her. And that meant, when it came right down to his will versus hers, she held all the cards.

No matter that a storm was brewing. No matter that all those cowboys she was dancing with were strangers. And she was beautiful and friendly and she gave her smiles to everyone.

There was going to be trouble with one of those strangers. One of them was bound to go too far as the evening wore on and the liquor kept flowing.

Then he would probably have to hurt someone. He didn't particularly look forward to that.

But then again, the more cowboys she danced with and the more he was forced to stand there and watch them put their common hands on her person, the more he felt heat building in his chest and behind his eyes, the more hurting someone began to seem like a good and necessary thing.

Rhia danced with yet another cowboy. It wasn't as much fun as it had been before Marcus appeared.

Somehow, with him there, observing her every move in that cold and disapproving way of his, no doubt judging her for not being a proper princess, it all seemed a bit tawdry. The pleasure had definitely gone out of her little adventure.

When the next cowboy stepped up to claim her, she thanked him, but said she was going to sit down for a while. She returned to the bar, where someone had bought her another tequila and a fresh beer.

Mona stepped up close. "Compliments of Bobby Dale," she said.

A few stools away, Bobby Dale raised his bottle of beer in a salute, grinning wide to reveal that space between his teeth.

Why not? She knocked back the shot and chugged the beer in a manner supremely unprincesslike. Somewhere in the shadows, Marcus was bound to be scowling in disgust.

She told herself she didn't care. Not in the least.

Bobby Dale signaled Mona to pour her another. The bartender had the shot poured before Rhia could stop her.

"Never mind about the beer," Rhia said. Without stopping to consider the wisdom of it, she picked up the shot glass and drained it.

Foolish. She knew that. The tequila made a fiery trail down the back of her throat and spread heat in her belly and she already regretted drinking it—and the one before it, too.

What was getting drunk going to prove? Nothing good. Plus, now she needed to pee.

She went to the ladies', where she had to wait for a stall. When she'd finished and was washing her hands, she saw that her hair was coming loose from its thick knot at the back of her head, her bangs were mussed and her lip gloss had long ago worn off. She looked way too much like she felt: forlorn and weary, a little bit woozy from those shots and the beer, with faint circles under her eyes.

She straightened her skirt and jacket, smoothed her bangs, repinned her hair, yanked her shoulders back and marched out the door. Of course, *he* was right there in the hallway, waiting for her.

One look at him, so stern and unwavering, patient as death, and she knew it was no good. The evening was over. It was time to go back to the Drop On Inn and try to get a few hours' sleep before boarding the family jet for home tomorrow.

Thanks to those shots and the beer, she shouldn't be driving. And she wouldn't. She would do the right thing and ride back with the man she'd tried so hard to get away from. Allie could have the rental people pick up the red truck tomorrow.

She looked directly at Marcus. "All right. You win. Let's go."

Without a word, he fell in behind her as she turned for the door.

"Hey, beautiful. Where you goin' in such an all-fired hurry?" Bobby Dale stepped in front of her. "Don't I at least get one little dance first?"

She felt Marcus moving closer behind her. There was no need. She could handle Bobby Dale. She put up a hand, warning Marcus back. "All right, Bobby Dale. One dance. And then I really do have to go."

Bobby didn't look drunk, exactly, but he didn't look quite sober, either. He bared the space between his teeth and narrowed his pale eyes at the silent man behind her. "Who's that? Your boyfriend?"

"No, he is not my boyfriend. Would you like that dance or not?"

"You bet I would, darlin'." He reached for her.

With some trepidation, she went into his arms.

Right away, she realized it was a mistake. He pulled her too close and whirled her away from the dance floor, into the shadows at the edges of the big barroom. When she stiffened and tried to put distance between his body and hers, he splayed a hand where he had no right to touch her and yanked her close again. "The minute I saw you, I knew you were special," he whispered in her ear, his breath reeking of stale beer. "All ladylike on the outside, hotter'n a bottle rocket underneath, just beggin' for the right man to set you off."

It was too much. "That's enough. Release me, now." Past Bobby's shoulder, Marcus appeared. She saw nothing but stillness and calm intent in his eyes. He was no more than a foot away.

Bobby Dale seemed to have no clue that Marcus was there. "Aw, now, sweetheart, don't go gettin' riled," Bobby whispered. He nuzzled her hair. "You and me got chemistry." Marcus reached out. "So you might as well—" Marcus touched Bobby's shoulder and Bobby stopped talking. The cowboy's mouth formed a round O and his eyes went flat. He let go of her, his arms dropping boneless to his sides as his knees crumpled and he collapsed to the floor.

Rhia blinked down at the unconscious cowboy, not really sure what had happened. "Is he…?"

"Ten minutes from now he'll be fine."

No one else in the bar seemed to have noticed. They were behind a pillar, just off the dance floor, out of the light.

And then, for the first time in eight years, Marcus touched her. She gasped as he took her in his arms and danced with her, turning her, moving both of them smoothly and swiftly toward the door.

She didn't argue. Beyond the fact that his touch had stunned her into silence, she was more than ready to leave Rowdy's Roadhouse behind. She only stared up into his haunting almost-green eyes and felt the deepest, saddest sense of longing. For *him*—a man who would hardly speak to her.

The longing made it all worse than ever. She looked in his distant eyes and saw herself: a complete disappointment, both as a princess *and* as a woman.

Marcus expected her to resist, to struggle free of his hold, to order him never, ever to lay a hand on her again. But she did none of those things. She let him dance her to the door and then when he released her only to grab her hand, she let him pull her along, out the door and down the steps, all without a single word.

It was snowing hard already and the wind was up. The sky overhead was starless, soot-gray, an anvil waiting to drop. He'd spent the worst of the winter in Elk Creek, providing security for Her Highness Arabella. He knew what was coming.

More snow. Probably a lot of it. The temperature was very cold and getting colder.

She staggered a little behind him and stared in a dazed way up at the sky. "You were right. It *is* snowing. It looks rather bad."

"Keep walking," he instructed. "The SUV is this way...."

She lowered her head and did what he'd told her to do. Her hand felt cool and small in his and he had to block out a few too-sweet memories of their forbidden weeks together at UCLA. During that time, they were always holding hands.

He led her down the middle row of vehicles. Since his arrival, the lot had thinned out a good deal. There were plenty of empty spaces now. Evidently, many of Rowdy's patrons had made their escape before the snow really started coming down. They passed the red pickup, the roof and bed of which were already wearing a mantle of white. And then, at last, they reached the SUV. He opened the backseat door for her and snow slid off the roof to plop at their feet.

She did jerk her hand free of his then. And she said one word, "No."

He had to actively resist his initial reaction, which was to scoop her up and put her in there bodily. "No, what, Rhiannon? No, you're not going, after all?"

She wrapped her arms around herself. She was shivering. "No, I'm not riding in back. I'll sit up in front, next to you."

It simply wasn't done, for Her Highness to ride in front with the driver. She knew that perfectly well.

But what did it matter at this point? If doing what was not done and sitting in front would get her into the vehicle, so be it. "All right. Hurry. We need to get on the road." He herded her around the front of the car, pulled open the passenger door for her and waited until she was safely inside. "Put on your seat belt," he said, and closed the door.

When he climbed in behind the wheel, she was shivering so hard that her teeth were chattering. He got the engine going and the heater running and then he backed out of the space and headed for the highway.

Something wasn't right.

And then it came to him. No one else was getting on the road. They had been the only ones leaving when they went out the door. No others seemed to have come out since then. The locals probably had the right idea. Those who hadn't left earlier were not going. They would wait out the worst of it.

He put his foot on the brake before pulling out of the parking lot and venturing onto the windblown, snow-thick highway. "It might be wiser to wait it out. Everyone else appears to be doing that."

She didn't look at him. She had her arms tightly wrapped around herself and her head scrunched down into her shoulders, like a turtle pulled into its shell. At least her shivering seemed to have abated a little. "No." She spoke softly. Without animosity, but with what seemed to him a deep and infinite sadness. "Please. Can we just go to Elk Creek? I couldn't bear to go back in there now."

He considered suggesting that they take rooms at the motel behind the roadhouse to wait out the storm. But she was in no condition to spend the night in some cheap motor lodge. The Drop On Inn was hardly the lap of luxury, but at least her family would be there, including her favorite sister, Alice. Sometimes Alice displayed bad judgment, but from what he knew of her, she had a good heart. Rhiannon trusted her absolutely and counted on her for support. It was a night when Rhiannon could probably use a little support.

"You're certain you want to risk the highway in this weather?" he asked one more time.

She nodded, still staring straight ahead. "Please. Let's just go."

So off they went.

The snow came down harder. And the wind blew the thick whiteness horizontally, straight at the windshield. He drove slowly, with care.

But it was bad and getting worse. Almost immediately, visibility went from poor to practically nothing. He started thinking about suggesting again that it would be safer to turn around and go back. But by now he wasn't sure if that actually *would* be safer. He couldn't see the shoulder on either side of the road. And if another vehicle appeared while he was trying to turn…

He kept going forward. The wipers labored to clear the snow from the glass. Rhiannon sat beside him, silent. And very still.

She would be all right. Of course she would. She was a strong and admirable woman with a core of steel. He just needed to get her back to safety with her family and everything would be all right. Just needed to…

Rhiannon gasped.

Another car had appeared, coming on way too fast in the opposite direction. He couldn't actually see the vehicle yet. Just four blinding lights: a pair of headlights and another pair higher up, the kind the local ranchers sometimes mounted above the windshield.

"Marcus!" Rhia whispered low. "Oh, my God…"

"It's all right," he told her, though she had to know that it wasn't.

"Marcus, I'm so sorry. So sorry about everything…."

"Shh," he soothed. And lied again. "It's all right." He leaned on the horn.

But it did no good.

The four blinding beams of light started turning. All at once, they illuminated the far side of the road as the vehicle itself appeared, a brown pickup skidding sideways, no longer in the opposite lane but straight ahead in theirs and sliding fast right for them.

Marcus saw the driver in the pickup's side window. An old fellow in a straw cowboy hat, eyes like two black holes, mouth agape.

There was only one choice and Marcus took it. He turned the wheel sharply toward the shoulder. The pickup whipped by, clipping them in the rear as it went, causing a bone-jarring second of impact, but then skidding on, vanishing into the maelstrom behind them.

He tried to swerve the wheel back into the lane. But it was no good. The snow-thick, icy road surface provided no purchase. The SUV kept going, right over the bank and off the road.

Chapter Four

Rhia's spinning mind couldn't keep up with the crash as it happened. She saw the brown truck skidding sideways at them, the face of a terrified old man in a big hat. And then, all at once they were over the side of the road, the front of the SUV suddenly pointing straight down. She closed her eyes, braced herself and waited to die as they dropped off the edge of the cliff.

But it wasn't a cliff, after all.

They hit bottom almost instantly, the nose of the SUV coming up a little and leveling out, the impact stunning enough to send a jolt of pure agony singing up her spine. A giant fluffy wall appeared, came straight at her and smacked her in the face and chest. It was already deflating when she realized it was the air bag.

By then, the SUV had stopped moving. The only sounds were the creaks and the cracking and strange airy sighs of a vehicle that would probably never be drivable again.

"Rhia. My God…" Marcus was half out of his seat, bending close to her. "Rhia, are you…?"

She dared to reach out, to touch his dear, forbidden face. Real. Warm. A little rough with a day's worth of beard, just she remembered it in her lonely, tortured dreams. "You just called me Rhia…" He'd never called her that, not since their brief time together. It was unacceptable for him to call her by her full first name. But to call her Rhia was, for him, beyond the pale.

"My God," he said again. "Are you injured?"

She closed her eyes, ran a quick physical inventory. When she opened them, she dared a nervous smile. "No. I'm all right. Pretty shaken up, but all right."

"Thank God."

"You?"

"Fine," he said quickly, dismissing his own condition the way he always dismissed everything concerning his well-being.

She thought of the other driver then, and stiffened.

"What is it?" he demanded. "What hurts? Tell me."

"That poor old man in the truck…" She reached over and unhooked her seat belt. "We have to get out, go to him. That pickup must have crashed."

"Wait."

"But, Marcus…"

"I'll call for an ambulance." He spoke to the thing in his ear. "Call nine-one-one." She waited anxiously for him to ask for an ambulance. But a moment later, he pulled his cell phone from his pocket and checked the display.

"What?" she demanded.

He looked at her again. "No signal. Must be the storm."

"Oh, no…"

He put the phone away and rehooked his seat belt. "Put your belt back on."

She did what he asked. "What are you going to do?"

"See if I can get us going again, get us out of this ditch."

It could be possible, couldn't it? The headlights were still working. They gleamed strangely, half buried in the snowbank the vehicle had scraped up like a plow as they hit the ditch. The windshield and windows were still intact. The front end looked pretty bad, though, all crooked and crumpled.

Marcus reached around his deflated air bag and started the car.

Or he tried to. All he raised was a click, after which the headlights went dark.

The whites of his eyes gleamed at her through the shadows. "Don't worry. I'll try again." He did. Another click. And again. More clicking, but not even a hint of a response from the engine.

"Uh-oh," she said softly. And she thought of that poor old cowboy again. "Marcus. We have to get out of this vehicle and get back up to the road. We have to make sure that man is all right."

He regarded her steadily through the gloom. "You're shivering."

The engine wasn't working—and that meant neither was the heater. She wrapped her arms around herself and ordered her teeth not to chatter. "It's nothing. I am fine."

His iron jaw was set. "Your high-heeled shoes are made of satin and you don't have a coat."

She despised herself right then. Stuck in a snowbank without proper gear. An old man could die because she'd just *had* to get away from the man sitting next to her. "I'm sorry, so sorry. It's all my fault. I know that. But we have to do something. At least we have to see if there's anything we *can* do."

He reached over the back of the seat and came up with

a lap blanket. "Wrap this around you." He shoved it at her. "I didn't hear a crash, so it could be that that cowboy regained control of his pickup."

"How could we have heard a crash? *We* were crashing."

He put up both hands. "Don't argue. Just wrap the blanket around you." He undid his belt again, reached across her, popped her belt open for the second time then slid the blanket behind her and closed it around her.

She stared into those eyes that would forever fill her lonely dreams, breathed in his still-remembered scent: plain soap, all man. "But, Marcus—"

"I will go, all right?"

"Oh, Marcus…"

"Take the blanket." He drew one of her hands from the warm folds. "Hold it close around you…."

She did what he said. He let go of her and she felt absurdly bereft. Then he told her again, in an even, calming sort of tone, "I will go. I will go and check and see if there's anything I can do." He slid over to the backseat so smoothly, she didn't realize what he was doing until he was behind her.

Bewildered, she turned to stare at him over her shoulder. Was it those tequila shots she'd foolishly drunk at Rowdy's? The accident? This whole awful day with Marcus right there every time she turned around, reminding her so cruelly of everything they would never have?

Probably all of the above. But whatever the reason, her brain seemed to be working as if in a fog, her reactions all out of whack, delayed. Wrong.

She'd pushed him to go out there and see about the old man. But now that he had said he would go, she suddenly realized how very foolish that would be. "Wait. No, I… That's not right. You can't go alone. It's a blizzard out there and it's not safe…."

He was bending over the floor of the backseat by then. But he stopped what he was doing and straightened enough that his shadowed gaze found hers. "We need to go see about that cowboy who almost ran us over. You *can't* go, you have to see that. So that leaves me. But now you don't want me to go. Make up your mind. Please."

What mind? "I..." She stared at him hopelessly. He let out a long breath and bent over the backseat floor again. She kicked off her ruined shoes, shoved the air bag aside and drew her feet up under her, hoarding her body's warmth.

He straightened again and light filled the cab.

She blinked. "A flashlight? Where did that come from?"

He dropped another blanket over the seat. "Put this around your legs and feet."

She hastened to do what he instructed. "But where...?"

"There's an emergency kit under the floor back here. Another blanket, a second flashlight, jumper cables, flares, a thermal tarp, things like that."

"It...came with the vehicle?"

"For a price. You know your brother."

Alexander. Of course. She should have realized. Alex was extremely security- and safety-conscious—almost scarily so. "I don't suppose there's a pair of size seven and a half women's snow boots and a nice down jacket?"

"Dream on." In the weird, slanting beam of the flashlight, she saw his mouth twitch. Good Lord, he had almost smiled. If things weren't so dire, that would have done her heart good.

"Marcus."

"What now?"

"I've changed my mind. I don't want you to go out there."

"Is that a command?"

"Oh, don't be ridiculous." She huffed out a hard breath and drew the blankets closer around her.

His gaze stayed locked on hers. Level. Unwavering. "It was an honest question."

"Can we just…dispense with all that, at least until we're safely back at the motor lodge?"

He considered. "Fair enough. Then *I* will decide. And I think it's best if I try to get up to the road, at least. I'll set some flares." He held them up. "And I'll see if that brown pickup is anywhere nearby—and if it is, I'll see if there's anything I can do for the driver."

She knew he was right in what he planned to do, even though she longed to beg him not to do it. "You won't go far?"

"No. My main responsibility is you, to keep you safe and well. You're the priority." She was so grateful to hear him say that—at the same time as she felt deeply ashamed to have gotten them into this awful situation. She had behaved badly on any number of levels and her evening of adventure had somehow gotten completely out of control. She sent a little prayer to heaven that God would be merciful and protect the man who was only trying to protect *her*. He added, "I'll stay well to the shoulder and I won't get out of sight of the flares that I set."

She took a slower, deeper breath. "Yes. All right."

He tried his phone one more time. "Dead air," he said softly. He flicked the door lock beside him. The front door on the driver's side was jammed against the bank, but the back door looked as though it might have some play. He pulled the handle and put his rocklike shoulder into it. With much crunching and groaning, the door slowly opened. It didn't open far. Too soon it was lodged in the snow on the bank. Freezing air swirled in. "Stay bundled up," he said. "I'll be back soon." And with that, he slipped out into the storm.

"Be safe," she whispered, as he wrestled the door free of the snowbank and pushed it shut behind him.

She stared over the seat, tracking the flashlight's glow as he slogged away from the car. He began to climb the bank. Too soon, she lost the light—and him. The view through the rear window was a narrow one from the front seat.

That was unbearable—to have lost sight of him so soon. She scrambled over the seat and then over *that* seat so she could look out the back. From there, she could see a faint glow up on the road. "Please, please God, keep him safe...." She had to resist the urge to bargain with the Almighty. She'd been foolish enough in the past few hours. She wasn't going to start trying to make deals with God.

Through the swirling haze of the snow, she saw a flash of sizzling brightness, followed by the red glow of a flare. Then came a second flash and there were two. The flares lit the upper rim of the ditch. His flashlight beam began moving along the shoulder, back the way they had come.

Too soon, the flashlight's glow was swallowed by the storm. She had only the red gleam of the flares to comfort her while she waited.

And waited. As far as she could tell no other cars had passed. She saw only the light given off by the flares. She didn't know what time it was. She wore no watch, had no phone with her. She had no idea if the car's clock might be working. And she wasn't about to scramble back over the seats to find out, wasn't about to stop staring out that back window, *willing* his return.

A glad cry escaped her when she saw the flashlight's glow again. It seemed to take form out of the spinning snow, materializing slowly from the whirl of whiteness.

It was coming closer, thank God. And it had probably only been ten or fifteen minutes since the beam had been swallowed by the storm. But somehow, those minutes had seemed like several lifetimes strung end to end.

At the bank, the light paused. There was the flash of another flare as a third warning torch lit up between the first two.

And then, at last, he began to descend the bank.

She scrambled back over the seat so she could push the door open for him when he reached it. The cold air and snow swirled in along with the big, cold man and the glow of the trusty flashlight. He pulled the door shut and she backed away to the far side of the seat in order to quell the powerful need to throw her arms around him and hold on tight.

"You're safe," she whispered prayerfully. "Oh, and I'll bet you're freezing cold...."

He turned off the light, set it aside and brushed snow from his shoulders, stomped it off his boots. She watched the shadowed, eagerly awaited shape of him as her eyes once again grew accustomed to the gloom.

Resignedly, he muttered, "Didn't I tell you to stay bundled up in the front seat?"

She laughed, a slightly hysterical sound. "I did stay bundled up. You never said a word about the front seat— and did you find him, the old man?"

"No. Not a sign of him or the pickup." He brushed snow off his hair.

Cold droplets touched her cheek. She swiped them away. "But...how could that be possible?"

"The snow's falling fast, covering our tracks. But the ones where he skidded sideways in our lane were so deep, they were still visible. I followed them—until they seemed to straighten out."

"Straighten out?" She considered the impossibility of that. "Surely you're joking."

"No."

"You're saying he somehow pulled out of that horrible slide?"

"It looks that way."

"Incredible."

"I told you. People who live here are used to driving in bad weather."

"He wasn't doing a very good job of it when he came flying at us."

Those big shoulders lifted in a shrug. "What can I tell you? It looked to me like he pulled out of it somehow." He wrapped his hands around himself and rubbed his arms.

"You're freezing," she said softly.

"I'll warm up, don't worry."

"Oh, please. It's almost as cold in here as it is out there." Cold and getting colder. Her nose felt like a small slab of ice. She gathered her feet underneath her and wrapped the blankets tighter. It had been a little chilly, even that morning, so she'd worn lacy tights, though she'd been tempted to go without them. Now, she was very grateful for at least that one good choice she'd made in a day and evening of really bad ones.

He tried his phone again. "Nothing," he told her after a minute.

"What time is it? Do you know?"

He pulled back the sleeves of the jacket and sweatshirt to reveal one of those military-style multifunction watches. "Twelve-forty."

She shivered a little. "Already tomorrow..." She watched as he bent and got the other blanket from the kit under the floor and settled it around himself. "You mentioned there's a thermal tarp in there, too."

He tugged the blanket closer, hunching his head down into the soft folds. "And?"

"You should use it, get your body temperature back up."

He just sat there, a large dark lump in the murky dimness of the cab. Annoyance nipped at her. The man made denial of his own basic comfort into something an art form. Just because she had gotten them into this mess didn't mean he had to freeze to death before help came.

And then he did bend over again. He brought out the tarp, which resembled nothing so much as a much-folded slab of aluminum foil. It caught what little ambient light there was and gleamed silver. "Here. You use it. You need to stay bundled up until help comes."

She made no move to take it. "You need it more than I do."

"Take it, Rhiannon."

She looked away. "How long will the flares last?"

"Rhiannon."

Slowly, she turned her head to face his shadowed form once more. She asked again, "The flares?"

He was still holding out the tarp. When she only sat where she was, unmoving, waiting for him to answer her, he dropped it onto the seat between them. "I don't know. Up to an hour, possibly."

"And if help doesn't come by then?"

"It will come eventually. The storm will end. In the morning, they'll have searchers looking for us. We're on a much-traveled highway and there will be vehicles we can flag down as soon as the road is passable again. We only need to keep warm until they find us."

She looked at him for a long time. Then she dared to say it. "We need to share our body heat. We need to share the blankets and the tarp."

He sat very still. She felt the intense regard of his gaze

through the gloom. Finally, he admitted it, too. "You're right."

They moved simultaneously. He picked up the tarp and started opening it. She helped. It was big, much bigger than the blankets.

When it was fully opened and billowed out over both seats, he said, "I'll sit back against the door. You sit between my legs. We can wrap two blankets and the tarp around both of us. You can take the third blanket for extra protection on your legs and feet."

It was a good plan—as much as it covered. "What about *your* feet?"

"No problem."

She peered toward the floor. She couldn't see his boots. It was too dark down there. But she had a very strong feeling that they were soaked through. "Are those boots waterproof?"

"They're fine."

"Wrong answer. You can't sit here all night with wet feet. You'll get frostbite."

"I'm all right."

"Oh, stop it. As soon as the storm ends, you're going to want to get out and stand on the side of the road to flag someone down. You won't be able to do that if your feet are frozen. But if you take off the boots and get your feet under the blankets and tarp, our body heat will dry your socks—all of which is completely obvious, and you know that it is."

He said with exceeding grimness, "You keep talking about body heat."

She didn't know whether to laugh or cry. He sounded so discouraged. Weary to the core. She felt bad about that— really bad. "Listen, Marcus. I mean this sincerely. I am very sorry about what's happened and I know that it's all my fault. I know the last thing you want to do is to share body heat with me."

"There. You just said it again."

"I'm sorry. Again. But it has to be done."

"And you have no idea what I want." His voice was deeper than ever. Rough in that delicious way she remembered from long ago.

Her silly heart got all fluttery. She commanded it to settle down. "We have to do this."

"Yes," he said. "I know."

"So take off those boots."

"All right." He lifted a foot.

"Here. Let me help."

He sent her one of those glances. Even through the dark, she could read it. She knew just what he was thinking. *It is not done for Your Highness to help a mere bodyguard off with his boots.*

But then he surprised her and swung one wet boot her way. She let go of her blankets, took the boot in both hands, by the wet toe and the soggy heel, and removed it, after which he offered her the other one. She took it off, too.

Yes, it did seem a very intimate thing to be doing for him. And it made her so sad all over again, made her think of those beautiful weeks all those years ago, when she was in her first year as an art major and he was only twenty-two, in California for a special Montedoran fellowship, a two-month intensive course of study in behavioral sciences, leadership and military psychology.

They'd met when he saw her in the student bookstore and recognized her. She'd caught him staring at her and boldly demanded to know what he thought he was looking at.

Her young heart had skipped a beat when he saluted.

"Your Highness, Sub-Lieutenant Marcus Desmarais of the Sovereign's Guard at your service."

She'd laughed in delight to find a countryman at UCLA. And she'd invited him to get some coffee with her. He'd surprised both of them and accepted her invitation.

They'd quickly become friends. It had seemed such a natural thing, with both of them so far from home. Their innate understanding of each other as Montedorans had seemed greater there than their differences. The chasm between them, he a commoner and she a princess, hadn't mattered at all.

At least not to her.

To her, it had never mattered. After all, her mother ruled her country—and *she* had married a commoner, an American actor from Texas. It was a wonderfully successful marriage. Born the last of her line to rule a principality crushed under the weight of massive debt, Adrienne Bravo-Calabretti had given her husband and her country four princes and five princesses. Under her mother's rule, with her father's unwavering support, Montedoro had prospered. The country was rich now. The throne had an heir and plenty of spares.

That was what had come of a princess marrying a commoner.

Rhia dropped the second boot to the floor and wished the man sitting there in the dark beside her could be as open-minded and far-seeing as her own father had always been.

"Come here," Marcus said. "You're shivering again."

With a sigh, Rhia turned and positioned herself between his hard thighs. They arranged the blankets into a nest to shelter them. She wrapped one of them around her feet and legs as he'd instructed. The others he drew around him and thus around them both, with the thermal tarp on top as he settled back against the door.

The tarp was big enough to cover them completely, wrapping around their bodies with plenty to tuck snugly over their legs and feet. He enveloped her in his big arms and pulled her back against his broad chest.

Instantly, she felt warmer, comforted. Safe. But how comfortable was he? "What about your back?"

"It's fine."

"But isn't it cold, against the door like that?"

"Rhiannon. It's fine." He held her even closer. It felt so good. She tried not to enjoy it too awfully much. His warm breath stirred her hair as he added downright cheerfully, "I'm feeling quite toasty, as a matter of fact."

"Toasty." She allowed herself a smile.

"Try to get some rest."

"Is it still snowing?" She struggled to sit higher, to see out the back window, rubbing against him intimately as she moved.

He made a low sound, quickly quelled. It might have been the beginnings of a groan. His big arms tightened, holding her still. "Stay here. Stay warm." His deep, wonderful voice rumbled against her back and lower down she felt…him. Heat flooded her cheeks as she realized that her wriggling about to see out the back window had aroused him.

She gulped and tried to sit still and reminded herself he couldn't see her blush. It was too dark and she had her back to him. She cleared her throat. "I just wanted to see if it was still snowing."

"It is."

"Has it let up any?"

"No. Rest."

She didn't think she could sleep. No way. This was too

strange and wonderful. It was…like all her forbidden fantasies somehow come to life: the two of them, in the darkness, all wrapped up together, nice and tight.

Yes, she felt a bit embarrassed at the thick, hard ridge of him pressing low against her back.

But she also felt…excited by it. Glad. To have such basic, undeniable proof that he still desired her, after all these years. That he wasn't as indifferent to her as he always tried to make her believe. It was a petty sort of triumph and she knew that.

She ordered herself to stop being smug. The man couldn't help his biological response, what with her all smashed up against his private parts like this. His physical arousal proved nothing—except that he was a man and she was a woman. He had done his duty by her tonight, and then some. She would be thankful for that and behave better in the future.

Her body slowly relaxed. Now that her teeth were no longer chattering, she could actually almost feel optimistic.

Yes, it had been an awful experience, all told. But there was a bright side. Neither of them had been injured. It appeared the old cowboy in the brown pickup had somehow escaped unscathed. And as soon as the snow stopped and daylight came, they would be rescued.

It could have been so much worse.

And she really was exhausted. She closed her eyes and rested her head back against the steady, sure beating of his heart.

Her eyes drifted shut.

And she remembered….

Chapter Five

Two weeks.

That was all it took in the easy, casual atmosphere of Southern California. Two weeks far from everything that defined them as worlds apart, and what began as friendship became a love affair.

A *secret* affair. Rhia was barely eighteen, after all. She told herself it was a fling, that she was much too young to settle down. And Marcus was a military man to the core, ruled by duty. He considered himself beneath her and felt more than a little guilty that he was her first lover—that he was her lover at all.

He told her more than once that he knew she deserved a prince. But in those magical, perfect days, he actually opened up to her, even relaxed with her. He told her of his childhood. He was raised by the nuns at St. Stephen's Orphanage. They'd found him as a newborn on the steps of Montedoro's oldest church, the Cathedral of Our Lady of

Sorrows. He didn't know who his people were, not his father, not his mother. He'd started his life with no one, and then been adopted as an infant.

"But the couple divorced. I was the glue that was supposed to hold them together. When I didn't do the job, neither of them wanted me. It was back to St. Stephen's when I was three. After that, I was a very, very good little boy— for the nuns. But evidently, I made sure none of the others who came looking for a child chose me. I don't remember how, exactly, I was so small. But I know even now that I didn't need that kind of heartache all over again."

She had told him she admired him, for what he'd suffered, for how he had managed to grow up both strong and good.

And he had captured her face in his two big hands. "Not so good. Not strong at all. If I were strong and good, I wouldn't be here with you now."

They stood out on the grass by the large and beautiful neo-Romanesque style undergraduate library. She remembered thick trees, dappled shadows, a feeling that they were the only two people in the world right then. She went on tiptoe, kissed him. "No regrets. None. I am very, very glad you're here."

And right then, he made her promise that they would walk away in the end, that it would be over forever once he finished his fellowship and returned to Montedoro. That the time they had together would be their secret. "Promise me, Rhia. When I go, we cut it clean. And no one else will ever know."

"Yes. Of course. I promise." She had nodded, beaming happily up at him, aglow with what she honestly believed at that time was a lovely mingling of warm friendship and delicious desire. She agreed to it ending, to it being their secret. She was so sure at the time that cutting it clean when he left was what she wanted. Not because he was "just" a soldier, but because she was only eighteen and had her whole life ahead of her and had never imagined she might find her true love in her first year of college.

At UCLA, they both stayed in dorm rooms, in separate halls. He had three roommates and she had one. They couldn't be together in their rooms.

When they decided they *would* be together—*really* be together—they had found a small, inexpensive hotel not far from the campus. It was beautiful to her, that hotel. In the Spanish style, with thick stucco walls and a red tile roof, all on one level, with each room more like a tiny apartment opening onto a central walkway than a hotel room.

La Casa de la Luna, the place was called.

The house of the moon.

She loved it there, in their own special house of the moon. One room in particular, the one they used the very first time, became "their" room. Their room had bright bougainvillea climbing the white wall outside the window and twin birds of paradise flanking the door. Their room had a small sitting area where they sometimes studied together. The bathroom had an old claw-footed tub and the mirror over the sink was streaked with age.

It was a magical place, their room. Every time they visited, she wished they might never have to leave. And when they did leave, she lived only for when they would go there again. But he was in America for only two months and that time flew by on swift wings.

They parted as planned. She drove him to LAX and kissed him goodbye and managed not to cry. As he left her to go through security, his broad back so straight and proud, never once turning to see if she was still there watching him go, she reminded herself that this was what she wanted. Their time together had been so beautiful. And now they would both move on.

Too bad she couldn't seem to forget him. Too bad no other man ever seemed to measure up....

"Marcus?" Her voice, soft. Tentative.

He stirred from hazy dreams where he was hard and aching and she was pressed tight against him. He couldn't push her away. He had, for some reason unclear to him but urgent, to keep her close, to hold her in his arms. He couldn't push her away.

But he couldn't kiss her, either. Couldn't take away all her clothes and bury himself in her velvety heat....

That was forbidden.

That could never be again.

It was torture of the most unbearable kind. And every soldier knew how it went when you were tortured. If your tormentor was good enough, eventually, you would give it all up—betray your family, your country, all you held dear.

Just to make the agony stop.

"Marcus?"

He blinked, opened his eyes to darkness.

And remembered. Her Highness Arabella's wedding. Rowdy's Roadhouse. The crash.

Rhia actually *was* pressed against him. His dream of being tortured endlessly by an unflagging state of arousal was real.

"Are you awake?" she asked.

"I am now," he grumbled and set his mind to blocking out the ache in his groin.

Wrapped in their cocoon of blankets and the tarp, they were warm, and that was what mattered. His socks were already dry and he didn't have to worry about her getting frostbite or pneumonia—or worse, freezing to death before rescue came.

"The snow?" she asked.

He peered over the seat. "Looks like it's still coming down."

"What time is it?"

He freed his arm long enough to look at his watch. "Ten to two."

"Your phone?"

He tried the headset. "Still out. Go to sleep. In a few hours, this will all be over."

She didn't do what he asked her to do. But then, she rarely had. "I have a confession," she whispered.

"Save it for a priest."

She made a low sound in her throat. A soft sound. A sexy sound. A sound that seemed to go straight to his tortured privates. "I told Alice about us. She's known for eight years. One week after I dropped you off at LAX, I called her and told her everything."

He wasn't surprised. "That wasn't wise."

"She would never tell anyone. She never has."

God in heaven, she felt good in his arms. And she smelled so good, like vanilla and jasmine flowers and something else, something that was only her. He would know her in the darkest part of the blackest night, in the crush of a crowd, blindfolded. "Rest."

"You keep saying that."

He almost pressed a kiss into her dark, fragrant hair. But he caught himself just in time. "We have to sit here like this to stay warm. We might as well get some rest."

"Or we could talk."

"There is nothing to talk about."

"Liar." She said it very low. And vehemently. "You are such a liar, Marcus."

He didn't argue. She was right. He had told the lies that he *had* to tell. And he had no intention of digging into the truth tonight.

Or ever.

She let out a sad little sigh. "We have so very much to talk about. If only you would."

"No, we don't."

She was silent then. Which was good. They only needed to get through this night without doing something foolish, without saying all the things that were too dangerous to say. Then they could both return to their separate and very different lives. Which was as it should be.

He rested his head back against the ice-cold side window and told himself to sleep, to block out the soft, tempting, never-forgotten shape of the woman in his arms—and not, under any circumstances, to think about the past....

Marcus did sleep.

And he dreamed about the things that he'd sworn not to think of.

He dreamed of that time six years ago, when she came home to Montedoro before her junior year at college and sought him out.

Somehow, she had learned his private email address. Three emails she sent him. He didn't respond to the first two. He consigned them to the trash and told himself that the wisest response to her was no response at all.

He never should have presumed even to speak with her in California. But something so impossible had happened the day before. And he was still reeling from it, his whole world tilted sideways, off its axis. Gone completely wrong.

She had challenged him and he had dared to respond as an equal might.

And after that, somehow he couldn't walk away—didn't

want to walk away. Not right then. He wanted to be with her, even though such a thing was completely forbidden.

To be her friend for that brief time had been unacceptable. To be her lover?

It was so much more than wrong. It was a desecration of all he held sacred. He owed everything to her family. Her Sovereign Highness Adrienne was a fair and just ruler, and a generous one. She truly cared for the lowliest of her subjects. She helped to fund St. Stephen's. And every year at Christmastime, Her Sovereign Highness would visit. She would come bearing gifts for each and every orphaned child and she would personally speak with every child who was old enough to form a recognizable sentence. Every year from the year he was three and his adoptive parents returned him to the orphanage like a defective toy, the sovereign princess spoke with him. And every year, she seemed to remember the things he had said the year before.

When he was six, he told her he wanted to be a soldier for his country, to join the guard, to serve the princely family. Her Sovereign Highness took him at his word. He received the education he needed. He began to train for the Sovereign's Guard at eighteen. But even before that, he was taken under the wing of Sir Hector Anteros, who was then the captain of the guard. Sir Hector was the closest thing to a real father that Marcus had ever known and Hector had seen to it that his protégé received an officer's commission after graduating from the University of Montedoro at the age of twenty-one. Marcus was no one, a foundling. And yet, because of Princess Adrienne, the future he'd only barely dared to dream of was his.

Essentially, Marcus owed the princely family his life, his education, his relationship with the man who paved the way for him and his livelihood. And he had repaid their endless kindness by seducing one of their daughters.

So yes. When Rhiannon sent him those first two emails six years ago, he had pretended that he didn't receive them. But then came the third email in which she threatened to seek him out in person, to come to the barracks not far from the palace where he lived and demand to speak with him. At that point, he'd agreed to meet with her in secret.

She chose the place. It was a short drive out of Montedoro, in the French countryside, a deserted farmhouse that belonged to her family. He arrived first.

He was standing on the front step, wondering if she had come to her senses and decided to stay away, after all, when a small yellow sports car appeared racing toward him along the dusty front lane. She pulled up a few feet from the steps and got out.

Her coffee-brown hair gleamed in the summer sun. She wore a sleeveless red cotton dress and she stood by the car and looked up the steps at him and he was in hell. Wanting to run to her, to reach for her, needing the feel of her flesh beneath his hands in the same way he needed to suck in his next breath.

And knowing that taking her in his arms could not, under any circumstances, be allowed to happen. Touching her would be too dangerous. Once he had his hands on her again, he might never be able to let her go.

He saw in those big dark eyes that she was going to say things that could never be unsaid. And so he had stood there, in the shade of the olive tree by the padlocked door of that plain farmhouse, and listened to her say those things.

"I think...I love you, Marcus. I think we made a giant mistake, to end it the way we did. I think of you often. All the time. It's as though you're somehow inside my heart. Here." She laid her slim hand above her breast. "As though you're somehow in my blood. Don't you…ever think about me? Don't you ever think you might want to try again?"

And then he said the lies he had to say. "No. I'm sorry. I don't want to try again. I'm content, I promise you, with the agreement we made two years ago. I wish you well. And now, would you please get back in that little yellow car and drive away and never try to contact me again?"

"But, Marcus…" She spoke gently. Carefully. Her enormous eyes beckoned him down to drowning. "Don't you ever even wonder if we might have made a mistake? Don't you ever wish or imagine that it could be different for you and me?"

"No," he said, again, his tone as deliberate, as carefully controlled as hers. "The mistake was on my part, to have ever dared to touch you or even to speak with you."

"But, Marcus, that's not what I meant."

He put up a hand. "Please. Hear me. The mistake was not that we ended it. The mistake was that it ever started in the first place. All I want from you, ma'am, is for you to keep the promise you made to me two years ago."

She had stood there, so beautiful it ripped his heart in two to look at her, and she had cried. "'Ma'am.' Oh, you can't be serious. *Ma'am?*"

"I would like for you to go now."

"Oh, God." She stood there in the dirt drive and stretched out her hands to him. "Please, Marcus. Please. Won't you just give us a chance?" The tears tracked down her soft cheeks, dripped over her chin. "I miss you. So much. Couldn't we just talk it over, at least, just… Oh, Marcus. Don't do this, don't just send me away."

But he had to. In time, he knew, she would thank him for it.

He made himself stand there, still and straight as any

statue. "You must go, ma'am. There is nothing more that I can say."

She stared at him through red, wet eyes for an endless moment. And then, with a ragged sob, she buried her face in her hands. He stood there, frozen to the spot, knowing that to move so much as a centimeter would destroy his control and have him running to her, grabbing her close. So he didn't move. He stayed where he was and he watched her slim shoulders shake as she strove to collect herself.

After forever, she dashed away the last of her tears, wiped her arm across her running nose and drew her shoulders tall to face him again. "I think you're a coward, Marcus." Her voice was cold now, frosty with disdain, though her swollen, red eyes remained turbulent, shining with the last of her tears.

He didn't speak, didn't move. He only waited, *willing* her to go.

"All right, then," she said at last. "Goodbye."

He watched her turn from him, hating himself for the pain he had brought her, a really bad emptiness in the center of his chest—and yet, even then, certain that it was the right thing he was doing. She got in the car and drove away.

And that was it. The end of it.

In real life, anyway.

But in this dream he seemed to be having, the ending at the farmhouse steps was…changing.

Morphing into something altogether different.

In this dream, he was hard. Aching for her. In this dream, she turned to the yellow car, as before. She pulled open the door, as before.

And then she pushed it shut again.

Not as before.

Everything went haywire then. She whirled and came to him, racing up the steps, her face flushed, still swollen from her fit of weeping, her dark hair coming loose from its pins, falling to curl around her unforgettable face. "Tell me again," she demanded. "Tell me how you want me to go...."

And it was too much.

Pure need took over. He reached for her. She came to him, sighing, twisting in his arms. He realized she'd been facing away from him, leaning against him. But now she had turned, so she lay against him face-to-face, her soft breasts smashed against his chest, her warm breath flowing across the flesh of his throat.

And suddenly, they were on some narrow padded surface inside the locked, deserted farmhouse. It was dark and cold in there, but they had their body heat to keep each other warm, a tent of blankets to shelter them.

She kissed him, her mouth opening, a night-blooming flower, under his, her breath flowing into him, their tongues meeting again, at last, after an eternity of loneliness and denial. He stroked her tongue with his, caressing, touching all those secret, wet, slick surfaces beyond her parted lips.

His arms were filled with her, so warm and soft and perfectly made. And so very eager. Her hair tumbled down, tangling around them, a dark web of curling silk.

So real, the taste of her. Nothing an ordinary soldier like him should ever be allowed to know. Honey. Ambrosia. The food of the gods. She tasted of all the things he had no right to touch. She tasted of paradise.

Real.

So real...

Better than all the hungry, lonely, longing dreams of her in all the years since...

She gasped.

And she wiggled against him, driving him wild, as she

slid her arms up his chest and used her soft, slim hands to frame his face.

"Marcus. Marcus, are you *asleep?*" Asleep? He tried to capture her mouth again, but she retreated, though her soft hands still held him, one on either cheek. "Marcus." Her voice was sweetly scolding now.

Awareness dawned: the heat between them, the hard door at his back. The cold just beyond their tent of blankets and tarp....

It seemed so real because it *was* real.

He opened his eyes. She was right there, her eyes waiting, shining at him through the dark.

"Sweet holy virgin," he heard himself whisper.

She moved, her body shifting a little between his legs, reminding him sharply all over again of how much he wanted her. He stifled a groan of need as she said, "And here I thought you had finally admitted you just *had* to make love with me...."

She was right. He had done exactly that, more or less. In his dreams.

Literally.

"Rhiannon, I..." He had no idea what to say.

She leaned closer again, sliding against him, stroking him with that fine body of hers. He gritted his teeth, absolutely certain he was going to lose it any second now. Her soft lips just barely brushed his. "I have a question."

He made a sound, a helpless, yearning, croaking sound.

Her lips moved against his. He felt the whisper of her warm breath across his mouth, over his cheek. "It's been a terrible night, Marcus. Worst of the worst."

"Er." Again, he had to swallow a groan. "That was a question?"

"I'm getting there."

Yet another tortured sound escaped him.

And she said, "My question is, *why not?*"

He didn't have to ask why not what. He knew exactly why not what.

She stroked the stubble-rough side of his face and whispered softly, in a voice of purest temptation, "Why not go ahead with it? Why not do what neither of us can stop wanting to do, just one more time?"

He knew exactly how he should respond to those dangerous questions. He needed to take her by the shoulders and put her gently but firmly away from him. But instead, he muttered in a rough, choked growl, "It would be…wrong."

She used the backs of her fingers to stroke the close-clipped hair at his temples. "I don't care, Marcus. I really don't care if it's wrong. I only want one good thing to remember about tonight, one sweet, naughty secret to make it…not quite so awful. I thoroughly understand that it's never going to be, between you and me. That it's over and it's *been* over. For years and years."

He tried to speak.

She put her soft hand between them and covered his mouth with her palm. "Shh. Not finished." He gulped and nodded. She took her hand away and brought her lips close to his once more. "But tonight, well, it's all been a complete and utter disaster. And now, here we are, waiting for the storm to end so that we can go our separate ways, waiting for the morning, keeping each other warm. And I say that now, tonight, is the only opportunity we're ever going to get to be together one more time. I say that the way you were kissing me just a few minutes ago, even if you *were* half-asleep, proves that you wouldn't mind doing exactly what I'm suggesting." She rocked her hips against him then—to prove her point, he supposed. And she did prove it. He groaned out loud that time. He couldn't stop himself. And she made a low, triumphant little sound. "*Yes.* That's what *I* say, Marcus. Yes. You and me. Tonight, right now. One more time...."

He exerted a superhuman effort of will and said, "We cannot. It's too dangerous. I've brought nothing to protect you." She knew his stand on contraception. He'd grown up without a father *or* a mother. He was adamant that his children would have both, and that he would only have children by his wedded wife.

"It's not a problem. I have condoms." She held one up.

He scowled at it through the dimness. "My God." She had actually planned to spend the night with a stranger from Rowdy's Roadhouse, then?

She slipped the condom somewhere back under the blankets and got up even closer, nose to nose with him. "Don't ask, all right? Just accept that I have them, and let's take it from there."

It was too much. The whole day of watching her, remembering and trying so hard *not* to remember, yearning and telling himself he didn't burn. Chasing her down when she tried to get away from him. And then being forced to watch her some more while she danced with one cowboy after another. Having to take down that fool who had dared to go too far with her.

The drive through the blizzard. The old man in the pickup. The crash.

And most of all, the hours with her pressed up close against him, making him burn for her, bringing all the old memories flooding back so powerfully he couldn't deny them, breaking his lonely, solitary heart all over again.

It was too much.

If she still wanted him for one last time, who was he to deny her?

To deny himself?

To hell with denial. For once. For tonight.

She made a small, hopeful sound.

And what was left of his resistance crumbled to dust.

He took her mouth, hard and deep. She opened for him. He wrapped his arms good and tight around her and he kissed her long and thoroughly, with no holding back.

"Oh, Marcus." She sighed when she lifted her mouth from his.

And then they were fumbling, getting their clothes out of the way without completely undressing, trying to keep the blankets and the tarp close around them as they got their bodies bare enough to touch, to stroke.

To join.

She opened his heavy jacket and pushed up his sweat-shirt. She unbuttoned his borrowed jeans and closed her soft fingers around him and he felt he would die right then and be glad to go.

He undid her satin jacket, unhooked her lacy little bra, freeing her breasts to his hungry hands. He pulled up her skirt so it was around her waist. And he tore at her tights until they split down the center seam.

It was awkward and groping.

And he didn't care. Judging by her eager moans and breathless, sweet sighs, she didn't mind, either. They were belly to belly, skin to skin at last, again, after all these years.

She was the same as he remembered her, the same, only better. Her breasts a little fuller, her skin still warm satin under his hands, her scent enough to drive him glo-riously mad.

At the last, before he finally claimed her, she brought out the condom and rolled it down over him. He blinked, dazed with need for her.

She gave a low, throaty laugh that seemed to dance

along every one of his nerve endings. "I mean it. Don't ask."

He didn't. He only lifted her on top of him, her legs in their tattered tights folded on either side of his thighs. He gathered the slipping blankets and tarp, tugging them back into place to preserve the wonderful heat they were generating, and he lowered her down onto him. She helped him, sighing, taking him into her by slow, delicious degrees.

Paradise. He had found it again at last. In the middle of a blizzard, stranded in a ditch on a deserted Montana highway. With Rhia.

Because wherever she was, there was paradise.

She rocked him, taking him with her to the edge of the world.

He went where she led him, all the way, surging into her softness, into the sweet, close, wet heat of her body. Too quickly, he felt the end rolling at him, closing over him, opening him up as it hollowed him out. He tried to hold on, for her sake, so she could go over first. He began to fear he couldn't last.

But then he felt her rising, felt the change in her breathing that meant she had caught the wave of her own completion. He knew then that she was close and he set his mind to holding out for her, holding on...

She cried out and stiffened above him, her hands against his chest, pressing at him, as below, she held him within her, hard and tight. He felt her inner muscles closing on him, the contractions of her climax gripping him, easing, gripping again.

It was too good. He couldn't take it. He was going over and there was no stopping it now.

He surged up hard into her and...something opened. Something gave way and suddenly he was feeling her even more acutely than before. It was perfect. A sensation like no other, as though he had found the secret woman's heart of her, as though he touched her, *knew* her in the deepest, most elemental way. He clasped her hips in his two hands and he let his own climax roar through him, turning him inside out as she whispered his name and he pulled her body down to him and claimed her soft mouth in a long, soul-deep kiss.

There was a time after that, the best kind of time. She rested against him, soft and lazy. He stroked her hair and kissed her forehead and wished those sweet after-moments never had to end.

Dawn came as they lay there, not talking, easy with each other in a way they hadn't been since Los Angeles, since their little room at La Casa de la Luna.

She was the one who finally said it. "I think the storm is over." He made a low noise of reluctant agreement. She kissed the side of his neck. "I suppose I'll have to let you up. We'll have to pull ourselves together and return to the real world."

They shared one more kiss. A long one, achingly sweet.

He didn't want to let her go. But of course, he had to. He clasped her hips and gently eased her away from him.

They both looked down at the same time and saw the condom. He was still wearing it, more or less.

It had ripped wide open.

Rhia hated the silence between them.

It was back, with a vengeance, as soon as they saw that the condom had broken.

Not much later, as she was struggling with her ruined tights, buttoning up her jacket and trying to smooth her tangled hair, Marcus leaned over the front seat and opened the glove compartment. He found a pen and a scrap of paper, on which he quickly scrawled a series of numbers.

"Here." His breath fogged on the frozen air.

She took it. "What's this?"

"My cell number. Don't worry, I use an excellent encryption program. No one will know if you call me."

For a moment, she actually thought that she'd read the silence all wrong. That he'd reconsidered and wanted to see her again. Her silly heart tried to leap.

But then she understood. "Oh, seriously. There's nothing to worry about. I'm not pregnant. The timing's wrong—plus, you're being ridiculous. If I were to call you, whatever the reason, I wouldn't care who knew."

"You *should* care. It's not fitting."

She opened her mouth to argue—and then shut it without a word. Arguing with him on that subject would get her nowhere. True, he had just taken her to heaven in the backseat of a freezing SUV. But that didn't matter. The barriers between them hadn't changed. Those barriers were unbreachable, even if they *were* all in his head.

She stuck the scrap of paper in the pocket of her jacket, with her permit and the electronic key and the one unused condom. "All right. What next?"

"We get out of here and up to the road and see if we can flag down a passing motorist."

The rear door of the SUV opened easily. They went out that way. Marcus insisted on putting her over his shoulder and carrying her up the side of the ditch through new snow that reached almost to his knees.

At the top, by the roadside, he gently let her down. "Are you all right?"

"Perfect." She aimed her chin high and gave him a regal smile. Yes, she did know that she wasn't a pretty sight. But except for her poor, cold feet in her soggy, stained Manolos, at least she was warm. She wore the blankets for a coat, glad that they covered her to her ankles as she'd had to remove her tattered tights, which she'd tucked into the front of her skirt when he insisted she not leave them behind in the wrecked SUV where anyone might find them.

He'd kept the torn condom and its wrapper, slipping the evidence of their indiscretion into a pocket for disposal later. Heaven forbid that someone might find proof of what they'd done together during the long, freezing night.

Marcus's phone still wasn't working. He lit more flares and they waited. It didn't take long. Within five minutes, a snowplow appeared, clearing the drifts of new snow from the highway. Following the plow was a highway patrol car.

The patrolman pulled over and stopped. He'd been looking for them since before dawn, he said. He put them both in his patrol car where the heater was going strong, and he had a Thermos of hot coffee for them. He called his station on the car radio and reported that he had found the princess and her bodyguard and both were uninjured.

They told the officer about the accident and described the old man and his brown pickup.

The officer shook his head. "I would bet my new quad cab that was Loudon Troutdale you almost got killed by."

"You know him?" Rhia asked, surprised.

"Your Highness, everyone in these parts knows Loudon. He's got some kind of record in the county for reckless driving. I'm thinking he's had his license for about a week now after the last big suspension."

Marcus said, "Last night, after the accident, I got out of the car and walked along the road looking for a sign of him. Judging by his tracks in the snow, he managed to regain control of his pickup and continue on his way."

"Can't tell you I'm surprised," the patrolman said. "Loudon always ends up in one piece. The people he runs into are generally not so lucky."

Rhia asked, "Do you think he'll lose his license this time?"

"That'll be up to the judge, but I can't say as how it would be a bad thing if Loudon never got behind the wheel of a vehicle again."

They returned to town. Marcus rode in front with the officer, as was proper—because Marcus was all about what was proper, what was *fitting*.

Rhia sat in back behind the security grate and tried not to feel like a very bad girl. She probably shouldn't have seduced Marcus there at the end after putting the poor man through hell the day and evening before.

To have sex with him on top of everything else? Well, it wasn't very nice. And it was foolish. Worse than foolish. He had said it himself: it was wrong. But she had kept pushing him, whispering to him, teasing him, until he gave in.

Because she still had that *thing* for him. There was just something about him that called to her, something that made her wish there still might be hope for the two of them somehow. Deep in her heart, she feared she would never get over him.

And yet, she had honestly meant what she said to him, that she knew it was finished between them. Their sad, lost love was never going to be resurrected. She accepted that. She'd had no expectations concerning Marcus for six years, not since their encounter in the South of France, in front of that deserted farmhouse that belonged to some distant relative of her mother's. Not since she had cried her eyes out right in front of him, throwing away every last scrap of her pride and her dignity, begging him to give them one more chance.

And he had just stood there, watching her, letting her

thoroughly humiliate herself. Before calmly and irrevocably sending her away.

So, yes. It had been rather a bad idea to have sex with him again.

A bad idea that had turned out absolutely perfect.

Something beautiful and real and honest in the middle of a terrible mess.

She probably *should* regret it. But she didn't.

Instead, she felt, at last, that she and Marcus had reached a certain peace with each other. That something good really had come of that horrible day and night. She felt she could let him go now without resenting him, without the bitterness that had clung to her heart for way too many years.

Yes. All in all, miraculously, it had been a good thing.

Well, except for the condom breaking. That was a bit worrisome.

But the time of the month was wrong. And they had only made love once. That she might become pregnant was very unlikely. Very.

In fact, she was certain that she wasn't pregnant. There was no need to worry on that score. She'd behaved badly, but she did have a lovely, wicked memory to cherish. Every once in a while even the most unimpeachable of princesses had to get out and misbehave a bit.

She had done just that and survived. And now, life would go on.

Rhia felt downright philosophical about the whole experience.

Or at least, she did until the next time her period was due.

Chapter Six

Two months later

"Just take the test," Allie pleaded. "Just get it over with so that you can move on."

"So that I can move on," Rhia parroted wearily. It was a balmy June afternoon in Montedoro. She sat across from her sister on the stone terrace off the living room of her villa. Sipping Perrier with lime, they gazed out over the Mediterranean. "As though taking the test will make everything all right."

"I didn't say that."

"What then? Are you saying you think I'm *not* pregnant?"

"Er, well…"

"Just answer the question."

"I'm saying I think you have to find out either way, so that you can decide what to do next."

Rhia sipped her Perrier. "Tell me. Where, exactly, did you buy those condoms?"

Allie winced. "In the ladies' at that little bar in Elk Creek called Charlie's Place."

"When did you have time to go there?"

"I, um, went in just to have a look, after I rented the red pickup."

"And decided to buy condoms?"

"Because I was hoping to convince you that we might, you know, get a little wild that night to help you forget your troubles. And I went into the ladies' and saw the condom machine and I thought, well, if we're going to be wild, we should be responsible about it."

Rhia watched a sailboat gliding smoothly on the wind-ruffled, turquoise-blue water of the harbor and softly advised, "I would not depend on the condoms from the ladies' at Charlie's Place again."

Allie made a sad little sound. "Oh, Rhia. I'm so sorry. I know this is all my fault and I'm...I'm just *so* sorry."

Rhia relented. "Oh, of course it's not your fault. I didn't *have* to run off to Rowdy's Roadhouse. And I certainly wasn't forced to seduce poor Marcus just because we ended up stranded overnight in a wrecked SUV in a Montana blizzard and I happened to have a couple of condoms."

Allie reached across and squeezed her arm. "You're a darling not to blame me. But I do see my part in what happened. And I'm turning over a whole new leaf, I promise. In the future, I'm giving up all my wild and ill-considered schemes."

"Oh, please, Allie. Your wild, ill-considered schemes are part of your charm. And everything I did that night, I did by my own choice."

"Still, I feel terrible..."

"Well, stop. Sometimes things just happen. You get in

an accident and the condom breaks. You pick up the pieces and you go on."

Allie squeezed her arm again. "Just take the test. Please. You'll feel better once you know."

The next morning, Rhia took the test.

The result should not have surprised her. After all, her breasts had become extra sensitive in the past few weeks and already that very morning she'd had to eat five soda crackers to settle her stomach. Also of late, just the smell of coffee or asparagus had her feeling queasy. She'd always heard that pregnant women developed sudden, strange aversions to various foods and beverages they used to enjoy.

No, the results should not have been a surprise. Since the day several weeks before, when her period was due and didn't come, she had known in her heart that she was going to have Marcus's baby.

Still, as she stared down at the result window of the test wand and saw that she actually, factually *was* pregnant, she had the strangest feeling of complete unreality.

She was shocked, after all. Shocked, stunned and very much surprised. Even though she'd already known. Because somewhere deep inside she'd been secretly expecting to find out that she *wasn't* expecting, after all.

That whole day, she walked around in a daze. At 9:00 a.m. as usual, she and her assistant, Leanne Abris, met in Rhia's office at the National Museum complex to go over Rhia's calendar and touch base on the progress of various projects. Leanne took one look at her and asked, "Ma'am, are you ill?" Rhia made some excuse about not sleeping well and they got on with business.

But then later she had a long conference with Claudine Girvan, the museum's brilliant director. They were

planning an upcoming exhibit of the works of the great
Montedoran-born Impressionist painter, Adele Canterone.
Three times during that meeting, Claudine asked in a worried tone if she was feeling all right. Rhia just kept smiling
vaguely and replying, "Of course. Yes. I am fine."

And she *was* fine. In a pregnant sort of way.

Allie came by that night as she'd been doing just about
every night for the past three weeks or so. They shared
dinner on the terrace.

Once Rhia's housekeeper had served the main course
and left them alone, Rhia told her sister that she'd taken
the test. "I'm having a baby."

"Oh, my darling." Allie jumped from her seat—and
then just stood there, her hand at her throat. "What will
you do now?"

Rhia straightened her shoulders and tried on a smile.
"Have this baby. Live my life—only now, I'll be raising
a child."

"Oh, Rhia…" Allie came around the table then, her
arms out. Rhia got up and Allie grabbed her in a hug.

In a whisper, as she held on tight to her sister, Rhia
confessed, "I don't think I even really believe it yet. But
I always did want to have a family, to have children. And
now I will. I'll just be doing it without a husband."

Allie took her by the shoulders and met her eyes. "You
will have to marry eventually. We all do." She referred to
the Prince's Marriage Law, which required all the Bravo-
Calabretti princes and princesses to wed by the age of
thirty-three or lose it all—their titles and the large sums
of money and various properties that were their birthright.
The Prince's Marriage Law was controversial. Many believed it wrong, in any circumstance, to set a schedule
for marriage. The law had been abolished in the past. But
then Rhia's grandfather had reinstated it. He had been the

last Calabretti heir and then managed to produce only one child, Rhia and Alice's mother, Adrienne. The Calabretti family had held the throne of Montedoro for centuries. The Prince's Marriage Law made it much less likely that they would lose the throne for lack of a legitimate heir.

Rhia shrugged. "I have seven years left to find the right man *and* keep my titles and property. I don't think I need to borrow any trouble right now. I have more than enough to deal with as it is, thank you."

"Mother and Father—"

"—will support me in my choice. You'll see."

"And Marcus...?"

Rhia chuckled. It wasn't a cheerful sound. "Don't look so worried. Of course I will tell him."

"When?"

"Right away."

At nine the next morning, Marcus entered the locker room from the training yard, dripping sweat and ready to hit the showers. He stripped down and grabbed a towel.

His cell rang. He scooped it off the bench in front of his locker and answered. "Captain Desmarais."

"Hello, Marcus."

Rhia. There was only one reason she would be calling him.

His knees went to jelly. He sank to the bench. This couldn't be real.

But it was real. "Marcus, are you still there?"

"Yes. Right here."

"We...need to meet."

"All right."

"Come to my villa. Do you have a pen?"

"Hold on." He shot upright and flung back his locker door. As luck would have it, there was one, way in the back on the upper shelf. He grabbed it. "Go ahead." She rattled off an address in the ultraexclusive harbor resort area of Colline d'Ambre. He had no paper handy, so he dropped back to the bench and wrote the address on his thigh.

"This afternoon?" she asked.

He'd just returned from a security assignment guarding Prince Alexander and didn't expect new orders for a couple of weeks, which meant he had nothing that day that he couldn't reschedule. "What time?"

A silence on her end. "You're making this so easy." She spoke with false brightness. "At the very least, I expected you to demand that the meeting be secret."

Had he misread the meaning of her call? He didn't see how he could have. They had been very clear with each other. But perhaps there was something else she was calling about, something he hadn't considered.

He glanced around the locker room. He was the only one there. It should be safe to come right out and ask her if she was carrying his child. But someone else could enter at any time. It was always safer to be discreet. Besides, at that moment, he couldn't have pushed the words beyond his teeth if his life had depended on it.

He said, with a formality that even he found ridiculous, "I *would* request that we meet in secret—if what's been between us can ultimately be *kept* a secret."

She made an impatient sound. "Well, it can't be for me. But for you? Yes. Absolutely, it can." Defensive. And angry.

He felt his own anger rise. What was she telling him? That she thought he might actually deny his own child—and that she would aid him in that?

He needed…to see her face. This was not a conversation they should be having over the phone. "Just tell me what time."

A careful sigh escaped her. "Four o'clock?"

He stared at the address on his thigh. It was smeared a little from his sweat. The unreality of this hit him all over again. "I'll be there."

"Wonderful." Her tone told him all too clearly that it was anything but. There was a click.

She had hung up.

At four on the dot a servant led him into a large sitting room furnished with excellent taste and a goodly number of fine antiques. A wall of glass doors opened onto a long terrace. The doors were flung wide. A pleasant breeze touched his cheek.

Beyond the central pair of open doors, Rhiannon sat at a small iron table, facing away from him. On the table beside her were two ice-filled glasses and two bottles of sparkling water.

"Thank you, Yvonne," Rhiannon said without turning. "Nothing else right now." The servant gave him a nod and left. "Marcus." Still, Rhiannon didn't turn. "Please." She gestured at the empty chair on the other side of the table.

He went through the doors. The villa was high on one of the hills overlooking the harbor, so that beyond the squat stone pillars that supported the terrace rail, the view was of clear blue sky and the hills across the water. Pleasure craft crammed the wind-ruffled harbor below.

Rhiannon turned her head to him. When her eyes found him, there was a sharp, jabbing sensation in the vicinity of his heart. She was as beautiful as ever, in a summer dress printed with bright flowers. She'd pinned up her seal-brown hair. He thought she looked tired. Her dark eyes gave him nothing.

He didn't know what else to do. So he retreated behind the habits of a lifetime. He'd worn his uniform. Somehow, civilian dress had seemed disrespectful. His visor cap was already tucked beneath his arm. He sketched a bow. "Ma'am."

Her soft mouth tightened. "Don't be absurd. Sit down." He sat. "Just put your hat on the table," she instructed wearily. He put it down. She offered, "Have some Perrier."

"Thank you." He made no move to touch it.

She poured the bubbly water over the ice in her glass and then set the bottle aside, resting her slim hand on the iron lace of the tabletop. "We are ludicrous. You know that. One time. How pitiful. This was not supposed to happen."

If he'd had a shadow of a doubt, he didn't any longer. He felt frozen in place, struck anew with extreme unreality. He attempted, badly, to reassure her. "It will…be all right."

She weighed his words, staring out over the terrace rail again. "Yes. Of course it will. Eventually." A small, strained laugh escaped her. "After my failures with fiancés, I had begun to believe I would never have children. I think that once I get over the shock, though, once I've become accustomed to the whole idea, I will actually be glad." She stopped talking.

He realized he ought to say something, to reassure her, to make it clear that he fully intended to do what had to be done now. "We must speak with Her Sovereign Highness immediately. And with the Prince Consort."

A frown drew her smooth, dark brows together. "Well, of course I will tell my parents. Soon. But I wouldn't say there's any huge rush about it."

He didn't understand. "Of course there's a rush. It's been two months since that night. The longer we put off the wedding, the more the world will talk. I don't want that for the child, growing up with people pointing, whispering, calling him hurtful names. We need to be married immediately—that is, if Her Sovereign Highness doesn't demand my head for this."

"Your head? Please." She looked at him again. "And what are you talking about? We're not getting married. You never wanted to marry me. You were very firm on that. There is no way you suddenly get to do an about-face now."

His ears felt hot. And his heart had set to galloping. This was a nightmare. "You deserve a prince. I know that. But the child is mine or you would not have called me here." *And no child of mine will be born without my name. No child of mine will grow up without his father, without two parents married in the eyes of God and man.* He swallowed. Hard. And spoke with a composure he didn't feel. "Of course, I understand your reluctance. I am so...sorry. But it can't be helped. It's necessary now that we go to the sovereign and somehow get her to see that we have to marry."

Her mouth was a thin line. "No, it most certainly is not necessary. Not in the least."

He gaped at her as a terrible awareness dawned. "Wait. No. You can't. You wouldn't."

She blinked. "Wouldn't what?"

He strove mightily for discipline. For calm. For reason. If ever there was a moment that demanded a clear head, this was it. And his brain felt like mush. Mush on fire. "I... understand that you don't want to marry me. That you've moved on from wanting much of anything to do with me. And of course, there would be more suitable prospects who would jump at the chance to make a lifetime with you. But that is not going to happen now. Not while there is breath in my body. I'm sorry to disappoint you, Rhiannon. Sorry on more levels than you could ever imagine. But I can't allow this. No other man will have my child. Never. My child will know his father. My child will grow up with parents who are married to each other and devoted to his well-being."

She stared at him for several endless seconds. And then she said with slow, careful deliberation, "Marcus. You understand nothing. You never have. I refuse to marry a man who only wants to marry me because I am the mother of his child. And as to those 'prospects' you mention? There are none. I'm not marrying you. I'm not marrying *anyone*. Not now, anyway. Not for years yet."

Of course she would marry him. She would have to now. There was no other way. He asked, just to be absolutely certain, "There is no one else, then?"

She huffed out a breath. "Do you actually believe I'm that reprehensible?"

He stiffened. "No. Reprehensible? Of course not. I never said that."

"That is exactly what you said—not in words, no. But it was clearly implied."

He knew he was in trouble here and he didn't even know why. Flatly, he defended himself. "I did not."

"You asked me if there was someone else."

"Yes, I did. But that doesn't mean I find you reprehensible."

"What else would you find me if you believe that I would have had sex with you while I was involved in a serious relationship with someone else?"

He hadn't thought of it that way. If the truth were known, he was having trouble thinking, period. Ever since he'd answered her call that morning, he'd felt as though he didn't have a brain inside his head. The last thing he could ever do was to marry the woman beside him. And now to marry her was the thing that he somehow, against all odds, must find a way to do.

Valiantly, he tried again. "I only meant, if you had someone…if you knew someone more suitable than I, someone who would marry you and give the child his name. I only meant, I'm sorry, but I cannot allow that to happen."

She picked up her glass, took a slow sip, set it back down. "Oh. Oh, I see. You were thinking I had perhaps planned ahead and cultivated the acquaintance of some random minor prince, or even some lesser aristocrat willing to call another man's child his own for certain… monetary considerations, or simply for the chance to marry up."

He could not sit in that little iron chair for one second longer. Rising abruptly, he went to the stone rail. Staring out over the harbor, his face to the wind, he spoke without turning to her. "Please, Rhia." He was so desperate to get through to her that he used the intimate form of her name, the form he had tried in the past eight years to completely eradicate from his vocabulary. "I did not mean to insult you." He turned and faced her then. "I don't judge you, not in any way. Except that I respect you deeply and…and you know that I care for you, that I always have."

She wrapped her arms around herself then, hunching her slim shoulders in a self-protective way. And for a moment, she closed her eyes. Her black lashes lay like small silk fans against her too-pale cheeks. When she looked at him again, her expression had lost the tension and anger of a moment before. Now she seemed defeated, infinitely sad.

"You're right." She spoke softly. "I want to be angry with you. I want to…take out my frustrations on you. But that's not helpful. I'm sorry, too, Marcus. I truly am. I've made a mess of everything. I shouldn't have seduced you that night in Montana."

"Don't blame yourself." The words felt scraped out of him, ragged and raw.

She drew back her shoulders, folded her hands in her lap. "But I *am* to blame."

He told the truth. They could have that at least between them. "I wanted you. I've always wanted you. I think you know that. We both…gave in."

"Because I pushed it."

He held her gaze steadily. "Let it be. Let it go."

After a moment, she nodded. "All right. Yes. I'll let it be. It's only that I…" The words wandered off. She glanced down at her folded hands and then lifted her head again. "At least I've told you. Now you know."

"Yes."

"And you know that I'm not going to marry someone just to give our child a name."

"Not *someone*," he clarified. "Me."

She made a small, pained sound. And then she rose, smoothed the slim skirt of her dress and approached him. They turned and looked out over the harbor together. The breeze brought her scent to him, sweet and exciting as ever. "Oh, Marcus. No. I could never marry you now. I meant what I said that night in Montana. What we had years ago, it's over. Too much has happened. There's been too much pain. We can't go back. Don't you see that it's not possible?"

He watched her profile, so pure and fine. One way or another, he would make her see that there was only one choice here. They were going to be married. It was going to happen. He would *make* it happen. "I don't intend to go back. I only intend to marry the mother of my child."

She did look at him then. The wind blew a few dark strands of hair across her soft mouth. She smoothed them away and tucked them behind her ear. "No."

He turned his body so he faced her fully and he tried

another line of attack. "You can't shame your family this way. The tabloids will have a feeding frenzy."

"I doubt that. They've always been more interested in my brothers than in my sisters and me." A faint smile tried to pull on the downturned corners of her mouth. "Except for Alice, on occasion, when she does something wild."

"You will become 'interesting' and you know it, if you're not married when the world learns of the baby."

She shrugged. "The interest will pass quickly. I'm sixth born—and eighth in line to the throne." His Highness Maximilian was the oldest, the heir, and he already had two children. "I'm an extra princess if ever there was one. And I don't see any shame in my decision. Yes, that this happened is completely my fault. I should have been more careful. I should have backed off that night when you said it was wrong. I should have...left it alone. But I didn't. And now there's a baby coming, a baby who will have my love and my complete devotion. And you can still be a father. You just won't be a husband. At least not to me."

He reminded her sternly, "You are a Calabretti, a princess of the blood."

"I am a *Bravo*-Calabretti, thank you very much. We marry for love. And *only* for love."

"Well, all right, then. I love you. I've always loved you."

She stared at him for a very long time. "I could slap your face for that," she said at last.

He reached out and clasped her smooth, bare arms. Heat seared him, just to have his hands on her again. "Do it, then. Only marry me."

Her eyes were dark fire. "No."

He went all the way with it, pulling her to him, lowering his head, claiming those sweet red lips. She gasped. And for a moment, her body went pliant and her mouth was so soft. A sigh escaped her. The past rose up, the days of their happiness. Fifty-eight days of joy and light, all those years ago. In another country an ocean and a continent away....

But then she stiffened again, whipped her hands up between them and shoved at his chest. "Don't. Stop it."

He released her.

She staggered back, her hand against her mouth. "You have to stop this, Marcus. It's too late for us. You know that it is."

He refused to believe that. "You're wrong. It's not too late. Whatever it takes, we are going to marry. I know what it is to grow up a bastard, unwanted. Unclaimed. That is not going to happen to any child of mine."

"The situation is in no way the same. Oh, Marcus, I know it was difficult for you, growing up. But things were different then."

"Not different enough."

She looked at him pleadingly now. "How many ways can I tell you? This baby will be wanted and loved. This baby will have everything. I will make sure of it. You have to see that. Please. Open your mind just a little, won't you?"

He fisted his hands at his sides to keep from grabbing her again—grabbing her and shaking her until she came to her senses at last. "How blind you are. How proud and thoughtless. You're a Bravo-Calabretti. You were nursed at your mother's breast and your father doted on you and on all of your brothers and sisters. You always had what every child needs. You took it for granted. *You're* the one who doesn't understand."

She gasped as if he'd struck her. And then she took another step back and tipped her chin high. "I think we're at an impasse here. I don't know what else to say to you to make you see."

He refused to give up. He would never give up. "I'll tell you what to say. Say yes. Say you'll marry me."

She made a low sound, impatient and regal. And then she went on as if he hadn't spoken. "I know this has been a terrible shock to you and I'm so sorry to have to put you through this—to put you through what will come, to make you a father when you never asked for that."

"Marry me."

She swallowed. Hard. "I want you to know that I will stick by you. I will make certain there is no...penalty for you with the guard or the CCU because of what's happened. And I hope that, in time, we will reach some kind of peace with each other, that we will find some way to work together, as parents, for the sake of our child."

He dared a step toward her. "The way for us to work together is as man and wife."

She put up a hand. "Don't. Do not come one step closer. I mean it, Marcus. You make a mockery of all we once had."

"That is not my intention. You know that it's not. I only want—"

She didn't even let him finish. "Please. I would like you to leave now."

He almost said no, that they had to come to an agreement, now, tonight, that there was no time to waste.

But he'd already said that. And she'd simply refused him.

He was a soldier, after all. He knew all too well that there actually *were* times when discretion was the better part of valor.

He needed to...clear his head. To think it through. He had no power. She was his princess and he was sworn only to serve her. She held all the cards. If she simply kept refusing him, what could he do?

But then he thought of the innocent child they had

made. And he knew he would do whatever it took. Whatever he *had* to do.

"Please," she said again, her voice so soft, full of hurt that they were doing this to each other. Again. "Go."

"Fair enough." With a last bow, he left her, pausing only to grab his hat from the table as he strode by it.

Rhia stayed rooted in place on the terrace until she heard the front door close.

The sound set her off at a run for her bedroom suite. She made it into the bathroom and to the toilet just in time to flip up the seat and drop to her knees.

Everything came up. It wasn't a lot, since her lunch had been very light. But still. It was awful.

And after it was over, she just sat there for a while. She didn't have the energy to get up—which was fine. She still had that queasy feeling, which meant she would probably only end up on her knees again, anyway.

His words kept playing through her head. *"I love you. I've always loved you...."* The exact words she had so longed to hear him say on the steps of that deserted farmhouse six years ago.

How dare he say them now? Her heart raced in sick fury at the very idea.

Which had her bending close to the bowl all over again.

"Ma'am?" It was Yvonne, her housekeeper, hovering in the doorway to the bedroom, her voice low with worry. "What can I do?"

"Some crackers. A glass of water..."

Yvonne helped her up a few minutes later. She led her to the bedroom and made her comfortable in her favorite slipper chair, with the glass of water and the plate of plain crackers on the small table beside her. Then she knelt and helped Rhia off with her sandals.

"Thank you," Rhia said. "Have Elda prepare me a tray. Something light, in an hour or so?"

"I will, ma'am. Anything else for now?"

Rhia shook her head. "No. That will do."

An hour later, when Yvonne brought in the tray, Rhia was able to eat most of her meal. She went to bed early but didn't sleep well.

She kept thinking about that look on Marcus's face when he left her. A look of purest determination.

The irony of the situation did not escape her. Marcus seemed as single-mindedly set on marrying her now as he'd once been determined never to speak to her again. She knew she hadn't heard the last of this from him.

She considered making the first move, calling him again, asking him if they might talk it over a little more in the hopes that they would manage to come to some sort of understanding between them. But she didn't really see how more talking was going to do either of them any good. Not until she had a new approach to the problem. Not until she felt she had a way to make him see what a bad choice it would be, to marry only because there was a child on the way.

Marcus had always been so determined to do the right thing as he saw it. He had no idea what went into a real marriage, had never seen one up close. The fact of the marriage itself seemed the main thing to him, that their child have married parents. He didn't know there could be so much more. He didn't understand that she wanted a chance at a *real* marriage, at a true partnership.

If she couldn't have that, she wasn't sure she could ever bring herself to marry at all—well, not at this point in her life, anyway. She supposed in a few years, when the specter of the marriage law loomed, she might change her tune.

Time would tell about that. What she did know was

that she wasn't marrying Marcus just because there was a baby coming. She had loved him too much once to settle for less than real, true love now.

Chapter Seven

Rhia went to Alice's villa that night and told her sister everything. Allie was wonderful. She hugged Rhia good and tight and told her what she needed to hear: that everything would work out fine.

Sunday was Father's Day. Rhia went to the palace for dinner with her family in the sovereign's private apartment. She gave her father a small oil painting by one of his favorite Texas artists. He thanked her with a hug and a warm, approving smile. Her father had always made her feel loved and appreciated—which for some reason brought Marcus's cruel words of the other day to mind. He had said that she was blind and proud and thoughtless. That her parents doted on her and she took their love for granted.

Her father tipped her chin up. "Is there something the matter, sweetheart?"

She looked into his eyes and thought how handsome and good he was. She was almost tempted to tell him about the baby right then. But no. The family celebration of her father's special day was hardly the time to go into all that. So she only answered, "Just a little…wistful, I guess."

He chuckled. "Wistful. It's a word that might mean just about anything."

"Thoughtful. Pensive. Will those do?"

"Do you want to talk about it?"

She shook her head. "Happy Father's Day. I love you."

"And I love you."

"You're my favorite father in the whole world."

"Well, considering I'm the only one you've got, I should certainly hope so."

They went in to eat shortly after that. Allie took the chair next to her. "I checked," she teased, leaning close. "No asparagus on the menu."

"Whew. I just might get through this meal without bolting for the loo."

They laughed together.

Overall, it was a lovely evening. Rhia watched her parents fondly—and with more of the wistfulness she'd confessed to her father. Her parents had been married for thirty-six years, yet sometimes they still behaved like newlyweds, sharing tender glances and, at least when it was only the family, touching often.

Her brother Rule and his wife, Sydney, were the same. When they looked at each other, it was obvious to everyone that they were in perfect accord. Max had been like that with his wife, Sophia. Now, three years after Sophia's death in a water-skiing accident, Max still seemed at loose ends without her. He had that faraway look in his eye, as though he'd lost what mattered most and didn't know how to get along without it. Alex and his wife, Lili, and their twins were in Lili's country, Alagonia, that night. But they were every bit as well matched and happy with each other as the other married members of Rhia's family. The Montana newlyweds, Belle and Preston, were the same.

No. Rhia wouldn't settle for less than what her parents and brothers and sister had found. She refused to settle for less. Did that really make her blind and proud and thoughtless?

Allie leaned close again. "You have that look. You know it, right?"

"Look? What look?"

"Stricken, sad and torn apart. Mother and Father are watching you."

"I'm just not ready to tell them about it yet."

"Then perk up and pretend you're having a good time."

Monday came. Rhia dragged herself to the museum to work. Tuesday was the same. And Wednesday, as well.

She kept expecting to hear from Marcus. After all, he'd made it painfully clear that he did not accept her refusal to marry him. She dreaded their next meeting at the same time as she wished they might somehow get it over with.

But he didn't call or try to get in touch with her.

She told herself that was good thing. Maybe he was reconsidering. Maybe he was learning to accept that a marriage between them was not going to happen.

By Thursday, after thinking the situation through from every angle, Marcus was deeply discouraged. He prided himself on being resourceful and focused and capable of strategizing effectively to accomplish any given goal. But every time he tried to plan how to get Rhia to see the grievous error in her decision not to marry him, he came up short.

He had known the truth the other night, when she told him about the baby and then flatly refused his offer of marriage: she had the power. He didn't. She had the wealth and the position and she simply didn't care if the tabloids said hateful things about her. She wouldn't listen to reason and she had no point of weakness he might exploit in order to further his suit.

The situation was dire.

And his powerlessness wore on him. It brought the truth all the more sharply home. The awful irony was not lost on him. She could refuse him now for all of the very valid reasons he had walked away from her before. She was above him and he had nothing to offer her.

The basic questions dogged him, dragging him down. What kind of man was he, if he wasn't going to find a way to claim his own child? If he couldn't make certain that his child didn't grow up a bastard like his father before him?

The answer to those questions was simple and clear. If he couldn't claim his child, he was not a man at all.

Finally, by that Thursday morning, he was desperate enough to accept that he needed input. He needed someone he could trust to help him find the solution that had so far eluded him.

He went to visit his old mentor, the former captain of the Sovereign's Guard, Sir Hector Anteros. Sir Hector, barrel-chested and gray-haired, owned a small house on a quiet cobbled street not far from the shops and open market of the Rue St. Georges. Sir Hector was an old bachelor, recently retired. But the members of the guard and even His Highness Alexander still consulted him on matters that concerned the safety and security of the princely family and of the country itself.

Hector ushered Marcus into his tiny living room and served him bad espresso. Then he sat in his big, tattered easy chair, his feet propped on a faded ottoman, sipping, and said not a word while Marcus confessed that he'd had sex with a member of the princely family entrusted to his care—and gotten Her Highness pregnant in the process.

"Is that everything?" Hector asked when Marcus was done.

Marcus decided that the secrets of the past didn't bear digging up right then. "Everything you need to know, yes."

Hector grunted. "Everything you're willing to tell me, you mean."

"Yes. That's right."

"You should probably be drummed out of the guard *and* the CCU."

"I realize that."

"Followed by disembowelment and a nice drawing and quartering."

"I agree," Marcus bleakly replied. "But that's not why I came to you."

"What is your intention?"

"To marry her. No child of mine will grow up without my name, without the clear and certain knowledge that I claimed him in the way that matters most."

"Did you propose to her?"

"I did. She won't have me."

Hector found that amusing, apparently. He chuckled and sipped from his demitasse. "Why should she? What do you have to offer her?"

"That's the problem. Nothing but my willingness to be a husband to her and a father to the child. And my name. Such as it is." There'd been no indication of what his birth name might be when he was discovered as a newborn on the steps of the Cathedral of Our Lady of Sorrows. So he'd been named Marcus after the priest who found him and Desmarais for one of the wealthy men who endowed St. Stephen's Orphanage. The nuns told him that the couple who adopted him had called him by their last name, but when they gave him up, his name was changed back to Desmarais.

"But Her Highness is having none of you, eh?" Hector's eyes twinkled merrily.

"Are you going to help me or not?"

"Perhaps you ought to try courting her, showering her with flowers and expensive chocolates, with poetry and romantic evenings *à deux*. You ought to put your mind to convincing her of your love and undying devotion."

"I told her I love her. It didn't go over well. I'm no Romeo. You know that. And so does she."

"Then what you need is mercy, my son. The mercy of Her Sovereign Highness and Prince Evan."

The light dawned. "Rhiannon cares about their good opinion. She will listen to them…."

"If you still have your head by the time that they summon her." There was more chuckling.

"You're enjoying this far too much, old man."

"The older I get, the more life amuses me. I have some hope that you will be allowed to keep that head of yours. After all, from the beginning, ever since you were a scrubby little urchin at St. Stephen's, Her Sovereign Highness has had a soft spot for you and your burning desire to grow up and be a soldier for your country."

"That's good, isn't it? That Her Sovereign Highness has kept me in good regard. That could work in my favor."

Hector made a humphing sound. "I will contact the princess's palace secretary on your behalf and arrange an audience for you."

"It must be soon. And if you could arrange for it to be a *private* audience…"

Hector waved a beefy hand. "You're hardly in a position to be making demands."

"They're not demands. They are…urgent requests."

* * *

The following Monday, Marcus received a call from HSH Adrienne's secretary. He was summoned to a private audience with the sovereign the next day at ten-fifteen in the morning. Somehow, Hector had managed to get him exactly what he'd asked for—and damn swiftly, too.

He went to see his mentor a second time to thank him.

Hector gave him more bitter espresso and ribbed him mercilessly about the likelihood that he would end up separated from his head. Marcus tried to take heart from the teasing. He told himself that Hector would hardly be so gleeful over the situation if he believed that Marcus's position was truly dire.

Then again, death wasn't the only penalty that could be considered dire. He could keep his head, but be thrown out of the guard and the CCU, thus losing everything he'd worked his whole life to gain. He could keep his head and be sent away in disgrace. There were any number of punishments short of actual death that he might be sentenced to endure. And how would he claim Rhiannon as his bride, how would he give his child his name, if he lost everything and was banished from his homeland?

In his heart, he believed he deserved whatever he got. At the same time, he knew he would crawl through hot coals naked on his hands and knees if he could only find a way to marry Rhiannon and claim his child.

Wearing his best dress uniform, his mouth as dry as the Sahara at midday, his belly in a thousand knots, Marcus was waiting in the luxurious anteroom to the sovereign's office at 10:00 a.m. At ten-fifteen on the nose, Her Highness's secretary ushered him through the gilded doors to HSH Adrienne's private office.

The sovereign sat behind her giant, heavily carved antique desk at the other end of the large, magnificently appointed room. The secretary announced him.

HSH Adrienne glanced up with a warm smile. She wore a simple white dress with short sleeves and she was, as always, stunningly beautiful. With those mysterious black eyes that seemed to know all and high, proud cheekbones and a wide, full mouth that would have made a movie star proud. She was in her mid-fifties, but looked so much younger—or maybe not younger. Ageless. A goddess of a woman. The most beautiful in all the world. Or so he'd always believed.

Until he met Rhiannon.

His throat locked up at the sight of her. And he was eight years old again and she was wearing a dress of Christmas red, smiling down at him so kindly, calling him by his given name, asking him how he was doing and if he still planned to grow up and join the Sovereign's Guard.

"Oh, yes, Your Highness. I want to be a soldier. I want to guard you always and to keep you safe."

Her smile grew even warmer, if that was possible. "Well, we shall just have to see about that, won't we, Marcus?"

"Oh, yes, please, ma'am."

"You must be a very good boy and work hard at your studies and do what the sisters tell you to do."

"I will, ma'am. I vow it."

And then the most wonderful thing happened. So lightly, her smooth, slim hand settled on the top of his head. His heart felt as though it might explode in his chest.

A moment later, she took her hand away and moved on.

Now, all these years later, she spoke as kindly to him as she had when he was eight. "Captain Desmarais, how lovely to see you. You are looking well."

He didn't feel especially well. His stomach gushed acid

and his pulse thundered in his ears. He remained where the secretary had left him, near the door. Too late, he remembered to salute. "Your Sovereign Highness. Thank you."

She rose from her enormous carved chair with its lush red velvet back. "Come in. Let's sit down."

She gestured at a grouping of fine antique wing chairs and a long velvet sofa near the side wall. And then she went over there.

He realized she intended for him to sit down with her.

Yes. All right. He could do that.

Stiffly, he approached. He waited until she had perched on the sofa and indicated one of the wing chairs. "Have a chair."

His hat under his arm, he went over there, slid in front of the chair and made himself sit in it, though the last thing he'd ever thought he would allow himself to do was to sit in the presence of his sovereign. "Thank you."

"What can I do for you, Captain? Sir Hector Anteros did tell me it was a matter of importance."

"Ma'am, I…" The words ran out. He had a careful speech planned and agonizingly memorized. But every last word of it had fled his panicked brain.

She tipped her head and studied him. Even in his desperate and determined misery, he knew it for a kind and gentle regard. "Please. Do speak frankly."

His throat had locked up. He had to cough into his hand to clear it. And then, somehow, he managed to ask, "Ma'am, if I might stand?"

She nodded. "Of course. If you wish."

He shot to his feet, locked his knees and snapped ramrod-straight. "Thank you, ma'am."

She nodded again. And she waited.

For a moment, he knew absolutely that he wouldn't be able to say what he'd come to say. But then he made himself think of the child. Of what had to be done, no matter the cost to him, no matter that this woman he revered above all would surely revile him, no matter that Rhiannon would likely never forgive him for going behind her back like this over an issue that was rightfully hers to broach to her mother at the time and place of her choosing.

He realized it was better, it was almost bearable, now that he stood at attention. The speech he'd so painstakingly rehearsed returned to him. "Ma'am, it is with great shame and consternation that I come to you today. I have done something unforgivable and been woefully remiss in my duty to our country, to your princely person and the princely family."

HRH Adrienne blinked. She appeared somewhat alarmed. "My goodness. Certainly it can't be as bad as all that."

"Oh, ma'am. It is. I have…that is, two months ago, when I was assigned as security to Her Highness Rhiannon for the wedding and wedding party of Her Highness Arabella…two months ago, when we were, er, stranded overnight together, we, er…" The words flew away again. He was making a complete balls-up of this interview and he knew it all too well.

Gently, she suggested, "Marcus. Whatever it is, I suggest you simply tell me."

So he did. "Ma'am, Her Highness Rhiannon is going to have my child."

The silence that followed was deafening. Marcus remained at attention, staring straight ahead as HSH Adrienne put her hands to her mouth and then rose and walked away toward her desk again, out of his line of sight. He didn't turn to her. How could he? He doubted he would ever dare to face her again.

She asked from way over there behind him, in a low, controlled tone, "Is that all, then?"

It wasn't. He knew he had to say the rest. And somehow, he did. He spoke to the landscape painting above the sofa. "I want only to claim my own child. But after she told me there would be a child and I proposed marriage, Her Highness Rhiannon then refused me. She insists she will have the child on her own."

"My daughter told you she would deny you paternity?"

He hastened to explain. "No. No, of course she would never do that. She freely admits I'm the father. She simply won't marry me."

"I see," said the carefully controlled voice behind him.

He dared to continue. "I realize that I am in no way worthy of her. And I will willingly bow to any punishment Your Sovereign Highness sees fit to inflict upon me. All I ask is that somehow you find it your heart to allow me to do the right thing by the child and marry your daughter." He paused, but the princess said nothing. So he confessed, "You...know of my history."

"Yes, I do," she said quietly.

"Then please, ma'am, do not allow the same thing to happen to this innocent child. Help me to convince your daughter that she must marry me and allow me to be a true father to our child."

There was another terrible, interminable silence. Then at last, he heard her quiet footsteps again. She reappeared in his side vision, returned to the sofa and sat. "You have come to me, then, without my daughter's knowledge."

He wanted to hang his head, but years of military training did not permit that. "Yes, ma'am."

Did she almost smile? Surely not. "Marcus. Sit down." He sat.

"Do you love my daughter?"

His sense of complete unreality, so overwhelming since he had entered this room, increased. Love. What an impossible conversation. He sat opposite his monarch whom he revered above all and she was asking him about love. What did he know of such things? "I am only a soldier, ma'am. I only want to do what's right."

She seemed to consider. But consider what? The things he had just said? Her next words? He had no idea. "I understand that for you the legitimacy of your child is of paramount importance."

"It is everything," he said too abruptly. And then remembered to add, "Ma'am." And then he couldn't shut up. "He must know, that I claim him. He must know that I am proud to...own him."

Her Highness swallowed and glanced away before drawing herself up and facing him again. "But for Rhiannon, the situation is not the same. You must see that. From her point of view, the child will not suffer merely because she hasn't married you."

"Not true. He *will* suffer. He—"

She put up a hand. "Please."

He subsided, shocked at himself that he had presumed to interrupt her. "Ahem. Forgive me, ma'am. Go on."

"I only meant that in this day and age, to be born to unmarried parents is not the terrible hindrance and shame it once was."

"That may be so, but—"

"Hear me out. I know that it was a very difficult life for you, as a child, without either parent to care for you. But this child *will* have two parents. Rhiannon has the means and the heart to raise a child as a single mother and I can see that you intend to be a part of the baby's life. And in this case, there is no throne at stake, no succession to secure, no reason the child *must* be born legitimate."

He couldn't let that stand. "Of course there's a reason. The child himself is the reason. Having a family can make all the difference for a little one. It can protect him from the cruelties of the world until he is old enough to face them on his own."

"I do sympathize," she said. "And I'm sorry, Marcus. But in this situation, coercion is not a tool I'm willing to employ."

His heart sank to his boots. "You won't help me."

"I didn't say that."

Hope rose anew. "You will at least talk with her, then?"

"I doubt that my going to her on your behalf will help you. I know my daughter. She won't think kindly of you when she finds out that you've come to me without her knowledge. Are you certain you've done all in your power to convince her that you love her and truly want to marry her?"

"I told her that I love her." He was careful not to add that she had instantly threatened to slap his face for it. "I... pleaded with her. I reasoned with her. I—" He almost said *I kissed her,* but decided that now was not the moment for speaking of kisses. "I tried everything. Nothing helped. She is adamant that she will not marry me."

One raven-black eyebrow arched. "You're certain she won't change her mind, given time and the proper incentive?"

"What incentive? I've done all I could to convince her."

"Ah. But sometimes one must simply try again."

"It won't help. She's made up her mind against me. Ma'am, will you speak with her? Will you try to make her see that our marriage is the right—the *only*—choice?"

The princess shook her head. "You are so very determined, Marcus. I thought I just explained to you that, for you and Rhiannon, marriage is *not* the only choice."

It was at that moment that he realized Her Sovereign Highness had not spoken of punishment, of what she would do to him for having seduced a daughter of the princely blood. But then again, perhaps she *was* punishing him— by not helping him make Rhiannon marry him. To be denied the right to be a father to his child was just about the worst punishment he could imagine.

And it was the child who would suffer the most.

No. He simply could not give up. He *had* to enlist her aid with this. "Will you speak with Her Highness Rhiannon about this, please, ma'am? It's all that I ask."

"Marcus," she chided, unfailingly gentle. "Have you heard a word that I've said?"

"Yes, ma'am. Every word, ma'am."

"Then you know that I don't believe my getting involved will work in your favor."

He drew in a long breath. "Please, ma'am."

The princess stood. Marcus followed suit automatically. "I must speak with her father," she said. "When the prince consort and I have talked this over, I will be in touch with you."

He dared to meet those knowing dark eyes. And he saw that she had said all she would say for now. The interview was concluded. It would gain him nothing to keep on. "Yes, ma'am. Thank you, ma'am."

With a final salute, he turned and left her.

Chapter Eight

That evening Rhia dined by herself on the terrace. After the meal had been cleared away, she lingered at the little iron table and stared out over the harbor and tried to ignore the nagging worry about what Marcus might do next.

If he did anything at all.

It had been more than a week—eleven days, to be precise—since she'd told him about the baby. In that time, she'd heard nothing from him.

She was starting to believe that he had simply given up, that he'd decided to accept her refusal to marry him. Should she have been content with that?

Probably. But she wasn't. The thought that he might simply let it go left her feeling sad and desperate and very much alone.

"Ma'am."

"Yes, Yvonne?" Rhia turned in her chair to smile at her housekeeper and saw that her mother was there.

Yvonne said, "Her Sovereign Highness, ma'am."

"Mother." Rhia rose and went to her.

"My darling." Her mother held out her arms.

Rhia went into them, glad for the hug, comforted by the subtle, familiar scent of her mother's perfume. "This is a surprise." She offered a drink.

Her mother shook her head. "No. I simply...well, I was hoping we might talk." She was strangely hesitant. And was that an anxious look Rhia saw in her eyes?

Something was going on. Rhia nodded at Yvonne, who left them, closing the doors to the outer hall behind her.

They sat together on the sofa. Her mother carried a lovely Fendi bag, which she set on the coffee table in front of her.

By then, alarm bells were jangling through Rhia. "What's happened?" She touched her mother's hand.

Adrienne clasped her fingers. "Marcus Desmarais came to see me today."

Rhia gasped and jerked her hand away. "He never."

Her mother nodded. "He did."

Rhia got up, went to the open doors to the terrace and stared out, hardly seeing the splendid view.

Adrienne said, "He told me you were having his child."

"Oh, Good Lord in heaven...."

"He is adamant that he wishes to marry you."

Rhia wanted to grab something breakable and throw it. And she also really, really wanted to throw up. But she wouldn't do either. She refused to. She swallowed hard, sucked in a long breath and drew her shoulders back. "Well, that's not going to happen. Which I made crystal clear to him the day I told him about the baby."

Her mother spoke tenderly. "Rhia. Look at me."

She made herself turn and face her mother's waiting eyes. She saw such love there. And wisdom. And true understanding. Rhia's throat clutched and tears filmed her eyes. She resolutely blinked those tears away. "I'm guessing you've already discussed me with Father."

"Yes. We love you. We respect you. We support your choices."

"It can never work with Marcus and me."

Her mother lifted both hands and then lowered them again and folded them in her lap. "I do understand that you...come from different worlds."

She made a scoffing sound. "You sound like him. I don't care about any of that. It's not what I meant."

Adrienne tipped her dark head to the side. Rhia recognized the movement. Her mother was thinking, putting things together the way she so skillfully could. Sometimes Rhia wondered if her mother could read minds. Adrienne said, "I seem to recall that years ago, there was someone. Someone very special. You never said his name. It happened when you were at UCLA, didn't it? And wasn't Marcus there, too, during your freshman year?"

Was her mother saying that she *knew*, about the affair so long ago? Or was she merely trying to add one and one and come up with two, dangling the hook to see if Rhia would bite?

It didn't matter. It was long over. Done. "I don't want to speak of the past. I truly do not."

"My darling, I only want to point out that you've been engaged twice since then and couldn't make yourself go through with the wedding either time."

"Oh, please. Do we have to do this?"

"He's a fine man. I don't think he has any idea how much he's accomplished from such difficult beginnings, or of how far he could go."

"You think I don't know that? You should tell that to him."

"I'm only saying, why refuse him out of hand? You aren't required to say yes or no right away. You could... make an effort with him, give the two of you a chance to find out if there might be a future for you together, after all."

A headache had begun to pound at her temples. And her stomach still threatened to rebel. "Please don't make me explain it all to you. I can't bear it right now."

"All right." Her mother was silent. She gazed steadily at Rhia, her expression thoughtful. And then she said, "You know that I love you. And so does your father."

"I do know. And I am grateful every day for all you have given me."

"I know you must be livid with Marcus about now, for coming to me about this."

"Livid doesn't even begin to describe it."

"But you could look at it another way."

"Oh, really? What way is that?"

"Think of his courage. His ingrained sense of honor and his absolute desire to do the right thing by you and by the child. Think of what it must have cost him to come to me, his sovereign to whom he's looked up from early childhood, to admit to my face that he had stepped so very far beyond the boundaries of his position, that he had become...intimate with you, my own beloved daughter, when his sworn duty was to see to your safety and well-being. Rhia, I'm certain he expected me to order his arrest."

Rhia sighed. "Yes. Well. I imagine he did expect that."

"And yet he came to me, anyway."

"He's like that."

"You would search long and hard to find another man so worthy. I think you *have* searched. And we both know what you've found."

"Mother. I just don't think there's any way it can work with Marcus and me."

Adrienne picked up her handbag and stood. "But you will give it some thought?"

"Honestly? Right now, it's *all* I think about."

"Good, then. Neither your father nor I can ask for more."

As soon as her mother was out the door, Rhia ran to the bathroom and lost most of her dinner. Once that unpleasantness was finished, she brushed her teeth and threw on a robe and asked Yvonne for hot tea and crackers. The housekeeper brought the bland snack to her bedroom and Rhia thanked her and told her she was free to retire for the night.

The bedroom had its own section of terrace overlooking the harbor. She opened the French doors to let in the sea breeze. She'd just taken a chair and picked up a cracker when the phone rang.

A glance at the display told her it was Marcus, which did not surprise her at all. Her stomach feeling a bit fluttery, but in a whole different way than earlier, she set the cracker down and answered. "Have you called to make your confession, Captain Desmarais?"

He knew right away what she meant. "You've spoken with Her Sovereign Highness, then?"

She tried to drum up a little of the outrage she'd felt before her mother started pointing out all of his sterling qualities. "You went behind my back."

"I'm sorry. I felt I had no choice. And now I find…" His fine, deep voice trailed off. He tried again. "I feel very guilty."

"And well you should."

"Rhia. I know it was wrong, but I had to do what I could to try and get you to reconsider."

"You just called me Rhia again." She felt absurdly gratified.

"Yes." Was that a hint of actual humor she heard in his voice? "Now that we're having a baby, it seems somewhat ridiculous not to use your name."

"It's always seemed ridiculous to me."

"I'm aware of that," he answered wryly. And then, with some urgency, "When can I see you again? When can we talk?"

She should make him wait, after what he'd done. But she couldn't. He was her greatest weakness and he always had been. "Now? Tonight?"

"I'm on my way."

Marcus had raised his hand to ring the bell when the door opened.

She stood before him looking beautiful and exhausted in a blue satin robe. Her gaze tracked over his casual trousers and knit shirt. "It's nice to see you out of uniform."

Anxiety for her well-being had him demanding gruffly, "Are you ill? Is the baby—?"

She waved a hand and commanded softly, "Come in." Stepping back, she gestured him forward.

He entered the stone-floored foyer and she shut the door behind him. "Rhia, are you all right?"

"I'm well. Stop worrying." She retied the sash of the robe and turned to lead him into living room.

He dared to reach out and pull her back. Beneath the smooth satin, her flesh was soft. Warm. And so well remembered. "You look worn out."

She glanced down at his fingers gripping her arm and then back up at him. He probably should have released her. But he didn't. "Marcus," she said finally. "I'm pregnant.

I have morning sickness. Except, well, the morning part? For me, it's more like morning, noon and night."

He didn't like the sound of this. "That can't be normal. Can it?"

She turned into him then and put her hand on his chest, as though to ease his racing heart. It didn't help. His heart only raced faster. "All the tension makes it worse," she said. "But yes, it's normal. I've been to see my doctor and he says I'm fine." Her soft lips were tipped up to him.

He wanted to claim them. It was harder than ever to resist her now that everything had changed, now she carried his child and he knew that he would do whatever he had to do to make her his. "You have to take care of yourself." His voice was rough with desire even to his own ears.

All those years of turning away from her, of denying the power she held over him, of waking from dreams of her and telling himself that dreams meant nothing. Those years were catching up with him now.

The fortress of denial was crumbling, leaving him openly yearning. Leaving him starved for the feel of her flesh pressed to his.

A dimple had tucked itself in at the corner of her beautiful soft mouth. "Marcus."

"What?" He growled the word.

"Are you going to kiss me?"

"What the hell." He took her mouth, hard. At first. She made a small, surrendering sound and tenderness rolled through him in a wave. He gentled the kiss. Jasmine and vanilla and the only woman who ever mattered filled his senses.

It lasted only a moment and then she was pushing him away. He let her go reluctantly, the taste and the scent of her making his head swim and his body burn.

She chided, "We do need to settle a few things, don't you think?"

He drew in a careful, steadying breath. "Absolutely."

She straightened her robe again. "Come into the living room. Please."

The night was balmy. They ended up on the terrace, staring out at the crescent of moon that dangled above the hills across the harbor.

She said, "My mother has urged me to give you a chance."

He sent a grateful prayer to heaven for the goodness and generosity of his sovereign. "Her Highness's wisdom is legendary."

The breeze lifted her shining dark hair, carried the scent of her perfume to him. "Yes, well. I must confess she can be very convincing."

Relief surged through him. "We can be married immediately. Now that it's settled, everything will fall into place."

She was leaning on the railing, staring out at the view. But then she straightened. "Hold on."

Hold on? He didn't like the sound of that. "What now?"

She turned to him, drawing her shoulders up the way she did when she prepared for conflict. She even stepped back, claiming distance between them. "I said a *chance*. I didn't say I wanted to race to the altar."

"But you said that Her Highness had convinced you." He kept his tone even and reasonable, though he didn't like the turn this conversation had taken.

She hitched her proud chin higher. "She did. She convinced me that you and I need to spend time with each other, to see if we might find a way to forge a future together."

"Time." He kept his voice level, but it wasn't easy.

Her dark gaze scanned his face. "Marcus. Don't look at me like that."

He pressed his lips together. "Like what?"

"Like you want to grab me and toss me over your shoulder and run for the nearest priest."

It was exactly what he wanted to do. But apparently, she wouldn't allow it to be that simple.

He took a moment to regroup, shoving his hands in his pockets, glancing away toward the moon before facing her again. "How much time were you thinking?"

She looked adorably anxious and she fiddled with the tie of her robe again. "Well, I don't know. I thought we could play it by ear. I thought you could move in here, with me—in separate rooms, of course, at first."

His pride jabbed at him. "Move in with you. Live off you, you mean."

She looked hurt and he instantly despised himself. "Well, um, where did you think we would live?"

He shut his eyes, drew in a slow breath. And confessed the truth. "I didn't think. Except for the necessity that we marry as soon as possible."

"You would want me to come and live with you?" She said it as though it were actually a possibility.

It wasn't. He had a one-bedroom unit with a single bath, in housing provided by the CCU. By his calculation, it would be another three years before he could afford his first house. It would be small and no doubt in need of repair—and certainly not in the luxurious harbor area. "No. No, of course not. You can't live with me, not where I am now. And you wouldn't want to."

"I can't?" She frowned.

"I mean, it's a single officer's unit. We would have to be married first and then I would have to put in for something bigger. And it still wouldn't be..." God. How to say it without sounding pitiable and so far beneath her he wasn't fit to kiss her pretty toes. "It wouldn't be what you're accustomed to."

She moved closer then and she put her soft hand on his chest again. "If we *were* married—which isn't going to happen right this minute—I would be proud to live with you in CCU housing."

There was so much to consider. He hadn't given much thought to any of it in his blind rush to get her to see that they had to marry, and do it quickly. "I don't think CCU housing will be appropriate for you," he said carefully, his body aching for her, his mind and heart once again all too aware of how very far she was above him, of how impossible their marriage was going to be in practice.

Impossible.

But absolutely necessary now.

"Oh, Marcus." With a tender sigh, she moved closer again and let her shining head droop forward on the stem of her neck, resting her forehead against his shoulder. "You're going to have to relax a little, you know? You're going to have to let loose of some of your pride and your hidebound sense of what is fitting."

He cradled the back of her head, eased his yearning fingers into her silky, fragrant hair. And then he whispered only a little raggedly, "Pride and what's fitting have served me well."

She lifted her head. Her eyes beckoned—dreamed of, longed for, never to be.

And yet, here they were. Together. After all these years.

They had made a child.

And somehow, he had to see to it that they *stayed* together, that they married and made some kind of settled life side by side. He had to give his child the essential things he'd never had.

"Less pride," she whispered, her breath so sweet and warm across his throat. "Forget what's fitting."

"I can never forget. Marry me."

She looked at him so tenderly. And shook her head. "We must have time first."

With a low growl of frustration at her stubborn refusal to do what must be done, he dipped his head and captured her lips. Because he *had* to, because the need was growing in him, to taste her again. To make her his.

They had to get married. She might say there was another choice. But for him, there was only one. Even if he could never be equal to her, even if she would forever be the princess he had no right to claim.

She kissed him back, eagerly, opening to him, sucking his tongue into her mouth where it was wet and slick and wonderful. He stroked those silky inner surfaces and pulled her closer, banding his arms good and tight around her.

Too soon, she broke the kiss. "Oh, Marcus...." She stood on tiptoe, pressed her tender lips to the side of his throat. "I mean it. Time." She breathed the words onto his skin.

He stroked her hair. Living silk. "How much time? The longer we wait, the more people will talk."

She chuckled, the sound a little bit sad. "It's not the Middle Ages. You really need to come to grips with that. I meant what I said. I want you to move in here. I want to...try and be close with you in the ways that matter. I want to see if we might have a prayer for a real marriage, you and me."

It wasn't what he'd hoped for. But he supposed it was the best he was going to get at this point. "I would have to keep my quarters. At least for now. Now and then, depending on my duties, I would need to stay there. And as you probably know I often travel, providing security for your sisters or your brothers."

"Yes. Of course. I understand that."

"But when I'm not on assignment, I could be with you here most of the time...."

She let out a happy little cry and clasped his shoulders. "You mean you will?"

He gave her the unvarnished truth. "I will do whatever I have to do to get you to marry me, to give our child my name."

She caught his face between her hands. "Do you have to sound so grim about it?"

He made his lips curl upward. "I shall try to be more cheerful."

"See that you do," she instructed sternly. And she brushed the hair at his temples with the backs of her fingers, the way she used to do all those years ago, when they were secret lovers in California.

He turned his head, kissed the soft pad of flesh at the base of her thumb and then nipped that softness between his teeth, enjoying the small, eager shiver that moved through her and the way her eyes got lazy, the twin fans of her thick, dark eyelashes lowering as she sighed. He couldn't help but wonder: If he took her to bed now, could he get her to give in and marry him right away?

His body responded instantly to that idea.

Her hips were pressed to his. She knew exactly what was going on with him. And she clucked her tongue and shook her head. "I confess, I *am* tempted...." She tipped her head to the side, studying him, and he saw the shadows beneath her eyes.

Seduction would have to wait. He ordered his body to back off and kissed her forehead. "You need a good night's sleep."

"Always so noble," she said with a teasing frown.

"Not as noble as I ought to be. But you have to take better care of yourself, starting with getting your rest."

"Oh, I suppose you have a point. Though making mad, passionate love with you would be so much more fun."

"I will be more than happy to oblige you—once you've had some sleep."

"Oblige me?" She groaned. "This is not how I planned it."

"Planned what?"

"This conversation. I expected you to try to seduce me into saying yes right away."

He shamelessly lied. "I would never do such a thing."

"Yes, you absolutely would. You've already confessed the truth, Marcus."

"What truth?" He tried to look innocent and knew that he failed.

"You'll do anything to get me to marry you."

"Yes, well. You have me there."

"It's all so very ironic, isn't it? You walked away before and wouldn't look back...."

He tried to see the humor in it. "And now you can't get rid of me."

"So I had a pretty good hunch that tonight you would try to seduce me. And then I was going to stand firm and explain how we not only wouldn't be getting married right away, we weren't having sex, either. Not until I felt we were...closer."

"Ah." He bent, nuzzled her ear. "Closer..."

She lifted her arms again and twined them around his neck. "But now, here you are, and I find I only want to... melt into you."

He didn't speak. He didn't dare. And he didn't move,

either. If he did, he would sweep her up in his arms and stride off down the nearest hallway in search of a bed.

She slipped a hand between them and he almost groaned at the thought of what she might be reaching for. But then it turned out to be only the pocket of her robe. She brought out an envelope. "I want you to move in right away. Tomorrow." Taking his hand, she put the envelope in his palm and closed his fingers around it. "Most of the time, Yvonne will be here to let you in. But if she's not, here's the key and the alarm code."

He explained, "I have training exercises in the morning and a couple of briefings. But I can get a few things together and be here in the afternoon...."

"If I'm still at the museum, Yvonne will show you to your room. You must make yourself completely at home." She said it as though she believed it, that he could ever be at home in a house such as this.

Regretfully, he put himself away from her. "Now I should go."

She pressed her lips together and nodded. He turned for the door. "Tomorrow." She said it softly. Almost hungrily. "Promise me."

"I promise," he solemnly vowed. "In the afternoon..."

Rhia called Allie right after Marcus left and explained all the latest developments.

"So he went and talked to Mother," her sister said with a smile in her voice. "The man's got stones, I have to say."

Rhia made a humphing sound. "He really shouldn't have gone behind my back."

"I don't know. I kind of admire a man who does what he has to do to get what he wants."

"That's certainly one way of looking at it."

"It's the *right* way to look at it. And I know you secretly agree with me, no matter that you feel you have to say that you don't—and now he's moving in with you. Good. Excellent, even."

"We'll see."

"Rhia, be bold."

Rhia made a face at the far wall. "Oh, please. What is that supposed to mean?"

"For eight years, you haven't been able to forget that man. Now, at last, the two of you have your chance together. Don't blow it."

"Oh, Allie…" All at once, Rhia's throat felt tight and tears filmed her eyes. "I'm so happy."

"That's more like it."

"And I'm afraid, too. What if we…can't find our way to each other in the end?"

"Don't think like that. You can't afford to think like that. Just concentrate on the two of you, on making it work. And it *will* work. Just watch."

"Oh, Allie. I do hope you're right."

Chapter Nine

When Rhia got home from the museum at six the next afternoon, Marcus was there. Dressed in jeans and a knit shirt, he rose from the sofa in the living room when she entered.

"Rhia." He set down the big coffee-table book he'd been looking at and stood to face her. His shoulders were broader than ever, it seemed to her at that moment. And his eyes…such serious eyes.

They regarded each other. She'd been thinking about him all day, trying to take her sister's advice and think positively. And it had worked, in the main. She'd found herself feeling a rather lovely sense of anticipation for this little experiment in intimacy of theirs.

But now that he was here and she was here and they would have some time to be together that wasn't secret or furtive or only for one night, well, somehow she felt a little awkward. And a lot nervous.

"Is your room all right?" she asked.

"It's beautiful. Very comfortable. Thank you." He studied her face. "You look more rested."

She laughed, a slightly off-kilter sound. "I... Yes. I am. Not long after you left, I climbed into bed and went right to sleep. I slept eight hours straight through. And when I got up, I felt better than I have in weeks. I actually ate a big breakfast. And it even stayed down."

"Good."

"Would you like a drink or a snack? Dinner is usually at seven-thirty...."

"A little whiskey, I suppose."

"Let me get you some." She went to the small wet bar in a corner alcove. "Ice?"

"Neat, thanks." He came closer.

She took the stopper from the crystal decanter and poured him two fingers in a short glass. By then, he was behind her. She turned and handed him the glass.

His fingers brushed hers as he took it and a lovely, hot shiver sang under her skin at the contact. "Thank you." He sipped.

She leaned back against the marble counter of the bar, her hands behind her, gripping the cool rim of smooth stone, and looked up at him. "I feel so...strange. Like this isn't quite real, you know?" He said nothing, only watched her, taking another sip, his eyes going slightly golden, somehow. And she heard herself rambling on, "After all these years, you and me, here in my house. Learning to be together in an everyday way. Sometimes I used to imagine, what it might have been. If you and I had managed to stay together, to make a life together...." Her sentence trailed off. For a moment, there was silence between them.

And then he said, "Marry me."

She shouldn't have, but she thrilled at those two simple words. He moved in closer, set the glass on the counter beside her and then stepped even closer, caging her neatly between his strong arms. More hot shivers cascaded through her.

He said, "If you marry me, you won't have to wonder anymore. We *will* be together. For the rest of our lives."

She felt breathless, mesmerized by the sound of his voice, the gold lights in his green eyes.

He bent closer, captured her lower lip gently between his white teeth, tugged lightly then let go. She let out a quivery sigh. He said, "I talked to your brother His Highness Alexander today."

She *had* to have her hands on him. So she braced them against his chest, which was hard and hot. She could feel the muscular shape of him through his shirt, count the beats of heart under her palm. "About us?"

He nodded. "It only seemed right. He is my commander in the CCU. He needed to know."

"Have you been stripped of your rank? Dishonorably discharged?"

He shook his head. "So far, your family has been amazingly forgiving. However, it's still possible that your father will come after me with a deadly weapon."

She knew better. "That will never happen. My father will always be there if I need him. But he—and my mother, too—are very much about letting their children make their own choices and lead their own lives."

"His Highness Alexander suggests that we marry immediately."

Rhia chuckled, thinking of Alex. Not too long ago Alex and his wife, Lili, had been in a situation very much like the one she found herself in with Marcus now. "Knowing Alex, I'm sure he did more that *suggest* that we marry right away."

"He's right, you know." He bent even closer and nuzzled her hair.

"We need time."

He nipped her earlobe. "You keep saying that."

She let her hands stray up over his big shoulders, along the strong column of his neck, over his nape and into his close-cut hair. "We could make a bargain. I'll stop saying we need time when you stop asking me to marry you."

"I'll never stop." He kissed her temple, her cheek. "Until you stand up beside me and become my wife." And then his mouth was on hers, hot and demanding and so very, very good.

Rhia sighed. He tasted so right. He was everything she'd resigned herself never to have.

And he was pushing her too fast. "Marcus..."

He stepped back instantly. "Too fast?"

She laughed, it was so exactly what she had been thinking. And oh, she did want to grab him and drag him to her bedroom. And maybe she would. In a little while.

But she wasn't going to rush to the altar. No. They did need time, time to fill the same space and find out if they both felt good about being there, time to speak of who they were and where they had been and what they wanted from life.

She touched his arm, letting her hand glide down over the hard, strong shape of it until she reached his hand and could twine her fingers with his. "Let's go for a walk before dinner."

He arched a straight eyebrow. "Trying to distract me from my purpose?"

"Oh, yes, I am. Definitely."

"It won't work, you know."

"Marcus. It's only a walk before dinner. Please?"

* * *

They went down the hill on which her villa was perched and strolled along the pier where all the giant luxury cruise ships were docked. People waved and called greetings to her and looked at Marcus somewhat curiously.

After they'd walked for a while, they got soft drinks from a street vendor and sat on a bench under a tree on the Promenade that rimmed the pier. Rhia sipped the sweet drink and thought how lovely and fizzy it felt, cool and welcoming on her tongue.

Marcus leaned over and tapped his bottle against hers. "You're smiling."

She looked at him and saw her own face reflected in the lenses of his aviator sunglasses. "I always feel free when I walk around Montedoro. You know how it is. We're so security conscious now when we travel outside the principality. But here at home we're still free to move about without trained men watching over us. I hope that never has to change."

He leaned closer. "You don't like having a security detail?"

"It's all right. Necessary, I know that. But it's nicer to be free."

His brow crinkled above the dark glasses. "I've been meaning to apologize...."

She frowned back at him. "Oh, no. What now?"

"I should have asked to be reassigned when I got the orders for the trip to Montana. But I was a coward."

She put her hand over his. "Don't. Please. Yes, I hated it, at the time. But even I understood that refusing your orders wasn't an option."

A muscle in his jaw twitched. "I should have thought of some workable way out."

"Marcus. I swear you have to learn to lighten up a little.

It's water under the bridge…or over the dam. Or however that old expression goes."

"You forgive me, then?"

"Completely. Don't bring it up again."

"Yes, ma'am."

"And don't call me ma'am."

He actually chuckled. And then, for a few lovely minutes, they just sat there, enjoying the shade of the tree, watching the people stroll by on the Promenade. It was quite companionable.

Or it was until two men in the uniform of the Sovereign's Guard came toward them along the Promenade. One was tall and very lean, the other shorter and stocky. They saluted her, murmured solemnly, "Your Highness." Marcus rose.

"Sir," the men said in unison, and saluted him. It seemed to her they made quite a show of it. Marcus returned the salute, but without all the fanfare. Rhia watched the exchange with interest. There was something—challenge, animosity?—in the way the two men looked at Marcus and the way he stared back at them.

The men moved on. Marcus sat beside her again.

She asked, "What was that about?"

"Just two soldiers, men of the guard."

"Do you know them?"

"I do."

"Do they have *names*?"

He let out a slow breath. "Private Second Class Rene DuFere—that's the shorter one. The tall, thin one is Private First Class Denis Pirelle."

"You don't like them?"

He took off his dark glasses, rubbed the bridge of his nose and then hooked the glasses on the collar of his shirt. "I like them fine."

"Marcus," she chided. "What was all that to-do about the way they saluted you?"

"I have no idea. They weren't required to salute, as I am not in uniform. Perhaps they decided going overboard couldn't hurt."

"Hurt what?"

"Rhia, I don't know."

She loosed an exasperated sigh. "Don't you see? This is what I've been talking about. You're always so guarded. Everything is a secret with you."

"It's not a secret. They are noncommissioned officers in the Sovereign's Guard."

"And?"

He glanced heavenward. And then he confessed, "They were at St. Stephen's with me. They are and always have been a...team, you might say. And I never really got along with either of them."

"A team? They're like brothers, you mean?"

He took her hand, held it between both of his and gazed directly into her eyes. "If you have to know..."

"I do. Absolutely."

"We were boys with nothing, no one to claim us," he said quietly, for her ears alone. "Sometimes we formed alliances. Sometimes we made enemies."

"Those two were—are—your enemies?"

He raised her hand toward his lips then. For a moment, she held her breath, sure he would press a kiss to the back of it. But he didn't. She felt regret, but she understood. It was a public place and she was the sovereign's daughter and he just couldn't go that far right then. He said, "We all do what we have to do, to survive."

"You're talking in riddles."

"I don't know how to explain it to you."

"Please. Try."

"You don't understand."

"But I *want* to understand. And I swear to you, Marcus. I would never tell anyone something you told me in confidence."

"I know you wouldn't."

"And I know that there's *something* you don't like about those two men."

"It's not that I don't like them."

"Oh, please. Don't lie to me."

"I swear on my honor. I am not lying to you. We've had our disagreements in the past—Denis, Rene and I—but I don't hold any of that against them now."

"But do *they* hold something against you?"

"I'm sorry. I can't answer for them."

Rhia let it go. She wasn't satisfied with his answers, but it was only their first evening together in this new, more open way. She could hardly expect to know everything in one night. Over on the pier, she saw a man with a camera snapping pictures of them.

Marcus saw it, too. "Now we'll be in the tabloids together."

"Maybe it's only a tourist taking shots for his travel album."

"Do you really believe that?"

"It doesn't matter, Marcus. If we're going to be together, the paparazzi will get pictures of us eventually."

"I don't like it."

She chuckled. "Learn to live with it. You've provided security for most of the members of my family at one time or another. You know how it can get sometimes. Especially if there's any hint of a scandal involved."

He leaned closer and said softly, "All the more reason we should marry immediately." She didn't reply. What was there to say? She'd made herself painfully clear on that subject. He looked at his watch. "It's almost seven. Time we were getting back to the villa, don't you think?"

They were quiet with each other on the walk up the hill.

At the villa, they shared the evening meal, just like a real couple at home alone together, dining in. She gazed across the table at him and remembered what her sister had said.

Rhia, be bold.

After dinner, she offered a tour of the villa, upstairs and down. That didn't take long. It wasn't a large house—not compared to the Prince's Palace, where she'd grown up, anyway. The master suite and the living area were on the first floor, with three more bedrooms above and a third floor where Yvonne and the cook had private quarters.

She purposely ended with the master suite. "And this is my room." She led him in there. "My private sitting room…" She led him through the door to the bedroom. "My bedroom." He made an appreciative noise low in his throat and she led him to the next door. "The bathroom." She took his hand and pulled him in there. He flipped on the light. They stood before the wide mirror above the vanity and twin sinks.

"Very nice," he said.

"The tub is big enough for two." She stepped right up to him, put her arms around his neck.

And kissed him.

He captured her face between his two big hands. "Rhia. What are you up to now?"

Be bold. "Well, as a matter of fact, I was just about to take you back in the bedroom and show you an intimate view of my bed." It came out slightly breathless. Lord. Was she making a hash-up of this?

But he reassured her—with another searing, perfect kiss. He covered her lips with his and he pulled her closer, so that her breasts flattened deliciously against his hard chest. He even pressed his hand to the small of her back, so she curved into him. He felt wonderful, so hard and strong. He wanted her. She could feel that, too.

Relief and desire swirled through her, making her knees a little weak. She clung to him. He didn't seem to mind.

When he lifted his head, she let her eyelids drift open. He regarded her gravely—or mostly so. There was also a definite flare of heat in his eyes. "I would love an intimate view of your bed."

She touched the side of his face, ran her finger around the neat rim of his ear. "You won't think I have no backbone, will you?"

"Why should I?"

"I said separate beds for a while, remember? That was the plan."

"Plans change." His voice was deliciously gruff. He bent close for another kiss—a sweet, quick, brushing kiss this time.

She stroked the side of his neck, breathed in the clean, manly scent of him. "Allie said I should be bold. And I've decided that I agree with her."

"Bold is good." He feathered another kiss against the tip of her chin and then lifted away a little. "Bold is excellent."

She wrapped her hand around the nape of his neck and drew him closer once more, close enough that they shared the same breath. "Oh, Marcus..."

"Anything."

"Tell me that we will be all right."

"We will," he whispered. "I know we will."

"Tell me we will work it all out."

"We will."

She brushed her lips against his, pressing herself up to him, feeling his heat and hardness, so acutely aware of everything about him: his strength and his goodness. His all-too-ingrained sense of propriety and his natural reserve. His fine, deep voice that made her want to rub herself all over him, the scent of him that had always drawn her. His very pigheaded insistence that she was above him and they couldn't make it work all those years ago.

His insistence that it *would* work—that it *had* to work—now.

"Take me to bed, Marcus."

His answer was to scoop her up high in his arms and turn for the other room.

Chapter Ten

Marcus reached the side of her high, turned-back bed, and didn't want to put her down. He feared she might change her mind if he let go of her even for a moment—change her mind and send him to the room she had originally assigned him.

She sighed and rested her head against his shoulder. "Um. So…are you just going to stand there holding me all night?"

He bent his head to her. "I might. I might never let you go."

"I might like it, if you never let me go…." She lifted her mouth for him.

He took it, hard and hungrily. She tasted of everything he had ever wanted, all he'd thought he could never have. He sucked her soft upper lip into his mouth, caressed the slick inner surface with his teeth. She moaned. He drank in that sound.

And then, still holding the kiss, he lowered her feet to the floor and began to undress her. She allowed that—more than allowed it. She sighed, swaying against him, whispering "Yes" against his lips as he unbuttoned her silk shirt and eased it off her shoulders, as he unzipped her snug skirt and pushed it down, taking the tiny lace and satin panties she wore along with it. With a flick of a finger, he undid her bra, quickly guiding the straps down her arms, pulling it off, tossing it aside.

She had her hair up. He speared his fingers in it, feeling for pins. "Let it down. Loose." He growled the command against her mouth.

She obeyed, lifting her arms, pulling at the pins until the heavy mass fell in a dark veil to her shoulders. He stroked the seal-brown strands, let the curls fall between his fingers, combing them.

He needed…everything. All of her. To touch her. Every smooth, soft inch.

And he took what he needed. He cupped those fine, full breasts of hers, and he played with her nipples as she bumped her hips against him, sighing, moaning, using her sweet, eager body to beg him for more.

More worked for him. More was exactly what he had in mind.

He pressed his hand against her still-flat belly, wondering at the miracle within, the baby they had made that had changed everything.

"Oh, Marcus. Yes…"

He inched his fingers lower, until he touched the short, silky curls that covered her sex. She lifted to him, moaning more yeses into his mouth.

So he went on touching her, parting her, delving in where she was so wet and sweet and ready for him. He found the hard little nub where her pleasure was centered and gave it special attention.

About then her knees gave way.

She clutched at his shoulders. "Marcus!"

"It's all right. It's good…" He eased her down across the bed, guided her slim legs apart and stepped in close between them. Bending over her, he pressed his mouth to hers.

She kicked away her shoes and caught his wrist to guide his hand. He knew already what she wanted from him. He gave it, caressing her the way she'd always liked it most, so long ago, in California. He dipped one finger in, then a second….

She cried out again. He cupped her, holding her, and let her rock herself against his palm as the finish took her.

A moment later, she went lax. She stared up at him through glazed eyes. He started to step back. She grabbed his arm and held him close and began pulling at his shirt. "Take this off. Now. All of it. Everything…"

Getting everything off sounded like a fine idea to him. He reached both hands back, gathered the shirt up and yanked it over his head. She got hold of it and threw it off the far edge of the bed.

He started to straighten again, so he could take down his jeans.

"Come back here," she insisted, reaching for him.

"One minute. Less."

She let him go long enough for him to kick off his shoes and tear off his socks, to pull his fly wide and shove his jeans down along with his boxers.

"There," she said approvingly. "Better."

He leaned close to her again, sliding a hand under one smooth thigh, lifting that leg, pushing it wider as she gazed steadily up at him, dark eyes full of night and wonder and sex.

"Oh, Marcus. At last. Yes…" She reached down between them.

He groaned at the pure perfect agony of it as she encircled his aching hardness and drew him to her, touching the tip to her wetness, guiding him where she wanted him to be.

He surged forward, filling her.

She cried out. She pushed herself up to him, taking him deeper. He went. All the way, burying himself in her wonderful heat, her unbearable sweetness. He went deep. The moment hung suspended.

The sight of her, below him, open to him, *his* in a way that he'd never allowed himself to think of her before….

That made him drive harder, move deeper within her, withdrawing only to surge close again.

It was glorious. Perfect. He wished it might never, ever end.

But of course, it did. The wave rose up, cresting over them. He went first, turned inside out by it, surging over, flying high.

And then he felt her contracting around him. He braced his arms on the mattress to either side of her flushed, beautiful face and he let her have him, let her move against him at her will. She called his name as she found the absolute hot center of her own pleasure.

She didn't give him long to recover before she was pulling at him again, arranging him to her satisfaction, dragging him fully onto the bed with her, so that they both lay with their heads on the pillows.

"There," she murmured. "Better. Wonderful…"

He nuzzled her hair, cupped one breast, flicking the

hard pink nipple so that she sighed. "You amaze me. You always did. So damnably beautiful...." He stuck out his tongue and licked the perfect, swirling shape of her delicate ear.

She laughed. "I have to ask..."

He nipped her earlobe. "What now?"

"Boxers? When did you start wearing boxers?"

"Boxers shock you?"

"It's just...you always wore briefs before."

"I like boxers. They're comfortable. And what does it matter?"

"It's a little thing," she admitted.

"Exactly."

"But little things do matter, especially now. I intend to know everything about you."

He grunted and thought of the biggest secret, the one he had never planned to tell anyone, the one he supposed he would now have to find a way to tell her. Because she wanted all his secrets and he'd more or less promised he would give her whatever she asked of him.

And he would. Just not right now. He couldn't bear to tell her now.

So he kept it light. "Everything? Be careful what you ask for, you just might get it."

She wrinkled her nose at him. "You've always been much too self-contained. When did you start wearing boxers?"

He smoothed her hair, loving the feel of it under his palm, catching a lock of it and rubbing it between his thumb and fingers. "If you must know, I bought some in a department store, in America, when I was providing security for your sister last fall. I tried them."

"*Silk* boxers?"

"What can I tell you? Silk feels good."

"I don't remember boxers, that night in Montana...."

"It was dark under that tarp, and we were..." He sought the word.

She offered it. "Urgent. It all seemed so urgent."

He remembered. And agreed. "Yes, it did."

She braced up on an elbow and stared down at him through somber eyes. "It was so strange, in Montana at the wedding, to see you shaking hands with the McCade men, and to realize that you had been there, lived in the ranch house there, with Belle and Charlotte..." Her voice trembled a little.

"Shh." He pulled her down to him again, kissed her hair, her cheek, the tip of her nose.

"It's only, well, it hurt. To think that you had been there for months, and I didn't even know."

"Rhia. Why should you know?"

She gave a slight shrug. "You're right." Her voice was thoughtful and more than a little bit sad. "Of course, you're right—but it's strange. When you come right down to it, I know so little of your life. And you know my sister's new husband better than I do."

"Not really. I like Preston McCade. He's a good man. Solid. Dependable. Strong. But we hardly became friends."

"It must be a lonely kind of job, watching over someone for months like that, having to stay close to them constantly, but not really being a part of their lives."

"I never thought of it that way. It's a job that I'm good at. And an honor to be chosen, to be counted on, trusted to protect the ruling family."

She touched his face again. "Lonely, though."

"Yes, I suppose. A little."

"Do you plan to be in security for all of your military career?"

He buried his nose in her hair, loving the scent of it. So sweet. So tempting. "We'll see."

She canted up on her elbow once more and gazed at him with reproof in those soft, dark eyes. "You're being secretive again."

"No. It's only that it's hard to know what opportunities might present themselves." She just went on staring down at him, waiting for more. So he continued, "The Covert Command Unit is a force of only fifty. And the Sovereign's Guard, of which the CCU is part, has two hundred and thirty-three men and women in total. I hope someday to reach the top rank of colonel."

"Would that be so impossible?"

"In such a small force, commissioned officers are few and far between. And as for earning more bars and stars, well, there are the French to consider. By tradition, French officers always claim the highest ranks among us. However, my prospects are even brighter now, with His Highness Alexander so closely involved. And I'm in the CCU, which he created, so that's also a plus in terms of my advancement. His Highness approves of raising up those of us who are Montedoran by birth. But still, we can't all be at the top, can we?"

She laid her hand against his heart. "I think you could achieve just about anything you set out to do."

He looked in her eyes and saw her sincerity. "Marry me."

She came back down to him, resting her head on his chest, where her hand had been. "Time, Marcus. Give us some time."

Rhia thought that things went well between them over the next few days. He left her early in the morning to go to CCU headquarters. But he came home for dinner. They took more walks down by the pier and along the beaches near the casino. And he moved his few toiletries to her bathroom, hung his clothes in her closet.

And every night they shared her bed.

That was wonderful. To spend her nights with him. And not only for the heady magic of their lovemaking. There was so much more. She loved to hear his even breathing beside her as he slept, to wake in the morning with him wrapped around her, so big and warm and strong.

He had always made her feel safe. Cherished. Protected in the purest sense of the word. But now, living openly with him at last, she felt more content and more truly at home than she'd ever felt in her life before.

She only hoped that it could last.

On Saturday, the first story about them appeared in a certain tabloid paper. It included several pictures of the two of them, pictures snapped on the Promenade that first night he'd moved in with her. The headline? *The Princess and the Bodyguard.* As usual with the tabloids, the story was full of trite phrases and heavy on the innuendo. The upshot was that there must be romance in bloom between Her Highness Rhiannon and Captain Marcus Desmarais.

Marcus hated it.

Rhia laughed and reminded him that it was only the truth. "And it doesn't say anything bad about either of us."

"It says that I was a foundling child raised by nuns and that you have been twice engaged and never quite made it to the altar."

"The truth. How terrible." She faked a shiver. "Honestly, we couldn't ask for more."

"Yes, we could. How about if they all learned to mind their own business?"

"Please. That is never going to happen."

He grumbled, "Even if I finally convince you to marry me, those bastards can count."

"Yes, I'm afraid that's true."

"The world will know that you were pregnant *before* the wedding."

"Undoubtedly so."

He tossed the tabloid aside and pulled her close. "Marry me now."

She kissed him. "Give it time, Marcus."

He grumbled something under his breath. But then he pulled her back to him and settled his warm lips on hers again. That led to a much more satisfying activity than arguing over what the tabloids would say.

Sunday, together, they went to breakfast at the palace. It was something of a family tradition. She and her brothers and sisters and their families would join her mother and father in the sovereign's apartments for a private family meal.

That Sunday, the last Sunday in June, Alex and Lili were in Alagonia, and Belle and Preston were in Montana. But everyone else came. Marcus didn't say much through the meal, but her siblings and her mother and father each made a point to engage him in friendly conversation, to show him he was welcome among them.

Rhia knew by the way they all behaved that her parents or Allie or Alex must have told the rest of them exactly what was going on.

Later, when she and Marcus were alone at the villa, he said, "They all know, you realize that? About the baby, and that I'm living here, that I want you to marry me and you haven't said you will."

"Yes. I gathered that everyone was up to speed on our situation."

"Our *situation?*" He repeated the word as if it were an

obscenity. "I'm surprised one of your brothers didn't grab a weapon and run me through."

"As a matter of fact, my brothers respect and like you. You're quite admired in my family, you know."

"Admired, humph."

"Everyone knows you're a good man to have at one's back. They know that you came up from nothing and have done very well for yourself. And that you will forever and always strive to do the right thing."

"They also know that I have no fortune and I seduced their sister."

"Well, *I* have a fortune, so if we do marry, we have that covered. And the seduction, as we both know, was probably more my doing than yours."

"That is not the point."

"Yes, to a great extent, it is."

"The point is that I presumed to have sex with a princess of the blood."

"Yes, but the good news is that you're a commissioned officer, which makes you a gentleman—self-made, but still. They see you as someone dependable who can be counted on to be a good husband and father. And as for having sex with me, well, these things happen."

He paced the living room. "No. No, they don't. Or they shouldn't."

"Marcus, you are such a complete snob. And so annoyingly straitlaced."

He stopped, whirled. Faced her with a lowering frown. "I am not straitlaced."

"No complaints on being called a snob, eh?"

"I didn't know which insult to tackle first."

She stifled a chuckle. "Marcus. You *are* a bit of a moralist, really."

He dropped to a chair as though the conversation had

exhausted him. "Never mind. It's enough. Believe I'm a straitlaced snob, if it makes you happy."

She told him gently, "Well, I suppose you're not really a snob...."

"Enough, I said."

"Very well." She went and stood over him and put her hands on his wonderful, hard shoulders.

He muttered, "Your family is wonderful."

"Yes, they are." She bent and kissed the top of his head.

He groused, "And I've never felt so out of place. Breakfast in the sovereign's apartments. Never in a hundred thousand years..."

"You got through it. And quite gracefully, I thought."

"You're just saying that."

"No. I do mean it. I truly do, Marcus."

He took her right hand from his shoulder then, and pressed his lips to her palm and tipped his head back to look up into her eyes. "Marry me."

She almost said yes right then and there. But she caught herself and gently withdrew her hand. "It's only been four days since you moved in here. I do think that we really need a little more time."

At ten on Monday, Hector Anteros showed up in Marcus's cubicle at CCU headquarters.

He shut the door, eased himself down into Marcus's one extra chair and said, "Am I hearing wedding bells?"

Marcus sent his mentor a weary glance. "I think she has to say yes first. The wedding bells come after."

"So you *have* asked her again?"

"And again. And again."

The space was small. Hector turned the chair so he could stretch out his legs. He groaned a little as he straightened them. "It hurts being old. Take my word for it—or don't. You'll find out for yourself one day."

Marcus closed the report he'd been working on. "You're working up to something. I can always tell. Just say it, whatever it is."

"I'm old."

"I'm clear on that. Go on."

"I find that living with guilt weighs on me."

"All right. You're guilty. Of what?"

Hector didn't look all that guilty. He looked a bit smug, really. He arched a bushy brow in Marcus's direction. "Did you really think that no one knew about you and Her Highness Rhiannon eight years ago?"

Marcus's heart lurched in his chest. His mouth dropped open. "You…? No."

Hector nodded. "At that time, as you are well aware, security was less of a focus. We didn't have round-the-clock protection for Her Highness while she was studying at UCLA. But of course, it was the duty of the Sovereign's Guard to see to her safety. We hired a trustworthy American security team to keep an eye on her, and—once you began spending time with her—on you."

We? "Who else knew?"

Hector named two officers of the Sovereign's Guard, good men, and discreet. "And the Americans who reported to us." But Marcus wasn't thinking of his fellow soldiers or the Americans. "Her Sovereign Highness and Prince Evan? Did *they* know?"

Hector gazed at him so calmly. "No."

"But it would have been your duty to—"

"Not necessarily. You see, Her Sovereign Highness made a special point, with each of her sons and daughters once they were of a certain age, to give them the freedom to make their own choices. I was instructed to allow Princess Rhiannon to test her wings, to find her own way as much as possible. It was most important to the sovereign and Prince Evan that their sons and daughters never felt spied upon. In my judgment, you posed neither a danger nor a threat, so I didn't approach the sovereign about what was going on." The explanation did make sense, given what Rhia had always said about her parents giving her the freedom to live her own life.

But that didn't absolve Hector from his responsibility to report what he knew to the sovereign. "You should have told Her Highness Adrienne."

Hector only grinned. "But I didn't. I chose to take my sovereign at her word and protect the privacy of Her Highness Rhiannon. And I don't think you're in any position to judge *my* decisions during that time. It was long ago, and it's over and done—and what happened way back when is not what I've come here to clear my conscience about."

"My God. There's more?"

"Consider. I knew about your past with Her Highness Rhiannon. And yet I was the one who suggested to His Highness Alexander that you be assigned to provide her security for the wedding in Montana."

"*You...?* I don't... You can't..." He seemed to be having difficulty forming actual sentences.

"Yes. I did. I provided, you might say, a window of opportunity for you. And for the princess you could never forget."

Marcus strove for calm as the man he respected most in the world sat there and told him that he had intentionally broken a critical rule. "But...it makes no sense that you would do such a thing. Hector, you know better. It wasn't safe. If you knew that she was important to me, that we had history, then you knew I didn't have the necessary objectivity to protect her effectively."

Hector waved a hand. "Perhaps."

"Hector, it was *wrong*. Dangerous. She ran away from the wedding party because she couldn't stand to be near me. Anything might have happened to her. We were in an auto accident. She could have been hurt. She could have *died*."

"But she wasn't hurt and she didn't die."

Marcus fisted his hands on the desktop to keep from leaping up and wrapping them around Hector's throat. "I have a powerful urge to throttle you, old man."

"Keep your shirt on. Hear me out. Yes, I took a risk."

"A foolish, pointless, dangerous risk."

Hector was unperturbed. "A risk that needed taking. For *both* of your sakes." With another pained groan, he pulled himself to his feet. "I'm an old man. And I'm alone. No wife to nag me, no children to give me grandchildren. I don't especially like being alone and I didn't want that for you. Now, because of what I've set in motion, you *won't* be alone. You will have a family. I don't regret the chance I took."

"Regret? You seem downright proud of yourself."

"Just get her to say yes. Be happy. That's all I'm asking of you."

Marcus gaped up at him. "And now you're leaving? Walking out, just like that? I should file a report on what you just told me."

Hector chuckled merrily. "What? To get me booted from the guard? That would be difficult, as I'm already retired."

"You could lose your position as advisor to the commander."

Hector limped to the door. "Do your worst, Marcus my lad. I'm going home where I can put my feet up."

That night, in the spirit of openness and sharing that Rhia had demanded—and also to ease his conscience a little for continuing to keep his deepest secret from her—Marcus told her what Hector had told him. They were in bed by then and had made slow, satisfying love. She'd already turned out the light and they lay beneath the covers, side by side.

He stared up toward the dark ceiling and told her what Hector had said that day.

When he was finished, she laughed in delight. "Oh, I knew it couldn't be only coincidence that you were assigned to me for that trip."

"It's not anything to laugh over, Rhia. It was a dangerous thing for him to do. A bodyguard cannot be allowed to have any personal relationship with someone he's assigned to protect. He must be cool-headed and objective at all times."

She made a distinctly undignified sound then. "I'm sure you're right."

"There is no doubt that I'm right."

"Well, I think it's very sweet that he wants you to be happy, to have a family, not to be alone. If he did something he shouldn't have, it was for a good reason."

"I should report him."

"Don't you dare."

He rolled to his side then and braced his head on his hand. "You are much too cavalier about this."

She gazed up at him, her eyes shining through the dark. "You're not going to report him. You couldn't do that."

He drew her close against him. "You're right. I couldn't." He smoothed her hair off her forehead. "Marry me." He kissed her.

She kissed him back.

But she didn't say yes.

The next day in the early afternoon, Marcus left for Italy to provide security for Prince Damien, who was speaking at a gala fundraising dinner for the victims of a recent flood. It was only a two-day trip.

Still, Rhia missed him. A lot. Wednesday, she got a call from Montana. Belle was happy in her new life and deeply in love with her new husband. Rhia told her older sister everything at last, about her past with Marcus, about what had happened the night of Belle's wedding and about the coming baby, too.

"So now you two are together," Belle said in a musing tone. "Will you marry him?"

"I want to. So very much. But I need to be sure that it's something that can last."

"I understand." Belle made a soft sound low in her throat. "Marcus. I never guessed it was Marcus that you loved all those years ago...."

"It was a secret he insisted I keep."

"He's a good man, Rhia. Considerate. Trustworthy."

"Yes, I know he is."

"Be happy, Rhia."

"Oh, Belle. I promise you, I'm working on that."

On Thursday evening, Rhia came home from the museum complex to find Marcus waiting for her.

Her heart lifted at the sight of him. She ran to him and he opened his arms to grab her close. He kissed her until her head spun.

And then, his mouth still fused with hers, he lifted her high in his strong arms. He carried her straight to the bedroom, where he swiftly took off all her clothes and showed her that he had missed her, too.

It was only afterward, as they lay there holding each other close beneath the sheet, that she sensed something wasn't right.

She lifted up so she could see his face. "Something's going on. You're much too quiet."

He ran the back of his finger down the side of her arm, stirring goose bumps in his wake. "I'm always quiet."

She wasn't buying. "Uh-uh. There's quiet. And then there's…quiet. You've got something on your mind."

He glanced away.

She caught his beard-rough jaw and made him look at her. "What's happened?"

He drew a much-too-careful breath. "You are not going to like this."

She held his gaze. She refused to let go. "Tell me."

"Before I get into it, I just want you to know that I honestly have been trying to find a way to explain this to you. I thought I would have more time to work up to it. But then, this morning, I found out I really can't afford to put it off any longer."

"Put what off? Marcus, you're scaring me. What are you talking about?"

"Just…wait." He put a finger to her lips, so gently. "Let me say this in my own stumbling way."

"Yes. All right. Of course." She gulped. "Go on."

He started in again. "I've been planning to tell you, trying to figure out how, exactly, to manage it…."

She ached to demand that he tell her and tell her now, but somehow she succeeded in keeping her mouth shut.

And about then, he gave up trying to ease into it. He said simply and flatly, "You're right. There's no good way to say this. I got a call from Los Angeles today. This morning, my father died."

Chapter Eleven

"B-but you don't *have* a father," she heard herself sputtering. "I mean, do you?"

He pulled away from her, pushed back the sheet and swung his legs over the edge of the bed. And then he just sat there. She stared at his powerful naked back. His big shoulders were hunched.

"Marcus?" She asked his name raggedly, barely making a sound. When he didn't answer, she reached out.

But he was already bending to grab his trousers from the floor. He rose and put them on. For a moment she thought he would pull on the rest of his clothes and walk out, leave her there gaping after him, naked in the bed where they'd just made love.

But then he did turn to her. He held out both arms to the side in a hopeless, bewildered sort of gesture. "All those years ago, I couldn't bear to tell you. I've never told anyone, except the investigators I hired to find out if he really might be who he said he was. The man is...*was* not a father to me in any way that matters. But biologically, yes. He's the man who fathered me."

She had to concentrate to draw breath. "I don't... All those years ago, when we were together, you knew of him then? At UCLA?"

He stuck his hands in his pockets, as though he couldn't decide what exactly to do with them. "Yes."

"But you always said—"

"I know what I said. It was... I couldn't talk about it then. I wanted to forget all about it, about *him*. I wanted it to be as if he'd never approached me, as if I'd never seen his face or heard him tell me I was his son."

"*When,* Marcus? When did he approach you?"

"Just before I first met you."

"In Los Angeles?"

He nodded. He still had his hands in his pockets and he seemed to be looking everywhere but at her. "I had only just arrived in California. He approached me the first day I was there. It was in Westwood. I'd gone to the drugstore to pick up razors and shave cream and toothpaste. He just came right up to me there on Westwood Boulevard. He said he was my father and that he'd hired people to keep track of me through the years, that he had learned of my fellowship at UCLA, had known I would be coming to Southern California. He knew where my dorm was. He said he'd followed me from campus just then...."

His words came at her. She heard them, but as though from far away. Her mind kept cycling back to the impossible fact that he actually knew who his father was. "I don't understand. You never told me. How could you never have told me something so enormous as that?"

"Rhia, I didn't believe him then. I *refused* to believe him, even though I couldn't deny, even on that first day, that I did look like him. I called him a liar. He grabbed my hand and put a piece of paper in it. He said if I ever wanted to know the story of my birth, I should give him a call. I kept that scrap of paper, but I didn't call. Not for more than two years. Not until after you came to me and told me you wanted to try again with me. After that, after losing you a second time...I don't know why that made the difference, but then, somehow, I *had* to know."

She longed to correct him, to remind him that he hadn't *lost* her. *He had sent her away.* But the pain in his voice stopped her. Yes, he should have told her all of this before. She was shocked and hurt that he hadn't. It cut deep that he hadn't. It was the harshest sort of proof of the basic problem she had with him. He kept himself apart. He kept secrets. She needed to be the one he told his secrets to.

But then she reminded herself that he *was* telling her his secrets. He was telling her right now. And it was agony for him.

His suffering broke her heart. She reached out her hand again. "Come here. Here to me. Please..."

He shook his head. He still didn't look at her. "I hate this. I should have told you, but I didn't know how. And I didn't want to think about it, about *him.* It makes me want to put my fist through a wall, whenever I think about him."

She scooted to the edge of the bed, until she could reach out and catch his hand. When she did, she pulled him toward her. "Come on. Sit down."

He hovered in place for a moment. But then at last he came to her and dropped to the mattress. Dragging the sheet to cover herself, she swung her legs over the edge so she could sit beside him.

She still had hold of his hand. And now, he was holding on, too. Tightly. He took her hand into his lap, twined their fingers together and looked down at them, as though the sight steadied him somehow. "Eight years ago, I thought I knew who I was. I fully accepted that I was alone, that whoever my parents had been, they had deserted me. For me, they didn't exist. What I would make of my life would be completely of my doing, on my own shoulders. I had graduated from university, had received my commission. You know how rare that is, for a commoner, for someone with no family, to receive an officer's commission?"

She nodded. "Yes. I know. Very rare."

"I was proud, of all I'd done, of how far I had come from such difficult beginnings. I was a university graduate with a commission. I was in America, sent there for a special fellowship...and then a complete stranger walked up to me and said he was my father. It blew my world apart. I considered just...leaving."

"Leaving what?"

"Leaving everything. Vanishing. Disappearing into America."

She pressed herself closer against his side, wishing she could somehow make it better for him. Not so annihilating. Not so full of pain. "But you didn't."

He shook his head again. "It's strange. I was so angry. My fury made me bold. Had I not been so angry, I never would have dared to approach you that day in the bookstore when you challenged me for staring at you. I never would have presumed to introduce myself so brashly, nor to go with you when you asked me to coffee. I never would have gone so far as to stare openly at you when I saw you and knew who you were. If I still hadn't been reeling from that encounter outside the drugstore, if I hadn't been burning with rage and ready for anything, I would have turned carefully on my heel at the very sight of you and walked away. Had you, for some reason, happened to smile upon me, I would have saluted, of course, and given you a proper greeting. But never in any way would I have allowed you to see me as more than a soldier at your command and sworn to serve."

"So then," she tried gamely, doing her best to look on the bright side, "in a way, we have this father of yours to thank, for…bringing us together."

He stared straight ahead. "We have nothing to thank him for. Nothing."

She wrapped her other hand around his bare arm. It was hard as ungiving rock, every muscle tensed. "You never had a chance to make your peace with him, then?"

He glanced at her sharply. "I think I have, yes. As much as I can. I never could forgive him for what he did. But I have accepted that he is—was—the man who fathered me."

"Marcus. You seem…"

"What?" He was looking at her now, his face set in a furious scowl. "I seem what?"

She braved his scowl to answer truthfully. "You seem far from peaceful when you speak of him."

He let out a slow breath. "All right. You have a point, I suppose. No, then. I have never managed to reconcile with him. And I don't imagine I ever could have."

Gently, she asked, "Will you tell me his name?"

"Roland Scala."

"Scala? Is that a Greek name?"

"He became an American citizen more than a decade ago. But he was born here, born Montedoran."

"And your mother…?"

"Her name was Isa Rhodes. She died the night I was born."

"Oh, Marcus. I'm so, so sorry…."

He gave a shrug. And then, bleakly, he asked, "Are you sure that you want to hear this? It's not a happy story."

She met his gaze steadily. "I do want to hear it, Marcus. Very much."

"Fair enough." He drew in a breath—and then let it out hard. "I don't know where to start."

"Anywhere. It doesn't matter where you start. It only matters that you tell me what happened, how it was...."

He gazed at her for several seconds, unspeaking. And then finally, he blurted, "My mother was a roulette dealer at the casino."

"At Casino d'Ambre?" She named the world-famous casino not far from her villa.

"That's right." He turned his eyes away and stared straight ahead. And then he seemed to gather himself. He started rattling off the story swiftly, as though he couldn't get it out and over with fast enough. "She was half French, half Montedoran. Roland met her there, at the casino. They were lovers. He said that by the time she knew she was pregnant, it was over between them. They didn't marry. He said they were always fighting and they both agreed that they would never make it as a couple. She left Montedoro and went across the border into France when she was six months along."

"To her family?"

"She had no family. Neither did he. They were both only children. With older parents. By the time they met, they were both on their own...." He was quiet. She wanted to prompt him to go on. But she didn't. She waited. And finally he continued, "Two months later, she gave birth to me in a small country hospital. As soon as I was born, that same night, she took me and left the hospital. She went back to the cottage where she'd been living and called Roland. She told him he had a son, and that she'd taken me home with her. He thought she sounded strange, confused. Delirious. So he went to her. She had hemorrhaged, he told me. He claimed she was already dead when he got there. He was afraid to call the authorities. And afraid to just leave me there, for fear no one would find me soon enough and I would die, too. So he took me back to Montedoro...." He seemed to run out of steam.

She finished for him, softly. Regretfully. "And he abandoned you on the steps of Our Lady of Sorrows."

He squeezed her hand harder. "That's right. He abandoned me. And then he went to America right after that. He had some money put by, he said. He gave up gambling. Opened a restaurant. Did well for himself. Applied for citizenship—and got it after he'd been in Southern California for fifteen years."

She pressed her lips to the hard curve of his shoulder, longing to give him comfort, knowing that nothing could ease him right then. "He told you all of this when you finally contacted him six years ago?"

"Yes. I returned to Los Angeles then, and met with him."

"And you believed him, believed his story?"

"Not a word of it. But he showed me the certificate of my birth, which he'd found on the kitchen table in the cottage where my mother bled to death after having me. The birth date was right. She had named Roland as the father. And so I...looked into it. I hired someone to investigate for me. The investigator found out that a woman named Isa Rhodes had died in the place and in the way that Roland said. Though the baby was never found, the district coroner had determined that she'd very recently borne a child and then the local police discovered that she'd given birth in the same hospital named on the certificate my father had taken from the cottage."

"Oh, Marcus." She leaned her head on his shoulder, rubbed her hand up and down his arm. "I don't know what to say. I'm so sorry...for all of it. For your mother and you. And even for your father."

He spoke low and intensely. "Don't feel sorry for him."

"But he—"

"Just don't. He left her there, with no one. All alone, even if it was too late for her. And then he took me...and left me, too."

She wanted to remind him that it was best not to judge. But what did she know about how it must be for him? She'd led a graceful, happy, sheltered life for the most part, with two loving parents who doted on her, with the world at her feet and brothers and sisters she adored. That day she'd told him she was having his baby, he'd called her proud and thoughtless. He'd said she took her happy childhood and her family for granted.

She'd been shocked at the time that he would say such cruel things to her.

But now she saw the truth in his words.

Now she knew that *she* was the one who had no right to judge.

She asked, softly, "He died just today, you said?"

Marcus nodded. "Or late last night. A lawyer contacted me through the CCU several hours ago. He said that Roland had sold his restaurant and retired. That he has a woman, a longtime housekeeper, who comes in to clean and cook for him every day. When the housekeeper went to make up his room, he was just lying there in bed, already gone. The doctor she called said it was some kind of aneurysm or a heart attack. They'll know more later. And I...I am his heir. The lawyer said I should come."

"Of course you must go."

"I don't want to go." He sounded slightly numb. But angry, too. A slow, seething, deep-seated kind of anger. "Why should I go? That man is nothing to me."

"Marcus." He looked at her then. His eyes were flat, the color leached from them. She said, "We'll go together, you and me."

He pulled his hand from hers. "I told you, I don't want to go. And there is no way I could ask you to go. That wouldn't be right."

"Of course it's right. And you're not asking me. *I'm* asking *you*. Please. Take me with you. Let's do this together. Let me be with you for this."

He put his head in his hands. "I don't want to do this."

"Marcus, you have to. You know that you do."

"No. I don't know that. I don't know that at all." He raised his head and looked at her wildly. "I don't want any of this. I haven't spoken with that man in over five years. I thought I had…accepted the reality that he was my biological father. But I certainly didn't want him in my life. I *am* the man I was raised to be. I am Marcus Desmarais. I own that name and I earned it. I never planned to tell a soul about him. Until you. Until now, in this past week…" He fell silent. His eyes were haunted now, guarded. And furious, too. But he did lift a hand. He cradled the side of her face. She melted inside at the tender touch. "Because you demanded that I tell you my secrets…."

She held his gaze. "I'm so glad that you've told me. I only wish you had told me sooner."

"I didn't want to tell you at all." The words were rough, very low.

She gazed steadily at him and didn't even try to hide her reproach. "Always guarding your secrets, so self-contained…"

He surprised her by answering with urgency. "But I swear to you, Rhia. I knew I needed to tell you. I *was* working up to it."

In spite of her frustration with him, she found she believed him—and she said so. "I believe you. And it does help me, Marcus, when you tell me the hardest things, the things you wish you could keep secret even from yourself."

He made a scoffing sound and dropped his caressing hand. "Helps you? How could knowing all this...this ugliness possibly help you?"

"It helps me to *know* you, to understand you better."

He grunted. "Why would you ever want to understand a nasty mess like this one?"

"Because that's what you do, when you care for someone. That's what you do for the ones of your family. You listen when they are able to tell you the truth about themselves, no matter how hard that truth might be. And then you do what you can to help them get through whatever difficult time might follow."

Chapter Twelve

The next morning, early, Marcus went with Rhia to the Prince's Palace to speak with HSH Adrienne.

He told the whole awful story all over again—to his sovereign this time. As always, the princess was serene and understanding and ready to smooth the way. He was given open-ended family leave from his duties at the CCU.

Back at the villa, Rhia called her director at the National Museum and explained that she would be out of the country for a while on urgent family business. Marcus called Roland's lawyer again and said they were coming. And then they packed their suitcases and flew to Los Angeles.

They arrived at LAX after midnight. A car was waiting to take them to the Beverly Wilshire, where a suite had been reserved for them. After they had checked in, Marcus stood on the balcony and stared out over the lights of Beverly Hills and Century City and wondered why he had come. He thought of Lieutenant Joseph Chastain, who had a small room adjacent to their suite and had been assigned to provide security during this trip. Marcus almost envied Joseph.

Joseph was a good man. And he knew exactly what he was here for. He would protect Her Serene Highness with his life. So very simple. So very clear.

Marcus would do the same for Rhia. But as her lover, the father of her child and possibly her future husband—if she ever said yes to him—he would never again be assigned to protect her. A bodyguard needed a cool head, after all, and that all-important emotional distance from the one he was charged with protecting.

Marcus had no emotional distance when it came to Rhiannon. He never had. But in the past, no one else had known—well, except for Hector and Her Highness Alice.

Now, everyone knew. Even the tabloids.

He heard light footsteps as she came out onto the balcony and stood at his side.

"Such a beautiful night." She took his arm and together they admired the view. He enjoyed the feel of her body so close, the touch of her fingers against his skin. He was treated to a faint, tempting hint of her perfume. But soon enough, she was pulling him back inside. "Let's go to bed. We have to be up early tomorrow." The lawyer had agreed to meet with them first thing in the morning, even though it was Saturday.

He stopped just inside the balcony doors and turned her to face him. "It's past 2:00 a.m., already tomorrow."

She gazed up at him, dark hair shining in the lamplight, brown eyes infinitely soft. "We can get a few hours of sleep, at least."

He knew she was right. She needed her rest. But he needed...her. He gathered her close and kissed her.

She opened for him, sighing. And then she tried to pull away.

He didn't allow that, but instead deepened the kiss, holding her even closer, wrapping his arms so tightly around her, using the taste and the feel of her, the wonderful scent that belonged only to her, to help him forget all the things he would have to remember when daylight came.

Eventually, he did lift his head. She stared up at him dreamily and whispered in a tender tone, "Marcus. Bedtime…" Taking his hand, she turned for the bedroom.

He didn't argue with her. She was leading him exactly where he wanted to go. Once they reached the side of the bed, he took off all her clothes and his own, as well, kissing her as he did it, caressing her tenderly, with practiced care.

By the time he was finished undressing them both, she wasn't thinking about sleeping, either. He took her down to the pillows and he kissed her some more. He touched her, the way he liked best to touch her.

Slowly. Everywhere.

Until she was pliant and eager, flushed and so willing— willing in every way except one.

She still wouldn't marry him.

But he would not despair. No matter how many times she told him no, he would never give up. His child would have a father who never, ever gave him up.

And she? No, he couldn't give her all the things she so richly deserved. But he would always protect her, always take care of her. He would be there, at her side, anytime she needed him. He would never arrive too late, never *not* be there when she needed him the most….

Turning her so she lay on her side, facing him, he traced a hand over the marvelous curve of her hip, sliding his palm along the taut smoothness of her thigh, lifting her knee and wrapping her leg over his.

She was so wet, so soft and sweet and ready, and she moaned when he pushed into her, moaned and canted her body up to him, taking him in all the way with that first stroke—at which point he couldn't hold back a moan of his own.

The sweetness, as always with her, was close to unbearable, the way any extreme pleasure tends to be. He had to go carefully, slowly, deliberately, had to try and be mindful of making it last, while his body constantly threatened to throw off all restraint and make that mad dash for the quick, hard finish.

He didn't want that.

He wanted more of her sighs and her soft, tender cries.

And he had them. They rocked together, arms wrapped around each other, for a fine, endless time.

He watched the finish come over her, saw the deep flush that flowed up her throat and over her cheeks, the glazed sheen in her almost-black eyes. Her breathing quickened, became a little bit frantic, and her hips jerked against him, harder, faster, with a sudden furious, hungry intent.

By then, he was gone, too, lost in the fine, swift rhythm she set. She cried out and pressed strongly against him. He held on tight as the rush of his climax shuddered through him.

It was perfect. Satisfying. Exactly what he needed.

But then, it always had been with her.

She took him to paradise so easily, brought him the best kind of forgetfulness. At least for a little while.

The lawyer's name was Anthony Evans. They met him in front of a Century City highrise. He was tall, tanned and fit, with silver hair. He grabbed Marcus's hand and pressed a business card into it. Then he turned a gleaming white smile on Rhia. "Hello."

She murmured her first name and took the hand he offered. He glanced past her shoulder at Joseph. She gave a
light laugh. "That's Joseph. He provides security." At the
mention of his name, the bodyguard gave a slight nod.
Rhia added, "I promise you, Anthony, Joseph won't be
in the way."

Anthony's office was on the top floor of the high-rise.
They sat in fat leather chairs in a large conference room—
except for Joseph, who stood near the door. Anthony explained that he and Roland often played golf together, that
he'd met Roland more than two decades ago at City Bistro,
the restaurant Marcus's father had owned.

"Your father had a very special kind of genius," Anthony said. "He made every customer feel special. Valued.
And he had a hell of a memory. The second time I ate at
the Bistro, he knew the table I preferred and that I wanted
Glenfiddich neat the minute my butt hit the chair."

Marcus had no idea what to say in response to that, so
he didn't say anything.

Rhia, sitting beside him, slipped her hand into his,
twined their fingers companionably together and made
the right noises. "This is all such a shock to everyone."

"Ahem, yes, well," said Anthony. "Difficult. Very difficult. My condolences. Roland will be missed." He put on a
pair of reading glasses and gestured at the folder with the
ring of keys on top of it that waited on the table in front
of Marcus. "Your copy of your father's will. It's all quite
self-evident. Except for a small bequest to the housekeeper,
everything goes to you. The house, the cars, the cabin in
the Sierras—and the money, of course. Your father was a
canny investor."

The house, the cars, the money. Marcus heard the words
and realized he could very well be a wealthy man now.

He really wished it mattered more.

Anthony was still talking. "It's all in there." He gestured at the folder again. "Roland asked that there be no funeral service and that he be cremated, that the ashes be entrusted to you and that you scatter them off the coast of Montedoro, in the Mediterranean Sea."

Ashes. He was expected to scatter Roland's ashes?

Rhia squeezed his hand. He saw that Anthony was looking expectantly at him.

So he nodded again. "All right. Yes. Of course."

"The autopsy will be performed by the first of the week, though it's merely a formality, due to the unexpected nature of the death. Once that's done, the remains will be transported to the Neptune Society. You can give them a call and they will tell you when you can come for the ashes."

"All right."

"And you've been to the house, I'm sure…"

He started to nod automatically, but then the words actually registered. "No. I haven't."

If that surprised Anthony, he didn't show it. "Ah. Well, it's no problem. There's a list in the inside pocket of the folder. Addresses, phone numbers, bank accounts, alarm codes. Everything you need to know. Your father seems to have assumed you will be selling the various properties." *Your father.* Marcus longed to tell the lawyer not to call Roland that. But what would that prove, ultimately? Nothing. Anthony asked, "Is that the plan?"

"Yes, I think so."

"Excellent. Because it's all set up that way. Roland's real estate broker will be contacted Monday to arrange to put the house and the Sierra cabin on the market. But still, it's all up to you now. Your father made it very clear that if you want the house, or anything else, you only have to say so and we'll make the necessary arrangements and adjustments."

"Thank you."

"And you have the keys."

Marcus glanced blankly at the folder again, and the keys that waited on top of it. "Yes. I see."

"Anything else, any questions, you have my number. Do not hesitate to call."

A few minutes later, they stood on the sidewalk on sunlit Century Boulevard. Rhia's driver pulled the limousine up to the curb at the sight of them. Joseph opened the door.

"Back to the hotel?" she asked him once they were safely inside behind the tinted windows.

"Yes, all right."

She took his hand again, scooted over next to him and put her head on his shoulder. He took comfort from the feel of her so close and thought about what a fine, good woman she was. Thought about all she deserved and all she meant to him.

And how he devoutly wished he might be…more, in so many ways.

At least he would have his own money now. If she ever said yes, he wouldn't have to live the rest of his life with her paying for everything. Too bad it was money that came from the man who'd abandoned both him and his mother. There was certainly some very rich irony in that.

His pride and his anger kept jabbing him to refuse it all. To call Anthony Evans and tell him he'd changed his mind, he wanted every penny of Roland's fortune turned over to St. Stephen's Orphanage in Montedoro.

But then he thought of the child. In the end, Roland's money would benefit the child, as well as allow him, Marcus, to contribute in a meaningful way to the financial support of his family.

That meant he couldn't indulge his anger and simply give it all away.

Once in the suite again, he sat down at the desk in the sitting room and read the will through. It was all true, what Anthony had said. There *was* a lot of money. There were a lot of *things*.

It would be enough that he could make a generous bequest to St. Stephen's *and* have plenty left for the baby's future, for Rhia.

And as Anthony had promised, Roland had it all worked out. Marcus didn't really have to do anything. If he took no action, everything would be sold and the money, in time, would be his, the funds transferred to the Bank of Montedoro into an account that had already been set up in his name.

Roland's only request was that Marcus would dispose of the damn ashes off the coast of Montedoro.

In the other room, he heard Rhia talking on the phone. He closed the folder and pushed back his chair, rising to his feet as she appeared from the bedroom.

She came to him, put her hands on his shoulders. "Well?"

He shrugged. "I am quite well-to-do now, as it turns out."

She smiled, but her eyes were sad for him. "I wish that I might have met him." He didn't know what to say to that, so he said nothing. And she soothed, gently, "Never mind." With a shake of her dark head, she brushed a kiss against his lips. "Do you want to visit your father's house?"

"I don't know. Maybe tomorrow. Or the next day." *Or maybe never.* "Who was that on the phone?"

"I talked to Allie. She sends her best. And then to my

mother. She wishes you well and wants you to know she keeps you close in her thoughts. And did I tell you I have Bravo relatives here in Los Angeles?"

"I remember. Jonas and Emma Bravo."

"They were wonderful to me when I was at UCLA. They invited me over for dinner often. I asked you to come with me once, if you'll recall. But you refused. Because we were a secret."

Her hair was down, the way he liked it best. He eased his fingers under the silky mass and clasped the nape of her neck, loving the feel of her skin, and the way the warm strands brushed the back of his hand.

He reminded her, "Keeping what we shared a secret was the only way for me then."

She pressed her lips together and hitched up her chin in that proud way of hers. "I hated it, that secret. The lies. Pretending for all those years that I hardly knew you. Everyone in the family knew that there was…someone. Someone I couldn't get over. Someone who had broken my heart."

He pulled her close, pressed his lips to her forehead. "I'm sorry, Rhia. You can't know how very sorry." He breathed the apology against her skin—and knew that it wasn't enough, that it couldn't make up for all he had put her through.

She tipped her head back to look at him again. Her eyes flashed dark fire. "I'm still angry about that, about the way you demanded that no one could ever know."

"It was a long time ago. Can't we let it go?"

Apparently not. She pinched up her mouth at him. "You mean the way *you* let things go? By refusing to speak of them. By…denying their existence? By walking away and not looking back?" She brought her hands up between them and pushed at his chest.

He released her. "My faults and sins are endless, I know it."

"Please don't become noble on me. I can't bear it right now."

How had they gotten here? A few minutes ago, she'd been all smiles, asking him so thoughtfully if he might want to visit Roland's house. He frowned down at her. "Is this a big fight we're working up to here?"

She remained defiant. "Maybe a big fight would clear the air."

He shut his eyes for a moment, drew in a slow breath. "Please, Rhia. I don't want to fight with you. I only want a chance to care for you, to help raise the child we made. I only want to be your husband."

Her mouth trembled then. She looked away. When she met his eyes again, he saw that her fury and defiance had fled. "You're doing the best you can, I know that. And it's been an awful day for you. I suppose the last thing you need is a hard time from me. That would be...unfair, I do realize. After all, I told you I was coming here to help."

He touched her hair again. She didn't pull away. He said gruffly, "I'm glad you're here."

Her brows drew together. "It's strange. More difficult than I imagined. Being here in Los Angeles again, where we met. Where we...loved so long ago."

"Too difficult?" Was she saying she didn't want to stay?

"I didn't say that."

"But you—"

She stopped him with a finger to his lips. "It may not have seemed like it a moment ago, but I do want to be here. I want it very much."

He wondered if he would ever understand the way a woman's mind worked. "You're certain?"

"Yes. And I spoke with Emma Bravo after I talked to

Mother and Allie. Emma has invited us to her house for dinner tonight."

Just what he needed. To spend the evening making idle chitchat with her Los Angeles relatives. "I don't feel like going out."

"We're going. Live with it."

He was grateful that she'd put aside her anger over the past. And that she really did seem to want to be here with him, to see him through the grim task of dealing with Roland's sudden death. Plus, he knew she was right about the dinner with her Bravo relatives. Sometimes a man just had to get out and deal with other people, no matter how disconnected from his real life he might feel. "Fair enough. Dinner with the Bravos. I cannot wait."

"That's what I needed to hear." She said it cheerfully and he realized he felt better about everything. "But we have hours until then. I think we should try and forget all our problems, all the sadness over Roland, the stress and the worries. What do you say? The pool? The beach?"

He traced the V-neck of the light blouse she wore, and remembered that she used to have a blouse something like it eight years ago. He had a quick, vivid image of her pulling that other blouse over her head, and her long hair crackling with static, lifting and then falling to curl on her shoulders as she tossed the blouse onto the rickety chair in the corner of the bedroom in the motel where they used to go. "Do you ever think of La Casa de la Luna?"

She scanned his face, her eyes seeming brighter suddenly, a glowing smile lighting her up from within. "I do. I have. Often—and let's do that, then. Let's go see how much has changed at the House of the Moon."

"I wasn't really thinking we should go there."

"But why not?"

"You said yourself that it's hard enough being here in Los Angeles, where it all started for us."

"No. Seriously, Marcus. I think we should go. I want to see if it's still the same...."

He realized that she was determined. And he *had* brought it up. Maybe it wouldn't be so bad. "A lot can happen in eight years. We should check first to make sure it hasn't been torn down."

She whipped out her smart phone and punched up the name. And then she grinned and turned the phone so he could see the display. "Still there. Let's go."

"It looks smaller, don't you think?" she asked when they stood on the sidewalk at the front of the Spanish-style motor hotel, with the limo waiting behind them and Joseph standing there at attention by the backseat door.

"Looks about the same to me." Aside from the fact that the stucco walls had more cracks than he remembered and the landscaping seemed a bit more overgrown.

She leaned her shoulder against his. "Let's try and get our room."

He wrapped an arm around her and whispered into her hair, "It won't be the same."

"Oh, Marcus. I know. I don't care. It's not supposed to be the same. Please."

So he signaled to Joseph, who led the way up the chipped tile steps. The bodyguard entered the lobby first to have a quick look around. A moment later, he opened the door for them and they joined him inside, where a rangy white cat lay in a pool of sunshine on the red tile floor and a different clerk stood behind the front desk, an old man with a white scruff of beard and a sour expression on his lined face.

"How can I help you?" The old fellow craned to the side

and peered around them at Joseph, who stood patiently over near the door, in front of a display rack full of brochures of things to do in Los Angeles.

"Is room one-twelve available?" Rhia asked.

The old man frowned. "Might be. But I'm not putting more than two in that room."

Rhia slid Marcus a glance. They both tried not to laugh. And she said, "Oh, that's not a problem." She tipped her head in the bodyguard's direction. "Joseph provides security. He will have to go in the room and give it a quick once-over, but then he will wait outside for us until we're ready to leave."

"Security?" The ancient fellow made a scoffing sound. "Come on, lady. You think you really need security?"

"Apparently, I do." She smiled at him sweetly. "May we have the room?" With a flourish, she indicated Marcus and then herself. "Just the two of us, I promise you."

The old man grumbled, but he let them have the room. Marcus paid for it with cash. They went out and along the central walkway to the room, where Joseph entered first.

They waited down the steps from the door. The birds of paradise were still there, to either side of the steps. They'd grown quite large and the birdlike flowers on their long stems sprouted wildly, hanging over the concrete walk, begging for a good pruning. Back at the entrance, the old man stuck his head out the lobby door, probably to make sure that no threesomes were being committed on his watch.

Finally Joseph emerged. "Safe and clear."

He came out and they went in.

Rhia headed straight for the cheap, scratched-up desk in the corner. "Same desk, remember?"

He did remember. In his mind's eye, he could still see her, sitting in the hard-seated chair, wearing cutoff jeans and a snug little shirt, one foot tucked under her, an art history book open on the table in front of her.

She wandered into the bedroom alcove, where the deep purple-red bougainvillea blazed on the far wall outside the window, just as it had eight years before. The worn-out box springs made squeaky sounds as she sat on the end of the bed. "I was imagining we might make wild, crazy love here, for old times' sake...."

He went and sat beside her. She'd pinned up her hair before they left the hotel, but a dark curl had already escaped and trailed along the side of her neck. He coiled it around his index finger. "Wild and crazy love sounds good to me. But why do I get the feeling you're not really in the mood?"

She sighed then. "It all looks a little...forlorn, somehow."

"It's just more proof that we can never go back."

Her slim shoulders slumped. "Ugh. More sadness. This was not my plan."

The curl of hair kept a corkscrew shape when he pulled his finger free. He wrapped an arm around her. "It's all right." She looked up at him and he kissed the tip of her aristocratic nose. "I *have* always wondered what became of the place."

She was studying him again. "Yes, well. There is that."

"Now we know." He wanted to kiss her, to say, *Marry me.* He'd bought a ring on Tuesday, before leaving for Italy with Prince Damien, and he was carrying it with him everywhere, waiting for the right moment.

Unfortunately, he had to admit that now probably wasn't it.

And then she asked, "Did you ever plan to marry and have a family, Marcus—I mean, marry someone else, before Montana and the baby?"

He didn't want to tell her. So he hedged. "Does it matter?"

She stood up and went to the window. For a moment, she stared out at the bougainvillea across the way. When she turned to face him, her eyes were stormy again, the way they'd been back at the hotel. "It matters. Yes."

Why? She didn't need to hear about the life he wasn't going to have now. "I don't agree. What matters is you and me. The baby…"

She made a circuit of the room, ending back at the window again. For a moment, she stared out. Then she faced him. "I keep waiting for you to see, to understand that I need to know…all about you. You keep telling me how you're going to be more open with me. And then, well, every time I ask you something about your life, about the past, about your dreams for yourself, you brush me off like I'm lint on your sleeve."

That was unfair. He stood. "That's not so."

"Yes. Yes, it *is* so." She wrapped her arms around herself in a protective sort of way. "I want…more than just a husband, Marcus. I want *you*. I want you in the deepest, truest way. I wish you could see that."

"I don't want to hurt you."

She blew out an impatient breath. "I can take a little hurting now and then. A little pain is worth it. Sometimes it's more important to know the truth than to be protected from the things that I might not especially enjoy hearing."

"But it doesn't even matter."

"How many times do I have to say it? Yes. It does matter. It matters to *me*."

By then, Marcus ardently wished he had just answered her question in the first place. He'd made way too much of it and now she was watching him with real anxiety, expecting some horrible revelation that would change everything.

So he went ahead and admitted, "I did plan to marry, yes. Eventually."

She gasped. "Oh, no." Her voice was much too soft, her eyes wide now, and worried. "I can't believe I was so selfish. I can't believe that I never even bothered to ask."

"Ask what?" He felt like a blind man plunked down in an unknown room, groping madly to gain some familiarity with the alien space.

"That night, I... Oh, Marcus, it was just all about *me*, you know? All about what *I* needed to get through what was happening. It never even occurred to me that you might have... Oh, God. I just feel terrible about this."

He dared to reveal his complete ignorance. "Do you know that I haven't a clue what you're talking about?"

She came and dropped down beside him again. "That night in Montana..."

"Er, what about it?"

"Marcus, was there someone you were seeing then, someone you had to end it with because of what happened with us?"

Chapter Thirteen

It was something of a relief to hear the question at last, because the answer was easy. "No, of course not. I wasn't seeing anyone."

She put a hand to her chest and blew out a breath. "Oh, thank God."

"Why would you imagine such a thing? Yes, it's true that I haven't been as forthcoming as I should have been..."

She actually rolled her eyes. "Understatement of the decade. I mean, given that we're here in America right now to settle the estate of the father you never mentioned that you had."

"But you must see. Roland is one thing."

"Roland is a very *big* thing."

"Rhia. If there was another woman, you can be sure I would have told you. I would have told you that night, under the blankets in the backseat of that SUV before things went too far. I would have told you and that would have stopped it. Not only because I would not betray some-one who trusted me, but also because you would never have made love with me if you thought I had someone else."

"You make me sound like a model of integrity when I just admitted that I wasn't thinking about anyone but myself."

He hooked an arm across her shoulders. "You couldn't do that to another woman. It's just not in you."

Reaching up, she brushed soft fingers against his cheek. "But you did plan to get married?"

Better, he saw now, just to tell her straight out. "Yes. I thought I would find a kind, even-tempered woman of my own class, someone who would look up to me, a woman who would be thoroughly impressed with my success and proud of my accomplishments, someone who wanted to raise a family."

Her mouth trembled a little. She asked, "So you thought you would marry some stranger just because she would look up to you?"

"Well, my hope was that she wouldn't be a stranger by the time that I asked her to be my wife."

She chuckled then. "Oh, Marcus." He pulled her closer and she settled companionably into the crook of his arm. "I always hoped you would be happy, I truly did. I just never wanted to imagine the particulars."

"Yet you asked…"

"Because I really did want to know."

Actually, he understood her conflicting emotions on this subject. It had been the same for him. "Both of those times you were engaged?"

She put a hand over her eyes. "Do you *have* to remind me?"

"I told myself how I *should* be happy for you—and then I went and took on all comers in the training yard."

She blinked. "Fighting, you mean?"

"A soldier has to keep in shape. And proficiency at hand-to-hand combat is part of the necessary skill set. Plus, well, hand-to-hand in the ring is the one place where rank doesn't matter. We're all equal there. As we are a small force, we have to practice on each other. Challenges are open to everyone in the guard and the CCU, so I had a good number of opponents to spar with and no end of opportunities to pound some heads."

"You're telling me that when I became engaged, you beat up your comrades in arms."

"All in the interest of peak fitness and battle-readiness, of course."

"Oh, yes. Of course." She slanted him a knowing look. "Did you take on those two we met on the Promenade last week, Denis and Rene?"

He hesitated to answer. He'd never carried tales. He'd taken his knocks and kept his mouth shut. But now, after finally telling her about Roland, after making himself admit that he had always planned to marry someone else, he was beginning to see why she asked for his secrets.

It was a way to bind them, each to the other. She should be the one in the world he could trust with the things he would never tell anyone else.

So he confessed, "As a matter of fact, Denis and Rene were first in line."

"Did you win your bouts with them?"

"I did, yes. I wish I could say I found those victories satisfying. But thrashing an old nemesis or two didn't change anything that mattered. You were still about to become another man's wife."

She made a small, throaty sound. "And then I didn't marry either of my fiancés, after all. I couldn't bring myself to do it. Both times I ended up having to admit that it wasn't going to work."

"And I was glad," he said low and rough.

She turned those shining eyes to him then. "I'll bet you hated yourself for that."

"I did. It was wrong. I had given you up twice. I had no right to be glad when you didn't find the happiness I kept telling myself I wanted for you. And I did want it. I *wanted* you to be happy—I just didn't want to think of you with anyone else."

Tenderly, she said, "We are ludicrous." They were the exact words she'd used the day she told him about the baby. Only now, somehow, the meaning was altogether different. Fond. And also gentle. Like the touch of Sister Lucilla's hand at St. Stephen's, when he was small. The sister would clasp his shoulder and smile benignly down at him and he would feel…blessed somehow. Reassured that in the end, though his birth parents had abandoned him and his adoptive parents had sent him back, though he had nobody to call his own, everything would come out right in the end.

Rhia suggested softly, "You know I want to know more about those two men you grew up with, about St. Stephen's, about your childhood there…."

He reconciled himself to giving her what she needed from him: another large dose of sharing. "It wasn't a bad childhood, really. In spite of what you hear about nuns at Catholic orphanages, the nuns who raised me were mostly kind. Then again, I was one of the good boys. I had no one and the only way I could see to make anyone care for me or pay attention to me was to be very, very good. The nuns approved of me."

"And Denis and Rene?"

"They got attention by making trouble and they were always suffering the consequences, forever being punished for some transgression or other. And they hated me. They were constantly engineering opportunities to make me pay for being a kiss-up."

"What ways?"

"Just the usual things that bad boys do to good ones."

"Such as?"

"Once they nearly drowned me in a toilet. They also lured me into the catacomb of cellars beneath St. Stephen's and then locked me down there in the dark. They stole my schoolbooks and my finished assignments and then destroyed them. And they beat me up every chance they got."

She made a low, outraged sound, as women tend to do when hearing stories of boys' inhumanity to boys. "That's terrible. You didn't fight back?"

"At first, yes. But I quickly learned that fighting back was an exercise in futility. They only beat me harder. So I would run away as fast as I could whenever I saw them coming. If I wasn't fast enough to escape, I would curl into a ball and bear whatever punishments they meted out. It went on like that for several years until I was strong enough to win my fights with them."

"Did you tell the nuns what they were doing to you?"

He gave her a patient look. "No."

"Well, you should have."

"Rhia, I survived. And I grew stronger. I started working out, studying up on martial arts and boxing. I was fifteen when I first took them both on and won. After that, they mostly left me alone."

"But they resent you to this day."

"How would I know? It's nothing I would ever discuss with them. And I have no way of knowing what goes on in their heads."

"Oh, of course you do. We all have instincts about such things."

"Yes, but now that I'm a grown man and not the least afraid of either of them anymore, I'm not especially interested in knowing what Denis and Rene are thinking."

She gave that some thought. And then she slid out from under his arm and stood.

He caught her hand before she could completely escape him. "Stay here."

She stepped up nice and close and he spread his thighs a little so she could ease in between them. Bracing her hands on his shoulders, tipping her head to the side, she studied him the way she often did. "I think that you are tired of sharing."

"You could say that, yes."

She leaned down to him. He breathed in the scent of her and thought about how fine she looked naked, how swiftly he'd become accustomed to being naked with her on a regular basis.

How he really would like to be naked with her right now.

But the room had a faint smell of mildew and the bedsprings creaked. He couldn't help wondering how clean the bedding was. They had some fine memories in Room 112. Making a new one right now?

He didn't think so.

She kissed the space between his eyebrows. "I'm ready to go if you are."

They continued their trip down memory lane. Visiting the places where they had been together before seemed to please her and he wanted very much to please her.

It also helped to keep his mind off the father who had deserted his mother and him.

The father he would never see again.

Not that he *wanted* to see Roland again. He didn't. Of course not.

They went to the bookstore at UCLA, the one where they'd met. And then for lunch, they tried the hamburger stand where they used to eat all the time way back when. They had cheeseburgers and fries and vanilla milkshakes and agreed that the greasy, heavy food was every bit as good as it had been eight years ago.

"When it comes to cheeseburgers," Rhia said, "you *can* relive the past."

They returned to the hotel for their swimsuits and went to Seal Beach, where they spent the afternoon slathered in sunscreen, basking on beach towels and wading in the surf, with the silent Joseph keeping watch.

That evening, they visited the Bravos at their estate, Angel's Crest, in Bel Air. Emma and Jonas had four children—two boys and two girls. They were also raising Jonas's adopted sister, Amanda, who was sixteen, something of a musical prodigy and stunningly beautiful, with enormous dark eyes and curly black hair.

Emma was a blonde charmer from a small town in Texas and Jonas doted on her. Their sons were three and seven and their daughters ten and five and Emma clearly believed that children should be both seen *and* heard. The children came to the table for dinner and laughter and happy chatter filled the elegant formal dining room.

The three-year-old, Grady, was an especially enthusiastic talker. He sat right up at the table in a booster chair. Marcus ended up seated on his right. Grady told him all about his plastic dinosaur collection and explained in great and nearly incomprehensible detail what levels he had reached playing Angry Birds.

Later that night, when they were alone together in the

hotel suite, Marcus told Rhia, "I liked them—Jonas and his wife, the children, Amanda, *all* of them."

They'd kicked off their shoes and stood barefoot on the balcony, admiring the lights of the city that spread out like a blanket of stars all the way to the Santa Monica Mountains. "I think you had a good time tonight," she said. "Though you didn't expect to."

"I assumed it would be four adults at a candlelit table making polite conversation. I had no idea there would be all those children, everyone talking over everyone else. It was all so energetic. And there was so much laughter, wasn't there?"

"Yes, there was."

"Was it like that when you were small?" Somehow, he'd never pictured the princely family being rambunctious at dinner.

"Often it was, yes. We would argue sometimes, and we would all grow excited. Except for Max. Maybe it was because he was the oldest. He always stayed in control and would try to calm us down. Damien was the biggest troublemaker. Once he grabbed the bread basket and began firing dinner rolls at Alexander, who then jumped up, ran around the table and punched Damien in the nose."

"Was there blood?"

"A river of it. Genevra, always so tenderhearted, became very upset and started crying." Genevra was eighth-born of the nine Bravo-Calabretti siblings.

Marcus laughed. "You will destroy all my illusions of the way young royals behave."

"I told you all this, didn't I, years ago?"

He took her by the shoulders, pulled her in front of him and wrapped his arms around her waist. "No."

She leaned back into him, resting her hands on his forearms. "We didn't talk enough, then—although, when I think back, I remember that I did feel close to you, closer than I ever have to anyone else, really."

"We were so young."

"And you were so incommunicative."

"Rhia, it was only eight weeks. And we spent a lot of the time we had together in that creaky bed at La Casa de la Luna."

"We always did communicate well with our clothes off, didn't we?"

He pressed his lips to her hair. "Yes, we did."

She stared dreamily out toward the mountains. "It was all just so heart-stoppingly romantic, that time. And I did talk about my family then, didn't I?"

"A bit. I seem to recall your telling me about the plays that you and your sisters and Princess Liliana used to put on."

"Yes. The plays were glorious—or at least, we thought so. Belle wrote most of them. They were full of princesses and knights and fire-breathing dragons. We made our own costumes. Our brothers and our parents and any available servants were called upon to be the audience. It was great fun. Oh, and we all enjoyed board games, too. We were quite competitive, especially the boys and Allie. In a horse race or a game of Risk, you will never beat Allie."

He bent to kiss the side of her neck and flattened a palm against her belly. Was it a fraction rounder than before?

She put her hand over his. "I watched you with Grady. You were wonderful."

"I was trying to keep up with what he was telling me and not exactly succeeding."

"I think you did very well."

He remembered that he was supposed to tell her the things that were hard to admit. "In the past couple of weeks, since you told me about the baby, I find I think about being a father. I think about it a lot."

She turned in his arms and gazed up at him steadily. "You're worried about this, about being a good father?"

He shrugged. "Maybe a little."

"Because you were raised without one?"

He nodded. "And don't start feeling sorry for me."

"I don't." A smile flirted with the corners of her mouth. "But I do feel some sympathy for the lonely and oh-so-well-behaved little boy you once were...."

"Rein it in."

"You will be a fine father. Because you *want* to be a good father. And that means you will work very hard to be one."

"I hope you're right."

"I know I am." She spoke with absolute assurance.

And then she lifted up on tiptoe and kissed him.

When she sank back to her heels once more, he said roughly, "Do that again."

She did. By then, he was hungry for the kind of communicating they'd always done so effortlessly. He picked her up by the waist. She wrapped those fine legs around him and he turned and carried her back inside.

The next day was Sunday. They called room service for breakfast.

As she poured him a second cup of coffee, he said, "I think I want to go to Roland's house today."

She didn't seem surprised. "Yes. Let's do that."

So her driver took them to Beverly Hills. The house was behind a tall stone fence covered in ivy, with an electronic gate. Marcus read the gate code to the driver and he leaned out the window and punched up the numbers on the keypad built into the wall. The gate slid open and they rode up a curving cobbled driveway with thick lawns and beautifully tended semitropical landscaping to either side.

"So green," Rhia said. "Beautiful and private."

The house was a one-story midcentury modern. The front door locked with another keypad. Marcus entered the numbers from the list of codes Anthony had provided. Joseph went in and Marcus read off the alarm code for him.

Once Joseph had vouched for their safety within, they entered. The slate-floored foyer opened onto a living room with a wall of windows looking out on the backyard. It was all very clean and attractive and well-maintained.

Rhia took his arm. He led her forward, into the bright central room, to the dining area and the modern kitchen, with its granite counters and stainless-steel appliances. She opened the refrigerator.

Empty. Spotless. She tried the door between two gleaming countertops. It was a pantry. There were rows of canned goods, dried pasta and boxed cereal.

"I do believe these cans are alphabetized," she said, and shut the door.

He went to another door. It opened to a laundry room. A door beyond that went to the three-car garage. He flipped on the light out there. A Jaguar, a Mercedes and a Land Rover, each one shiny and new. He could hardly bear to look at them. He turned off the light and quickly shut the door.

She was waiting in the kitchen. "Marcus, are you all right?" She searched his face.

He muttered, "Let's just go through the rest of it."

"All right." She followed him out of the kitchen and down a long hallway with a study, three bedrooms and two baths branching off it. The rooms were painted in deep colors—reds and forest greens, jewel blues and deep browns. Overall, the impression was inviting, Marcus thought, and attractive. He hated it, every inch of it.

"It's all so impersonal," Rhia said sadly. "Not a single snapshot of a friend or any family photographs. And all the art has that look."

"What look?"

"Generic. As though he bought it all framed and properly matted at some gift shop or art emporium."

They entered the big bedroom at the end of the hall. The room was a deep maroon color, with plain, dark, well-made furniture. Marcus knew from the size of it and the full bath branching off it that it must be the master suite. There was a sitting area and a sliding door led out to a small patio. He set the list of codes and the ring of keys on the sitting area table and opened the walk-in closet, which had been designed for maximum use of the space. Roland's clothing hung so neatly. All the shoes were clean and polished, lined up with soldierly precision.

"Everything is so neat and tidy," Rhia said from behind him. "The housekeeper even made the bed. It's hard to believe a man died here just three days ago."

He stared at the long row of dress shirts, each perfectly pressed, hung by color, from light to dark, and spoke without turning. "I wouldn't be surprised if he left that housekeeper detailed instructions as to what to clean up in the event of his death. Judging by his will and the look of this house, he seems to have been a very organized man."

"Too organized."

He agreed. "You would almost think that nobody lived here."

"Well, Marcus. Nobody does anymore...."

He felt a flash of heat under his skin. Annoyance. Worse. He turned to her. "You think I should have made up with him, don't you?"

She took his hand. He had to actively stop himself from jerking away. She wrapped that hand around her waist and then took his other hand and guided it behind her, too, so that he held her in a loose embrace. After she'd arranged his hands to her satisfaction, she put her own on his shoulders. Softly, she told him, "I think you're a good man and you did what you could. I think you had a lot to forgive him for. Maybe too much."

"That's no answer." He growled the words at her.

She kept her chin tilted up, her gaze on his. "Sorry. It's the only answer I've got right now. This is all very sad. He did well for himself in America, but it looks like he was all alone."

"And whose fault was that?"

"Marcus. Does it really have to be someone's fault?"

He was the one who looked away. "There's a safe in the study." He took her hands from his shoulders and stepped back from her. Grabbing the list he'd set on the table, he turned for the door to the hallway.

The study had cherrywood wainscoting to waist height. He pressed a panel. It swung wide. The safe was behind it. He went on one knee to enter the combination. It opened.

Inside there was a small stack of cash on top of a large yellow envelope. He counted the money. Two thousand dollars in hundreds. He supposed it belonged to him now—like everything else in this too-orderly, too-quiet house. But for some reason, he couldn't bear to take it. So he set it aside and picked up the envelope.

"What is it?" Rhia had followed him. She hovered in the doorway to the hall.

He rose, carried the envelope to the desk and poured out the contents.

Disappointment tightened the skin on the back of his

neck and made a hard ball packed with nothing in the pit of his stomach. "Just another copy of the damn will."

She came to stand at his shoulder and asked in a low and careful voice, "What is it you're looking for?"

He sank into the desk chair. "I don't know. Something more than this. Letters. Photographs. Something... personal. Something *real*."

She put her hand on his shoulder. "I think we should look through the house, open all the drawers, go through everything. See what we can find."

He reached up and clasped her fingers. They felt good in his. They felt right. Funny how just the touch of her hand did so much to make the emptiness bearable. He shouldn't be so gruff with her. But somehow, gruff was the only way he could be right then. "Doesn't that seem a little disrespectful, going through Roland's drawers and closets when I never even knew the man?"

She moved in closer, wrapped her arms around his neck and bent close to him. He breathed in the faint scent of jasmine and the knot of nothing in his gut eased a little more. She whispered, "What I think is that you need more than an empty house, a pile of money and another copy of your father's will. And I think we are going to keep looking until we find what you need."

Beneath the orderly rows of matched, perfectly rolled socks in Roland's sock drawer, Marcus found two pictures. In one, a pretty, very serious-looking woman wearing dark trousers, a black vest, a white shirt and a bow tie stood by the world-famous Fountain of the Three Sirens in front of Casino d'Ambre. On the back of that snapshot was one word: Isa.

The other picture was of Roland and the same woman. They sat at a table in an outdoor café. His arm was across her shoulders, an open bottle of wine and two half-full wineglasses in front of them. Roland was grinning at her. Isa was smiling back at him. It was a joyous, open smile with just a hint of mischief in it.

He called Rhia in from the other room and showed her what he'd found.

She clapped her hands at the sight. "Personal pictures. Oh, I'm so glad. I knew we'd find *something*." She read his mother's name on the back of the one by the fountain, then turned it over to study the image on the front. "Oh, Marcus. She looks so…subdued. It's hard to tell much about her from this one."

"The other one's better, I think."

She took the second one and stared at it for a long time. "This is the good one. She looks like she doesn't want to be anywhere else but right there, at that table, with that man. He looks like he feels the same about her. As though they have it all, don't you think?"

He wasn't willing to go that far. "They look as though they're having a good time. I'll say that much."

"Well, *I* would guess from this picture that they were happy together, at least for a while…."

What did it matter? They would never really know. "All right. Let's think of it that way. Once, they were happy."

"Yes. I like that. I truly do." She gave him back the photo and left him to return to the search.

It was only a few minutes later that she called him into the study and showed him a four-drawer file cabinet in the closet. The bottom drawer was labeled "Marcus." It contained a series of reports and a large number of photographs compiled by the investigators Roland had hired to gather information about the son he'd abandoned. The first report was fifteen years old.

"It fits," Rhia said, excitement vibrating in her voice.

"He came to America, spent several years building his business. But he never forgot you. When he had some money, he started trying to find out what had happened to you."

He wasn't impressed. "Too little, too late, as far as I'm concerned." The more he thought about it, the more he realized he didn't need to know any more about the long-dead past.

She was giving him a look that seemed to speak volumes, but she didn't say anything.

That look got under his skin. "He abandoned both my mother and me. In the end, that's all that really matters to me."

She did speak up then. "And he spent his life paying for that one terrible decision."

"I would say he did all right for himself."

"Marcus, he was alone. He never married, never had a family."

"Because he threw away his family. And what do you mean, *one* terrible decision? I would say that there were at least two of those. He didn't call for help when he found my mother's body. And then he took me, only to abandon me."

"Because he was afraid. He didn't know what would happen if he called for help. I can see that he might have thought he would be blamed for her death."

"Why would he even think he would be blamed if it wasn't in some way true? And now I say it all out loud I'm seeing that it's more than two bad decisions. There was a whole ugly string of them. And that's if we can even believe his story that she was dead when he got there."

"Marcus. Come on. I'm sure that he wouldn't have—"

He shoved the file drawer shut. It slammed hard against the frame. "I'm finished here. None of this stuff means a damn thing to me."

She wouldn't give it up. "My mother always says that forgiveness is everything, that when we forgive, we free *ourselves* more than the one who needs our forgiveness."

"Heard that before," he told her flatly. "Raised by nuns, remember?"

"I'm only saying that the more you learn about who Roland and Isa were, about what really happened between them, the more you'll begin to see that they did the best they could."

He took her arm and pulled her out of that closet. "Enough."

"But, Marcus..."

He didn't need to know any more about his mother and Roland and their tragic love—or whatever it was between them that had ended with his mother dying all alone and him abandoned on a cold cathedral step. It was over and done. Isa and Roland were gone. Beyond suffering. Beyond retribution for their sins.

Whatever their sins might actually have been.

What mattered was now. This moment. What mattered was this fine, true-hearted, beautiful woman before him. His child that she carried inside of her body. What mattered was this chance he had with her.

Against all odds. In spite of everything—his own blind, foolish pride most of all.

"Marcus, have you heard a word that I've said?"

"Every word, Rhia."

"I only think that it could help you, to know more about them."

He reminded her, gently now, "You said that already."

"But I'm trying to—"

"Shh. No more." He put his finger under her chin, tipped her soft mouth up—and claimed it.

She stiffened at first. And then a choked little sigh escaped her. And then she slid her hands up over his chest and clasped them behind his neck. She melted into him.

He tasted her sweetness and knew that, no matter what happened, no matter if she refused to marry him every time he asked for the rest of their lives, he would never leave her. He would be there, for her. And for the child. He would never be a man who walked away from the ones who mattered most of all.

They left that house soon after. He took the two pictures from the sock drawer with him and the list of codes and the ring of keys. Everything else, he left behind.

He told the driver to take them to their favorite burger stand. And then they went to a movie—a comedy—at Mann's Chinese Theater.

That evening, they stood out on the balcony at the Beverly Wilshire and he told her that, no, he didn't want to go to Roland's cabin in the Sierras. "What I want is to call Anthony Evans and find out if there's anything else I need to do to settle my father's estate. And then I want to call the Neptune Society and ask them to ship Roland's ashes to me. And as soon as all that's done, I want to go home."

She caught her lower lip between her pretty white teeth. "I know I should just let it be...."

Her hair was up. He wanted it down, wanted to sift the strands between his fingers. So he started pulling out pins, letting them fall where they might. One pinged against the railing. And another after that.

She didn't object—not to his taking her hair down, anyway. "We might find more pictures, up at that cabin, learn more about your mother...."

"Forget the cabin. It doesn't matter."

"But—"

He bent close, pressed a quick, hard kiss against those

sweet red lips. "Shh." He whispered against her mouth, "I want to go home." He combed her hair with his fingers. It felt so warm and soft and silky. And then he took her by the waist. "Come here. Closer..." He slid his hands down, cupped her firm bottom and pulled her in tight to him. He was already half-hard.

And he was getting harder. He wanted her. All of her. He wanted her clothes off. He wanted that now.

"Marcus..." She sounded slightly breathless. He liked her that way. He started unbuttoning the sleeveless pink shirt she wore. She pushed at his chest. But not all that hard. "We should really...talk about..." He covered her mouth and sucked the rest of that sentence right out of her.

She tasted so good and he didn't want to talk anymore.

He was through talking for one day. More than through.

He wanted her smooth, pretty body. He wanted her ardent sighs. He wanted to kiss all her most secret places.

And then he wanted to bury himself in her sweetness for a long, satisfying ride.

He had all of her clothes off in less than a minute. He'd always been good with his hands. Her little pink shirt and her short skirt, the red thong she wore underneath. And the lacy pink bra, too.

About then, she started pushing at his shoulders again. "Marcus, I'm standing here on this balcony naked as the day I was born...."

"You still have those sandals." He tried to capture her mouth again.

"Anyone might glance up here and see me."

He scooped her high against his chest. "Then we should go inside."

She made a sound that might have been a protest, but then she wrapped her arms around his neck and tucked her head against his shoulder. He carried her in and set her down in front of a fat wing chair. She blinked up at him, bewildered. "What are you *doing?*"

"Here. Let me show you." He took her velvety shoulders and pushed her gently down into the chair.

"Marcus..."

"It's fine." He knelt before her and eased her shapely knees wide. "Just keep saying my name."

"Oh! Marcus..."

"That's the way." He bent close, nuzzled the soft dark curls that covered her where she was hot and wet already—and open for him.

She said his name more insistently and breathlessly, too, as he kissed her. He started with quick, teasing kisses. And then he made those kisses longer. Deeper. He used his tongue and his fingers, too.

In no time, she reached for him. She kicked off her sandals and braced her feet up on the arms of the chair. She held his head tight and close. He breathed in heat and vanilla and jasmine and musk, tasting her in that most intimate way as he kissed her, coaxing her, driving her steadily to the brink.

And over.

She held him tighter than ever then. He could hardly breathe and he didn't care. The slick, hot center of her pulsed against his mouth. He drank her in as she cried his name out good and loud. When she sagged back to the chair cushion, he gathered her limp body into his arms again and carried her to the bedroom, where he set her so carefully onto the turned-back bed.

He got rid of his clothes. She reached for him as he came down to her. He buried himself in her glorious wet heat and forgot everything but the feel of her beneath him, the miracle of her flawless skin under his hands.

They made it last. By the time she went over the edge,

taking him with her, he was lost to all but the wonder of her body locked to his.

Afterward, he held her. He stroked her hair and ran his hands down the sweet, tender bumps of her spine. She fell asleep and so did he.

In the middle of the night he woke. She lay against him, smooth and tempting, smelling of sex and flowers. He drew her even closer and made love to her all over again.

By the time they returned to Montedoro on Wednesday, Rhia had resigned herself to the fact that Marcus was not going to try and find out any more about his lost father—or about his mother who had died so tragically on the night of his birth.

Yes, she felt it would be better for him to know more, to find out everything he could. But he'd been through so much in his life. Too much. If he'd had enough, who was she to tell him he had to find out more?

In the end, although she could try and get him to see the wisdom of making real and lasting peace with his past, she couldn't do it for him. If he said he was satisfied with the way things stood now, it was her job to accept his decision.

Acceptance was part of loving.

And Rhia did love. She loved Marcus. She knew that now.

Maybe she had always loved him. Or maybe, since Montana, she'd learned to love him again. She didn't know for sure which. And it didn't really matter. What mattered was that at some point during their second time together in Southern California, she had come to grips with the fact that she loved him *now*.

She loved his bravery and his goodness, loved his unflagging determination to do the right thing. She loved that he wanted so fervently to be a good father. She loved how, though he'd started with less than nothing, he'd manage to create a meaningful, productive life for himself. She loved how hard he was trying to tell her about himself, to share with her all the secrets he would never tell another.

She loved the way he laughed—just a little unwillingly, as though someone might catch him at it and steal the moment of humor away. She loved his intelligence and his wonderful, powerful body.

She loved *him*. It was that enormous and that simple. And she understood now that it was very likely she always would love him.

For her, the decision was made at last. She wanted to make a life with him. To be his wife as well as his devoted lover and the mother of their coming child. She was ready to say yes as soon as he asked her to marry him again.

Unfortunately, though he continued to stay with her at the villa and to treat her with tenderness, consideration, passion and what seemed like deep affection, he never actually said that he loved her. And a month after they returned to Montedoro from Los Angeles, he had yet to mention marriage again.

Chapter Fourteen

"It's so simple," Allie said.

Rhia braced herself for a lecture.

It was a little past noon on the second Wednesday in August and they were sharing lunch at Allie's villa, which was smaller than Rhia's, not in the harbor area and without nearly as nice a view. But it was closer to the palace and the stables where Allie spent most of her time, so she was perfectly happy living there.

What Allie was *not* happy with was Rhia and the way she was handling this problem with Marcus. She scolded, "You have to tell him that you love him. And then you have to say that you *do* want to marry him, that you've made up your mind at last."

Rhia picked up her water glass, but plunked it back down without taking a sip. "You don't understand."

"Oh, yes, I do. *You're* the one who's making this way too complicated and impossibly difficult."

"No. No, I'm not."

Allie ate a scallop and then stuck her fork in her linguine and twirled up a nice big mouthful. "Yes, you most definitely are. You know what the Americans say."

"Please don't tell me."

"No guts, no glory."

"Didn't I ask you not to tell me?"

Allie ate her fat forkful of linguine with obvious relish. "You're the one who went on and on about how you would never marry a man just because you were having his baby. Well, now you don't have that problem anymore. You *want* to marry Marcus because you realize he's the man for you. So do it. Tell the man you love him and can't wait to spend your life with him."

"But what if he's changed his mind?" Rhia's stomach churned. She pushed her plate away. This conversation did not lend itself to the enjoyment of scallops, even if they were fresh-caught and perfectly prepared. She put her hand on her stomach, which was growing rounder by the day. She had a definite baby bump now. Yesterday, at the museum, as they ticked off their progress with the final preparations for the Adele Canterone exhibit in two weeks, she'd caught Claudine eyeing her belly. Rhia was certain that the museum director had guessed she was pregnant—not that it really mattered that Claudine had guessed. After all, it wouldn't be long now before everyone would know.

Everyone including the paparazzi. Rhia knew how such things went. She would be all over the tabloids, seen from the side, her bump prominently displayed for the whole world to ogle and gossip about. She could picture the headlines now: *Bodyguard's Love Child. Princess Rhia's Baby Bump. A Baby But No Wedding Bells for Princess Rhia.*

Ugh.

All right, yes. She had known this would happen. She

had told herself that she was prepared for it, that she would get through all the unpleasantness of being just scandalous enough to get the attention of the tabloids even if she was only a far-down-the-birth-order princess in a family full of potential heirs.

And she *was* prepared.

But now that she knew she loved Marcus and wanted to marry him, it didn't have to be all that bad. If they got married, the scandal would quickly fade away.

But they *couldn't* get married.

Because Marcus hadn't asked her and she was too afraid to ask him.

Allie was not through lecturing. "What are you worried about? He's not going to change his mind about marrying you. I mean, please. How many times has he asked you already?"

"Um. Seven? Nine? I'm not sure."

"Well, and there's another reason why you should do the asking."

"What are you talking about now?"

"Rhia. It's your *turn*."

"My *turn?* There are no *turns* when it comes to proposing marriage."

"In your case, there ought to be."

Rhia pushed her plate a little farther away. "All right. I admit that I really *should* just go ahead and ask him."

"You admit the simple truth. Will wonders never cease?"

"But I *can't.*"

Allie gave her a look of pitiless disapproval. "Oh, yes, you can. You're not a wimp. Stop acting like one."

"You don't understand."

"You're right. I don't."

"Allie…" Her voice failed her. Her throat had clutched

and her eyes burned with hot tears. "What if he turns me down?" There. She had said it.

And Allie was not impressed. "He's not going to turn you down. Even if he wasn't crazy in love with you—which it's obvious to everyone but you that he is—he wants to be married to you because of the baby."

"How many times do I have to explain that I do not want a husband who only wants me because of the baby? And besides, he's…different lately. He's more relaxed. Happier."

Allie threw up her hands. "You're making my arguments for me. He is different. He's a happy man now. I know that he'll say yes. Just do it. Just ask him."

"But what if he says no?"

"Then you'll still have turned him down six—or eight—times more than he did you."

"Five or seven," she corrected in a tiny little voice that was cracking around the edges.

Allie blinked. "Huh?"

"Allie, I begged him."

"Wait. What? I thought you hadn't even said 'I love you' yet."

"But I did."

"When?"

"Six years ago." A rough, ugly sob escaped her. "I stood in the dirt in front of a run-down farmhouse in the South of France, and I pleaded with him to give our relationship a chance. I cried right there in front of him, like a pathetic, hopeless fool with no pride whatsoever and I told him that I loved him. And he said it was over and he wasn't interested and would I please just go away."

"Oh." Allie gulped. "That."

"Yes. That."

"I guess I had kind of put all that old awfulness right out of my mind."

"Well, I haven't. And I…I can't do that again." The tears overflowed then. She couldn't stop them. They rolled down her cheeks and her nose started running. She tried to swipe the flood away with the back of her hand.

Allie gave up all pretense of talking tough. "Oh, my darling. I'm sorry. I shouldn't have jumped all over you. I'm an ass. Don't…" She got up, grabbed a handful of tissues, scooted to Rhia's side and gave them to her. Then she bent to wrap her arms around her. "Dearest. You mustn't."

"I can't help it." Rhia tried to mop up the flood a little, but the tears just kept coming. "I want to tell him, but I can't do it. I just…I can't, that's all."

"Well, all right. All right, then." Allie patted her hair, stroked her back. "You go ahead. You just cry it out…"

"Oh, Allie, you're right. You are. I am being so very, very stupid over this."

Allie had totally surrendered her tough-love approach. She said what a good sister should say. "My darling, you are not in any way stupid."

"Yes, I am! Stupid, dumb and way too emotional. It's the hormones. Or at least that's what I keep telling myself…." She broke down and sobbed some more.

Allie held her and tenderly stroked her hair. "Whatever it is, it doesn't matter. Sometimes a woman just needs a good cry."

So Rhia cried. And Allie went on holding her, whispering that it would be all right.

When the tears finally stopped, Rhia blew her nose and wiped her eyes and retired to the powder room to try and repair the ravages before returning to the museum.

As she was leaving, Allie couldn't resist getting in the last word. "Just tell him you love him. If you could only do that much…"

That evening when she got home, Marcus was waiting.

He had a big bouquet of fire lilies for her and a bright-purple bruise high on his cheekbone.

The flowers cheered her up. A man who didn't want to marry her wouldn't be bringing her flowers.

Would he?

She thanked him with a kiss, gave Yvonne the flowers to put in a vase and took Marcus to the kitchen where she found a bag of peas in the freezer and made him hold it to the side of his face.

He told her he'd trained that morning with Denis and then with Rene.

"You fought with them, you mean." She tried not to sound disapproving and knew that she probably failed.

He didn't deny it. "That Denis has a deadly right hook." He said it with what could only be called admiration. "He's not a bad guy, really. Neither is Rene…"

He was coming to *accept* his childhood enemies? Would wonders never cease?

She said, only a little bit smugly, "Do you realize you are sounding almost forgiving?"

He shrugged. "Won't the sisters at St. Stephen's be proud?" And then he told her the important news. He'd had a meeting with her brother Alexander and Sir Hector Anteros that afternoon. "My days providing security to the princely family are numbered. I'm being promoted to commandant and over the next few years I will be groomed for the leadership of the CCU."

"Alex is stepping down?"

"He says he will be spending more time with Lili and their twins in Alagonia and focusing more on his duties there. He is the father of the future king, after all."

It really was exciting news. "Oh, Marcus. Congratulations. How wonderful."

"Yes, it is, isn't it?" He was so confident, so self-assured, standing there in the kitchen with a bag of frozen peas against his handsome face. "I'm the man for that post and it's satisfying that I'll have it." His eyes sparked with wry humor. "Even if I do have something of an unfair advantage...."

She frowned up at him. "What advantage?"

He reached out, caught a lock of her air and tugged on it. "Well, Rhia. You."

She tried to read his thoughts in his expression, and failed utterly. So she asked, "Does it bother you that your relationship with me would make my brother more likely to choose you as his successor?"

He chuckled then. It was a real chuckle—good-natured, lighthearted. "It might if I didn't know that I fully deserve this promotion and will give it my all."

"So then, it doesn't bother you?"

"Not in the least."

Rhia tried not to gape at him, not to demand to know what he'd done with the real Marcus. He'd always been so proud. Too proud. And she'd dreamed that he might somehow become a little more relaxed about things. That he might see his own value and simply accept the good things that came his way. Like for instance, that a princess might have fallen in love with him all those years ago.

Apparently, he had finally learned to do just that—at least when it came to his military career.

What else had changed about him? Had he come around to her original way of thinking about the baby, too? Had he come to agree that they didn't need to be married for him to be a hands-on, loving father?

He must have sensed her distress. He took the peas away from his cheek and set them on the counter. "Rhia, are you all right?"

I love you and I want to marry you. I want that so much.

It's making me crazy how much I want that. "Ahem. I, well, I have been feeling a little bit weepy today." *And I am a complete coward lately. I seem to have no idea how to say what I want.*

He reached out and laid his big hand on her rounded belly. "You're all right, though? Both of you?"

She bit her lip and nodded.

And he took her hand and led her out of the kitchen and into the bedroom they'd been sharing for almost two months now.

He took off her clothes and pushed her down to the bed, where he rubbed her feet and then massaged her back. He told her she was beautiful, even though she knew that she looked haggard and that her eyes were still red and swollen from her crying jag at Allie's. He put his big hands on her belly and he talked to the baby. He'd been doing that for a couple of weeks now, talking so softly and soothingly, saying the sweetest things.

Dear Lord. He was turning out to be an absolutely wonderful man.

If only he loved her. If only he wanted to marry her not only for the baby, but for her sake, as well. If only it could all *not* turn out the way it had six years ago.

When he finished his conversation with the baby, he kissed his way up over her belly and her breasts. He brushed a warm, soft row of kisses over her throat and her chin to her mouth. She opened for him, sighing. He kissed her some more. He kissed her everywhere. He made beautiful love to her. At the end, she almost forgot her fears enough to shout out her love for him as her climax rolled through her.

But she didn't. She held it in.

And in the morning when she woke, he was already gone for his predawn workout at the CCU training yard.

He called her at the museum later that morning. "Did I tell you that Roland's ashes arrived?"

"That's a relief." It was a complicated process, shipping cremated remains internationally.

"They came yesterday afternoon before you got home." *Home.* He had called the villa *home.* That was a good sign, wasn't it? "I got all wrapped up in telling you about my promotion and forgot to say that they were here."

"Well, I'm glad they arrived safely."

"Yes." His voice sounded far away, suddenly. "I've reserved a motorboat. I was thinking I would take care of them this afternoon."

He would take care of them. So, then. He wanted to do the job alone. She could accept that, could understand that it was something he might want to do without company. Still, disappointment settled on her shoulders, heavy as a cape made of lead. She yearned to be the one he needed with him at a time like this. Then he asked, "Will you meet me at four? Can you get away?" He named a slip at the pier not all that far from the villa, down in the area where the smaller boats were docked.

He wanted her to go with him! The cape of lead lifted. She felt light as air. "Yes. Of course I'll be there."

She considered going home and changing into something more casual to go out on a small boat. But then, really, this was the only sendoff the mysterious Roland was going to get. So she wore what she'd worn to work: a lightweight, fitted sheath of raw silk and a contrasting raw-silk jacket. She had a scarf in her bag in case the wind came up.

He was waiting when she got there, looking so handsome in the white uniform he'd worn the day she told him that there would be a baby. The bruise on his cheekbone from the bout with Denis was already fading. He helped her into the boat, which was larger than she'd expected, with a small cabin and a roomy cockpit.

She took a seat. The wind tugged at her hair, so she put on her scarf as he dealt with the mooring lines. When he took the wheel, she asked him, "The ashes?"

"In the cabin." He put on his aviator sunglasses, started the engine and backed the boat from the slip.

They were quiet with each other as he eased the boat through the obstacles in the crowded harbor. It wasn't long before they passed between the twin points at harbor's end and into the open sea.

He turned the boat and followed the coastline south for a time. She watched the glorious, gray-green hills of her country moving by, the red roofs of villas so inviting through the lush canopy of trees. The Prince's Palace, home of her childhood, appeared on its high, craggy promontory, growing larger as they came even with it. The sun was warm on her shoulders, but the wind had a bite to it. Seagulls soared on the air currents overhead. She could hear their distant calls.

Finally, he said, "I think it's safe to drift for a little." He left the wheel, ducked below and emerged with a plain black box.

He took off his sunglasses, put on his hat and took the box to the landward side, where the wind was at his back. Then he turned to her. She remained in the seat by the wheel, unsure of what her involvement should be. He tucked the box under one arm, and held out his free hand to her.

She had that light-as-air feeling again as she rose and moved to his side.

He caught her hand, brought it to his lips. "I know you're going to want to say a few words...."

She gave him a wobbly little smile. "Yes. Please."

They turned together toward the coast. He opened the box.

The wind pushed at her back. He folded down the plastic lining and tipped the box so the ashes drifted out slowly. She started the Lord's Prayer. When she finished that, she recited the Twenty-Third Psalm, all while he carefully shook free the grainy gray powder studded with white bits that had to be bone. Some of the powder made a film on the surface of the blue water, some the wind carried away toward the shore.

When it was finally done, he took the box below. Then he put his sunglasses back on and went to the helm once more. She reclaimed her seat beside him. He started up the boat and drove them back the way they had come.

It was all strangely dreamlike, she thought. Dreamlike and so peaceful.

They reentered the harbor. He maneuvered the boat back to the slip, eased it cleanly into place and tied it down again. He took her hand and helped her back onto the pier.

"Let's walk a little," he said, and tucked her fingers around his arm. He led her to the Promenade and they strolled along it for a time. There was a man with a camera back on the pier, snapping pictures of them. And another man, also armed with a camera, who seemed to keep popping up in her side vision as they walked.

She didn't care. She tuned them out. Marcus didn't seem to mind, either.

People called to her and waved. She smiled at them, returning their greetings. Eventually, they came to that same bench beneath the tree where they'd sat together on that first night he moved into her villa.

"This looks familiar," he said. They sat side by side in the shade. He took off his hat and his sunglasses and turned to her. "It meant a lot to me, that you were with me."

"To me, too."

"I think it was…nice." He touched the side of her face. She smiled into his eyes as he untied her scarf. "Peaceful." She made a sound of agreement as he pulled the scarf away. He gave it to her and then began removing the pins from her hair.

That made her smile. "You do know that we are probably being photographed."

"I don't care. You're here with me. That's what matters. Give me your hand." She did. He put the pins in it, on top of the scarf. She wadded the whole thing up and stuck it in her bag as he combed her hair with his fingers. "There."

She gazed into his almost-green eyes and felt tears welling in hers. "Oh, Marcus…."

He touched her cheek, wiped a tear away with his thumb. "Don't cry. I love you, Rhiannon. I've always loved you."

She blinked in amazement. The miracle had happened, just like that. He'd said the words she needed so much to hear, said them so she knew he meant them. At last. She sniffed, shut her eyes, willed the tears down. Because she knew then. She knew…everything. "Oh, Marcus…"

He gazed at her so earnestly. "You made me tell you about that other woman, the one I never actually met. But that was only a sad little story I told myself, a pitiful consolation for the hard fact that I couldn't let myself have you. You were always the only one. Always. Please believe me."

"How could I not?" she whispered. "It's been the same for me."

"I know I hurt you."

She let it out then. The old, awful, brutal truth. "I begged you to give us another chance. While you just stood there on the steps of that empty house and looked at me like you only wanted me to stop. I *pleaded* with you, threw my poor heart at your feet. Still, you sent me away."

"I was wrong."

"You were. Terribly wrong. I so longed to hate you for that."

"Say that you didn't."

"No. I wanted to. I couldn't. I could never hate you, not really. I love you. More than anything. I will never, ever stop loving you, Marcus."

He took her hand again. "I've been waiting. Trying to show you that I can be the man you need for a lifetime. That we can be together in every way. Stand together. Love together. Be the ones who make the future. Raise our baby together."

"Oh, God." Tears scalded the back of her throat again. She swallowed them down and made herself come clean. "I thought...that maybe you had changed your mind."

"No. Never. I've been an idiot, but not anymore."

"Oh, Marcus...."

"Marry me, Rhia. Be my wife."

She looked down and he was slipping a diamond onto her finger. "Oh! Oh, it's beautiful."

"Just say yes. Tell me yes."

And she did. "Yes," she said clearly and firmly. "Forever and for always, Marcus. That's how I want it to be."

And he grabbed her close and kissed her long and slow and deep, right there on the Promenade for all the world to see.

Epilogue

The pictures of the bodyguard's proposal on the Promenade at Colline d'Ambre appeared in various tabloids worldwide three days later.

Noah Cordell saw them. Not because he was a big fan of the stuff they printed in the scandal sheets, but because Noah made it his business to keep up with everything that happened in the Bravo-Calabretti family.

Noah dreamed big. They called him brash and bold. Difficult to know, yet charming with a boyish quality that had helped him to get ahead.

He had started out on the mean streets of Los Angeles with nothing. At the age of eighteen, he'd enrolled in business school at night and gone to work days as a laborer for a guy who flipped houses—and loved horses. Within two years, Noah was flipping houses himself. And getting invited to his new boss's ranch, where he quickly learned to love horses, too. Noah moved up and he moved up fast.

By the end of his real estate career, Noah was building office towers in all the major real estate markets. But then, with his unerring feel for the markets, he sensed the crash was coming. He got out just in time, and he took his fortune with him. Since then, he'd been living the good life, looking after his investments, watching his money grow.

Noah thoroughly enjoyed the fruits of his ambition and labor. Five years ago, as a thirtieth birthday present to himself, he'd bought a sprawling, luxurious horse ranch in Santa Barbara. He'd moved in, bringing his frail younger sister, and the housekeeper who'd once been his sister's foster mom. More recently, while pursuing his interest in fast, expensive cars and beautiful women, he'd wrangled an introduction to Prince Damien of Montedoro. Noah and Damien found they had a lot in common. The connection to Damien was a big step in the right direction. Noah now had a friend in the Bravo-Calabretti family.

He wanted two things from the Bravo-Calabrettis.

One, the princely family bred and trained Akhal-Teke horses. The tough, ancient, hot-blooded breed from the deserts of Turkmenistan fascinated Noah. He wanted an Akhal-Teke stallion from the palace stables of Montedoro and he intended to have one.

Two, Noah had decided it was time he got to work on his dynasty. To start a dynasty, a man needed the right woman. Noah thought that a princess would do very nicely.

But not any weird, inbred, frail kind of princess. Noah wanted a woman with guts and brains and a sense of humor. Oh, and with a family history of fertility. After all, a dynasty is predicated on the production of heirs.

It was a tall order. But Noah knew where to look to fill it. The Bravo-Calabrettis were a large, loving family. There were five sisters in that family. One of them loved horses as much as Noah did and was closely involved with the breeding and training of the Akhal-Tekes he coveted.

So Noah had concentrated on the horsey one, on finding out more about her. He'd learned that not only was she a genius with horses, she had something of a wild streak. She liked riding fast motorcycles and dancing all night in working-class bars.

There were a lot of pictures of her on the internet. Noah had studied them at length. She had brown hair and dimples, eyes that sometimes looked gray and sometimes blue and sometimes a strange, haunting color in between. Her smile dazzled.

Yeah. She was the one, all right. Her Serene Highness Alice would definitely do.

* * * * *

LET'S TALK
Romance

For exclusive extracts, competitions
and special offers, find us online:

- facebook.com/millsandboon
- @MillsandBoon
- @MillsandBoonUK

Get in touch on 01413 063232

For all the latest titles coming soon, visit
millsandboon.co.uk/nextmonth